A GLOBAL WARNING

Paul Zedane

Published by Skyscraper Publications

Printed in Great Britain

ISBN 978-1-911072-64-5

"Any sufficiently advanced technology is indistinguishable from magic."

Arthur C. Clarke

Prologue

In one of the rings of Saturn, which everyone knows are not solid rings but collections of pieces of rock and ice of different sizes circling the planet, there was one component, the size of a large hospital on planet Earth, which was distinctly different from its irregularly-shaped neighbours. Over the years it had become encrusted with irregular layers of impacted rock, ice and dust, but these were regularly melted away or brushed off to expose its original regular shape, a parallelepiped, a shape like an Earthly brick – but much larger – which was pristine when it arrived in the solar system 300,000 years ago. It was made up of six smooth surfaces of an enduring, carbon-based alloy, designed to withstand the hostile rigours of temperature and vacuum which obtain 900 million kilometres from the Sun, a star known to the builders of the three-dimensional structure by a very different name.

In its interior, the structure, which became known on Earth as 'the Outpost', was a honeycomb of nanofabricated units. Some were quantum computers, others were factories, able to manufacture a range of items ranging from viruses, genes and protein molecules, to space probes, power generators, satellites and antennae, using nanotechnology and supported by fusion energy generators which could run almost indefinitely, occasionally supplied with the necessary tritium and deuterium extracted from the space environment.

The Outpost's own radio wave receivers took up one whole surface, with moveable antennae which had been pointed at Earth for millennia, alert for the first signs that living beings had developed the technology to communicate using radio waves, communications on which the vastly powerful and sophisticated (by Earth standards) computers on the Outpost could eavesdrop, and which they could interpret, understand and learn from, until the time had come to send a message, which became known on Earth as 'the Message', with content which would change the history of the race of intelligent beings who had been anticipated to evolve, since the civilisation which built the Outpost had first genetically manipulated their ancestors 250,000 years ago.

Chapter 1

"Lunch!" called out Olga Cheliuskina, as she pushed the outer door open with her shoulder, letting a blast of cold air into the central hall of the SETI Institute in Moscow. It had been her turn to take her colleagues' orders today, sandwiches and pies from the Daily Bread café on the other side of the Garden Ring.

"God, those traffic lights take ages," she said, "and I dropped somebody's pirog in a puddle, when I crossed the other carriageway."

"It must have been yours, Olga Mikhailovna," said Pavel, the deputy director. "Only two of us ordered pirogi, and it wouldn't have been mine you dropped."

"You are not allowed to pull rank, Mr Deputy Director."

"Why not?" he said. "The era of equality died with the Soviet Union."

There were ironic laughs from the group around the large mahogany table that took up the centre of the hall.

"The era of equality died when Adam met Eve," said Igor Schmidt.

"I'm sure Eve would agree with you," Olga said, dumping the paper bags on the table. "Sort them out for yourselves. And Pavel, you and I will share the remaining pirog – it's big enough and so are you."

Olga took off her fur coat and shook the rain off it in the porch area between the outer and inner doors. She went to her shopping bag hanging on the coat rack, took out a towel and dried her long brown hair. There was the sound of paper bags being opened as people looked at the lunch ingredients and found their own.

"Did you see that *Scientific American* article on brown dwarfs?" Irina, one of the graduate student interns, said to Igor, the institute's astronomer, a shaven-headed man in his thirties with a limp acquired from an accident during his military service.

'Brown dwarf' was his nickname, since each person at the Institute was christened with the name of a type of astronomical object. Boris Veselov, the director, out to lunch at Moscow University today, was 'Red Giant'. He was tall, true, but neither a communist nor a redhead.

"Is that meant to be a joke, Irina?" Igor said.

"No, it's really there," Irina said, "It's by someone at Northwestern. She writes about the crowdsourcing work looking for brown dwarfs in data from the Wide-field Infrared Survey Explorer. Maybe we should do that with SETI data. There's so much of it to go through."

"The Americans do it already. They've got a much more sophisticated approach to looking for extraterrestrial intelligence," Olga said, and she sat down at the table and broke the pirog in half, pushing one half across to Pavel.

The Russian SETI Institute was in a former villa just off the inner ring road in Moscow, the Garden Ring. The villa – and the Institute – had seen better times. It had been the home of Lavrenty Beria, the Russian chief of secret police, who had done dreadful things there, until he suffered a dreadful fate himself. Then the villa was left to become derelict for decades after his death in 1953 before undergoing renovation so that it could be used to house a series of minor government departments. During the renovation, human bones were found in the grounds, bones which no one looked at too closely since, in the light of Beria's known tendency to murder people in the villa, it would have been surprising if bones had not been found.

Whether it was the villa's gruesome history, or just the fading fortunes of each department that was housed there, the villa saw a series of tenants come and go - mainly go. Eventually, with the downgrading of any Russian efforts to search for extraterrestrial life, the rump of what had been a thriving institution was given the choice of Beria's villa or Akademgorodok, a science city 3000 miles from Moscow. The decision, when put to the staff was, as the Russians say "simpler than steamed turnips" - a no-brainer - and the much diminished team, formerly in a handsome building on Tverskaya Street, moved to their new premises and tried not to think about human remains, or any of the ghosts that were said to haunt the place.

It could have been the beginning of a dispiriting time for the staff, but the director, Boris, was a motivator. He had long given up hope of any serious advancement through the Russian science hierarchy after his former wife, whom he loved, had had an affair with an oligarch who fell out of favour with Yeltsin, and she fled with him to London to start a new life as the man's mistress. Knowing that promotion was not on the cards, Veselov decided to gather the small SETI team around him and organise a 'make work' programme to fill their days with interesting science projects while they - of course - kept an eye on that remotest of possibilities, that a message from some extraterrestrial civilization might actually arrive at their small unit before any of the other SETI programmes, in China, the US and the UK, were aware of it.

All this explains why, when Olga came across what looked like a message from an extraterrestrial civilisation the day after the lunch where she dropped the pirog, and took the news to Boris, he was almost disappointed. Many of their other little projects were going well - looking for faces in the James Webb telescope galaxy photographs (Pavel found Bob Dylan in NGC 628), organising school groups to tell children about SETI, finding new constellations in highly magnified star fields (Igor pinned up a print of a group of stars which looked exactly like an N 308 bus) - and so a real message, or rather the tiny chance of a real message, was almost a distraction. But of course the 'make work' programme was a pose, a desperate measure to give his employees something to look forward to at work, and Veselov was intrigued and excited when Olga put on his desk a printout from a radio telescope in the Caucasus.

Miles Cadogan, Master of St James College, Cambridge, was returning from a very enjoyable dinner at Sidney Sussex College. It had been an annual custom for each college to invite the master of the other to the

Founder's Feast each year. The two colleges had been founded within twenty years of each other, and there were rumours that Lady Frances Sidney and Sir Ferdinando Freckleton, founder of St James', had been what is called today 'an item'.

Cadogan felt that his own college's cellar was better than Sidney Sussex's, thanks to a fellow who spent more time in the vineyards of Europe, and occasionally the Antipodes, than in teaching Classics, but there had been a superb wine with each course tonight and he had no complaints on that score.

Cadogan was proud of his achievements: Fellow of a leading college at the age of 27, Senior Tutor at 30, and Master at 37, although it has to be said that he was a compromise candidate between two bitterly opposed factions on the college council. He was also stylish, some saw it as vanity, wearing a wide-brimmed fedora which he hoped would be seen as a fashion statement when in fact it was to cover a thinning patch on the back of his head. His shoes struck some perceptive people as a little thicker than normal shoes, although at 5' 7" even his normal height was nothing to be ashamed of.

He was a social anthropologist, a world expert on gender and society, and his propensity to accept any invitation to an international conference even vaguely related to his research had led to his nickname in the college of 'Frequent Flyer Miles'.

As he walked across Market Square he threaded his way through the traders' stalls which were sometimes colonised at night by homeless people. It was a cold night and all Miles could see was sleeping bags or bundles of clothes. He tried to give the huddled figures a wide berth, protective of his expensive cashmere overcoat, but as he turned a corner towards King's Parade, he trod on the edge of a sleeping bag with a man in it.

"Wha...?" the man said, "Fuck...! Spare some change?"

'Well,' Miles thought, 'you're not trying to endear yourself, are you?'

"Prick! Sorry, just a quid?" the man said.

The man knelt up with an outstretched hand.

Miles looked around. A couple of students on the other side of the square were sitting on the low wall outside St Mary's church, and one was watching him. Miles thought he recognised him as a St James' student.

He reached into his overcoat pocket and looked for some coins, but there was none. He was about to walk away but thought that would look callous, so he looked in his wallet for a five pound note, but there were only ten pound notes there. Reluctantly he took one out and handed it to the man, making sure it was seen by the students.

"Here, take this."

"Fuck!" said the man, spluttering with excitement. "Cocksucker! Th..th..thanks!"

Miles thought the man's swearing was pathological. Tourette's perhaps? He turned and walked towards Trinity Street in the direction of St James'.

"Evening, Dr Cadogan," said one of the students.

"Evening..." Miles paused and then went on "...Charlie," pleased to have remembered the young man's name.

The following morning in college, on his way from the Master's Lodge to a college seminar, Cadogan dropped into the Senior Combination Room. It was a means of being approachable, as well as picking up on gossip and spotting new research fellows. He felt that 'people management' was an important part of his job, unlike some previous Masters who barely recognised some of the newer Fellows.

The room was surprisingly full. At this time in the morning, there were usually only two or three people, socially distancing themselves, not for health reasons but because of an aversion to conversation with other fellows so early in the morning. As Miles approached the coffee machine he saw a knot of fellows, four or five, clustered around a circular oak table covered with the day's newspapers. There was a low hubbub of conversation.

With a disposable cup of double espresso in hand, he nudged his way between Katie Flynn, a fellow in palaeolinguistics, and Ravi Chandra, the director of studies in mathematics.

"Hello, Master," Ravi said.

"Oh, Ravi, hi," Cadogan said. "What's got so many people up early this morning?"

"Apparently the Russians have detected an extraterrestrial message, but they won't tell anyone what's in it. Not yet anyway." He smoothed his hair and straightened his tie in the presence of the head of the college.

Ravi was always neatly dressed, whatever the time of day. As a professor of mathematics at Cambridge University, a job he would never have dared aspire to, he was always on his dignity, and secretly abhorred the slovenly way some of his colleagues dressed, even when giving lectures. A 60-year-old man wearing trainers? What was the university coming to?

"Is the story in the papers?" Miles said, peering down at the pile of newspapers.

"No," Ravi said, "That's what we're looking for. It must have been released too late."

Miles looked around the table for a scientist to ask about the news story and spotted Paul Spearman, an astronomer. *The* astronomer, really, since he held the symbolic title of Astronomer Royal, a largely honourable post with a salary of £100 a year. Miles Cadogan rather envied Paul his post and the access he imagined it gave him, but the Royal Household seemed to be in even less need of an Anthropologist Royal than of an Astronomer Royal. As a result Miles felt a little in awe of Paul. Spearman also made Miles uncomfortable because he knew about real science - physics and astronomy and cosmology - and Miles barely scraped through GCSE chemistry at school.

"Do we believe this, Paul?" Miles said. "Is it likely the Russians have detected such a message before anyone else? Do they have a SETI programme?"

Miles was pleased that he could at least show off his knowledge of the acronym. He remembered it from one of the recent admissions interviewees, a pimply boy who was passionate about astronomy and had submitted an essay about the search for extraterrestrial intelligence.

"I was unaware that they had one," Paul said. "They've never expressed much interest in the search for extraterrestrial intelligence. Years ago, a Russian wrote the standard work on the topic but after that, as far as we know, the Russians focused all their efforts on Mir and Soyuz, and manned space travel. Their radio telescopes were used for tracking orbital stuff more than looking for signals from alien intelligence."

This was more information than Miles needed.

"Must get to a seminar," he said. "Can't keep thirsty young minds waiting," and he turned away.

Moscow was basking in autumn sunshine, as Sergei Gromov's official car drove towards Red Square, past electronic signs advertising American brands - Marlborough, Macdonald's, Calvin Klein, Marriott. Gromov thought back to the late 1980s when, as a young soldier, he had been taught to hate anything - and anyone - American, at a time when the streets of Moscow were grim and grey and devoid of the kind of light or colour that now painted every available building or billboard. It had been a time when the restaurants were so dark you could barely see the menu, and if you lit a match to read it, you found little variety and you knew that what you ordered would be plonked down in front of you, tasteless and badly cooked. Moscow was so different now; full of American hotels, Swiss watches, French fashions, and an entire luxury shopping mall under Manège Square.

As the car entered Red Square, he wondered if he was doing the right thing. When Boris Veselov, his squash partner, had called and asked if he could fit in a quick game at seven in the morning, Gromov said "Do you really think the head of the FSB has time for such frivolity? Saturday mornings are fine, but seven on a weekday?"

"You will thank me, Sergei Alexandrovich."

"For what? For feeling good because I will beat you yet again?"

In fact, of course Sergei would take up the invitation, and Boris knew it. They were old friends from student days at Moscow University and, like Alexander Herzen and Nikolai Ogarev, they used to walk on the Sparrow Hills, talking the night away. And Boris had sounded excited about something.

Now Sergei was taking that something to the President, knowing that intelligence was power and Pavlov would want to be the first to know about this. Well the fifth or sixth, it seemed.

He patted his jacket, outside the pocket containing the extraordinary printout, three pages which, if genuine, would transform the future of the world. When he had gone over the printout, with Boris filling in some of the detail, he knew that a copy had to be sent by messenger straight away to President Pavlov, and that as soon as he had it, the phone summons would come to a meeting at the Kremlin.

As his car approached the Kremlin gates, Gromov wondered how Pavlov would react. He was an unpredictable man, often keeping you guessing. His motivations were not always clear. Of course, his prime aim was the promotion of Russia – its image – its power – but he sometimes seemed to take a delight in disruption for disruption's sake. In that respect, he took after the late Vladimir Putin, assassinated when what he did to try to destroy Ukraine disgusted even the Russian military.

The car stopped and Gromov got out on to the steps of the Presidential building. As a reflex, rather than through nervousness, Gromov wiped the tips of his brown, well-polished shoes on the backs of his trouser legs, and tightened the knot of his tie. Unlike some of his colleagues, he still wore a tie for important meetings, taken out of his office wardrobe if he had a meeting at short notice.

There was a yapping sound as the president's Yorkshire terrier came running out of the large, heavily-ornamented doorway, pursued by Oleg Kozlov, Pavlov's factotum, a short, wiry man with a perpetual smile.

"Mr Gromov, sorry about this. Ninotchka escaped from the president's suite and ran down the stairs," Oleg said.

"Do you want me to carry her up, Oleg Nikolayevich?" Gromov said.

"No, no, hairs will come out on your nice suit. I'll carry her up. Please…" He gestured towards the door and the marble steps beyond.

As Gromov entered the presidential office, Dmitry Ilyich Pavlov sipped tea from a Fabergé teacup with a chip out of the rim and a crack halfway down the side.

"Did I ever tell you the story of this cup, Sergei Alexandrovich?" he said, looking across a pile of papers at Gromov, who was standing at a respectful distance from the massive 1950s walnut desk.

"I don't think so, Mr President," Sergei said, lying.

"It was passed down to me by my father who found it among *his* father's things after he died. My grandfather had been one of the revolutionaries who stormed the Winter Palace. I knew him when I was very young and he used to tell me the story himself while he drank from the cup."

Pavlov took a sip, made a face, and put a lump of sugar in the tea.

"When the doors of the palace were smashed down and the crowds rushed in, most of them raced off to find the wine cellars, and ended up sloshed and incapable hours later, surrounded by empty magnum bottles of Château Lafite. But all my grandfather wanted was a cup of tea – he had been demonstrating for hours in the square outside – so he wandered through the palace and found one of the many kitchens, and a samovar still lit. He sat there drinking tea from a cup he found in a dresser, looking out of the window at the square crammed with shouting people, and he knew that tsardom was over and Russia was about to change. Absentmindedly, he slipped the cup into his greatcoat pocket, and found it several hours later when he returned home. I think he drank from it for the rest of his life."

"It's a good story, Dmitry Ilyich," Gromov said, politely.

"I sometimes wish he had taken the whole tea set," Pavlov went on. "He could have sold it on the black market in the 1930s when he was so poor. Of course, now we have such tea sets in my dacha, but without the sentimental connection."

"It helps to explain why you drink tea from such a disreputable looking cup," Gromov said, wondering when Pavlov would get to the point.

"Somehow," Pavlov said, "with this cup in my hand I feel a sense of continuity with Russia's history, good or bad, and I think about what my grandfather would have thought if he could see me now."

He put the cup down on its saucer and picked up one of the sheets of paper Gromov had sent him.

The text over the three pages was about 600 words long. Pavlov started reading it for the umpteenth time. He then picked up the phone and told Oleg to come in. Turning to Gromov he said "Do we know where it came from?"

"It appeared on the SETI feed from the Ratan-600 telescope in the Caucasus."

"How many people know of its existence?"

"Just the people at SETI. The director, Boris Veselov is an old friend, someone I trust. That's why he brought it to me first." Gromov wanted to establish some priority in this matter as early as possible.

Pavlov got up from his desk and paced back and forth in front of the huge fireplace. He was wondering if there was a way to use this, this extraordinary unprecedented message – if it was genuine, and if no one else had it – to help Russia in some way.

"Does anyone else have it?"

"I asked Boris Nikolaevich this question, and he said that clearly the signal would have been detectable anywhere on earth, but it was a matter of chance. Any radio telescope would have to be pointing at the same small part of the sky as Ratan-600 in order to get it."

"Can you find out?"

"Well, there's bound to be internet chatter if anyone has. We'll send out a general message to our people to look out for it."

"And of course it could be a hoax? Chinese? American? To make us look silly. Can you authenticate it as soon as possible, and find out where it comes from?"

Pavlov drummed his fingers on the desktop.

"Sooner or later, probably sooner, we should tell the world about this message. But it is so momentous that the ramifications could be enormous. It needs to be handled very carefully. We don't want to miss any opportunity to use it in our favour. No one must let anything slip. Do you trust the SETI people?"

"Well, they are committed to secrecy, and they know what happens to people who betray state secrets. I assume they will abide by all the documents they have had to sign to be working for us at all."

Pavlov looked thoughtful.

"Never assume... he said. "I think we need a bit of time. We should release something about it, that the message exists, before we release the full message. I'll talk to Irina Semyonova about it. You can go now, but be ready to come to the dacha next weekend. I'm thinking of a small group - you and Irina for the PR side - and Ivanov, from the military. It could be quite fun..."

Sergei Gromov left the Kremlin feeling uneasy. 'Fun?' What does Pavlov mean by that? The contents of the message were astonishing, and they had the ring of truth. But what was it in the message that Pavlov needed to think about, that might be 'quite fun' when they released the message to the world?

TASS: FOR IMMEDIATE RELEASE

RUSSIAN SCIENTISTS INTERCEPT FIRST EXTRA-TERRESTRIAL MESSAGE.

It Contains Vital Information Of Global Significance.

MOSCOW, MONDAY, SEPTEMBER 30 2024 12 MIDNIGHT.

Russian scientists and cryptographers have been working intensively to transcribe and interpret the first ever message from non-human life in space, detected by radio telescopes earlier this month. Many of the details are still under wraps. Sergei Gromov, supervising the team working on the message, said "We do not want to release the message until we know its significance. It is such an important step forward in understanding our place in the universe that the early release of a garbled or mistranslated message could cause alarm and panic. What I can say is that the message is of about 600 words or semantic units and has been transmitted in several different world languages. As far as we can tell, the content is all identical, allowing for differences between vocabularies."

President Dimitri Pavlov said, "I am proud that Russian scientists have detected and are working on this message. We hope to publish the full text within a month, along with an analysis of the significance of its contents. Russian astronomers are working on the task of analysing the origin of the message. The work they have done so far suggests a nonhuman source but the nature of the raw data does not give a precise location for the transmitter." A spokesman for TASS said that when the content and source of the message had been fully authenticated, and understood, it will be released to scientists and political leaders around the world for discussion of its implications.

Chapter 2

It was with difficulty that NASA had maintained funding for a SETI programme at all in the latest round of US government funding. Like a giant protoplasm, the Mission to Mars programme had slid pseudopodia into every crevice of the organisation, absorbing 20% here, 50% there, and the SETI programme was only saved by the efforts of Sherry Walker, a manager in the unmanned planetary exploration programme. She pleaded to be allowed to supervise a much-slimmed down search for extraterrestrial intelligence with a team of three, in addition to her duties processing data from several interplanetary probes, including Juno, now orbiting Jupiter , and New Horizons, the first spacecraft to study Pluto up close.

Sherry was passionate about SETI. Ever since her first visit to the Natural History Museum Planetarium while she was a girl growing up on the Lower West Side of New York she had been convinced of the possibility – the inevitability, really – of some kind of communication from the intelligent societies scientists calculated must exist in the Universe. And recent data made this even more likely, as billions of sun-like planetary systems were being predicted, using results from more and more sophisticated telescopes and data analysis programmes. A place at the Manhattan Science College, as one of its few black female students in those days, led her inexorably to study physics, maths and astronomy at SUNY, Stony Brook. An internship at NASA at the beginning of its affirmative action hiring policy (long before the movie *Hidden Figures* came out) put her foot on the bottom of a ladder she hoped to climb, perhaps all the way to the top.

As it turned out, by 2022 she had been at the same grade for ten years, supervising the processing of data from probes which had either reached the end of their natural life or sent faint little messages back from the outer reaches of the solar system, long after the official end of their mission. The SETI operation was a kind of consolation prize from her boss, Kent Branton, Director of Science at NASA, when it looked as if Sherry might decide to leave NASA and go somewhere where she could earn some real money.

Sherry's department was at the Goddard Space Flight Centre, in Maryland, just outside the Washington Beltway, and space was found for the SETI operation in a large area of the basement of Building 3A, previously used to store old paper printouts of data from the 1970s and 80s. It was given a lick of paint and equipped with an array of mainframe computers and monitors, which received data from telescopes around the world which might or might not be pointing at an area of the sky where known sun-like stars had been detected. The coverage was by no means comprehensive. Who knew where the first message – Sherry knew there would be one – would come from? Any direction was as likely as any other.

On September 30th, at about eight in the evening, Sherry was stirring a can of tomatoes into a pasta sauce. She liked to entertain, and about once a year she invited groups of staff – who she saw as friends as well – to supper and excessive wine-drinking, with her departmental budget paying for taxis to take them all home. Tonight was the turn of the SETI team, a smaller gathering – just three of them – than her last such occasion when the ten members of the Juno team crowded into her small flat in Georgetown.

Sherry heard the sound of the three of them, all younger than Sherry, chatting in the other end of the open plan area, and was pleased at how they were getting on with each other. Tom Sullion was the newest and youngest, and rather quiet, but the wine she had laid out along with the nibbles, seemed to have loosened his tongue a little.

He was arguing with Gary Dorval, a computer scientist in his late thirties.

"You can't think the Police are better than Fleetwood Mac," Tom said.

"You can't like Fleetwood Mac!" Mary Onofrio shouted, "You're just an embryo. They were formed before your grandmother was born."

"So what," Tom said. "People still listen to the Beatles, for God's sake."

There was a burble of overlapping chatter, and Sherry heard her cellphone ringing, on the kitchen island. Quickly, she dried her hands and answered the phone. It was from her boss, Kent Branton, who never called her outside office hours

As she listened, Gary, Mary and Tom carried on their noisy banter.

"Ssshhh!" Sherry said, holding up her hand, as she listened to what Branton was trying to say.

"Of course. Will you email it to me?" she said.

She closed the call and looked at her phone, waiting impatiently for the email.

The SETI team looked at Sherry's expression and fell silent.

She sat down in an armchair, and said "This could be important. Very important."

There was a ping and Sherry opened the email from Branton's office. It contained the Russian press release. Sherry read it out, to wide-eyed gasps from the other three.

"Fuck!" said Gary, and then, "Sorry."

"Your 'fuck' is entirely justified," Sherry said. "And why did it have to be the Russians? I thought their SETI programme was more moribund than ours."

"Did Kent Branton say anything else about it?" Gary said. "There seems to be nothing useful in what you read out that could tell us anything about the contents, or where in the sky it came from."

"Zilch," Sherry said, "But that shouldn't stop us drilling into our recent data, in case we missed something."

Mary, petite, with short hair and a perpetually worried expression, said "'Earlier this month' probably means between, say September 1st and about the 25th, giving them a few days to decipher it."

"Probably in the first half of the month," Gary said. "They'd need some time after deciphering it to decide what to do with it, and so on. Them wheels grind slow."

“Of course, Gary, you know Russia,” Sherry said. She remembered that his CV mentioned a Russian course at Moscow University.

“Do you want us to go back to the office now?” Mary said, ever the conscientious one.

“I’m not sure that would achieve much,” Sherry said. “If we don’t know where or when to look, we’d just be spinning our wheels. Let’s eat some pasta, drink some more wine, and maybe I can find out more before tomorrow. There’s a few people I can ring.”

“There’s someone I can ring too,” Gary said. “It’s a long shot, but I think my Russian teacher was moonlighting from a job somewhere in the Russian astronomy sector.”

The following morning, October 1st, in her office at the White House, President Jennifer Billings was perplexed by the territorial battle that was going on in front of her, among the people she had called together for an emergency meeting: Kent Branton, from NASA, ‘Tonk’ Wilbraham (‘where do men get these weird nicknames?’ she thought), director of CIA, Natasha Firestone, from the State Department Russian section, and Bob Newberry. the National Security Adviser, who had been close to her throughout her presidential campaign.

“Calm down, calm down,” Billings said, “I can't hear myself think. Does any of you have the actual message?”

The men looked sheepishly at each other.

“How much do we spend on the various organs of national security in this great state of ours?” Billings asked.

There were murmur of ‘billions’ among the assembled group.

“We only got the press release last night,” Natasha Firestone said.

“Press release?” Billings said in mock astonishment. “Is that how we spy these days? Espionage by press release?”

“To be fair, Madam President, messages from outer space have never been a very high security priority,” Bob Newberry said.

“Our SETI programme was downgraded in the last Mars rebudget,” Branton added.

“So, Natasha, do we know what the Russians are going to do next?

“Well, Madam President, we have to assume that they’ve decrypted it already. They wouldn't have released the news unless they have the whole message and were planning their next steps.”

“Mr Director Wilbraham,” Billings said, (she couldn't bring herself to say ‘Tonk’ in this setting, though she knew him well enough), “Do we have any intel on Pavlov's intentions?”

Wilbraham paused and then said, “There’s been chatter between the Kremlin, the FSB and a couple of university departments. That was last week when they would have reached peak decrypt, but nothing specific.”

“Don't you have anyone inside their SETI programme, or anyone to hack their data?” Billings said.

"As far as we knew, their SETI programme went the same way as ours," Branton said. "To be frank, I'm surprised they've been able to detect anything at all. The best receivers of galactic sources are everywhere else but Russia. I checked last night and they just have very old technology used mainly for planetary radio astronomy."

"But of course the Russians could have hacked any of the other major SETI receivers round the globe." Wilbraham said.

"And if they can, we can," Newberry said.

"But I'm pretty sure – even with our limited resources – we have an open line to any of the likely receivers," Branton said, "and we'd have been told within seconds if they'd received anything promising. And nothing's come across my desk in the last month."

"Right," said Billings, "I want to avoid breaking the hearts of fifty Boy Scouts waiting in the Jefferson Room merely because the world has been contacted for the first time in human history by extra-terrestrials – or not. I'm going to slip out now for fifteen minutes. When I come back, I want a full action plan for what we do next. Bill, can you keep these clowns in order?"

She swept out of the room leaving several disgruntled senior executives staring at their feet.

When Billings returned twenty minutes later she opened the door of the Oval Office on to a gabble of angry voices which fell suddenly silent.

"Jeez!" she said as she sat down, "Have I got to make all the decisions in this benighted country?"

"It's okay, Madam President," Newberry said, "We were just finishing our recommendations."

"So what was the arguing about?"

"It was less to do with what we recommend and more…" He looked meaningfully at Branton and Wilbraham. "More to do with who gets a budget increase for the next stages."

"Right. What are we going to do? Bill?"

Bill Newberry looked at his scribbled notes."

"Step One, don't do anything publicly until the Russians release the text. Maybe even cast doubt on the whole thing. Say that maybe it's a hoax…"

"Maybe it is," Billings said.

"Well, they're unlikely to make a fake message stand up for long, and if they're being played by someone else, it's certainly not us."

"Step Two?" Billings said.

"Two, move heaven and earth, not literally, to find out what's in the message and where it's from. NASA and the CIA can do that. Three, once we are absolutely sure of the source, propose to the UN that a conference of all major nations is held within six weeks, no later, and offer to chair it. The Russians will want to too of course…"

"Okay," Billings said, "Next."

"That's it," Newberry said.

"That's what you produce when I leave you alone for fifteen minutes?"

The room fell silent. Billings made a note on a yellow pad in front of her. Then she swivelled her chair round and looked out of the window, across the lawn towards the city.

"Your list is not all shit, Bill. Step 1 is terrific. And that's all we are going to do, publicly, anyway."

Bill Newberry looked down at his list.

"Let the Russians release the text?"

"Yup. But in private, of course, Kent and his merry men – and women – can scour the world's telescopes for the message, and Tonk and his merry men and women can spy the hell out of the Russians to find out what they are on about. Now shoo!"

The general chatter over the guest night dinner in St James', presided over by Miles Cadogan, was that if there was a genuine message it was likely to be some sort of 'Hello, here we are' message, a bit like waving a flag in the distance to attract the attention of someone on a distant mountain top.

"Even that would, of course, be exciting," Paul Spearman explained, to the fellows and guests around him at High Table, "but bear in mind, even the nearest earthlike planet, Proxima Centauri B, is four light years away, so any dialogue started by this first message is going to be pretty slow. Four years for them to receive a reply from us and another four years for us to receive their response."

"So Professor Spearman," said one of the diners, husband of the college bursar, "How would we read this message once it's received?"

"Well, I would have expected just a string of prime numbers, the sort of thing that could only come from an intelligent mind. That's all we'd need to be sure that the message was genuine – I mean, once we'd established that the whole thing wasn't a hoax – by the Russians or by someone trying to fool the Russians."

"But Paul…" Miles Cadogan chipped in, "The Russian press release talks of several languages, so it sounds more sophisticated than a string of numbers."

"That's right, Miles. It is puzzling that the first ever message like this is plunging straight into some detailed content," Paul said. "Most unexpected. We are all agog for what happens next."

Ravi Chandra, the mathematician, played with a warm bread roll he had just been given by a waiter. He wanted to chip in but as usual felt a little overawed by the company. He had been at the college only a year and still couldn't even bring himself to call Miles Cadogan 'Miles', but called him 'Master' instead, like the College Butler or Miles' secretary. However, he decided to plunge in.

"Of course, prime numbers can do more than just list themselves," he said. "They can be used to carry information, like letters in a language. They could even be used by the … aliens to demonstrate some mathematical proof no one has yet cracked on Earth. The Riemann Hypothesis, for example." (This was a hypothesis Chandra himself had been trying to prove for a decade or more, and he felt he was near to a solution.)

"How disappointing," Miles said. "I feel at the very least we should be looking forward to the secrets of the universe, not something only a handful of people can understand."

"Master, there are more than a handful of good mathematicians in the world. In this college, even."

"I know, Ravi, I was making a poor joke at your expense, because my knowledge of maths stopped at differentiating x^2. The answer's 2x, right? I will rely on you to explain the secrets of the universe to me if that's really what the message is about."

At the end of dinner, Miles walked back to the Master's Lodge with Paul Spearman, who was going to collect his bike from the rack by Skimbles Bridge and cycle home to the Madingley Road.

"Is this message thing going to go anywhere?" Miles said.

"Who knows?" Paul said. "There have been false alarms before. The Wow! signal in Ohio 1977. Even Jocelyn Bell's discovery back in 1967, which turned into pulsars. But nothing with any actual intelligible content."

"So if this was an actual message it would be significant whatever it says?"

"Jesus, yes, Miles! Wouldn't you be excited? That someone up there..." He pointed to the star-studded night sky. "... is trying to get in touch with us?"

Miles thought for a moment as they walked under the archway that led to the chapel.

"You know, I can't get worked up about it. I prefer immediate communication with humans in societies, some kind of dialogue. By the sound of it, any conversation with these ... entities would be very slow."

Paul laughed. "You're not much of a romantic, Miles, are you?"

Miles felt slightly affronted. "Sure I am. I love a mystery. Look at the structure of the society of the Khasi in Meghalaya..."

"I would if I knew how to," Paul said with a smile, but Miles was already in explanatory mode and in no mood for flippant remarks.

"...But if there is a society up there that's talking to us," Miles said, "It seems we're not going to get much further than 'Hello, how are you? what's your name? how many legs do you have? where do you live?' before we all die."

"I think it's just possible we could be in for a series of events that put the piddling preoccupations of human societies in the shade. Stay tuned. Here's my bike."

"Well, it would certainly increase applications to study science," Miles said. "Although we're pretty well-supplied at the moment, thanks to an increase in climate science."

"Please, I don't want to increase my teaching load," Paul said as he walked away. "NGC 4885 is just getting to an interesting stage. I've never seen a galaxy like it."

Miles let himself into the Lodge. As he took his coat off he heard the strains of Arab music from upstairs.

"Loo, I'm home!" he called, but there was no reply from his wife.

'Deep in her photos,' he thought, and went into the sitting room to switch on the news. The BBC seemed to be taking the Russian press release as seriously as Paul had. There were the usual reporters and pop science interviewees who knew no more than was in the press release but tried to generate some kind of spurious excitement out of it.

Miles opened his laptop and read an email reminding him that there was only a week to go before he had to submit the final version of the paper he was giving at a conference in Boston early next year. He started to type a reply to the conference organiser.

In British government circles, officials were slow to react to the press release. The Prime Minister, Carla Baxter, had enough on her plate: a meeting with a rebellious clique in her party who threatened to reduce the government's majority of 19 at a vote on China, an uncomfortable appointment with her inadequate transport secretary who really had to go but was clinging on, and a potential security breach at GCHQ which its director wanted to keep out of the media. But Baxter fitted a briefing about the Russian press release into her diary, with Cardew Bateman, President of the Royal Society who favoured the 'hoax' theory.

"Dr Bateman," she said to the scientist, "If this did turn into something, who would deal with it in the science community? Would we set up some kind of working group to handle it?"

"It depends what handling is required. It sounds as if the Russians are doing all the necessary processing, and will just release the message in clear – in ordinary language. We can't really decide how to handle it until we know what's in it. If it isn't a hoax, that is…"

"Shouldn't we have someone standing by? The Astronomer Royal for example. Isn't this the sort of job he should be doing for his nugatory stipend."

There was no love lost between Bateman and Paul Spearman. They invariably clashed at Royal Society Council Meetings, where the Astronomer Royal had an ex officio role. Of course, people always argued for their own specialties when it came to funding, but Spearman was quite happy to argue against someone else even if it was way outside his own areas. Bateman's own lab, working on reverse transcriptase, had suffered when Spearman gave a casting vote against supporting the research.

"I really don't think Spearman is the man for the job," he said. "Let me think about it further when we know what's in the message. It's unlikely to be earth-shattering."

Unfortunately, earth-shattering is exactly what the message was, or promised to be, when the Russians released the text two weeks later.

Moscow TASS Agency, October 15th 2025

URGENT RELEASE, NO EMBARGO

FULL TEXT OF MESSAGE RECEIVED FROM EXTRATERRESTRIAL SOURCE ON SEPTEMBER 15TH, 2025

[This message was written in binary code which, after deciphering was shown to repeat the same text in seven world languages. This press release is issued in each of the languages to the relevant nations or peoples. Russian scientists and astronomers are actively trying to confirm the nature and location of the source. The original sequence of binary digits that carried the message in its various languages can be accessed at: www.messagebinary.gov.ru]

"1.) This message has been composed by the fully automated Outpost of a civilization on a planet round a star which appears on Earth star maps in a constellation you call Cetus. The star is 3.5 magnitude and you have given it the name Tau Ceti. Our planet is the only planet orbiting the star and is approximately 1.7 Earth masses.

As you know, Tau Ceti is about 12 "light years" from your solar system. Our civilization sent probes to a number of likely exoplanets 400,000 of your years ago, and the probes, which are like the rovers you sent to your moon, Mars, and other planets in your system, although much more sophisticated, were programmed to send radio signals back to us with analyses of possible life forms.

We were very interested to discover a range of life forms on your planet and by analysing the data, we were able, over a number of years, to work out the microbiology and physiology of Earth creatures, including the common genetic basis of transmission of characteristics and how species evolved.

None of the other life forms detected by our rovers showed signs of intelligent life, and in particular, any indication of language, necessary for the evolution of an intelligent civilization. So we decided to accelerate the evolution of life on Earth towards intelligent life. As a result, over many centuries, we developed another type of probe, small, compact and versatile, carried in a large 'factory ship' which we launched about 300,000 years ago, containing thousands of the small probes designed to seek out life forms which were capable of being accelerated towards intelligence by genetic manipulation, to facilitate the development of language.

We had to wait many thousands of years for evidence that this attempt to accelerate your evolution had succeeded but in your year 1900 our 'factory ship', now an Outpost in your solar system, detected radio waves from Earth. These increased over the next few years and their nature suggested that at last, the civilization we had seeded had reached a high level of civilization.

2.) Our Outpost was fully equipped to monitor your communications of all types and build up a 'picture' (though we have no word for this since we do not use light patterns to perceive) of your progress towards the heights of civilization, which as, in a sense, your progenitor we wished you to advance towards. This Outpost is now sending you this message, composed in some of the major languages used by your species. The Outpost includes quantum computing facilities with sophisticated artificial intelligence and neural net learning abilities. It also includes nano-factories capable of manufacturing any objects, devices, or substances whose molecular structure is known. Now, after fifty years of observation, we have decided to communicate with you.

3.) We have become increasingly alarmed at the state of planet Earth and fear that it is reaching a point of no return as a result of the actions of homo sapiens, the species we feel responsible for, and of its failure to take corrective measures to prevent a series of catastrophes, evidence for which has been accumulating. We do not need to remind you of the threats posed to the human race by the following: one million species are at risk of extinction; ecosystems are disappearing at an alarming rate; deserts are spreading; wetlands disappearing; forests being cut down; oceans overfished and stocked with plastic; air pollution killing more than 9 million humans a year; and of course, the inexorable rise of greenhouse gas emissions. (We have been only too aware of the dangers of this as a result of our observation of Venus over millennia, which has shown the disappearance of a previously varied biosphere.)

It is almost as if humankind, one of a handful of intelligent civilizations we have detected in our galaxy, is waging war on nature. We cannot allow this to continue. So we propose to intervene.

4.) It is clear that our experiment of developing a life form capable of matching and eventually excelling our own level of civilization has failed. We have no alternative but to prevent further negative consequences for the nonhuman biosphere by a painless and instantaneous annihilation of the entire homo sapiens species, to take place five years from the receipt by any Earth inhabitants of this message. (Outpost monitoring of your media will indicate when this is) The method by which we will carry out this cleansing process will be revealed nearer the time."

NOTE BY RUSSIAN GOVERNMENT

We believe this message to be authentic and are taking steps to establish its source. It is clearly the case that there is a 3.5 magnitude star in the constellation Cetus, which astronomers have named Tau Ceti. Although it is a similar stellar type to our sun, we have not detected any planets around it which might bear life. But, as part of an attempt to communicate with possible extraterrestrial civilizations, the star was targeted by the so-called Teen Age Message, sent from the Yevpatoria Planetary Radar to six solar-type stars during August–September 2001. The structure of this message was suggested by Alexander Zaitsev, Chief Scientist at Russia's Institute of Radio-engineering and Electronics. The message's content and target stars were selected by a group of teens from four Russian cities, who collaborated in person and via the Internet.

The scientific facts do not, course, prove an extraterrestrial origin for the message. However, nothing in the message contradicts what we know of science and the universe. While we attempt to gather more information about the source, we believe the likelihood that the message is genuine is so strong that the world must act. We are prepared to coordinate that action, and suggest ways in which, using Russian technology the threat contained in the message can be averted or eliminated.

People familiar with the story of Orson Welles' radio play based on H.G. Wells' (no relation) novel, *War of the Worlds*, and the panic it caused in 1938 among Americans at the time, gave a knowing nod when the Russians released the message, or the Message with a capital letter, as it came to be called. In fact, Miles Cadogan himself had actually written a paper for a journal called Social Anthropology, with the title 'Why People Panic'. He showed, using a number of case histories, that even in extreme situations, mass panics were very rare. People internalised their perceptions of a new situation, and made risk assessments which had far more to do with their rating on the 'Structure of Temperament Questionnaire', devised by a Russian psychologist, Vladimir Rusalov, than with any fact-based assessment of true risk.

So on the evening of October 15th, when Miles and his wife Leila sat down to eat a late supper of quiche and salad, and Paul Spearman rang to tell them to switch on the news, Miles was less worried than Leila at the torrent of coverage of the full text of the Message.

EXTRACT FROM TRANSCRIPT OF THE EVENING'S TELEVISION TRANSMISSIONS, OCTOBER 15TH, 2024.

BBC News 24

20.53. NEWSREADER: Now some breaking news. The Russian government has released the text of the message it claimed two weeks ago came from an extraterrestrial source. It states that scientists have been working on the message to interpret it and understand its significance and that they believe the text released tonight is accurate. Our science correspondent, Baz Franklin, has been taking a first look at the message. Baz:

BAZ FRANKLIN: At first glance, the message claims that a civilization in the constellation Cetus, which means 'the Whale', has been following the evolution of life on earth over millennia and has observed the deterioration in the conditions on Earth that threaten the survival of life on earth. Because of that, they say, and I quote, "We have no alternative but to prevent further negative consequences for the nonhuman biosphere by a painless and instantaneous annihilation of the entire homo sapiens species."

NEWSREADER: That sounds a bit drastic, Baz. Why would they want to do something like that? What's in it for them?

BAZ FRANKLIN: They say in another part of the message – *(he scans the paper in his hand)* Yes, this is it. They say they sent a probe 300,000 years ago to infect the species – they mean pre-human primates – with a virus that implanted genes for intelligence and language. So they claim to have created humans, effectively. And so they seem to claim the right to destroy them.

NEWSREADER: And who are 'they', do we think?

BAZ FRANKLIN: Well, I mentioned the constellation Cetus. So the most we can say is that they must be a civilization on a planet round a star in that constellation?

NEWSREADER: And how far away is that constellation?

BAZ FRANKLIN: Actually, Anita, the stars in a constellation are not all at the same distance.

NEWSREADER: So they're like a galaxy, a collection of stars?

BAZ FRANKLIN: No, not exactly.

The newsreader turns away and listens to her earpiece.

NEWSREADER: I've just heard that the Prime Minister is preparing to address the country about the message. Let's go over to Downing Street.

Outside 10 Downing Street, a BBC political correspondent is shuffling papers.

CORRESPONDENT: Anita, we understand that the Russians have released this message simultaneously around the world and that they have not given sight of it in advance to world leaders. But Carla Baxter, the Prime Minister, wants to make a preliminary announcement to prevent panic and reassure – oh, we're going over now.

P.M.'s Outer Office

CARLA BAXTER: Many of you will have heard about the message which the Russians claim is from an extraterrestrial intelligence. Now, our scientists are looking closely at the wording of the message, alleged to be translated by Russian linguists from texts sent in several different languages by the intelligent civilization. We think it is too early to accept the truth of claims in the message that humankind was 'created' in a sense by the civilization, from lower life forms, and that because, in their view, we have failed to take care of the planet and that the situation can only get worse, they are making plans to destroy mankind in the future. All of these statements are hypothetical. And indeed, we do not yet have evidence that this is not some kind of hoax from a hacker or even by the Russian government. I urge people to stay calm and not to act as if their lives are going to end in five years' time, the period mentioned in the message. And even in the worst case, if this message turns out to be true, I plan to talk to other world leaders in the next 24 hours to cooperate on a plan to prevent the course of action set out in the Message.

I have given instructions to the London Stock Exchange to remain closed until further notice, and other countries are following suit. His

Majesty King Charles has been informed and he proposes to address the nation tomorrow morning at 11 a.m. Thank you, and God bless us all.

CORRESPONDENT: Well, I don't think there's ever been such a prime ministerial message to the country as grave as that. I understand from a Downing Street source that the PM received the Message only twenty minutes ago, at the same time as the media, and thought it essential to say something to reassure people. What is important to cling to in that broadcast is that no one is sure that the Message is even from aliens, or that what it says is correct. Since the Russians are the only people who have seen the original message, we cannot even be sure that they have translated it correctly. Mrs Baxter and other world leaders will be pressing the Russians for the raw data so that other scientists can check that the translation is correct. One source told me that only with detailed information about the raw signal that was first detected can we ever discover whether it is genuinely from an extraterrestrial source. For now, back to the studio.

NEWSREADER: Thank you, Laura. We'll be following that story closely. Meanwhile, there is news that a panda at Chester Zoo has given birth to a cub after three failed attempts to mate her with a panda on loan from China…

21:13 p.m.

ITV Love Island – The boys and girls are in a villa on Mauritius.

DENISE: Get your fucking 'ands off me. When I said I liked you, I didn't mean you could get into my knickers…

GARRY: Sorry, sorry. When I said I liked you, I didn't realise what a stuck-up bitch you were…

Denise lunges at Gary. Picture goes blank. Caption on screen:

"Important announcement follows"

ITN Newsroom

NEWSREADER: We interrupt this programme for very important announcement. The Russian government has just released the text of a message which it claimed two weeks ago had come from an intelligent source outside the earth. If confirmed, this will be the first ever such message, the culmination of fifty years of monitoring space by scientists from all around the world. We will provide a detailed account of the message in our news bulletin at 10 p.m. It contains information which world leaders are already discussing because of the implications for the future of mankind. Now back to Love Island…

Sherry Walker was at her local gym in Georgetown when the text of the Message was released. As she reached three miles on the treadmill, with her earbuds tuned to some Howard McGhee jazz, something made her look around and she noticed a group of other gym users clustering round a TV set fixed high on one of the walls. She stepped off the treadmill, seized a towel and went and stood behind about a dozen people. One of them, a hedge fund manager called Drex Beamsped, turned and saw Sherry.

“This is your thing, isn’t it?” he said. “The Russians have released that message they talked about.”

Sherry could see but not hear the newsreader, against a background of – yes, what else ?– an image of ET and a hammer and sickle, even though the Soviet Union died more than thirty years ago.

“Can someone turn the sound up?” Sherry said.

“No one can find the remote,” said a young woman in a tracksuit.

‘Oh, shit,’ Sherry said to herself and headed for the dressing rooms. She knew she was going to have a late night, whatever the news. Every media outlet in the US had her cellphone number as the go-to person whenever anything extraterrestrial came up. Sure enough, when she took her phone out of the locker, there were already twenty or so messages, including one from Kent Branton.

Sherry didn’t even bother to go home but set off straight for the Goddard Space Center. But while she was on the Beltway, she received a call from Kent.

“Where the fuck are you?!” a furious Kent Branton said.

“I tried to return your call,” Sherry said, angry at his tone. “You obviously didn’t listen to your messages.”

“How could I? The world and his grandmother’s been ringing me. Including the president. Wherever you’re going, turn round, ring a number I will text you, give your ID details and head for to the White House. Your name will be at the East Gate.”

Turn round? Sherry didn’t bother to ask how he knew what direction she was going in.

“The White House? Who to see?”

“The President of course.”

Sherry was aghast.

“I’ll have to go home to change!” she said.

“No time. What are you wearing anyway.”

“Sweats,” Sherry said.

“Oh, shit. I know someone in the Press Office. I’ll see if she can help. Come straight here.”

Sherry’s mind raced as she found the next turn off the Beltway, stopped in a layby and looked at her text messages.

“Call Mary-Ellen Pomfret, 202-456-1400 NOW”

A pleasant sounding woman seemed ready for Sherry’s call, and took down her social security number, passport number and car registration. “Your details will be at the East Gate,” she said.

As she drove back to central Washington Sherry wondered what she could possibly say to the President, whom she’d never met, which would possibly cast new light on the Russian message, which she hadn’t even read. She rang Mary’s number and hoped she was not at a movie or somewhere else where she couldn’t answer.

“Sherry!” Mary said excitedly, “Have you seen it? It’s amazing!”

"No, I haven't. That's why I'm calling. I'm on the way to the White House and feel a little under-briefed for my meeting with the President." She had to admit it felt rather good saying that.

"The President! Jesus! That's exciting."

"It'll be even more exciting if I tell her I haven't read the Message. Will you read it to me as I go along?"

"Sure," Mary said, "Hang on."

There was a pause while she found the Message on the screen of her laptop.

"Here's how it starts," Mary said, and started reading. "Full text of message received from extraterrestrial source on September 15th, 2025…"

Sherry made a mental note of the date. It would help to try to find other copies of the Message if it had been detected by any other radio telescope.

By the time Sherry gave her name to the security man at the East Gate, she had heard the whole Message, and asked Mary to email the text to her phone. It was so momentous she couldn't really process the core of the message, the annihilation threat. Not so much a threat, more a promise.

But there were some interesting inferences to be made, based on the wording and the Russians' own brief account of how they had obtained it. She hoped that would be enough to justify being summoned by the President.

Half an hour later, wearing an ill-fitting tunic dress lent her by Kent's friend in the Press Office, Sherry sat facing the President of the United States, her heart racing. Her hand was trembling a little as she tried to drink a cup of very hot White House coffee, wrapped with a White House paper napkin to insulate her hand, and hold a plate with a brownie on it.

"So Dr Walker, I understand you are the SETI Queen?" President Billings said.

"Hardly the Queen, Madam President. More like a lowly princess."

"But Kent told me you were in charge of the whole US SETI operation?"

Sherry looked across at Kent Branton who was expressionless.

Sherry thought 'Does the President know the *whole* US SETI operation is three men and a dog, metaphorically speaking'.

"Yes, but we've not had that much SETI material to work on recently," she said, "so I'm also running a couple of data analysis programmes on Juno and some defunct probes."

"OK, let's cut to the chase. Here are my questions." The President looked down at a yellow legal pad she was holding.

"1. Is it a hoax? 2. If it's not a hoax, where has the Message come from? 3. What is the likelihood that a civilization…" She looked at her pad again "… twelve light years away could destroy humanity anyway? Let's start with those."

Sherry did her best to answer, but she was sure she sounded vague and uncertain. How would she know if it was a fake? She heard it read to her once and then skimmed it while she was changing out of her sweats. 'Where it had come' from wasn't easy to answer either. The messengers identified themselves as from a planet round Tau Ceti, a star which had been on every SETI watchlist for a number of years because of its sun-like characteristics, but what was this about an Outpost in our solar system?

"The most interesting thing, Madame President, is this mention of an 'Outpost'. Clearly, they imply that this is far away from their planet and presumably near enough to ours to make monitoring and sending 'nanobots' and stuff not too time-consuming. That could put it in the Oort Cloud or more likely in the solar system. The interesting thing about that is that it might explain why no other SETI telescope has spotted it. Or at least we haven't heard if they have."

"Why not? They're all looking in the sky aren't that?" President Billings said.

"Yes, but they are looking at the fixed stars. If the Outpost in actually in the solar system, its signals would only be picked up by a telescope pointing at a planet, say, or one of the asteroids, which move across the sky each night."

"So Kent, can we use that information to look again?"

"Our SETI programme's never considered looking for intelligent life in the solar system. We haven't found any life outside the Earth so far. What do you think, Sherry?"

'Passing the buck,' Sherry thought.

"The best we could do," she said, "is tap into an entirely different group of observatories which might have been doing different types of observations, not SETI work. But this Message may have come in a one-off burst and the chances of catching it might be slim."

"Do these places record their data?" Billings said, becoming more interested in the whole matter. "Maybe if you know when the message was received they could go back into their records?"

"Sure," Kent said, "We'll look into it."

"And my other question?"

Sherry remembered.

"Well, the only way they could carry out their threat of annihilation would be if they have the means in this 'Outpost' they talk about. At twelve light years away, they could hardly destroy us in five years' time. I suppose the 'Outpost' could do it but it would have to be unimaginably complex and versatile, something very different from just a monitoring and messaging probe. It seems unlikely."

"Unlikely or nor, I think we have to take it seriously. I'm about to have a meeting with the joint chiefs of staff. They will want to destroy half the universe to prevent our own annihilation, so if you can narrow down the location of the Outpost a bit I'd be grateful."

As Kent Branton and Sherry walked back to their cars, they were both thoughtful. Then Sherry said "Is she serious? How can I and three willing but inexperienced enthusiasts save the world by finding this Outpost?"

"I might be able to find you another member of staff," Kent said.

"Ten more would be better," Sherry said.

"Or you could use human ingenuity instead of brute force?" Kent said.

The following morning, the US SETI team assembled at 8 a.m. raring to go if only they knew where.

Mary Onofrio was still on a high, after her vicarious trip to the White House. Well, it was her reading out of the Message to Sherry which meant Sherry was briefed to meet the President.

"What was it like?" she said excitedly to Sherry.

"Oh, same old same old," Sherry said, to general laughter. Then she reached into her laptop case. "Have a souvenir."

She handed a slightly crumpled paper napkin to Mary who looked with amazement at the White House logo.

"Now, down to business," Sherry said to the group.

"What is the business?" Tom said. "We've all read the Message over and over, but it is what it is. Either we're going to be annihilated or we're not. There doesn't seem much we can do about it."

"Never mind the annihilation threat..." Sherry said.

"Oh, no, of course not. I have no plans for 2030 anyway," Tom said.

"No, I mean it's not our job to do anything about that. Let's concentrate on something we know about. The location of the senders of the Message. The President would really like to know. Because, in fact, if you think about it, there's no way a civilisation twelve light years away could annihilate humanity in five years."

"Except through a wormhole, maybe," Gary said. "If they're as far advanced as they seem, they may have mastered the technique."

"Park that idea," Sherry said. 'Unlikely,' she thought 'but a smart idea.' "So what about this 'Outpost' in the solar system? What do we think that is?"

"Probably just some probe to relay the prepared Message when the time was right."

"It needs to be a bit more than that," Mary chipped in. "They say it's been monitoring us at least since 1900, and it must have enough AI to interpret the increase in radio transmission and analyse human communication. That's not some poky little satellite."

"Any ideas for how we pin down the location of the Outpost?" Sherry said.

For the next hour, the team discussed every element of the solar system where an extraterrestrial civilisation might have left a probe, undetected during more than sixty years of study by astronomers. Then Sherry set each of them to write a summary of their ideas: Mary to write about Mercury out to Mars, Gary to take Jupiter to Pluto, and Tom to deal with the asteroids and moons of the solar system.

"This is the best we can do," she said, "until the Russians release the raw signals on which they base their decrypting. That may have more information in the metadata."

Chapter 3

Within 24 hours of the Message being released, the world's press did its best to deal with the massive implications it contained, but usually fell short, often doing what newspapers do and trying to fit it into the ideological framework each media outlet was comfortable with.

THE LONDON TIMES, November 2nd, 2025

FIRST LEADER

In the hours following the release by Russia of the alleged message from an alien civilization, the world was in turmoil. No single event has ever attracted the attention of every citizen from world leader to ordinary members of the public in every nation in the world with the impact and reach of yesterday's news.

But in spite of its potential importance and of the assertions of authenticity emerging from Moscow, the message cannot yet be taken as a basis for making plans, even though the news it purports to carry – if correct – has profound and worrying implications for the whole of mankind.

Let us, even now, while most of us have barely absorbed the significance of the message for our lives if it is true, consider the following cautious steps which any government, including ours, should take before reacting precipitously.

1. Whatever the Russian recipients of this message say, we should demand cast-iron proof of the extraterrestrial origins of the message.
2. So far, the world has read only a series of translations into major languages, made by Russian translators. While it is possible that other countries, including the USA, have received or at least analysed the original data, there is no external corroboration of the Message or its content. This corroboration must be obtained, perhaps by authentication of the original raw data received on Earth. Only then can the world consider what action needs to be taken to forestall or otherwise respond to the assertion in the Message of the destruction of humanity in five years' time.
3. Whatever action is taken in response to the Message, if it is genuine, will need the collaboration of the nations of the world with a unanimity which has seldom if ever been obtained. The doleful progress of the coronavirus pandemic of a few years ago, a far less serious threat than the annihilation promised by the Message, showed how difficult it was for world leaders to adopt an agreed and effective policy in the face of a global threat.
4. The laudable decision at very short notice to keep the world's stock markets closed is an essential step which must be maintained until a decision emerges about future actions. If the message is correct, and the intentions of its writers are genuinely expressed, any attempt to prevent the annihilation or, if it is even

possible, to contact the Messengers will require a huge economic effort and the collaboration of world economies. The short term drain on resources which might occur if the markets remain open could make far more difficult any effective response.

Clearly, the next few days are going to pose many challenges to world leaders and their governments. As we said often during the coronavirus pandemic, it is important to 'follow the science'. Since with the Message and its implications the science is the only way through the minefield of interpretation, analysis and risk assessment, it will be very important for the world's scientists to concentrate all their efforts on guiding a global scientific response to this epoch-making event.

GUARDIAN, October 17th, 2025

FIRST LEADER

Never has the world faced such a potentially momentous event as the Message which Russia claims has come from an extraterrestrial source and which predicts the annihilation of the human race in five years' time.

Of course, as has been pointed out in most of the global reaction in the hours since the content of the Message was announced, its authenticity must be verified. Russia has form in issuing misleading or mendacious information, but the import of the Message has such grave implications for mankind that no time can be lost in formulating a global action plan. If it takes a week to validate the source of the Message, that week must not be wasted. The world will heave a sigh of relief if the Message is a hoax. But no harm will be done if that week has been spent starting to devise a global system for addressing the myriad issues posed by the Message. It might even be that such activity will lay the groundwork for a better response to the problems faced by the world, defined so expertly in the message.

There is another issue in the Message that has been overshadowed by the threat of annihilation. We may well ask why such action would be contemplated by a civilization so much more advanced than ours. What threat does our neglect of our planet pose to them? The answer lies in paragraph 2 of the message, where the civilization claims to have created homo sapiens by genetic manipulation of our ancestors. If this is the case, we are, as they say, their progeny. Their attitude to us may be that of a parent whose child has gone astray. It would be harsh, certainly, to kill such a child, but there have been cases where criminals in our society have been disowned by their parents. Nevertheless, there are other responses to a child who has gone bad. Perhaps this parent civilization can be persuaded – if there is any way of communicating with them – that mankind can reform even at this late date and undo the harm that it has caused.

The one thing that must be avoided, if it turns out that the Message is genuine, is panic and despair, and here, too, a global response by world governments has a part to play. Whatever plan emerges over the next weeks and months, it must be calm, measured, unanimous and hopeful. Very few national governments showed themselves capable of such qualities during the coronavirus pandemic. Let us hope that this far graver crisis can unite the world in a more effective and ultimately more beneficial response.

NEWSPAPER HEADLINES, OCTOBER 17TH 2025:

Daily Mail

'ET message is Russian hoax' says Megan Markle's astronomer cousin.

The Sun

'ET' drink and be merry. For tomorrow we (may) die

Financial Times

ALIEN THREAT TRIGGERS FALLS IN CONSTRUCTION, AVIATION AND ENERGY SHARES, RISES IN PRIVATE SPACE INDUSTRIALS AND PHARMACEUTICALS, BEFORE STOCK EXCHANGES CLOSE.

New York Times

OP-ED

The rush to believe the dramatic news from Russia could be a dangerous phenomenon. Within twenty-four hours of the release of the alleged text of the Message, statesmen, politicians and ordinary members of the public were falling over themselves to propose actions to defend the Earth from annihilation or, conversely, to 'negotiate with' the extraterrestrial civilisation from whom the threat is said to come.

The issue has divided Congress along predictable lines. Republicans argue for an immediate programme to revive and expand the abandoned Star Wars project, in order to defeat a threat which, if it exists at all, is likely to involve weapons or techniques which are far beyond the skills of us earthlings to defeat. Meanwhile, Democrats argue either to 'wait and see' or to increase scientific efforts to understand more about the so-called Outpost and its intentions. And predictably, Donald Trump, from his prison cell, has claimed that the message is a hoax dreamed up by the climate change lobby, afraid that they are losing the argument among the ordinary people of America.

Of course, as the next few hours and days pass, 'wait and see' will surely be the correct option. What difference will a few days inactivity make to the eventual dangers of annihilation if the message is genuine?; how foolish will those people seem who call for action – and expenditure – today if the message has an alternative explanation? And there are several explanations which are more likely:

A Russian-organised hoax, to terrify the world for some motive of international politics? A hacker holed up in some student dorm or Israeli start-up? A Chinese attempt to destabilize Russia and the US?

There is no doubt the Message is cleverly written. This is exactly the sort of wording we might expect from a super-intelligent civilisation which had been observing Earth for millennia and had good enough AI and computing power to understand the culture and languages of humans. But then, of course, it is also the sort of wording that a hoaxer or malicious government could infer that such a civilisation would use.

We will make a prediction. If the nations of the globe hold their collective breaths for a month, the situation in November will look very different, and be much more nuanced than anyone can possible anticipate in the current mix of panic, calls for action, and forebodings of doom. And you read it here first.

New York Daily News

BS from ET

So the aliens are taken in by the climate change lobby, and are threatening to destroy us? Even their super-intelligence has been fooled by the torrent of lies and fake statistics alleging disaster for the globe in a few decades. If ET and his friends are so concerned about man's alleged destruction of the environment in the next fifty years, why are they planning to destroy it in five? We should send a message back to them, telling them where to get off, and saying we don't believe that their threat is serious. In even five years, if the defense industries of the world collaborate, we could develop a shield that would make it impossible for any weapon, however sophisticated, to destroy the entire human race. And combine that with deep shelters for the nucleus of a future population, and their threat will be shown to be what it really is: BS from ET.

A hundred or so new students in their first few days of term were lined up for a photograph in Skimbles Court in St. James's College. They were in rows perched precariously on a rather rickety wooden framework brought out each year for just this purpose. It was a three step structure, and one of the assistant porters was creating a space in the middle of the front row.

"That's for the Master," he said. "He should be along in a minute. Oh, there he is."

Miles Cadogan hurried across the grass. He didn't notice that his assistant, Debbie, was hurrying along behind him.

"Dr Cadogan," she called, breathlessly. "There's a call for you, an important one."

"Debbie, can you take a number? I'll call back. This will only take ten minutes."

"It's from...", she said and hesitated. Then she mouthed something which Cadogan couldn't lip read.

"What?" he said.

She came closer and spoke in a low voice. "It's 10 Downing Street."

Miles looked puzzled

"What about?"

"Wouldn't say. They're still holding, back in your office."

"Mr. Patch, would you mind? Apparently, there's an urgent call, a very urgent call," Miles said to the assistant porter.

When he walked back towards the Lodge, Patch apologised to the photographer waiting by his tripod, and turned to the students.

"Relax, but don't change your position. It took a long time for you to work it out. I don't want to go through that again. Anybody would think you didn't know your ABCs."

In his office, Miles Cadogan picked up the phone, pressed a button and said "Hello."

"Professor Cadogan, it's the PM's private secretary," a male voice said.

"The PM?"

"The prime minister."

"That's what I thought you meant. If she has a son who wants to come to St. James', I'm afraid she'll have to go through proper procedures." He meant it as a joke.

"I'll pass that on to her," the voice said dryly. "Now, can you come here for a meeting tomorrow? It's about the Message. The PM is getting a small group together."

"Really?" Miles said. "How could I help?"

"She's concerned about panic, panicking crowds. We think you wrote a paper about that."

'"We think",' Miles thought. 'Google thinks, more like it. And that was ten years ago. I've moved on since then.' He supposed that John Drury at the University of Sussex must be out of the country, and he was the best they could do at short notice.

"There'll be someone from GCHQ and someone from the Met."

Miles assumed it meant the Metropolitan Police rather than the New York art museum.

"Do they think only Londoners might panic?"

"I don't have time to go into that. I have a lot of calls to make. Tomorrow morning at 10.30? Your name will be at the door."

"Well, I'll have to cancel a tutorial and a Senate House meeting. But I suppose it's important."

"Very. We'll see you tomorrow."

"Since it's for my country, yes. Do you want me to bring anything?"

"No, it will be a brainstorm session. The PM will lead a heads up."

"Oh well. I'll bring my brain," he said, "and my head."

"If you need to get in touch my name is Martin."

"Thank you, Martin."

"No, Paul Martin."

"Oh, well. Thank you, Paul. Goodbye."

Debbie put her head through the door with a quizzical look on her face. Miles wondered for a moment and then remember the matriculation photo.

"Sorry!" he said, "I'm coming."

In all his career, Miles Cadogan never dreamed that there would be a reason for a social anthropologist to be invited to 10 Downing Street, other, perhaps, than to some rubber chicken buffet to burnish the intellectual credentials of the government.

When he went back to the Lodge for lunch, he dropped it into the conversation as Leila was serving out an aubergine stew.

"I shall be in London most of tomorrow, Loo" he said.

"This is rather sudden," she said. "You know I've got a charity auction of some of my prints for Medical Aid for Palestine. I need you there to get the bidding going in case it's slow to start."

"I know I said I would, but when my nation calls, I have to respond."

"And which bit of our nation? Any Questions? The Moral Maze? The BBC isn't the whole nation, you know."

Miles ate a forkful of the stew.

"Delicious," he said. "And to answer your question, our beloved prime minister called today and wishes to see me tomorrow."

"You spoke to Mrs Baxter?"

"No, actually. I spoke to one of her spads. I imagine that's what he was. He sounded spaddy. You know – spotty, still in short trousers, bumped up to be a 'special adviser' when I doubt if he could advise the way from Marble Arch to Oxford Circus. You must have come across them when you were the Number 10 photographer."

"A Number 10 photographer? I filled in occasionally for Tom Miller."

"Lucky for me you were, or I'd never have met you."

"And I'd never have fallen for you. But that was one of the more boring Number 10 receptions – forty administrators from UK universities. You didn't have much competition."

Miles flicked his napkin at her across the table.

"Anyway," Leila said, "It's about the Message, presumably. What does she want? Your astrophysics is a bit shaky, isn't it?"

"Cheeky. She wants to know whether there is going to be increasing panic over the next few days and weeks, and what we should do to prevent it."

"And what are you going to tell her?"

"Christ knows! I'd better reread some of my old research, and other people's newer stuff."

As Miles waited on the platform at Cambridge station, he was quietly pleased at the invitation to 10 Downing Street. He had put on his best Armani suit, and although he was against wearing ties for the most part, he chose one that Leila had given him at Christmas – she really liked to see him in a tie – with the double aim of pleasing her and looking smart to the Prime Minister. As the train came in, he saw a figure he recognised cycle into the forecourt and padlock his bike in a rack. It was Paul Spearman, looking familiarly unkempt, in old cords and a bomber jacket. 'I suppose he's going off to a meeting with astronomy nerds,' Miles thought.

The two men got on reasonably well. Miles actually admired anyone who could wrestle with the abstract ideas of cosmology, but just didn't see why science and bad dress sense should go together. As he found a carriage with a table to put his laptop on, Paul hurried, a little breathless, between the seats.

"Miles!" Paul said, "You've bagged a table. Mind if I join you? I promise I won't talk. I've got a paper to referee for Proc Roy Soc A."

"Of course," Miles said, and Paul sat down and put down a backpack which was somewhat the worse for wear. Miles clicked open his Montblanc leather briefcase and took out his laptop. He was hoping for an opportunity to tell Paul where he was going.

"Just a day trip?" Paul said, as he booted up his computer.

"Yes," Miles said. "A meeting at 10 Downing Street."

"Oh, me too," Paul said. "What time's yours?"

"Ten," Miles said, curtly.

"Mine's at eleven," Paul said. "They're having meetings on the hour to deal with this Message stuff. Mine's about the genuineness of the Message and the science of its transmission. I actually toured the Russian observatories last summer so I know a bit about it. What's yours about?"

"It's about crowd control, I suppose," Miles said. "They're worried that as the days go by it will sink in. About the annihilation, you know. I did some work on mass panics, so I may be able to help."

"Trouble is, until we know whether it's genuine, it could be a huge waste of emotional energy."

"You're not worried?" Miles asked.

"I'm not. Any worry I might have is swamped by the sheer excitement that this might actually be a genuine message from an extraterrestrial civilisation. The world has been waiting for this for so long, we'd almost given up. Of course, Dee is worried. Our daughter has a child on the way and she doesn't like the thought of him only having five years on this earth. I'll start worrying when we've explored every other avenue and there's no alternative."

The train started moving, and Paul looked down at his screen.

"Now, Dr Xi, what's all this about the black hole at the heart of NGC 4486b…?"

At 9.50, Miles was shown into an anonymous meeting room on the first floor with windows looking on to the Number 10 garden, with trees turning brown and highlighted in the autumn sunlight. There were several other people there, none of whom Miles recognised, apart from Richard Murchison, a psychologist from Trinity Hall.

"Hello, Richard," Tim said, "What's a psychologist doing here?"

"Everyone welcome, apparently. There's a bishop over there." He indicated a woman sitting opposite, talking to one of the other participants. "But I think they want me here to talk about the effects of the Message on individuals. Total annihilation and all that. You too, probably."

"Don't you think meetings like this are taking place all over the world?" Miles said, "Politicians running around like headless chickens. It sure beats making decisions."

Three or four more people came into the room from the staircase, and then a door opened at the other end and the prime minister came in, accompanied by a young man Miles assumed to be Paul Martin – or was it Martin Paul? – and the two of them sat down. Miles rather liked this Prime Minister in spite of the fact that she was a Conservative. She had a way of getting to the point in public and out of it, and also gave the appearance of actually listening to what people said, and thinking about it.

"As you will appreciate," the PM said, "this situation is unprecedented, and has so many ramifications – scientific, social, political, security issues – that I am having wall to wall meetings when I could actually be running the country. And before anyone says 'What if the whole thing is a hoax?' that's what I said to COBRA last night, and the feeling is, if we're to 'follow the science' as people have been known to say, we must treat it as genuine until proved otherwise. Can I introduce my team – this is the Home Secretary, whom you may know, and this is Quentin Stewart from GCHQ, who hopes you might not know him."

There was a titter round the room.

"I have two questions," Baxter went on, "and I'd like people to keep their answers brief. What are the public order implications of people believing that the annihilation of the human race will happen in five years' time? In other words, are people going to panic and will it get out of hand? And what are the best approaches we can use as a government to keep people informed as more information becomes available? If we take the first question, maybe I could ask Dr…" She looked at the notes that had been prepared for her. "…Cadogan."

Miles' head was in a whirl. He was just processing the fact that he was sitting in a room in 10 Downing Street, with the Prime Minister, the Home Secretary and some top secret spook. He'd rather hoped that someone else would speak first so that he could gauge the level of the discussion. But it was not to be, and he started to speak.

"What I have found…" (He should have said 'what anthropologists have found' but he felt he might never have a similar opportunity to blow his own trumpet) "is that an important characteristic in the behaviour of crowds is the matter of control. If people feel in control of their own lives, they are mentally attuned to trust that their own decisions will see them through almost any situation. Now clearly, if this Message is genuine, there is nothing people can do to prevent annihilation, and they well may panic or lose the will to live, or despair over their families and the future they won't see. But if they believe there is even a small chance that the dreaded event will not happen, they will feel more in control of their lives. Some people with cancer who've been told that 90% of people with their condition will die within five years cling to the belief that they are in the 10% who will survive. Others take the 90% as a death sentence. In the two groups, as Patterson, Globniak and Cadogan showed in their survey of 5,000 cancer patients, the 10 percenters had a 200% better quality of emotional life than the 90% and on the Hungerford Optimism/Pessimism Scale, which links negative feelings to hope versus fear, there was no doubt that, on drilling into the data, the 10 percenters felt that had more control of their lives and that correlated with the quality of life index."

"That's all very interesting, Dr Cadogan, but is there any way that knowledge will help us form policy," Carla Baxter said.

"Well, the bottom line is that if there is a way to reduce people's hopelessness so that either they believe the Message is not genuine or they believe the government has a plan to prevent the annihilation, a significant proportion of the population – the 10 percenters as opposed to the 90 percenters – will handle things well, and not do anything rash. Like panicking for example."

"So are you suggesting we lie to the public?" the Home Secretary said, leaning forward.

"Well, it won't be the first time – for reasons of national security of course," Miles added hastily, although he could think of at least three recent occasions when the Home Secretary herself had lied and been found out.

"Professor Bendixen, as a psychologist do you agree with Dr Cadogan's assessment?"

"Up to a point, Prime Minister, but I think Dr Cadogan thinks in mass terms – populations rather than people…"

Miles bristled but kept silent.

Bendixen went on, "The influence of individuals on crowd behaviour can be difficult to predict, particularly when they are magnified by the mass media and, even more these days, by social media. You need to take that into account. Unfortunately – some would say fortunately – we have free speech in this country so there's not a lot you can do to prevent the media saying what they want. But I would recommend that you try to get at least one major media influencer, the *Daily Mail*, for example, onside by giving them extra access to government information…"

"Government lies, do you mean?" the Home Secretary said.

"No, I just mean if there is any progress on finding out whether the Message is genuine or not, a leak or two ahead of time to a friendly media outlet might calm people down."

"Unless the progress is in the other direction, and suggests that it is genuine…" the Prime Minister said. Then she turned back to Miles.

"You've presumably looked at the Message in as much detail as the rest of us, Dr Cadogan. Is there anything in it that would allow us to assess the genuineness? I don't mean the science – COBRA is looking at that – but in the wording. Maybe some of your Cambridge colleagues have spotted something…?"

Miles looked for a sneer in that remark – Baxter had been at St Andrews – but found none.

"It's all happened so quickly, Prime Minister, that I've barely discussed it with anyone."

"Can I ask you to ask around among your colleagues in case someone has a brilliant insight that has escaped the rest of us? Now…" she said, looking at her list, "…what help can we provide via gov.com? Caroline French, you're our internet behaviourist. Is there a way we can help people who are worried, perhaps interactively. Some kind of psychotherapy AI?"

"I think we have to be careful that we don't terrify people in a different way. The more 'human'…" she made air quotes "…AI seems, the more it can remind people of the whole weirdness of this crisis. They need real human contact, or at least the more familiar means of using the internet rather than something which might seem like an alien itself…"

Various other members of the group joined in the discussion and then Paul Martin looked up at the clock, said a word in the Prime Minister's ear and said "Well, we'd better stop there. I hope we can come back to any of you if we want to pursue points you've raised. Now we've got to meet some scientists."

'Cheek,' thought Miles, who'd always jealously guarded the idea that the social sciences were every bit as scientific as chemistry or biology or physics, even though he knew they weren't quite there yet.

As Miles travelled back by train to Cambridge, he looked around at other people in the carriage: an elderly man with a hearing aid trying to hear a woman talking in his ear; a mother with two small children fighting over some electronic device that was beeping irregularly; two young people with piercings who looked like students in love; none of them looked anxious or terrified. And yet already, the newspapers, not just in the UK but around the world, were filling with stories of street demonstrations calling for action, an increase in the suicide rate among older people, conspiracy theorists flooding Twitter with two contradictory theories: that it was a hoax and part of a plot being organised by Russia to release some lethal organism in five years' time and blame ET, the other that another country – China? America? – had fooled Russia into believing that the Message was genuine with some indeterminate rationale to blame them in the future for creating panic.

When he got off the train. Miles saw what seemed to be the last taxi on the rank and rushed towards it at the same time as another man. They both got there together and then Miles saw it was a man he had met once on a University finance committee.

They each deferred to the other, and then Miles said, "Professor Walgrave, isn't it? Where are you going?"

"North Cambridge. Girton," the man said,.

"Shall we share?" Miles said, "You could drop me at Magdalene Bridge and I can walk to college, St James, from there. I'll give you a fiver towards the fare."

"Sure," said Walgrave, "And don't worry about the fare. It will all come out of the same pot. You're the Master of St James, aren't you?"

"Yes, that's right."

Walgrave walked around the cab to get in on the other side and gave the driver his address, telling him where to stop on the way.

Miles had a sudden thought. "Have you been to Number Ten today?"

"That's right. I gather they've had several meetings about different aspects of the Message. Mine was to do with what the Russians might be up to."

"And what might they be up to?" Miles said, intrigued.

"Well, there's something odd about the way they're dealing with the Message: the initial 'preparation' press release, 'the world awaits' – I'm sure they loved the tension they were causing – and then the dénouement of the message itself, with its stark, even terrifying content, which somehow they are treating as if it was a report of the Duma Subcommittee on the Next Five Year Plan or something."

"Interesting," Miles said. "I've not thought of it as some kind of plan or campaign, just as a series of events as they happened."

"I may be over-suspicious, but it'll be interesting to see what the Russians get out of it, as things develop. I always ask *cui bono* in any situation involving the current Russian government, or past ones, for that matter, because it's usually only Russia that benefits. Even in the last 24 hours, their UN delegation has suggested that there should be a committee to consider contingency plans if the threat seems genuine. I wouldn't be surprised if they insisted on chairing it and already had some plan up their sleeve that would benefit Russia in some way if things go the way they want."

"So what does our government think about it all? Or shouldn't I ask?"

"Well, we were asked to keep things to ourselves, but I must say I wasn't very impressed with the gung-ho attitude of the military people there. They were keen to destroy this alleged Outpost before anybody knows if it's genuine or not. 'Not a day to be wasted' said one of them. I should think the Russians would be keen on that too. They have a stalled space weapons programme that they could offer to reactivate with a donation of a few trillion from the nations of the world."

The roads were deserted and Miles was soon dropped at Magdalene Bridge. A week ago, he knew nothing about SETI and the alleged imminent destruction of humanity. As he walked down Bridge Street past St Johns and turned into the porter's lodge at St James, he now had a lot to think about. And it was all rather interesting…

Chapter 4

It was clear to the SETI team at Goddard that wherever in the solar system the Message came from, the radio telescope that received it must have been pointing directly at the source, somewhere in the solar system. Furthermore, it was unlikely that anyone would be looking for extraterrestrial messages so near to hand. So it can only have been an accidental alignment between the source in the solar system and some distant star which might be a target for a SETI search, or it might not.

The team gathered the morning after they had been given their assigned tasks. Their basement office showed an unusual state of disorder. Usually, the pace of work in this area was hardly frenetic. There were always data analysis tasks, checking in on SETI colleagues – a dwindling number – in other countries, and revisiting astronomical sources which had been only mildly interesting in the past, in case they had flared up in some exciting way. But during the last 48 hours, with the bit between their teeth, the team had lived off Diet Coke, Macdonald's hamburgers and Crispy Kreme donuts and the evidence of this was all around the area.

When Sherry arrived, she swallowed hard and bit back any critical comments about the mess. There was clearly a buzz in the room that she hadn't seen before among her young team. Mary, usually the tidiest and neatest of the four of them, had a dishevelled look, with a wool jacket buttoned up asymmetrically and ruffled hair, but she had the light of discovery in her eyes. Tom and Gary were comparing notes, looking at a star map on a large computer screen, as Tom checked the position of a particular asteroid and its relationship to one of the planets Gary had been investigating.

"Gather around, my chickens," Sherry said, and couldn't think why that expression had come into her head, but she felt warm towards her team for rising to the challenge.

In fact, the individual reports from Sherry's team were thorough, but provided slim pickings so Sherry assigned them the task of following up on their own list of planet/target alignments, trawling the world's astronomers to see if any of them had noticed any odd signal some time round about September 15th. It seemed a tall order.

And Tom's report, about the asteroid belt, didn't even have that small lead to follow. If somehow the Outpost was on one of the asteroids, there were between a million and two million of them larger than a kilometre, and they were scattered across the sky. Any one of them could have passed across some astronomer's target star without her even noticing.

But on further consideration, there was something in Gary's report which might be worth following up, and Mary spotted it. Gary charted the positions of the larger planets, and he noted that the Russians had had a long-standing interest in HD 164595 in the constellation Hercules, and that between September 13th and 15th, Saturn had passed very near it.

"Wasn't that the spike at 11GHz that they detected a few years ago, and then they ruled it out?" Sherry said.

"Yes, the Ratan-600 telescope detected it. Maybe their curiosity was piqued and they've been looking at it again."

"Saturn, eh?" Sherry said. "Pretty inhospitable for any life form, but if the Outpost was all silicon and metal, maybe it could survive."

"Except there'd be nowhere for it to land," Gary said, "since there's no actual surface. Just swirling gases and liquids. I'm not sure if a message could even get out."

Mary Onofrio bounced up and down in her chair and went a little red. "How about the rings?" she said, excitedly. "Maybe it's lurking in the rings, like one of the millions of rocks and chunks of ice that orbit the planet."

"That's a big leap, Mary," Sherry said, "But you know, it's worth thinking about. I have an idea. Leave it with me, while you get on with calling the world's astronomers."

Sherry left the basement and went up to a central area in the Planetary Science section. One of the rooms off an open plan area was labelled 'Planetary Image Archive.' Although all desks had access to NASA's library of images gathered by decades of planetary probes, this room had large, high resolution monitors, and main frame computers storing the raw image data before it had been processed and simplified and colourised. After she booted up one of the terminals and accessed the archive, she noted that there were 395,927 images gathered by the Cassini probe to Saturn between 2004 and 2017. 'Better skip lunch,' she thought, but knew that it would be possible to narrow them down. First, she selected only images of Saturn's rings rather than the planet itself. Gary was right about it being unlikely that the Outpost could be somewhere on the planet. The conditions would be too unfavourable for survival over thousands of years or for transmission through the gases and liquids that made up the bulk of the planet.

There were 81,875 images of Saturn's rings. Sherry flicked through and stopped to gaze at some of them in wonder. Many were abstract curves looking like computer generated graphics rather than the reflected rays of millions of pieces of icy rock orbiting in rings separated by mathematically determined regions into which the rocks couldn't stray. She wasn't sure how she would find what she was looking for. 'Has any human eye looked at these images, more than a third of a million?' she thought. And if they had, they wouldn't have been looking for what she sought now – some anomaly, perhaps only a few pixels wide, which might be a space probe hiding among the rocks that made up the rings.

As she scrolled through the thumbnails, occasionally expanding one on the large screen to full resolution, an idea formed in her mind. This needed some software, probably quite simple, which would look for sudden jumps in luminance within the uniform brightness of a ring image. It would have to exclude jumps in the black background – they could just be stars or asteroids – but she was sure the limits could be set so that there weren't too many false positives. She'd also have to exclude jumps in brightness from the borders of a ring to the black background, but that could be done by programming the target area as a circle.

There were programmers at NASA who could do the job, but she didn't want to share the idea - rather off-the-wall really - with too many other people until she felt a bit more certain about it. Then she thought of an old teacher of hers, an Associate Professor at the University of Arizona ten years ago, who was a brilliant mathematician, as well as an inspired software programmer. Maybe if she could track him down, and put the problem to him without revealing too much about why she needed a quick answer, she could find out whether the Outpost really was in one of the rings of Saturn.

Ravi Chandra often thought back to his childhood in an Indian village, and – as the expression goes – had to pinch himself to believe how far he had come from a house built of cow dung in Pulivalam, a village in Madras. He had developed a thirst for learning that meant that nothing could stop him walking seven miles to school every day, sometimes – in the monsoon season – having to cross a rushing river, holding his books wrapped in a plastic bag, high above his head, and trying to keep his balance. It was pure chance that the maths teacher, Mr Jassy, in the government Melapulam High School happened to be a grand nephew of the famous mathematician, Srinivasa Ramanujan, and never tired of telling the class – or those boys who weren't throwing chalk at each other – the story of the boy whose passion for numbers took him all the way to Cambridge, England, during the First World War, and to the peak of his profession, before he died suddenly because he couldn't get the Indian food he needed. (At least, that's how Mr Jassy put it.) Ravi's own fascination with numbers meant that he would stay on after school pestering Mr Jassy with questions even Mr Jassy couldn't answer, like why do prime numbers come in pairs – 5 and 7, 11 and 13, 17 and 19, however far you went. Ravi himself sat one night near a guttering oil lamp, with a scrap of sugar paper writing the pairs down with the stub of a pencil. On and on they went, up to 281 and 283, and then he nodded off and his father had to pick him up and lay him down on his bed in the corner of the kitchen.

His brightness and concentration led to him passing the exam to the University of Madras, when he joined the department of computer science and got a taste for the sort of programming that you needed to know to search for patterns in prime numbers, a field which continued to be his passion.

Wanting to emulate Ramanujan, he applied in writing to Trinity College, Cambridge, but his English wasn't good enough to demonstrate the originality of thought that was actually lurking in his brain. But, thanks to the US waking up to the fact that foreigners could actually be as clever as Americans, the government sent circulars round to American consuls in different countries encouraging students to apply to US universities – not the Ivy league, of course, but there were some state universities which would be good enough. After sending a written application over which he took a lot of care and then being invited to sit an examination in the American consulate in Madras, Ravi was awarded an undergraduate place and an English Speaking Union scholarship, and after a sendoff by the entire population of Pulivalam who almost blocked the bus from leaving, he travelled to Phoenix, Arizona, to start the next phase of his life.

He took maths modules and computing modules, and sometimes solved problems in ways that even his teachers didn't understand until he explained it to them. Like Ramanujan, he hadn't had access to the university-level books and journals that were readily available to other students, and so he had been compelled to devise his own methods for dealing with the kinds of problems that came up in number theory and computer programming on his course. As a result, of course, he sometimes made silly mistakes, but he more than made up for this by some of his inspired insights which seemed to come from nowhere. A paper was actually accepted by the *Journal of the American Mathematical Society* while he was still a sophomore, and as a result the professor in the maths department asked to meet him.

Of course, he went on to do a PhD and was offered an associate professorship, spanning the two departments, which is where he met a brilliant black student called Sherry Walker. In India, as a fairly light-skinned Indian himself, he shared the suspicion, even distaste, for the darker Indian groups from the far south of the subcontinent, but he was disarmed by Sherry's open manner and impressed by her grasp of number theory, though he felt her heart was really in the course she was taking on mathematical astronomy. With his natural reserve, and his feelings of inferiority towards America and Americans, he never plucked up the courage to be more than a rather distant tutor to Sherry, and of course, any attempt to start an actual relationship would lead to instant dismissal. But he remembered her fondly and knew he'd miss her when, as a result of an epoch-making paper on the Riemann Hypothesis, something Ramanujan also had tried to crack, he was offered a research fellowship at St James College, Cambridge, fulfilling his original ambition to study at Ramanujan's old university. St James wasn't Trinity but it was next door, and that was good enough for Ravi.

During his research fellowship, he won a Field Prize, the maths Nobel, for development of his Riemann work, and was offered a permanent fellowship and the job of Director of Studies in mathematics.

Ravi Chandra didn't usually answer phone calls while he was giving a tutorial, but this student was driving him mad with his slipshod analysis of Gauss's law of biquadratic reciprocity.

"I don't quite see why the solvability of the congruence $x4 \equiv p(\text{mod } q)$ should be related to that of $x4 \equiv q(\text{mod } p)$," the boy was saying despairingly, when the phone rang.

Ravi picked up the phone.

"Hi, Dr Chandra, it's Sherry. Sherry Walker. Remember me?"

"Sherry!" he said, "Of course. How nice to hear from you."

He listened and then said "No, I'm giving a tutorial on Gauss. I still remember how you thought you'd found a new approach and it was actually a variant of Euler's criterion."

He looked across at the student and said to him "I'm sorry, we'll have to stop early today but at least it saves you from being strangled. Get out and come back next week with a foolproof proof, fool."

He immediately regretted his flippant remark, but he hadn't been able to stop himself. The boy gathered up his papers and crept out.

"It's been a few years," Ravi said to Sherry. "Are you coming to the UK?"

This was the only reason he thought she might be calling. He was a dab hand at giving tours of Cambridge to visiting Americans.

"No," Sherry said. "I have a small problem which might be up your street."

"How can I help?"

"I think I could work it out myself but I've got a deadline, and I thought you might be able to give me a quick answer. You know, I think, that I work for NASA now, and I'm doing some analysis of a large database of photographs and I'm trying to find a way, maybe a small software programme, to simplify the task."

Ravi looked across the room at the departing student and waved him out of the room.

"Fire away," Ravi said, "and give me your phone number in case I have to get back to you."

"Take my email - it's more secure." She gave him an anonymous-sounding email address. "It's fully encrypted," she went on, and then regretted it.

"Okay," Ravi said, "tell me the problem."

"I'm looking for sharp luminance differences across small areas of an image."

"That shouldn't be difficult. You just need linear scans at whatever grating interval is appropriate."

"No, but that would give too many false positives. Every star on the dark background would register."

Sherry was thinking of a way she could put the problem without revealing that the rings of Saturn were involved.

"So are you looking for bright areas on the surface of a planet," Ravi said.

"Sort of..."

There was a pause.

"Go on," Ravi said.

Sherry knew she'd have to give Ravi more information.

"Well, I'm going through several thousand images of the rings of Saturn and I'm looking for areas of unusually high albedo in the rings."

"So you need to set the target radius and exclude sharp changes in luminance due to the edges of the rings?"

"Exactly, I knew you'd get it."

"It rings a bell. I think I once devised a programme to pick out different sizes of gaps in the field of primes. I could maybe adapt it. Would next month do?"

Ravi was joking. He sensed the urgency in Sherry's voice and wondered what could be so important.

"Whaaat! No!" Sherry said.

"It's OK. I was joking."

"You shouldn't do that to a girl." Sherry said, and it brought back in Ravi the unexpressed feelings he had for her ten years ago.

"You'll owe me," he said.

"Anything you want," she said, "If it works."

Ravi looked at the time. He was planning to have a cafeteria lunch in Hall before going to a meeting in the Mathematics faculty. Before he left his rooms he Googled 'Sherry Walker'. He knew she'd got a job at NASA after her PhD but hadn't really kept up after that:

> Sherry Walker is at the Goddard Space Laboratory with responsibility for several interplanetary probes. In 2020 she was put in charge of the US SETI project after the SETI Institute in Albuquerque was defunded by the Trump government…

"SETI," he thought. "Then she must be working on the Message…"

There was a low buzz of conversation in the Hall, from undergraduates at long tables with benches. In Michaelmas Term, quite a lot of undergraduates ate in Hall at lunchtime, the majority of them first years who hadn't discovered the culinary and financial advantages of making their own lunch from Aldi's finest convenience foods. Actually, St James' kitchens were pretty good, but knowledgeable students who wanted a meat and two veg meal would normally dine in the evening and 'snack' at lunchtime.

On a dais at one end of the Hall was a long table with chairs for those Fellows who wanted to eat a little more than the sandwiches available in the Senior Combination Room. Ravi avoided the curry on offer at the food counter. He was sure it was OK as food, but not as curry. He tried it once and tasted the faintest hint of curry powder, but nothing like the Madras cuisine of his youth. He took some grilled fish and rice, and a steamed jam pudding.

At the table, Katie Flynn and Paul Spearman were sitting side by side. Ravi usually found both of them friendly and approachable and hovered over the other side of the table.

"Mind if I join you?" he said, and they both smiled in welcome.

On his walk across Snape Court, Ravi had been thinking about Sherry's call and whether it had something to do with the Message. Now, as he sat down across from Paul Spearman – the Astronomer Royal, after all – he realised he had an opportunity to test out his theory.

"We were just talking about the Message," Paul said. "I was asking Katie what she thought about the claim in the Message that aliens planted some kind of gene for language in homo sapiens."

Katie was a fairly new fellow. She'd done her PhD at University College, London, and impressed the Fellowship Appointments Board with her grasp of palaeontology, linguistics, and genetics. She hadn't expected to get the fellowship but applied out of bravado, to test whether Cambridge was too elitist to take on someone as young, female and non-Oxbridge as herself.

Having now settled into Cambridge life, she still sometimes felt overawed by the people she mixed with, like now, with the Astronomer Royal picking her brains. Somehow, the Message and the puzzles it proposed, was bringing together disparate elements of the academic community. This was the point of the college system, of course, but this kind of cross-fertilization was usually confined to High Table chats.

She took a breath and plunged in.

"My research has been looking at a gene called FOXP2, which seems to be associated in some way with the development of language. People who don't have it, or have a defective version of it, have problems with language. And it even seems to have something to do with mimicry in birds."

"Did it just evolve like other characteristics?" Ravi asked. "Once people had it, it gave them a big advantage over those who didn't?"

"Except that there's something unusual about this particular gene. What seems to be the case is that this gene 'swept through' the primates, according to a key piece of research, much more quickly than other characteristics evolved."

"So what do people think might have caused that change? How long did the gene take to sweep through that population? A century? A millennium?" Ravi asked.

"Many thousands of years, but still short on an evolutionary timescale. People have looked for a sudden geographical change that could have stimulated that change – a sudden new evolutionary niche, for example, but nothing convincing."

"So now," Paul said, "there's one possible explanation, that fits the timescale. Alien genetic engineering."

"Really?" Ravi said, looking at Katie.

"Hold on, hold on," she said. "I just raised it as a faint possibility, and anyway I can't think of a way to prove it."

"So you're both treating the Message as if it's genuine?" Ravi said.

"It's more fun that way," Paul said. "That's why we're in this business, isn't it?"

"Fun?" Ravi said.

"Sure. Think how exciting it will be if it's genuine. Give us a few days of excitement before some wet blanket shows that it's a hoax. The government's taking it seriously, anyway. Number Ten was red hot with meetings yesterday. I went to one and bumped into Miles on his way to another."

Ravi was impressed.

"Did you meet the Prime Minister?" he said.

"I did actually. I've met her before, when I was appointed. She handed me my first stipend. £100 bought Dee and me a nice dinner at the Ivy."

"What was your meeting about?" Katie said.

"I can't tell you very much" Paul said, "but if I tell you that the head of the joint chiefs of staff was there, you can see that they are taking it seriously."

"Crikey," Katie said, "what do they think the military can do prevent total annihilation at the hands of a civilisation immeasurably more advanced than ours?"

"If you have a hammer, you have to treat everything as if it was a nail," Paul said.

"And I suppose they wanted your help in directing the hammer towards the nail," Ravi said, taking a mouthful of sea bream.

"I wasn't much use at that," Paul said. "Although the Message implies the Outpost is in the solar system, nobody has any idea where."

"I might," said Ravi.

He explained his call from Sherry, and how putting together her SETI role and the fact that she was analysing the rings of Saturn, might suggest that she believed the Outpost was somewhere in the rings.

"That's extraordinary," Paul said. "I mean it's as good a place as any. Better than some - the surfaces of the planets apart from Mars are pretty inhospitable - but you think she might be able to narrow it down?"

"Well, I said I'd adapt a piece of software that would help. Until then she's got a lot of photos to go through manually."

"Do you think she'd tell you if she finds it?"

"I doubt if she'd volunteer the information."

"Was there anything in the raw data that could help narrow it down?" Katie said to Paul, joining in the excitement. "You helped to analyse it, didn't you?"

"No. We looked in the metadata at the beginning and end of what the Russians made available. There was also a lot of guff between each language version. But there was nothing which could pinpoint where it came from. And of course, directional information would only be at the telescope which detected it."

"What difference would it make if you did know that the Outpost was on the rings of Saturn?" Ravi said, excited to be involved in something more earthshattering than hammering number theory into skulls which were too thick to receive it.

"I've been thinking," Paul said. "All the Russians have given us is their version of the Message plus the string of digits that generated it. Whoever detected the Message will have recorded the really raw version of it, unfiltered, un-error-corrected, before it was treated to extract the zeroes and ones. If we had that signal, much more difficult to fake, we'd be really sure that it was genuine."

"Do you think some other SETI telescope might have that signal?"

"I'm not sure any SETI telescope would have it. No one looks in the solar system for extraterrestrial intelligence. SETI telescopes follow the stellar background, which the planets move across. So the only SETI astronomer who would receive it would be someone who's looking at a galaxy or star when the Outpost passes across that region of the sky. If we knew where it was – the Rings of Saturn, for example – we could then do a trawl of all SETI targets being monitored and see if any of them was in the same line of sight as the Outpost and gathering data at the time the Message was transmitted."

"That's quite a leap," Ravi said, impressed.

Paul was becoming more excited.

"So if there is any way your friend can pin the Outpost down, that would increase our chances of finding the original message and proving that it wasn't a hoax."

"But if course," Ravi said, "If you don't find the original, it won't prove that the Russian message is a hoax."

"Correct," Paul said, as he picked up his tray. "But one can dream. Let me know if you hear anything."

Chapter 5

On October 15th, Olga Cheliuskina had come up the escalator at Okhrizhnaya metro station on her way home after work. In the month after the intensive period spent translating the various elements of the Message, she had thought often of its contents. Difficult as it was to believe, she was convinced that the Message showed the wisdom and concern of a higher intelligence, expressed in words which were as clear as they had to be to convince mankind that there were consequences to their actions, consequences, which some had been warning about for fifty years or more. The solution suggested by that higher intelligence might not be to everyone's liking, but it could be the only chance to address the plight of planet Earth and ensure some kind of future for its biosphere.

As she was sworn to secrecy, with the highest level of secrecy in the government, Olga had not, of course, told anyone else about her work on the Message. She knew in any case that the plan was to release the contents to the world, and after that she would be able to take quiet satisfaction at her contribution to the task of decryption and translation.

Up until today, when the text of the Message was to be released, she had obeyed Boris Nokolaevich's strictures to the team at their last meeting to tidy up the multilingual text of the message, and then take a welcome break.

"After today, you will have nothing further to do with the Message," Boris said, "You have all done good work, you will receive a bonus, and whatever happens next, whatever our government decides to do with the Message, you are to tell no one of your role or even of your knowledge. These have been three days with a magnificent end result. Now we disperse, move on and stay silent!"

This didn't seem an insuperable task. Once the message was released at six p.m. today, introduced by a television address from the Kremlin by President Pavlov, Olga would have no reason to discuss its content further, other than as an interested citizen of Russia.

At the top of the escalator, Olga noticed that it was snowing heavily outside. There were already several inches on the ground and the road and pavements were a mix of untouched snow and nasty black slush. She was glad she had worn her boots that morning. As she neared the bus stop, she saw that she had just missed the t78 bus that took her to her block of flats in the suburb of Severny.

She swore to herself and looked at her watch. She wanted to watch Pavlov's TV announcement to see how he presented the text of the message. But she still had forty-five minutes and would get home in time as long as the next bus came soon.

Impatiently, she stamped her feet to keep warm. She looked around her at the crowd waiting for the bus: an elderly man with a fur hat, and spectacles mended with sticky tape, a young woman with a painfully short skirt – 'Her legs must be freezing,' Olga thought – 'and why does she wear so much makeup?'; two men in their forties in workers' overalls and badges identifying them as power station workers; a woman in her 50s in a nurse's uniform, holding a small puppy in her arms and trying to control a young boy – 'her grandson?' Olga thought. She felt a quiet buzz of pride and awe that she knew something none of these people knew yet, that would affect their lives so dramatically.

Squeezing onto the bus, Olga smelled the warm, wet odour of soaked clothing. Thank God smoking was forbidden these days. She remembered her bus trips to school as a child and the fug of smoke and sweat she had to sit in. People seemed cleaner these days too.

As the bus headed for the junction at the outer ring of Moscow, she listened to the steady swish of the vehicle ploughing through the snow and slush. Suddenly, as the bus navigated a curve in a complicated junction, turning north of the Outer Ring, the back of the bus skidded in the slush. There was a loud bang as the side of the bus collided with a lamppost, showering glass on the passengers and blocking the door at the back, near where Olga was standing. She felt a sharp pain in her hand and saw a shard of glass sticking out and blood starting to ooze. Quickly, she pulled the shard out and threw it through the broken window. Stemming the blood with her scarf, she stood among the passengers, some of whom were moaning, others shouting "To the front!"

Olga's first thought, after she realised that the scarf had stopped the bleeding and she wasn't seriously hurt, was to get out, find another bus and get home for Pavlov's broadcast. But no one was getting out quickly. A few startled passengers had left the front of the bus, but some were prevented by a pile up of an old couple on the floor in the central aisle who were being tended by the nurse who had been at Olga's bus stop. Her puppy was yapping, adding to the sense of chaos.

Olga eventually extricated herself from the bus, refusing treatment for her hand from a passing doctor, and waited around with the other walking wounded, and some passengers who were unharmed. The next bus and the one after were full. Eventually an empty bus arrived to pick up the passengers who were able to travel.

By the time Olga got home, it was 6.45 p.m. and she came into her flat to find her husband watching the last few minutes of the Pavlov press conference.

"Olgotchka!" he called as she came in, "You missed the extraordinary news about a Message from the aliens!"

She took off her coat, went into the bathroom and ran her wounded hand under a cold tap.

"The message he announced last month?" she called.

"Yes, but they quoted from the actual Message. It's extraordinary if true, and Dimitri Ilyich promises that it is. It seems the earth is doomed! I can hardly believe it!"

And then her husband told her the details of the Message that had been shown on the screen and recited in a solemn voice by Russia's leading TV presenter. And Olga sat down heavily in a chair.

'It can't be' she said to herself, 'it just can't!'

It had been a month since she and the rest of the group had finished the task of transliterating the Message in its various languages, and of course, she hadn't been able to keep a copy on her laptop. The whole team's laptops had been taken away to be erased. But she remembered enough of it, particularly the all-important Paragraph 4, to know that her husband's summary – and therefore Pavlov's – could not be accurate. It's true Sasha wasn't interested in science. He wrote children's books and might not have grasped the full implication of the Message. But how could he have got it so wrong? She quickly booted up the computer in a corner of the sitting room and found the text that TASS had released.

"What is it, Olgochka?" her husband asked her over their supper of thick vegetable soup, black bread and fruit.

"Nothing, Sasha," she said, "Maybe I was a bit shaken by the bus accident."

She was in a state of utter confusion. What had happened between the translation she and the rest of the SETI team had worked on and the message released today, and why?

It was this confusion, and the internal battle in her mind between her loyalty to her State, and her membership of the human race, that eventually led her to decide to make a call to an old university friend, currently in the USA, a call whose content was cryptic enough not to get her in trouble if it was ever overheard or transcribed.

Gary Dorval was jogging his usual route around Lake Redington on the Patuxent Nature Reserve on a Saturday morning when his mobile phone rang. The screen said 'Number withheld'.

He was ready for a break to get his breath back and take a drink, so he slumped on to a nearby tree stump and answered the call.

"Gary, this is Olga. Olga Cheliuskina."

Gary's mind raced back over fifteen years, to his time at Moscow University. Had he really had the same cellphone number back then?

"Olga!" he said, with a note of surprise.

As if Olga read his thoughts, she said "I'm so happy you still have the same cellphone number."

"I'm still the same old stick in the mud," he said.

"You taught me that phrase," she said. "Look, I must be quick. Do you remember the song whose words you taught me? Don't say it."

Gary thought back to a song by the Police that was all the rage among the students at the time, and how Olga had asked him to teach her the words and what they mean.

"Yes?" he said, puzzled."

"Well, suppose the title was wrong" she said. "Suppose someone had changed it?"

"Can you be a bit clearer?" Gary said.

"No, Gary. Just think about it. Much depends on it."

With that, she disconnected the call.

Gary wanted to call back but her wariness suggested she wouldn't welcome his call, and probably wouldn't say any more anyway.

By the time Gary had run back to his bike and put his helmet on, he knew the purpose of Olga's call, and was overwhelmed with its implications. As he cycled back to his apartment to change, he knew he had to see Sherry as soon as possible. There was a to be a team meeting at 10, but he wanted to talk to her alone.

When he reached Goddard an hour later, he went to the sixth floor and walked into the Solar System Explorer Department, an open plan area with several glassed-in offices at one end. He could see Sherry in one of them, talking to her boss, Kent Branton. She was showing him something on her laptop. Gary hovered outside, talking to a rather pretty data analyst he had met once at a Goddard Christmas party. He regretted having to stop in mid-sentence as Branton emerged, in order to try to grab Sherry on her own.

"Gary," she said. "Aren't we meeting in the basement in half an hour?"

"Yes, but I have something to tell you. Can I come in?"

"Sure," she said, "But keep it quick. I've got something to tell you, the team I mean."

"Do you remember a song called 'Message in a Bottle', by the Police, sung by Sting?"

"What is this? Some kind of quiz question?"

Gary quickly summarised Olga's cryptic call.

"She said 'Suppose someone had changed the title?' But that seemed nonsensical. The title is the title and even it had once had a different one, so what? But then I thought, suppose she means that someone had changed the 'message in a bottle' – the Message from Tau Ceti?"

Sherry thought, and then said "That's a pretty slim basis for a global sigh of relief and the world ignoring the Message. And is she someone who would know this anyway?"

"I don't know. She was a high flyer in the math department, and she was pretty cagy about telling me what she was going to do after we both left university."

Sherry looked at her watch. "It sounds weird enough to be true," she said. "Keep it to yourself for now. Don't tell the team until I've discussed this with Branton. He was here just now. I was showing him something I want to tell you all about at the meeting."

When Sherry walked into the basement room, the members of the team abandoned their computer terminals and went and sat round the table in the centre of the area, like birds waiting for a worm.

“Well,” Sherry said, “thanks to some help from an old teacher, I think I have found the Outpost.”

She sent an image from her laptop to a large screen on the wall.

“Using a small piece of software, I scanned many thousands of images from the Cassini mission looking for spots on the rings which were of unexpected brightness. This is one of the images,” she said, “and here is another.”

There was a gasp from the others in the room. Sherry had found a closer view, and it had visible sharp edges and what looked like a flat surface reflecting sunlight.

“That bright spot near the edge of the inner ring of Saturn is unlike anything else in Saturn’s rings.”

“Why didn’t anyone see this before?” Mary said. “These images have been available for how long? Ten years?”

“Sometimes, you only see what you are looking for. And there are 80,000 photos, remember. Some of them only in raw form, so they haven’t even been enhanced. I was looking for something that no one expected, and the software I used narrowed down the list to a few worth looking at more closely.”

“Have you ruled out every natural explanation?”

“All the ones I could think of. That angular shape with reflective planes is nothing like the irregular chunks of rock that make up Saturn’s rings.”

There was a silence in the room as people took in Sherry’s news.

“What difference does it make, practically?” Tom said. “I mean, we’re still going to be annihilated, wherever the Outpost is.”

“Well, it will be easier to communicate with them,” Sherry said. “We might even be able to spot it now. Cassini’s long gone, but we could try to get time on the JWS telescope, maybe even monitor it. It will make it easier to communicate if we know exactly where it is. Now, I must tell the Director and he can tell the White House and President Billings can tell the world. It might even persuade Congress to increase our meagre grant next year.”

Dr Jane McReady was working in A&E at Addenbrooke’s Hospital in Cambridge when the ambulance team brought in the homeless man. The frost had been particularly hard that night and his core temperature was very low, in the eighties, and she worried about whether he would survive. But with careful warming and monitoring his vitals, he gradually thawed out. He didn’t resist the nurse’s attempts to bath him when he woke up, and unlike many similar arrivals on cold nights at Addenbrooke’s his breath didn’t smell of alcohol. Of course, he didn’t have an address, but gave his name as Douglas. All his worldly goods seemed to be in a grubby cloth carrier bag, which had seen better days. When Jane was next on duty she went into his cubicle but he was asleep. In an attempt to find out more personal details, she opened his bag and moved aside the residue of broken biscuits, an old shirt, a battered plastic folder with some snapshots, and a much-thumbed collection of sheets of paper held together at the corner by a bulldog clip.

"Heyyy!" The shout startled her. Douglas had woken up and when he saw what she was doing he shouted out.

"Leave my things alone! Fuck!"

"I'm sorry," Jane said. "I was only trying to see if there was any more information about you. We should really have your name and last known address."

"Papers! Give me!" he said urgently.

Jane handed over the dog-eared papers and Douglas held them close to his chest.

"Is there anyone we can contact for you?" she said. "You could be out in a couple of days and we don't want you back outside in the freezing weather."

Douglas concentrated for a moment. "Fuck! Cadogan!" he said.

Jane sighed.

"Look, I suspect you've got Tourette's but that's not very helpful."

"NO! Doctor Cadogan! He… Give me," he said, "the bag."

She handed it to him and he took out a baseball cap, grubby like everything else. He reached into the torn lining and produced a ten pound note.

"He gave me this. He is my friend. Prick!"

"Someone called Dr Cadogan gave you this?"

"Yes, college…"

"What college?"

"Bugger, I don't know… Wait. James?"

Jane McReady found two Dr Cadogans on the university list. One was a graduate student and one a fellow of St James', as Douglas had suggested. In fact, he was the Master. She looked at the college website which showed pictures of all the fellows.

"Is that him?" she said to Douglas, showing him Miles' portrait.

Douglas went into a paroxysm of ticcing and swearing which Jane took as a 'Yes'. The outburst exhausted him and he flopped back on the pillows.

"Leave it with me," Jane said.

When Debbie told Miles there was a call from Addenbrookes, he was worried.

"Yes?" he said, anxiously.

Jane McReady introduced herself and told Miles about Douglas.

"I don't know anyone called Douglas," he said.

"He's a homeless guy. We think he's got Tourette's."

It came back to Miles.

"Oh, yes, he must be that man in Market Square. But I just gave him a bit of money. I don't know him."

"Well, there's another thing…"

"What?"

"He's clutching some papers as if they're the crown jewels. From the glimpse I had they're full of symbols."

Miles' heart sank. "These people often think they've discovered perpetual motion or the alchemist's stone or something like that. Is it written in green ink?" he said.

"No, it's printed, or at least typed, like a scientific paper. But he claims that it's a genuine solution to an important problem that's been ignored. He says if he'd been taken seriously he might have got a job and been able to lead some kind of normal life in spite of his Tourette's, but that possibility was snatched away, he says. And he thought you might be able to help."

"I hardly know the man."

"Oh, he implied you were more than a passing acquaintance."

"'Passing' is what I was, literally."

"OK, I'll get the social worker along and we'll see if we can get him a hostel place."

"No, wait," Miles said. "Do you have time to scan a page, or even just photograph it, and email it to me? I'll show it to someone who will tell me if it's gibberish. I'll look at it when I can."

That afternoon, Debbie showed Ravi in to Miles office.

"Have a seat, Ravi," Miles said, "I want to show you something."

"Of course, Master," he said.

Debbie had printed out two copies of pages emailed to Miles by Dr McReady, and she handed them to Ravi, before leaving the office. Ravi looked curious and then intent. He took a minute or two to read the words and symbols. The first page was an abstract, headed "The Ternary Goldbach Theorem is True, Douglas Burnside, Submitted March 17th, 2002." Ravi flicked through ten pages and the last one finished with some mathematical symbols and the sentence "The main theorem is hereby proven: the Ternary Goldbach conjecture is true." Ravi sat back in the chair, thinking for a moment.

"This could be nonsense," he said. "Where did you get it?"

"Well, obviously from someone called Douglas Burnside," Miles said

"Never heard of him," Ravi said. "When I edited the *Mathematical Journal,* this was the sort of thing that used to arrive on a weekly basis, and turn out to be rubbish. They say a little knowledge is a dangerous thing…"

"What is the Ternary Goldbach Theorem," Miles asked.

"The Ternary Goldbach conjecture says that every odd number above 5 is the sum of three prime numbers. For example, 19 which is prime – you can't divide it by a lower number – is 3 + 5 + 11. It's the ease of describing it that makes anyone who can do mental arithmetic think they can solve it in a few hours."

"Is it worth seeing this man? If he's really a genius, it would be a shame if he was sent back to Market Square" Miles asked.

Ravi read through the pages again. The 'proof' had a ring of plausibility about it.

"Helfgott actually presented a very good proof in 2013, but this man – if he's genuine – took a rather original approach in 2002, it seems. I'll read it through properly and let you know if there's something in it."

Ravi Chandra read Douglas Burnside's paper several times, occasionally stopping to scribble in a notebook, testing some of the assumptions Douglas had made on the way to his 'proof'. He had to admit that it was a considerable achievement, even if occasionally Douglas arrived at a subsidiary result, a lemma, in a complicated way which showed that he hadn't kept up with the developments in the field.

'This man clearly has unusual talent,' Ravi thought, and leaned back in the comfortable armchair in his study that had seen better days but which always gave him a feeling – superstitious of course – that his better ideas came when he sat in it.

He remembered how G.H. Hardy had seen Ramanujan's potential when he first received the letter from India containing some unusual mathematical theorems, some without proof. Perhaps this Burnside man could be a project to develop and nurture. Ravi's own mathematical work was stuck in a rut, and he couldn't get past a particular stage that required him to prove that the value of a function was 'equal to or greater than' a certain value on a curve, and he could only prove that it was greater than the point on the curve. He even wondered if Burnside, with his obvious facility for number theory, might be able to help.

He picked up the phone and dialled the number of the Master's office.

Two days later, Douglas Burnside, erratically shaven and smartly dressed – for him – apart from some disintegrating trainers, walked into the Porters' Lodge and asked for Dr Cadogan. Fortunately the head porter, Harry Farlow, had been forewarned, otherwise he would have been tempted to send the man packing, for all his attempts to look smart.

Instead, he answered Douglas politely and walked with him into First Court to point the way to the Master's Lodge. In Miles' office, Ravi was perched uncomfortably in an Eames chair, more a sculpture than a piece of furniture but Miles was proud to have earned enough once, as adviser on a feature film about New Guinea, to be able to afford to buy one. Also in the room was the senior tutor, Mary Sheridan, a computer scientist. She was describing the options for funding a research studentship, to study for an MA, for a year.

"But whoever it was would still have to go through some sort of entrance examination, usually covering more topics than just the subject of their MA, and they'd have to attend an admissions board."

"There would be rather a lot of swearing," Miles said.

"Oh, the applicant would have to put up with that," Mary said. "I presume you mean one of our esteemed colleagues…?"

No, I mean the man has Tourette's," Miles said with a laugh.

"Is he as good as you make out, Ravi?" Sheridan said.

"I know it sounds improbable," Ravi replied, "But unless someone else wrote this paper, he's a kind of mathematical genius."

The office door opened and Debbie showed Douglas in. He stood on the threshold, blinking, and making a strange clicking noise with his mouth. Miles jumped up from behind his desk and held out his hand. Douglas wiped his hand on his trousers and shook hands hesitantly with Miles.

"This is Dr Chandra and Professor Sheridan," Miles said. "Have a seat."

It took a while to convince Douglas that he was being offered a lifeline by the college. Ravi explained that he he'd like to talk to Douglas for an hour or so about his paper, and then if this confirmed that he had a special mathematical talent, that the college would like to try to give him a chance to develop it further. He said that he would be happy to work with Douglas on his paper and perhaps on other aspects of mathematics that Douglas was interested in.

Mary Sheridan said that there might be a way he could have a room in college and a computer to work on his ideas.

"I'm not sure how long I can stay in – fuck! – Cambridge," Douglas said.

"Oh," Sheridan said. "You have plans to go somewhere else?"

"No, but I might have to. The fucking council..." Here he displayed a volley of twitches. "...They're going to clear out the Market Place at night. We'll all have to find somewhere else. Pricks..."

The three others in the room didn't grasp at first what Douglas was saying. Then Miles spoke up.

"You didn't think you'd have to sleep outside? We'd provide you with accommodation!"

"She said a room to work in..." Douglas said, nodding at Mary Sheridan. "I thought I'd still have to sleep outside."

"No, no," Mary said. "Your room would be to live in while you were here. In Skimbles Hostel."

Douglas erupted in an explosion of swearing and tics.

"I don't want no fucking hostel!" he shouted. "They're full of druggies and thieves! The food is shit and they lock you out in the middle of the day!"

Miles realised the depth of Douglas's misunderstandings and between them they reassured Douglas that he would have a room with a bed, a bathroom, a desk, a computer, food supplied by the college and, on top of that, a regular stipend to cover other necessities.

"And I think," Mary tried to say tactfully, "we might be able to set you up with any new clothes you might want, from the Supplementary Accoutrements Fund."

Chapter 6

Within hours of the translation of the Message having been released, intelligence agencies around the world had downloaded the original binary code from the Russian government website and carried out their own transcription of the digits and confirmed that it did, indeed, say what the Russians said it said. Of course, that didn't prove that there was a message - anyone can forge a list of binary digits - but each security service felt it would have been remiss not to carry out this check. In fact, of course, the code was so simple that anyone could check and thousands of amateur computer buffs did the same. There seemed to be nothing unusual about the digital version apart from what seemed like a random sequence of binary digits, preceded and followed by eight zeroes, between each language version of the message. Nobody paid much attention to them. The zeroes obviously marked the beginning and end of each version, all that anyone needed to know to pick the right starting point for the translation.

Meanwhile people grappled with the idea of the annihilation of mankind - every man and woman and child on earth - but life seemed to go on largely as usual. The range of beliefs and anxieties ranged from "Something will happen to stop it", rather like many people's attitudes to the climate crisis itself, to immediate terror and despair. But at some level, Miles Cadogan's suggestion at the Number 10 meeting that the Message might actually create an increased cohesion among communities seemed to be working, the feeling that "We're all in this together."

Katie Flynn, and her research assistant Rosie Kim, got off the train at Kings Cross and pushed their way through the crowds on the concourse. There were signs everywhere of the public reaction to the dramatic message from space. She noticed a group of people around a man standing on a small stepladder, holding a banner which said "The end is <u>really</u> nigh: Five years to salvation."

A newsstand nearby had a display of periodicals, and Katie noticed that every one of them, from the Spectator to the New Statesman, *History Today* to *New Scientist*, *Tatler* to the *New Yorker*, had covers emblazoned with captions that reflected the Message and offered wisdom, consolation or advice to a troubled readership.

Why did she not feel it more strongly, this extraordinary situation? Perhaps because she hadn't taken it in? But she had. Like everyone, she had pored over every paragraph of the Message, looking at its syntax, its assertions, its science, for indications of human origin - the Hoax Theory.

But it couldn't be true, she decided, none of it. The interconnectedness of world communications and the fiendish ingenuity of hackers and fake newsmongers meant that really one just had to apply Occam's razor to this whole situation and act on the basis that it was all a fake, and that over the weeks or months the truth was bound to come out. But she could do one thing, which was relevant to her research anyway. She could think a bit more about that extraordinary sentence in the Message, about the Message's claim of facilitating the development of language in primates, leading to the evolution of human intelligence.

Katie had planned a London day to look at a new skull found in Africa at the Natural History Museum, which Chris Stringer had said she could look at for evidence of brain development. There was no brain left, of course, but Chris had prepared a plaster cast of the inner surface of the skull so she could look for evidence of bumps and clefts associated with the language areas of the brain. She decided to give a day out to Rosie, who was a good and assiduous worker for whom nothing was too much trouble, but Katie felt she needed to see the world a bit more, think a bit more 'outside the box'. Rosie's upbringing by working class parents on the outskirts of Cambridge, and an HNC at the technical college, had not stretched what seemed to be a good mind, and Katie felt some responsibility to help broaden her horizons.

Sure enough, having been warned by Katie not to be overawed by one of the world's leading primatologists, Rosie asked intelligent questions and challenged Stringer when he said that one of the grooves in the cast might be an artefact.

"But isn't that the sulcus of Rolando?" Rosie said, and the scientist was taken aback.

"It's not, actually," he said, and pointed to a deeper groove a few millimetres away. "But you've done your homework," he went on, and Rosie blushed.

On their way back to King's Cross, Katie took Rosie to tea in *Freshfoods*, off Tottenham Court Road. They found a table near the window and Rosie went to the counter to get drinks and cake "Choose want you like," Katie said, giving Rosie a ten pound note.

At a nearby table, a mother sat with a child, a boy of about eight. They were both drinking smoothies, and the boy wore a decorative cap with two alien eyes on springs which wobbled as he sucked the last drops of his drink through a straw. On the cap, as he turned his head, Katie saw the words "We're on our way!" She wondered at the skills and ingenuity of entrepreneurs who would quickly seize any opportunity to make money, however inappropriate it might seem. It was a rerun of the UK's covid PPE scandal, on a smaller scale.

"The world has gone mad," Katie said to Rosie as she put a tray on the table. "There are people who don't believe a word of it and others who think that we're doomed. How do you feel about it?"

She had not really had a serious conversation with Rosie about the annihilation, but she had the impression from students at St James that young people were so preoccupied with their day to day lives that they didn't feel the sense of panic that many older people did.

"My dad says it's just another conspiracy theory, designed to make working people do what the government says."

"But what do you think?"

"Well, it sounds awful. I don't want to die in five years' time. Sean and me can't afford to get married at the moment but we want to one day."

"Maybe the doomsayers are adopting Pascal's Wager," she said.

Rosie looked puzzled.

"Pascal, the philosopher, said, about belief in God, 'Act as if it's true because not doing so if it *is* true, is worse than doing so even if it *isn't*'."

"So I'm right to be worried, then?"

"Well, it's true that if it doesn't happen, we'll all be happier than we've ever been."

"So don't you believe the Message?"

"There's a theory that it may be a hoax," Katie said, "but I suppose that, à la Pascal, even if it is, if we act as if it's going to happen, we may get the world into a better shape than it would have been without the Message."

They took a bite of their cakes.

"How's the carrot cake, Rosie?"

"I'm glad you recommended it. I could hardly believe it wouldn't taste of carrot, but got it because you said so."

"Just be careful about believing things because people in authority say so," Katie said. "You were right in this case, but it doesn't always work. Look at my research, for example – our research I mean. People think I've got a bee in my bonnet, quite knowledgeable people too. But something funny happened about 250,000 years ago when *homo sapiens* acquired language in quite a short time. And this Message has even suggested what, though many people would think me mad to suggest it. But of course, there's no way to prove it."

"Do genes have patterns that we could recognise that are nothing to do with their chemistry?" Rosie asked, taking up the challenge

"Well, they're made up of four chemical units which we call C, G, A and T, so I suppose we'd notice if they spelled 'CAT' occasionally, as they would do by chance. But the only real significance those units have is in the functions they cause the genes to perform."

"So if you found a complex, repeated pattern in a gene, in FOX whatever you said, you might be puzzled?"

"I don't understand. Do you mean if one gene had the same pattern as another?"

"No. I mean if there was something different somewhere in the FOX gene that you'd never seen in any other gene. Something that, say, a random alien civilization might have put in to show it had a different origin from 'normal' genes."

Katie thought about what Rosie had said.

"That's a pretty big leap to make."

"Couldn't we look?" Rosie said, really excited now. "You've been showing me how to use the CRISPR technique to show gene sequences. Couldn't we do that with the FOX gene?"

Katie looked at her phone.

"Jeepers, we'll miss our train if we don't hurry. You might have something there, Rosie. Let's talk about it on the train."

Miles received an email from Number 10 asking him if he would draft a paper to use some of his research insights into the behaviour of crowds to help the government plan an approach to allaying public fears, and perhaps distract them a little from the 'annihilation message'.

"It's quite a responsibility," he said to Leila when they were having a drink before supper, the day of the phone call.

"It's not often you sound unsure of something," she said," particularly in the area of your research..."

"I'm not unsure about the research," he said, "but it's a big leap from data gathered from samples of 1000 or even 5000 to making recommendations about an entire population."

"When do they want it? Number 10."

"Tomorrow?"

"Well, you'd better come and eat this shepherd's pie and then get to work."

Miles sat with his laptop in the room he and Leila used when they wanted some quiet, up in the attic area of the Lodge, looking down into Snape Court. He saw a boy coming out of N staircase with his arm round a girl. He knew them both. The boy was the son of an Old Jacobian, a man who had pushed Miles hard for his son to come to St James, and Miles had to say that the college was no longer able to make allowances for the children of former members. Fortunately, the boy was bright and had got in on his own merits. The girl had applied reluctantly, persuaded by her comprehensive school that she had a chance, and thanks to a female fellow on the admissions panel who saw potential in a rather disorganised mind, had got in and risen to the challenge, getting a First in Part 1 Classics.

'Are those two really going to be destroyed in five years' time?' Miles thought. 'What a waste. Surely the Message's threat can't be true? Or at least, surely something can be done to stop it?'

He was used to writing scientific papers but he had occasionally been asked to write Opinion pieces for the *Guardian* or articles for *Prospect*, so he felt he had a talent for popularising. He decided to use sociological research on the happiness of the population during the Second World War as a comparison with how people's morale could be raised under the similar, though graver, threat in the Message:

> It may be illuminating (he wrote) to compare the state of public happiness under the threat of annihilation, with public attitudes during World War 2, about which there is a mass of sociological data. (E.g. review papers by Blight and Meredew, 1951, Hassler, Barley, Quantock and Fairbrother, 1963) To suggest that people were happier during World War II, a period marked by death and destruction on a scale previously unseen in human history, may

seem counterintuitive. However, there are several reasons why people might have felt happier during this time.

Firstly, World War II was a time of great solidarity and national unity. The war effort required the entire country to come together and work towards a common goal. This sense of shared purpose and sacrifice created a strong sense of community and belonging, which is known to contribute to happiness. It may be possible to create a similar sense of community, provided some leeway can be found in the Message that can be used to imply that there may be a chance, however small, that by approaching the Outpost 'they' can be persuaded to cancel, or at least delay, the threat....

Miles went on to look at other causes of people's feelings of well-being in World War 2 – significant economic changes, a shift in people's sense of independence and empowerment, and the creation of a sense of optimism for the future, even at the darkest times in the War, and made suggestions to the PM for lessons to be learned.

The following day, after tweaking his draft, Miles put his head into his secretary's office

"Debbie, do you have a phone number for that young man in the prime minister's office? He said he was Paul Martin, or was it Martin Paul?"

Debbie looked in her notebook, flicking back a few pages.

"Here it is," she said. "I think it's Paul Martin but…"

"But what?"

"Well, I sometimes put the surname first and then a comma. It hasn't got a comma so it's probably 'Paul Martin', but it could be 'Martin Paul."

Miles was irritated – with Mr. Martin (or Mr. Paul) as much as with Debbie.

"Why couldn't the man have a less ambiguous name," he said, "Or at least be called James James, or something else where it doesn't matter."

He took a Post-It with the number on from Debbie and went into his study.

When he dialled the number, a voice answered "PM's office."

For a moment Miles thought his name must be Paul Martin. But who answers his phone with his initials?

"Ah," Miles said, and without mentioning the man's name, he said "It's Dr Cadogan calling from Cambridge," and then felt that he sounded like somebody on what used to be called trunk calls, where it was a novelty to place a call to someone outside your local area.

"St James College," he hurriedly added.

"Cadogan?" the voice said.

"Yes. We spoke a couple of weeks ago when I was invited to a meeting with the Prime Minister.

"Of course. Miles, isn't it?"

"Yes," and once again Miles was facing a dilemma. "Yes, Martin," he risked

"What can we do for you today?"

Miles was so pleased at having got the man's Christian name right, that he almost forgot why he was calling.

"Oh, yes, I have drafted something along the lines the PM suggested but I have one query before I send it.

"Do you want to tell me?" the man said.

Miles didn't, and said so.

"Well, the PM's rather busy as you can imagine. Put your query in an email with the draft and someone will get back to you." He sounded rather irritable and rang off.

Miles took a final look at the draft, called up the Number 10 email address and wrote a short note to go with what he had written.

Ten minutes later, his phone rang. Debbie was on the line.

"It's Paul," she said, hesitantly. Miles had sent a draft of his suggestion to his colleague Paul Spearman for his comments but hadn't heard back.

"OK," Miles said, and waited till he heard a click.

"Paul," he said, "I spoke to the sixth former, the PM's clueless advisor. They needed the draft pronto. What do you think?"

The line was silent.

"Hello?" Miles said.

"Hello," said a voice that was not that of his colleague, Paul Spearman.

"Hi, who is that?" Miles said, his heart sinking.

"It's the PM's clueless advisor. You know, the sixth former?" Paul Martin said coldly.

Tim knew there was no point in taking the bait. "Oh, hi," he said.

"We received your email but there was no attachment."

'Shit!' Miles thought. Could he seem more incompetent?

Miles finished the call, sent the email and then picked up the phone and pressed a button.

"Debbie," he said coolly, "Can you get Paul – Paul Spearman – on the phone?"

"Wasn't that him just now?"

"No, it was the man in the PM's office. He appears to be called 'Paul Martin'. Can you make a note of that in red capitals somewhere?"

But Miles was pleased that he had been admitted into the inner circle of people who were considered worth consulting by the Prime Minister, and he received an acknowledgment from Paul Martin that Carla Baxter had appreciated what he had written and that the paper would be put before COBRA. But later events were to render his advice superfluous.

While journalists and politicians focused on feeding the public appetite for facts, probabilities and answers to the question, "What is the government going to do about it?", the scientific community was as interested in the many scientific questions raised by the content of the Message.

Informal internet groups of scientists across the world came together to share data about the location of the civilization that sent the Message, the size and spectral type of the star Tau Ceti, possible types of planets around it on which civilizations might live, the likelihood that a civilization at that distance, any civilization, could build an Outpost – whatever that was – that was capable of monitoring Earth at close quarters, and a myriad other questions.

Paul Spearman was a participant in the WhatsApp group called 'Who are the Messengers?' and regularly dipped into the different threads when he felt he might have something to contribute.

Some time in October, he logged on from his office in St. James' College and found the following new messages in the thread called The Outpost:

> GAVIN BRUCE, CALTECH: If they really seeded Sapiens they must be at least, say, 500,000 years old –200k seeding event preceded by 300k to develop from their initial life form to acquire the technology to design and build the Outpost.

> CHEN WU, SHANGHAI: ...and how old is the Outpost? How could survive in solar system? Asteroid and meteorite impacts will surely erode.

> PIERRE ASTIER, SCI PO, PARIS: Surely with technology Outpost must have, and advanced intelligence/technology of Messengers, protecting Outpost from impacts would be simple for them.

> CHARLES CHAPMAN, DURHAM UNIVERSITY: As Arthur C Clarke said technology of civilizations more advanced than ours would seem like magic to us.

> CHRISTY HAWKESWORTH, ST. ANDREWS: What he actually said Charles was "Any sufficiently advanced technology is indistinguishable from magic."

Paul decided to focus the group's attention specifically on questions whose answers he felt would be more useful as the world came to grips with the Message and its implications:

> PAUL SPEARMAN: DEPARTMENT OF ASTRONOMY, CAMBRIDGE: Does anyone have any ideas about the likely computing power the Output would require to monitor and interpret the totality of information from Earth needed to convey to 'them' an accurate picture of the damage to the environment that the Messengers are so agitated about?

> PIERRE ASTIER: Paul, it may not need to be very much with good technology, maybe with probes sent from the Outpost, they would easily have seen over the last five decades that the atmosphere and the biosphere are going to pot.

> PAUL: It seems to me that they could need more than physical measurements to be sure that it is mankind that it is to blame and that

we are not doing anything, or enough, about it. Surely, they are monitoring our communications – radio, TV, telephones, internet – with enough AI, presumably based on machine learning and neural nets – to understand it all. Also – and this is the clincher – the Message is in clear in at least seven of our languages. There must be a whole section of the Outpost which has learned human languages enough to understand and write them

PIERRE: Magic indeed!

PARVO VARTIAINEN, UNIVERSITY OF HELSINKI: Hello, Paul, Parvo here. This is not my field but surely quantum computers could do any of this. Imagine where our faltering steps will have got us in this field in only 10,000 years!

PAUL: Hi, Parvo. Sure. But think of the peripherals the Outpost needs – energy supply, protection from radiation and collisions, built in self-repair, effector organs for transmission and reception – all a tall order.

PIERRE: As I said, magic.

Paul sat back in his chair. 'This is ridiculous' he thought. 'How can we all be getting worked up over a message we still don't know is genuine?'

Sherry Walker was on a high. She had been able to tell Kent Branton both about the Outpost on the rings of Saturn and to suggest tentatively that the Message the world was worried about might not be genuine. Kent was astonished, not so much at the possibility - everyone had kept that as a hope, in fact - but that it had come about through some kind of leak from a lowly Russian to a lowly NASA employee, rather than as a result of high level espionage.

When President Billings heard of this possibility, she ordered her National Security Adviser to set up a working party straight away and do again what they had presumably done before, look for evidence of fakery, either in the Message itself or through some characteristic of the raw data which the Russians had released, although of course everyone assumed that the Russians would be capable of making a fake message which seemed entirely authentic. They weren't likely to make silly mistakes.

Chapter 7

Back in September, the weekend after the Message had been received and transcribed, President Dimitri Pavlov had been digging up a flowerbed at the presidential residence, at Novo-Ogaryevo, when Oleg Kozlov called to him from the veranda that ran all around the two-story home, built in the so-called Stalin Empire style, with ochre walls and white columns supporting a classical pediment.

As Pavlov looked up, Ninotchka, his dog, ran yapping away from where she had been harassing Pavlov's spade, towards Oleg, whom she loved, and back towards Pavlov, whom she loved too.

"What is it?" Pavlov called.

"Your visitors are here," Oleg replied.

Pavlov brushed his dirty hands on his overalls and looked at his watch.

"Ten o'clock already," he said. "Give them tea and cake. I need to wash, then I'll be there."

General Yuri Pavlovitch Ivanov, Chief of Defence, Sergei Alexandrovich Gromov, Head of the FSB, and Irina Semionova Lyubimova, Director of TASS, the Russian press agency, appeared behind Oleg on the veranda.

"Go and make yourself comfortable, unless you want to do some digging," Pavlov called, "I'll be with you in fifteen minutes."

In the sitting room, with an entire wall of doors open to the garden, Oleg had placed pads of paper, pens, and some typed pages on small tables by the armchairs. In the corner, a samovar bubbled, next to a tray of Pyrex cups and saucers.

As the three visitors entered, Ivanov said to Irina, 'Do you know what this is about?" She replied "No" and looked at Gromov who said, "I do, but I think Dimitri Ilyich should tell you himself."

As they sat down, Oleg said "Mr. President asked me to give you this to read before he comes in," gesturing at the tables in front of each of them.

The visitors settled into their seats, and picked up the papers.

Gromov knew already what was in them. He had helped to write them. Irina Lyubimova was there to discuss any publicity moves Pavlov might want to make. And as Ivanov was Russia's senior military commander, Pavlov needed some information from him before Russia released a text of the Message.

There were gasps from Ivanov and Lyubimova as they read through the papers, which contained the full text of the Message passed on to Gromov by his source.

"Is this genuine?" Ivanov said.

"We believe so," Gromov replied, "That's one of the things we need to work on."

Pavlov strode into the room, showered and wearing a sweat suit and trainers. He slumped down into his favourite armchair and took a sip of tea.

"I hope you have read this," he said.

Ivanov and Irina started to speak at once, both sounding concerned. Pavlov waved his hand.

"Before you say anything," he said, "let me speak."

He took another sip of tea and then started.

"Sergei Alexandrovich and I have discussed this message, which we believe to be genuinely from an extra-terrestrial civilisation. We believe that we are the only nation to possess it at the moment, because my Director of the FSB assures me that he has spoken to a scientist in the Caucasus who tells him that the device that detected the signal was looking for something else and stumbled on it, in a way that would be unlikely with some other device."

Pavlov gave a slightly menacing look at Sergei as if to say 'You'd better be right.'

"He also assures me that there has been no 'chatter' on message boards or websites suggesting that other astronomers have caught wind of such a message. Now, that may not last, and I have an idea that needs speedy consideration, followed by action. Let me ask you one question, for a brief answer: Yuri Pavlovich and Irina Semyonova, what do you think of the message?"

Lyubimova spoke first.

"Well, if it is true, it is astonishing. Setting aside all the practical objections, it is understandable that they want to do what they suggest…" – she looked down at the paper – "in Paragraph 4. God knows how they would do it but from their point of view it's the right thing to do. If they really did cause, or at least facilitate, the creation of humanity, through language and intelligence, it is understandable if they are disappointed in how they – how we – have turned out. Their proposal is certainly a drastic way of dealing with their disappointment but…" She shrugged her shoulders.

Pavlov turned to Ivanov.

"Yuri Pavlovitch?"

"Mr. President, are you absolutely sure that this is a genuine message? It could have been carefully contrived by someone on Earth to destabilise global politics in some way. Not every nation will agree on the correct response to such a message, and China or the US, once they know about it – if they haven't faked it themselves – may seek to use it to their own advantage in some way."

"It is safer to assume it is genuine, at least among ourselves, in order to discuss what to do," Pavlov said. "Obviously, we won't release it – or a version of it – if we think it is fake."

"A version of it?" Irina Malchyk said.

"Sergei Alexandrovich and I have discussed releasing an edited version."

"Edited how?" she said.

"Sergei?"

Gromov spoke.

"We are not terribly happy with Para 4," he said. "We would like to replace it with something which will benefit Russia more, possibly by doing a bit of global destabilising, and also by selling to the world a type of technology which only we have at the moment, or which we can develop quicker than anyone else."

"Yuri Lyubimova" Pavlov said, "how is Project Papirosi coming on?"

"Well, as you know, Mr President," the general said, "We mothballed it last year to save money."

"I also know that you only appeared to mothball it, but kept the team going and continued to develop the atmospheric firestorm technology, using some underspend on the missile program that you unaccountably failed to declare."

Ivanov went pale.

"Sergei Alexandrovich would not be doing his job if he didn't keep me informed of such things. Now, Yuri Pavlovitch, how easy would it be to convert the satellite-destroying capability of Papirosi into a shield that would destroy incoming space vehicles?"

"It would need to be reconfigured for a much higher orbit, which would make it much more expensive to manufacture and launch."

"Don't worry about the expense. The rest of the world will pay."

"I don't understand," Irina Malchyk said.

Pavlov sat back. "Tell them the plan, Sergei."

"We will replace Para 4, with a paragraph which says that the people sending the message will destroy homo sapiens in five years' time, before the Earth's inhabitants can do any more harm."

Ivanov looked at Lyubimova and back at Gromov.

"That's a pretty big change," he said.

"Inspired!" said Irina. "The world turns to Russia so that we can save it from annihilation..."

"Yes," General Ivanov said. "It is brilliant, because Papirosi doesn't even have to work."

He was relieved at this, because the project had faced some severe challenges.

"And yet, we have done enough work on it to be able to convince others that it is the best hope to avoid annihilation."

"But what happens when we are not annihilated?" Irina said.

"We can say we have prevented it," Pavlov said, and they all laughed.

"No, but Irina Semyonova has a point, Mr President," Ivanov said. "Something will happen in the next five years, some global response to the message. And we are not going to be very popular if people discover we changed the words of the message..."

"First," Pavlov said, "people must not discover that. That's your job, Sergei Alexandrovich. And second, if necessary, we can 'discover' evidence that the whole thing was a fake dreamed up by the devilish CIA and callously causing untold distress to people all over the world."

"What do you want me to do, Mr President?" Lyubimova said.

"Help Sergei draft a new Para 4. Sergei Alexandrovich will then get that translated into the seven languages of the message. This will take a few days, but meanwhile, you need to draft a press release to prepare the world for the message itself. Say we are still working on decrypting it, and will release the full version on a certain date. October 15th, maybe? I've written something for you to work on."

He opened a drawer in the small table by his chair.

"Show your version to Sergei and he will discuss it with me.

Then Pavlov called "Oleg Nikolayevich!"

Oleg came in with a tray of glasses and vodka, and poured out a glass for each man.

Pavlov lifted his glass. "To the annihilation of mankind," he said, and the other three repeated it.

The events that led to the replacement of the original Paragraph 4 with a new version, required a new team of cryptographers. Sergei Gromov did not want to deal with the puzzlement of the team who had translated the original, including Olga. They were scientists rather than spies and he needed people in his own organisation whom he could trust absolutely not to reveal the deception. But time was short and it was a complicated task...

In mathematics, it can sometimes be useful to show that some concept or value must exist without having to describe it exactly. It's known as an 'existence proof' and it can advance a researcher's activities merely through the psychological value of knowing that if she perseveres she has a chance of getting an answer. A 'non-existence proof', of course, would be useful too, stopping her wasting time on a fruitless task.

It wasn't long before the world's scientific community knew that NASA, and therefore the US government, was taking seriously the possibility - the likelihood really - that the Russian version of the Message, or part of it, was faked. The rumours were so rife that Sergei Gromov, as chair of the newly organised UN Alien Communication Committee, UNACC, was compelled to deny it at the first meeting of the Committee, being careful to say that "all evidence is that the entire Message is genuine."

President Pavlov had been furious at the rumours and he and Gromov were already devising a backup plan that blamed anyone but themselves if someone discovered their deceit.

Ravi Chandra at St James' College, Cambridge, loved a puzzle, and when Paul Spearman saw him at coffee time in the Senior Common Room and asked him if he had any ideas for how to test the idea that the Message was partly faked, he was pleased with the challenge.

"We did take a look at it all together in my office, Ravi," Paul said, "And it wasn't so much that it looked genuine as that we couldn't think of a way to test for fakery. But now we know that there's a realistic chance that it could be fake, or that someone in the know thinks it is, is there anything we didn't try?"

"I'll look at the raw data when I get back to my office. Douglas Burnside is coming to see me to plan his research but I'm sure he won't mind."

The raw data of the Message, freely available, was a string of 0s and 1s derived from the variations in the radio signal. The original analysis of the string of digits, carried out by all major SETI enthusiasts round the world, had found nothing suspicious or anomalous in the seven versions, each separated by the string of digits including eight 0s, markers of the beginning and end of each language version.

But there were what appeared to be random sequences of 0s and 1s between those markers. No one had paid them much attention up till now, since it was the text of the Message itself that was important.

When Douglas came to Ravi's office with his dog-eared notebook and the brand-new laptop the college had given him, he asked what Ravi was looking at on the computer.

"Well, we should really work on your Goldbach Conjecture proof, but I'm happy to tell you what we are doing."

Ravi explained the rumours that the Message as released might not have been the original version and explained the structure of the raw data, with strings of digits between each translation with unknown significance.

"Here's where the Message begins," Ravi said, "With the first 10 prime numbers in binary. That's what must have alerted whoever detected the Message in the first place."

He pointed to a sequence:

10111011111011110110001100111011111101.

Douglas peered over Ravi's shoulder.

"Can you print it out?" he said.

"Sure," Ravi said, "But that's not at issue. Everyone agrees that that's the sort of way a message would begin - with something that humans recognise as non-random."

Ravi took a piece of paper from the printer and handed it to Douglas who inspected it closely.

"I see what you mean," he said, "2, 3, 5, 7, 11, 13, 17, etc, in binary. But how do you know that's what they mean... fuck!"

Ravi had a hard time ignoring Douglas's tics, but he did his best.

"I don't understand."

"Well, you've divided them up the way you want, into primes. But it could start 10111, which is 47 in decimal, and then go on to ..." He paused.

"Ah, I see what you mean." Ravi said, "But as you've probably just discovered, if it started with 47 in binary the next number would begin with 0, which no binary number does, just as no decimal number does."

"OK. Supposing the zeroes were used as dividers. So you'd get 47, then a zero, then 11111, which is 31, then a zero, then 1111, which is 15..."

"Which is not prime," Ravi said. "I think you'd find that even without dividers, this sequence would strike any astronomer as so unusual, so non-random, as to be intentional. But I'm impressed with your facility with binary numbers."

Douglas looked disgusted.

"Shit! Easy peasy! Any number theorist could do it."

"You should teach my elementary computing class..." Ravi said. "Some of them have to do it on their fingers."

"So why are you looking at this now? Ain't everyone inspected it to buggery?"

Ravi decided to abandon the Goldbach Proof session he had planned. Perhaps Douglas's unusual skills could be of some use with the task Paul had given him.

"Can you print out the whole thing in binary?" Douglas said. "I'm so used to doing stuff on paper – don't get me wrong, fuck! this laptop is great, but sometimes it's easier to work it out with a pencil, as the constipated mathematician said... Sorry."

Ravi sighed, called up the whole message and printed it out.

"There are seven languages, and four paragraphs in each. Here's the clear text of the English. The beginning and end of the language versions is marked by 8 zeroes."

"What about the digits between the two lots of eight, between the versions," Douglas said.

"No one's quite sure. It's a string of binary digits that don't seem to have any significance."

"Can you give me a few minutes?"

"Of course, make yourself at home."

Douglas did just that, sinking to the floor, lying on his stomach on the rather worn Indian carpet, and starting to scribble in the margins of the printout.

"Coffee?" Ravi said, standing up and walking to his coffee machine.

"Have you got instant?"

"Good God, no!" Ravi said. "You're at St James' now."

The two men worked quietly in their separate corners of the room.

After about ten minutes, Douglas looked up and said "Did anyone try to see if these were checksums? The binary digits between the eight zeroes?

"I think someone did." He looked on his computer for a specific file. "Here's an email from Jacob Dolgopolsky at Caltech."

Ravi skimmed it.

"He says he tried parity byte, sum complement, and position-dependent checksums but none of them seemed to be relevant."

Ravi was surprised that Douglas knew about encryption methods and ways of safeguarding them with checksums. Ravi did, because he had done some work for GCHQ. To protect against tampering, encrypted messages had an extra few digits after a message which were related in some way to the content. It could be as simple as a coded version of the number of letters in the message, a 'checksum'. If somebody changed the message, leading to a different number of letters, without knowing how to change the checksum, anyone could see that it had been tampered with, because the two wouldn't match.

"It may not be as complicated as that. Look," Douglas said. He held up a piece of paper. "Look, the number after the eight zeroes following the English version is 1011100101110. In decimal that is 5934." He jumped up, excitedly.

"M-m-m-aybe that's the number of letters in the English version! Quick, do a count."

Ravi called the English version up on his screen and went to Word count.

"3754," he read out.

"Fuck!" Douglas said. "That's a long way from 5934."

He was disconsolate and slumped to the floor. Then he leaped up again.

"Spaces! Spaces! Try the count to include the spaces between the letters!"

This time the count was 4521, still seemingly with no relation to the figure in binary after the end of the message.

But Ravi was impressed with Douglas's quick-wittedness.

"It was a good try. I don't think anyone has even thought of that approach. Not that I've read, anyway."

Douglas leaned over his notebook again.

"I'll try it with the other languages."

For the next fifteen minutes, the two men worked together. Douglas worked out the binary 'checksums' while Ravi calculated the numbers of letters in each message. The results were tantalising. With each language, the 'checksum' number was consistently larger than the number of symbols and spaces in each translation.

While they were looking at the figures, Ravi's phone rang. It was Paul enquiring if Ravi had looked at the text of the Message yet.

"Yes, I've been looking at it with Douglas, Douglas Burnside. The h…" He stopped himself from saying "the homeless man" and said instead "the highly gifted new research fellow I'm working with."

"Anything interesting?" Paul said.

"Well, Douglas thought the figures at the end of each message might be a checksum… Yes, I know Dolgopolsky tried that, but we – Douglas – thought of a simpler idea. But it's not working out at the moment."

He explained that they had hoped that the number after each language indicated the number of symbols and spaces, but it was always larger.

Paul exploded on the other end of the phone.

"Whaaat?"

"I said…" Ravi started to say.

"I know what you said. Don't you think it would have been much less interesting if the number had been exact?"

Ravi was puzzled. "It would have been a new discovery about the Message," he said, a little aggrieved. "We might have got a Letter to *Nature* out of it."

"Think about it, Ravi. If what we have is the original Message, why would these figures be nearly correct but not exact? But if someone had altered the original, and not realised the significance of the figures between each version, the figures would be bound to be different, and all in the same direction. They are all larger than they should be, right?"

"Yes, " Ravi said.

"Here's another task. Work out how much larger the checksums are for each language. If they are the roughly the same percentage, it may reflect the fact that the original message was changed in each translation and made shorter for some reason, deleting or changing what the Messengers tried to say.."

It didn't take Douglas long to work out that each translation was about 30% shorter than the 'checksum' predicted. It could mean that someone, the Russians presumably, had altered the Message, cutting 1400 characters from it in the process.

"Give us back our 1400 characters," Paul said and rang off.

Chapter 8

The SETI team at NASA were getting nowhere. While the National Security team picked apart the raw data from the Message once more, looking for evidence of fakery, Kent Branton asked the team, now augmented by an English data analyst from Jodrell Bank on a sabbatical, if they would look again for any telescopes which might have picked up the Message in addition to the Russians and therefore have a copy of the original version.

"Come on Bernard," Sherry said, as the team sat around a table littered with pizza boxes, "Shake us out of our rut. What are we not thinking of?"

Bernard Oldroyd was the English researcher and as a newbie he didn't have the courage to correct Sherry, and other Americans for that matter, when they kept calling him 'BerNARD'.

"I think it always helps to restate the problem as clearly and in as much detail as possible," he said.

"OK. Does restating it produce new insights?"

"Not really. It just delays the time when you actually have to do something about it."

There was a pause. 'Was this man serious?' the others thought. Then Sherry laughed.

"Oh, I see. The famous British sense of humour..."

The others laughed politely.

"No, but also it would help me if I knew what you had done."

"Mary? Would you summarise the problem and the failure to get an answer?"

Mary took a bite of pizza, a swig of Diet Coke and started to speak.

"On or about the 15th of September, a signal arrived at the surface of the Earth from somewhere in space. In fact, if we believe the Message, it came originally from Tau Ceti – which perhaps should be called Tau SETI – with an 'S' – from now on..."

"Nice one," Tom said.

"The Message said that it was transmitted from an Outpost somewhere in the solar system, and our revered boss discovered something which could well be the actual Outpost in one of the rings of Saturn. Gary then got a mysterious, pop-song-related tipoff that the Message that stunned the world was a fake, or rather was an altered version of a genuine message. We then – well, Gary mainly – contacted every SETI researcher on our database, plus other astronomers who might have contacted us in the past, to see if anyone had their telescope programmed to point in the direction of Saturn, or at the patch of sky which Saturn would have passed though, on the night of September 15th."

"Did you only contact SETI researchers, Gary?" Bernard said quietly.

"Well, yes," Gary said. "They were the only people who would have been on the lookout for a SETI message."

"But they might not be the only people who detected it..."

"How do you mean?" Sherry said.

"Any device pointed at Saturn might have received the signal."

"I suppose that's true. But surely the frequencies used for planetary observation are different from any likely interstellar message?"

"I think we have to assume that the Outpost will be clever enough to use the frequency they think is most likely to be detected, and so we should maybe widen the net."

"Do it," Sherry said. "That's a good idea, Bernard."

"In fact," Bernard said, hesitantly, "We could do worse than start with a colleague of mine, Terry Farron, who works with me in Manchester. He's been studying SKR for some years - Saturn Kilometer Radiation."

"Right," Sherry said. "We discovered that with Cassini and then traced it back in data from previous missions - Voyager and Ulysses. But that's a very different wavelength from what you might expect."

"Exactly," Bernard said. "But it can still carry a message. That may be how the Russians found it. One of their Saturn astronomers, maybe."

As part of his role as Astronomer Royal, Paul Spearman tried to earn his symbolic stipend by visiting centres of astronomy around the UK, giving a popular science lecture at a public meeting to astronomers, staff and local enthusiasts, and then touring the laboratories or research centres to get a sense of the work they were doing. As a member of the Science Research Council, he needed to be informed

A scheduled visit to Manchester University and the Jodrell Bank Observatory had been planned for some months and although he now had Ravi's - or rather Douglas's - insight to think about, and would rather have stayed in Cambridge, he didn't want to cancel the visit.

In the afternoon of his visit, he had a round table meeting with the Astronomy Department where the members, from professors to PhD students, gave five minute intros to the work they were doing. Paul made notes and made occasional comments when he thought it would be helpful.

In the light of the heightened public interest in astronomy caused by the Message, he had changed the subject of his public lecture, in the early evening, from "Stunning Secrets of the James Webb Telescope" to "The Message and the Messengers - The Meaning for Humankind". The session ran on far longer than intended because there were so many questions from the audience, most of which Paul couldn't answer with any certainty. Of course, he didn't even hint at the discovery that the Message might have been altered, though he wanted to raise it with a former Cambridge colleague, Terry Farron, over supper. Terry had always been a good sounding board for new ideas even if they were some way from his own line of research.

As they settled into an alcove in a gastropub near Jodrell Bank, Paul picked up the menu.

"I'm starving," he said. "That went on far longer than I expected."

"Well, one good thing is it's got people interested in science," Terry said.

"We-ell," Paul said, dubiously, "I'm not sure they're any more interested in positron-dust interaction and the charging of interstellar dark clouds today than they were last month."

They both laughed.

"How's that research going, by the way?" Terry said.

As Paul started to answer, Terry's mobile phone rang, and he put up his hand to stop him.

"Bernard!" he said to the caller, "How's life in Nasaland?"

He listened, and then said "I'm pretty sure I have data from that night. Yes, a number of frequencies, but I haven't been though all of them yet. It's only a month ago, Bernard. Out in the sticks here we don't work as hard as you… September 15th? Any idea what time?..."

Paul leaned forward quickly, pulled down Terry's hand holding the phone and pressed the red 'End call' button.

Terry was astonished.

"What did you do that for?" he said.

"Was that someone in NASA and did they ask if you had Saturn data from September 15th?"

"Yes. It was Bernard Oldroyd. He's on a sabbatical from Manchester."

"Don't you realise what they are after?"

"Well, I was a bit puzzled. NASA has a lot of data on Saturn radio waves from Cassini. I'm just using the Very Large Array to tickle the fringes, frequencies which can be detected from Earth."

"You know, you might have the only genuine copy of the Message outside Russia."

A waitress appeared.

"Can I take your orders, gentlemen?"

Paul was irritated at being interrupted.

"Have you got a curry?" he said.

"Butter chicken," she said.

"I'll have that," Paul said, "And so will he."

Terry was about to intervene but he could see that Paul had something important to say.

"My dad's right," he said to the waitress. "He controls my diet rigorously."

But Paul ignored this remark and ploughed on.

"We believe - we heard via the Americans - that the Message the Russians released was an altered version of an original message. What's more, some nifty number work in Cambridge - at St James, actually - suggests that the original was longer, by about thirty percent. But no one has come forward with a copy of a version which might be the original. But your friend in NASA who just rang probably wants to fish in your data pool to see if you have a copy. Obviously, they think that the Message might have been picked up not by a SETI researcher but by someone - like you -

who's been recording radio waves from Saturn, where the Outpost is believed to be."

"Well," Terry said, thoughtfully, "It's clever of them to come up with the idea. Maybe I should send them all the data to look at."

"Don't you dare!" Paul said. "Your country needs you."

"I was joking. But shouldn't NASA have it, really? They've got all the tools to analyse it and if they find the real message, to do something about it."

"Look, British science is chronically underfunded. If we find the original message, it will give us real leverage. And who knows, maybe a chair for you?"

"I've already got a chair," Terry joked, "But it's a bit wobbly. Maybe a new one would be nice."

Spearman ignored his friend's flippancy.

"How long would it take for you to go through the data?"

"I'll start when we finish supper. Any idea what frequency I should look through first?"

The waitress brought their curries, and the two men discussed a strategy for looking through a mass of data gathered in the space of a single night at a whole range of frequencies.

"Think like an alien," Paul said to Terry. "You know Saturn better than I. Its magnetic fields, and so on. What frequency would you use to penetrate the field around the planet and the rings, as well not being too attenuated when it reached Earth. And Terry, don't tell anyone about this. Do you understand? Not even your wife."

"I don't have a wife. We're just living together."

"You know what I mean. And call me as soon as you find anything. I'm getting the first train back from Manchester tomorrow morning."

"Is there anything you can give me that will help narrow the search down. Do you have some content I can search for?"

Paul thought.

"I think I can get you the first few hundred digits. The Russians won't have changed the metadata. That will enable you to search. One other thing: if you find anything, don't do anything with it until you've spoken to me again. Don't send it anywhere outside your own secure storage. Where is it?"

"It's on a 5 terabyte removable disk."

"Remove it if you find anything, and let me know in a brief innocuous email."

"Oh, and what do I tell the Americans?"

"Stall them. You can tell them you'll look."

"Bernard won't be happy when he finds out."

"It's a tough old world."

By noon the following day, Terry had found a file with the same initial identification digits, and he sent an email to Paul:

“Congratulate us on our new twin. Let’s hope it’s non-identical.”

When Paul read Terry’s email in his office at the Department of Astronomy, he knew that he would have to find a secure method for Terry to get the file to Cambridge. If any government – American or Russian – suspected that astronomers interested in Saturn might have access to copies of the original file, they would scour university and research intranets.

“Can you bring the twin to Cambridge in a safe way?” Paul wrote in his reply.

“Will you pay our fares?” was the reply.

“Yes,” Paul said.

“First Class?”

“No.”

“OK, I can get there this evening.”

“I’ll book a room in college. Come in for dinner in Hall. It's guest night.”

“I can't Paul. I have to read to my kid the very last chapter of *The Lion, the Witch and the Wardrobe*.”

“Can’t she read?

“Of course she can. But it's our bonding time. If I skip supper I can get to Cambridge about ten.”

“Okay,” Paul said “I think I'll round up a couple of people to help. Tell the porter to call me when you arrive. I'll warn them.”

Paul was on call for the guest night as one of the college's leading figures. His popular science books sold well, and he was often called on to comment on television news programmes when astronomical stories came up, though with the Message making such huge media demands, he sometimes sent one of his PhDs.

Miles liked to have Paul around at dinner to sit between distinguished guests who – you never know – might end up donating to the St James’ Development Fund.

Before supper, as the diners assembled, Paul took Miles aside.

“Look, I don't want to get too excited,” he said, “But there may be a development about the Message, one that only I and one other person know about at the moment, but we may have to act fast. Can we meet after dinner?”

“Where?

“It might be best in the Lodge.”

“OK. Leila might not stay up. She's got a shoot tomorrow.”

“I'd rather no one else was there anyway, apart from Ravi. I'm going to give him a call.”

At about ten thirty, Paul, Miles and Ravi, the last two wondering about Paul’s suppressed excitement, assembled in the sitting room in the Master’s Lodge. Leila had left them a thermos jug of coffee and some Lebanese biscuits and waved them good night, as puzzled as her husband.

The three men sat down.

"Right," Miles said, "You'd better tell us what this is about."

"We're expecting one more," Paul said.

Miles and Ravi looked at each other.

"Someone we know?" Miles said.

"Unless you've studied planetary radio emissions," Paul said. "I doubt if either of you would."

Paul's mobile phone rang and he answered it.

"That's him," he said, "I'll go and get him."

The two others took sips of coffee.

"These are delicious," Ravi said, eating one of the biscuits. "Did Mrs. Mason make these?" Ravi Chandra had been unable to shake off his unease at calling the master 'Miles' and his wife 'Leila'."

"No, she buys them from a Lebanese bakery in London."

Paul came into the room, accompanied by Terry Farron, and he explained the story so far: the discovery of the checksum data between the language versions, Ravi's - or rather, Douglas Burnside's - estimate that there might be an original message which differed by a few percent from the one the world was so exercised about, the lucky accident that Terry had been recording radio emissions from Saturn, among them a copy of the Message file that might be different from all the other copies, and the call from NASA which gave the whole matter extra urgency .

"How do you know it might be different?" Tim said.

"Because all the others are 2.3 megabytes exactly. This one is about 3 megabytes, and that fits with Ravi's new data."

"Douglas's actually," Ravi said.

"I haven't drilled down into the binary version of what the text might be," Terry said. "I'm not sure I'd know how. Our signals usually require a different sort of analysis. And do you mind if I take my coat off and sit down. Otherwise I feel like a DHL delivery man."

"Of course!" Miles said, leaping up. "I'm so sorry. What can I get you? Have you eaten?"

"I haven't actually. Avanti West Coast unaccountably failed to provide a sandwich service this evening."

"I can bring you some bread and cheese…"

"I'm vegan actually. Bread and bread will be OK."

"I think we've got some Flora. Is that vegan?"

"Yes. And maybe a stick of celery?"

"Okay," Miles said, and left the room.

"Where is the message at the moment?" Ravi said, "On your computer?

Terry took a small memory stick out of his pocket with a flourish and put it on a coffee table.

"And the only other copy in the universe is on my portable hard disk, which is detached from the computer."

"The Earth, only," Ravi said. "There must be copies somewhere on the Outpost."

"And in Russia," Miles said.

"I told him not to send it even by an encrypted route," Paul said. "That's why he's brought it by hand from Manchester this evening."

Miles came in with the food for Terry. He saw the memory stick and playfully held it up to the light.

"I see no Message," he said. "So what next?"

"That's why I've asked Ravi here. If we open up a file on a secure computer, one isolated from wi-fi and the internet, how easy would it be, Ravi, to find somebody trustworthy to transcribe the first thousand or so characters after the identifying primes? We would then see if it resembles the message at all, and decide whether it's worth transcribing the whole thing."

"Let me have a go," Ravi said. "Or rather, me and Douglas, if he's free. He did an amazing job spotting the checksum. I think we need to hold on to that man, in spite of his peculiarities."

"Well, well," Miles said, "And all because I gave a beggar £10."

"OK, Ravi," Paul said, "I'll bring you the memory stick tomorrow, once you've devised a programme to analyse the data. I don't want to let it out of my sight." Then he thought. "You couldn't do it tonight?" he said, pleadingly.

"No, Paul, I couldn't. Give me an hour tomorrow to set up a programme to do it. I'll use the raw data from the Russians' version to test it out. And if I can get it to work, I'll call you to bring it over. You'll be at the lab?"

"No, I'll be in my college office, waiting."

Ravi got up, a little dazed.

"Thank you, Master. I hope I haven't bitten off more than I can chew."

"You won the Field Prize, Ravi. If you can't do it, no one can," Miles said, and got up to show Ravi out.

"Paul," he said as he started to leave the room, "Can you wait a few more minutes?"

"Of course," Paul said, "Though I was going to show Terry to a college guest room I booked. He's had an eventful day."

"He can stay here," Miles said. "The Lodge guest room is much better. King Charles III once stayed in it. There's an orchid on the windowsill that Leila heard him talking to. Can you show Terry up to the room while I show Ravi out? Top of the stairs, second door on the right."

When both men were back in the sitting room, Miles said, "There's something we need to talk about."

"There's many things we need to talk about. What in particular?" Paul said.

"Should we tell the PM about the situation?"

"Look, it'll only take us a day to find out if there's anything significant. I doubt if she's got anyone else involved yet. Who knows what we may be able to tell her in two days' time?"

"You're right. Just checking. The next twenty-four hours could be extraordinarily interesting."

At about eleven the following morning, Ravi rang Paul, who had been on tenterhooks, unable to concentrate during a budget meeting with his departmental administrator. He leapt like a scalded cat each time his mobile phone rang, until finally Ravi's name showed on the screen.

"Well," Ravi said, "I've now got a programme which transcribes the original raw data file to reveal the message we already have. Do you want to bring your file over so I can put it through the same programme?"

"On my way," Paul said, leaving the 2026 budget unfinished.

In his office, Ravi sat in front of his computer. He'd asked Douglas along to help and now he was leaning over Ravi's shoulder looking at the screen.

"You could simplify it a bit by making that exponent 'mod n'," Douglas said, "You would have to discard the negative values anyway."

"You're right," Ravi said, admiringly.

As Paul came in, Ravi put his hand out for the memory stick.

"No," Paul said, holding onto it. "Do you have a laptop?"

"I do."

"Let's work on that. But switch off the Wi Fi first."

"My, you are being cautious," Ravi said, and pulled a laptop from his briefcase. "But I'll need to copy the software that I've set up on my computer."

Paul sat in a rather saggy easy chair, which had suffered under generations of maths students' bottoms.

"You should apply to the bursar for new furniture," Paul said as he looked around. "In fact, maybe a new study."

Ravi took a spare memory stick and copied the software he needed, then installed it on his laptop.

"What's wrong with the room?" he said.

"The worn carpet, the sagging bookshelves, the nail in the door instead of a coat hook. How much was the Field Prize worth?"

"That's long gone. I spent it all before I came to St. James's."

"On wine, women and song?"

"Just song, and one woman," Ravi said. "I took my wife to the full Ring Cycle at Bayreuth in the best hotel. Now, finally, will you give me the memory stick?"

Douglas, squatting on the floor and leaning on an old armchair, was uncomfortable with the small talk, and felt inhibited by it.

Paul handed it over, and Ravi prepared to insert it into a USB socket.

"Wait!" Paul said, and Ravi paused. "Did you switch off the wi-fi settings?"

"Yes, Paul, I did."

"Then you may go ahead."

For the next few minutes, Ravi typed away at the keyboard and moved the mouse. Paul asked Douglas how he was settling in to the College, and got a mumbled reply with a couple of swearwords.

Then Paul said to Ravi, "Do you have the English text of the Russian version?"

Ravi went back to his computer, found the English text and printed it out, handing the sheets of paper to Paul.

"If this works. I'll read out what we get, so you can compare the two."

Paul jiggled his leg as he sat sunken in Ravi's armchair. He could see the computer screen from a distance but didn't want to crowd Ravi by looking over his shoulder.

After a few minutes, Ravi said "I seem to be getting gibberish at the moment."

Douglas leaped up and peered at the screen.

"What interval gap did you use?"

"Four?"

"Try five."

Ravi pressed some keys and sat back.

Some text appeared on the screen.

"That looks more promising. Ready?" Ravi said.

"Ready," Paul said.

Ravi began reading:

"'This message has been composed using artificial intelligence and triggered by automated observation of your planet and the problems it faces.'"

"Is that the same as the version the Russians released, so far?" Ravi said.

"So far," Paul replied.

Ravi then read the rest of Paragraph 1, and the whole of Paragraphs 2 and 3. They were all were identical to the Russian version. There was a mounting sense of disappointment in the room.

Then Ravi started reading paragraph 4:

"'We have become increasingly alarmed at the state of Earth and we fear that it is reaching a point of no return as a result of..."

"Wait," Paul said, "Are you sure that's what it says?"

"Yes," Ravi said.

"What about 'It is clear that our experiment of developing a life form capable of matching and eventually excelling our own level of civilization has failed...' The original para 4?"

"See for yourself."

Paul stood up and walked over to the screen, and saw a Paragraph 4 which was entirely different from that in the Russian message. It read as follows:

> 4) We have become increasingly alarmed at the state of Earth and we fear that it is reaching a point of no return as a result of the failure of homo sapiens to take corrective measures to prevent a

series of catastrophes, evidence for which has been accumulating over the last half century. We do not need to remind you of the threats posed to the human race by the following: one million species are at risk of extinction; ecosystems are disappearing at an alarming rate; deserts spreading; wetlands disappearing; forests being cut down; oceans over-fished and choked with plastic; air pollution killing more than nine million humans a year and of course the inexorable rise of greenhouse gas emissions.

It's almost as if humankind, the species for which we had such high hopes after we engineered its acquisition of language and intelligence, is waging war on nature. We cannot allow this to continue. So we propose to intervene, using levels of artificial intelligence and nanotechnology which we have developed over a much longer period than your own technology. This will require you to set up a global organisation, setting aside political differences, to liaise with us or rather with our Outpost, over the course of time, sooner rather than later, in order to stop and undo the harm that is being caused to the global biosphere, and create the conditions for humankind to resume normal life and progress towards a fulfilling and sustainable life for all peoples on Earth. We will supply blueprints, computer programmes, AI software, and nanotechnology devices in high volumes to address each of the above problems in ways which your technology is far too primitive to address. We anticipate that accepting this offer may be difficult for you to agree quickly, but we urge you to make every effort to coordinate a total global response that all nations will sign up to. The sooner this happens the sooner we can start the tasks which face us all.

While Paul and Ravi were reading this, Douglas was rapidly counting the characters in the new paragraph.

"Shit!" he said, "An extra 1400 characters! I was fucking right!".

As the two men finished reading this, the door opened and Miles Cadogan put his head in.

"Anything interesting?" he said.

Part Two

Chapter 9

The clock on the Porter's Lodge at St James' struck twelve, followed as it always was by St. John's clock which overlapped with Trinity Hall's. Douglas had asked if he could get back to his number theory work. Although he sensed that something important was happening, he lived in world where the principal reality was numbers, and he was happy to leave it to others to make the more practical decisions of life. After he left, Paul, Miles and Ravi sat in silence.

The sounds of everyday life went on outside. Although it was late in the year, because of a spell of nice weather there were still shouts on the river of exuberant students showing off punting skills to their girlfriends. A rumble of trolley wheels on the cobbles came from the assistant porter Bob Patch transporting several parcels of books to the library. From the music room in the floor below, the college string quartet was tackling one of Beethoven's last pieces. It all seemed so ordinary.

"This is big, isn't it?" Ravi said.

"It is," Paul nodded

Ravi had printed out the new version of the Message, or rather the old version before the Russians altered it.

"We are the only three people in the world who know this?" Miles said.

"Don't forget the Russians," Paul said,

"Well, maybe the only dozen in the world, and the only three in the west."

"It changes things utterly," Paul said.

"So we are not going to be annihilated?" Ravi said.

"Far from it," Miles replied, "It looks as if we shall be saved from our own misdeeds."

"People will need to know this," Paul said, "as soon as possible."

"I agree that's important," Miles said, "But it's such a momentous discovery with so many ramifications. We need to think carefully what to do next. We can't just ring up the *Guardian* or the *New York Times* and tell them. Surely something needs to happen at a government level? They have people that plan for this sort of thing. We - or they - need to answer questions like, do we tell the US or the Russians? Do we tell the UNACC committee before anyone else? Are we even 100% sure that we are right or do we look for another copy?"

"Why would we need another copy?" Paul said. "This one is as clear as day. Obviously the Russians felt they had some advantage to gain by inventing the annihilation story. But we can nip that in the bud."

"We need to be careful," Miles said. "We know it's genuine. The trail from Terry Farron's data to here is unbroken. But are people going to believe it on our say-so? Conspiracy theorists will have a field day. They'll say we've made it up to dampen public fears and promote the climate change lobby. They've already tried to pretend the Russians made up the original message - or rather the second version, as we know it to be. This should knock that idea on the head, but could replace it with another hoax theory."

"Well, we can't just sit on it," Paul said.

"I'm suggesting that we can. At least for a couple of days. I'd like to suggest that, once again, we approach the PM."

"The PM?" Ravi said, astonished, "How will you get to her?"

"There's a back story here, Ravi," Paul said. "Miles and the PM are old buddies."

"Buddies of a month," Miles said. "Look, I'd like to talk to Leila about it too – get the view of someone who isn't as wrapped up in it as we are."

"Do you mind if I tell Dee? I've talked to her a bit about the original message."

"OK, but don't tell anyone else. And stay out of earshot of Ellie..."

Ravi seemed stunned.

"I presume you don't want me to tell anyone?"

"No, certainly not. Is Terry safe too, Paul?"

"I'll talk to him," Paul said, "but he doesn't even know the content, merely that he found another copy of the file. I'll play it down, tell him there were just a few interesting differences and I'll keep him posted."

"Thanks for this, Ravi," Miles said, getting up, "And thank Douglas, too," he added. "You have probably both saved the world in ways none of us yet realise."

"It was nothing," Ravi said with a smile. "Any time."

As Miles walked back to the Lodge, his mind was in a whirl. What do you do when you have a world-changing piece of news which it is 99% certain? There seemed to be no way of independently corroborating the Message, proving that even in its new form it wasn't a hoax. There was nothing that could be checked scientifically that wasn't already known. If the Outpost had given the location of an obelisk they'd planted on the Earth – as in the film *2001* – which could then be discovered, that would be some sort of corroboration. Except, of course, it couldn't, because whoever faked the Message could plant an obelisk and then include the location in the fake Message.

That evening, Miles had been due to take Leila out to an anniversary celebration meal at a new restaurant on Midsummer Common. It was their fifth anniversary, the first Miles felt they could mark as a significant milestone, though he wasn't sure which. Paper? Wood? Plastic? He knew she wouldn't be back from pitching a photography idea in London until early evening, so he spent a restless afternoon in his study, unable to concentrate as Debbie asked him questions about her draft of the College Council minutes.

He came into the residential part of the Lodge about six, eager to talk to Leila about the Message. As he put his keys on a side table, Leila came out of the sitting room, dressed smartly in a Palestinian dress with silver bangles on her wrist and her hair up.

"How do I look, Miles?" she said, twirling around. "I've dressed up to celebrate."

Although Leila had a good dress sense, she usually wore 'casual smart' with trousers and Miles had to admit that it made the occasion rather special when she did dress up.

But tonight he was going to have to disappoint her, but delight her as well, with his news.

"Darling, I'm afraid we're not going out to dinner," he said, and her face dropped.

"Oh, Miles, not work again? Even on our anniversary you have to work?"

She started letting down her hair. "Oh well, I've got some prints to produce for that exhibition I've been putting off."

"You can't do that either, Loo," Miles said, "We need to talk, and I don't want to be overheard."

"'We need to talk'", Leila said, "That's what they say in the movies when husbands want to divorce." She was only half joking.

"No, no," Miles said. "Look, let's get something out of the freezer and open a bottle. Some college champagne will be appropriate. I promise that when I tell you what I'm going to tell you, you won't regret missing the meal. It could be the best anniversary present you've ever had or are likely to get."

Leila had been worried – like everyone else – about the contents of the Message. She wasn't someone who brooded, and she usually took the bad news – even the worst – on the chin and somehow got on with life. But Miles knew that the thought of five more years and then nothing had led to a rethink of their lives and of life itself. When she and Miles married they had not ruled out having children, but Miles had wanted to get established in his college role as well as complete an important program of research, before – as he saw it – saddling himself with extra responsibilities, and extra work. He knew, and accepted, that his role in bringing up children would be as important as Leila's, and he wanted to have the time to do it properly.

For Leila, the Message meant the idea of having children was gone. No one should bring children into the world where they might not live beyond the age of three or four, however much she hoped that the combined efforts of human ingenuity and global cooperation might prevent the annihilation.

Miles knew that the contents of the real message would bring a rush of relief to her. He also valued her advice on exactly what to do next, with only four people in the world outside Russia – him, Paul, Ravi, and Douglas knowing about the discovery.

After Leila had changed out of her smart clothes and put on a long house gown, she came into the kitchen.

"I warmed up some mujaddarah," Miles said, "The batch you cooked for the buffet with the new intake."

"Oh, just what I would've done," Leila said.

"Sit down," Miles said, as he brought the dish to the table. "Don't turn over that piece of paper yet," he went on, pointing to a sheet he had put on the table. "I want to tell you about it first."

"Mysterious," Leila said, and helped herself to some of the lentil and onion dish.

Miles opened a bottle of champagne, poured two glasses, and then took a swig of champagne. He looked across at Leila.

"There is no way of saying this other than straight out," he said, "The human race is not going to be annihilated in five years' time."

"Oh, Miles, is this a joke? Or have you found a way, single-handed, of preventing a highly advanced civilisation doing what it promised in the Message?"

"The Message is not genuine, or rather there is a Message but not the one the world has been told about."

She looked puzzled.

"The message Russia released," Miles said, "was an altered version of the real Message, changed to threaten annihilation, when the real Message did nothing of the sort. That's the real Message," Miles said, reaching across and turning over the printout of Ravi's deciphering of Terry Farron's file.

Leila picked it up gingerly, as if it would burst into flames, and started to read it carefully.

"But this is the same," she said.

"Keep reading till you get to the fourth paragraph."

Leila read on and read the fourth paragraph three times.

"My God!" she exclaimed. "Can I really believe this? Promise me it isn't a trick. My heart is racing." She put her hand on her chest.

"Why would I show you that if I didn't believe it was true?"

"Of course you wouldn't. You're not a cruel person. But can you be sure?"

Miles described the chain of events ending with the discovery of one copy of the original file in the computers of the University of Manchester.

"Who knows about this?" Leila said. "Can I tell anyone? I'd love to call my mother and my sisters"

"No!" Miles said, "Absolutely not! Now we have the real Message, we have to decide very carefully what to do, how to 'tell the world', you could say. It's a weird position to be in, and as well as setting your mind at rest I wanted to hear what you had to say. Your advice is always good."

"It's lovely of you to say so, husband mine, but there's a big difference between helping you decide to apply for the Mastership of St James, and advising on how to break a piece of news to the world that would cause huge relief but possibly create havoc too. And what about Russia? They must have a big reason for faking the Message in the first place – wouldn't it unleash a can of worms if someone just shows them up overnight? And anyway, is it up to you, or you and Paul, even to make the decision?"

"Well, we definitely have one decision to make – what to do next. Who to tell and when."

"Let's stand back a moment," Leila said, "What about the new content? It sounds too good to be true. To go from annihilation of the human race to saving the globe with unimaginable technological solutions. Do we believe they – the aliens – can do that? And here's another thought. It's one thing to remove the threat, but surely if everyone comes to believe the problem will be solved by someone else, we'll stop doing all the things the nations are beginning to work on together – carbon capture, renewable power, reduction in emissions."

"That's a good point, Loo. But it's not an argument for letting people believe in the fake Message."

"What are the options?" Leila said. "One, do nothing, and let the world panic as we get nearer to 2030. At the other extreme, tell everyone everything, stop all the anti-climate change measures, and wait for the next message, or even millions of carbon-removing bots to descend from the sky. Or…" She said.

"Yes?"

"How about you – or the government – says that we've established that the Russians altered the message to create the 'annihilation threat', and that a committee will analyse, or even – telling a little white lie – try to find out what the original Message says, pretending you don't know."

Miles thought about what Leila said.

"How would that help?" he said.

"It would separate out the issue of annihilation – and the fact that it was no longer a threat – from the next stage, to help the world get to fix its problems."

"Hmm. That's a really interesting idea. The trouble is, I, or we, don't have control once the genie is let out of the bottle. If we tell the PM about the real Message, whatever we recommend – about not releasing it – she may decide differently."

"How many copies are there of this, as computer files or printouts?" She held up the printout.

"There's one printout – you're holding it – and no other print copies. There are no versions of the text on any computer. Ravi destroyed it after printing it out. And there is one copy of the raw, undecrypted data, on a memory stick which Paul has. Terry agreed to destroy his copy of the file."

"So don't give Carla Baxter the real Message. Just tell her the Russian version is a fake, and make sure no one can get at the real version until you say so."

"You are a devious woman," Miles said, admiringly. "Have some more champagne. This has been very helpful. I'll talk to Paul first about all this."

That night Leila had the best night night's sleep since the news had first broken about the Message. During the period after she had settled down, she lay awake thinking of the revived possibility of starting a family, and she realised that the anxiety she had over the Message was less to do with fearing death and much more about missing out on having children, something she had long desired since she was a girl.

When Rosie Kim had asked Katie if the Outpost could have planted something, some kind of signature, in the FOXP2 gene, the two women had talked on the train from London to Cambridge about how such a 'signature' could be looked for. Katie explained that even one gene was a molecule made up of thousands and thousands of the four bases C, A, T, and G, as well as lots of other apparently extraneous sequences of atoms and molecules. She didn't know where to look and what to look for. But Rosie said that, surely, the aliens would want their signature to be found so wouldn't they put it somewhere obvious?

Katie felt a bit out of her depth, so she decided to seek out Mary Sheridan, a computer scientist who had helped crack the problem of using computers to predict the shapes of protein molecules. Mary had also been a source of good advice for Katie when she first arrived at the college, and made Katie at home in the college women's group.

Over dessert and wine after High Table, Katie described the task she needed help with – finding an unusual or unexpected sequence in a very long sequence of many thousands of bases.

"What do you mean by 'unusual'?" Mary said, "and don't forget to pass the wine trolley clockwise even if you don't want any. You're being glared at."

Sure enough, the fellow on Katie's left, a wispy-haired historian past his sell-by date (full fellowships were for life), was staring at Katie as if his eyes could drill into her head.

"Sorry, sorry!" she said as she wheeled a small silver trolley with madeira, port and dessert wine, along the polished table surface from in front of Mary to the man, who knew more about mediaeval builders' tools than any other human being, but little or nothing about personal relations.

"I was hoping you would know some clever mathematical way to define an 'unusual sequence'," Katie said.

"There's an old mathematical query: what is the largest uninteresting number? The answer is, there can't be one because if there was, it would be interesting because it was the largest uninteresting number."

"And that is relevant because...?" Katie said.

"You're asking for the opposite," Mary said. "You're asking how to find an interesting sequence among thousands and thousands of interesting sequences. They must be interesting because they all do something in the genes. It's just that we don't know what. Your alien message, if it's there, is likely to look just like any other sequence of bases."

"What about if they scattered the same sequence throughout the gene?"

"As you know, DNA is full of repeated identical sequences, as well as some with small differences. It might be difficult to pick out any that were 'unusual' enough."

"So who do you think should win Celebrity Come Dancing tomorrow night?" Katie said, and Mary laughed.

"We don't have to give up so easily. I'll look at the genome project page for FOXP2 and see if I can come up with some software to do the job," she said, "And I think that Japanese sumo wrestler partnered with Fiona Bruce should win."

Three days later, Katie received an email from Mary Sheridan:

> To: Katie Flynn
>
> SUBJECT: UNLIKELY BUT POSSIBLE
>
> I won't bore you with the details but I thought of a way of looking for repeated sequences but filtering out those of a length or type that were unlikely to have been artificially inserted. I assumed that the 'aliens' would not insert some hugely long sequences for example, and so I put an upper limit on number of bases. The application came up with the following repeated sequence of bases. As you know, there are four bases, names simplified as A, C, G and T. I found an apparently meaningless sequence at intervals throughout the plasmid map for RC215021. I say 'apparently meaningless' because sets of three bases usually code for one amino acid but the triads in this sequence, however you slice them up, don't relate consistently to the amino acids necessary for expressing this gene. I think it needs a cryptanalyst or at least a mathematician to work out whether this sequence means anything, and specifically, whether it contains anything that might be of extra-terrestrial origin. Good luck. PS: And the sumo/Bruce combo did win!

Attached to the email was a sequence of the four bases, A, C, T, and G, in an apparently random order:

GTCCCTGTTCCACCATCCTCTCCTTGCCGGCGGTGTTTCCTGT

Katie had looked at this, bemused. She supposed there might be something significant in the difference in numbers of the four bases – there seemed to be fewer Gs, for example, but she knew that she could stare at the sequence for hours and not find anything meaningful. She didn't have that sort of brain. She needed some help.

When she bumped into Ravi Chandra in the queue at Sainsbury's, he looked a little shame-faced. Among the contents of his trolley was a pink gift set of bath bombs, talcum powder, and shower gel, clearly not the sort of thing he would be expected to need. He had bought it as a birthday present for a new lecturer in Indian history he had met at dinner in Trinity, invited by the Professor of Mathematics, and he hoped Katie hadn't noticed.

Katie was behind Ravi in the queue and deliberately didn't watch closely while he put his groceries on the conveyor belt. Somehow, she felt, people's choices were so personal that it gave you an uninvited glimpse into their soul. Even so, when it came to the bath time kit, Ravi slid it forward under a floppy pack of exotic flatbreads.

As he finished packing his bag, Katie leaned forward.

"Do you have a moment, Ravi? Just let me pay for these."

"If it is a moment. I have a supervisee in fifteen minutes."

"Of course," Katie said, and waited while the assistant totted up her purchases – not too many – and took her credit card.

"Time for a coffee?" she said as they walked towards the exit."

"I'm afraid not. Can it wait?"

"I need your brain to look at a sequence of symbols and tell me if there is anything unusual about it. Can I email it to you?"

"Is this for some competition?" he said.

"No, no, much more important than that."

Ravi had an idea.

"Look, do you know Douglas Burnside, the new research fellow in maths? He's got the sort of brain that likes puzzles. Why not try it on him? He'll be on the college phone list."

"Is he that ... man who I see sometimes with you in the SCR, that rather strange man?"

"Well, he's got a condition called Tourette's syndrome, which make communication rather difficult – or even offensive, I should say. But he's a brilliant mathematician. He spotted something in ..." Ravi hesitated. He knew he mustn't say anything about the real Message. "Anyway, he might be able to help you.

Later that day, Katie tapped on the Douglas's door on the first floor of Skimble's Hostel. There was a noise inside – it sounded like swearing – and then Douglas opened the door a crack.

"Dr Burnside?" she said. "I'm Katie Flynn. I'm a fellow."

"I...I know," he said, opening the door wider. "I seen you in Hall."

"I have a problem Ravi – Dr Chandra – said you might be able to help with."

Over Douglas's shoulder she glimpsed a chaotic scene. There was a mattress on the floor although there was a perfectly adequate bed, but that was covered with books and papers. Also on the floor was a laptop and next to it a pad with scribbled mathematical symbols.

"What sort of problem?" Douglas said, suspiciously.

"It's a kind of puzzle, but maths might be involved. Or cryptography."

Douglas became more interested.

"Can we talk about it somewhere ... else," she said. "The SCR later?"

Douglas looked dubious.

"Not so keen on 'Fellows' stuff," he said. "How about the *Live and Let Live*, Mawson Road? It's a pub, off Mill Road."

Katie didn't really know that part of town but knew she had to humour this man to get his help.

"Six o'clock?" she said.

Later that day she found herself sitting opposite Douglas in the public bar of a rather noisy pub. There seemed to be a mix of building workers in hi-vis jackets and other workmen in overalls. There was a beer-stained table between them and Katie found a pile of paper napkins to wipe it dry. As she was doing this, a plump woman with untidy hair and a shapeless floral dress under a denim jacket came up to Douglas.

"Douggie!" she shrieked. "Ain't seen you around for months. Whatcher been doing with yerself?"

"Get yer fat arse out of here," Douggie said cheerily. "Can't you see I'm busy?"

He reached into a pocket and pulled out a five pound note.

"Buy yerself a rum and coke – fuck! – and then leave us alone."

The woman grabbed the note and saluted.

"Right you are, sir. Over and out," and she scuttled away.

"I 'ad a different life once," Douglas said, "You prob'ly heard."

Ravi had told her a bit about Douglas's background, but she was still a little dazed by the situation. She took the printout of Mary Sheridan's sequence and put it on the table.

GTCCCTGTTCCACCATCCTCTCCTTGCCGGCGGTGTTTCCTGT

Douglas leaned over to look at it. He was silent for a moment. Then he said:

"Four different symbols. Forty-three of them. Uneven distribution. Only two As but seventeen Cs. That's odd. Do you know anything about this?"

"The four symbols represent the bases of DNA. In threes they code for amino acids. Do you know what they are?"

"Anyone with time on their 'ands in Cambridge reads about Watson and Crick. So do I need to know what amino acids these are?"

"Well, apparently that doesn't get you very far. You can split it into triads, which would code for specific amino acids, but you end up with an isolated 'T' at the end. And the sequence doesn't seem to have any biological significance. We think – the researcher who found this – thinks it might be some code where the biological significance is irrelevant."

Douglas took a swig of his pint and jotted something down on the edge of the paper. Katie read it upside down.

It said 'Try 1,2,3,4.'

Douglas scribbled a list of numbers and then looked at it:

3422243442212214224242244322332334344422434

"Well, there's no pi in there," he said.

"Oh, would you like something to eat?" Katie said, jokingly, but Douglas was absorbed in the sequence.

"There's somethin' about only four numbers. Maybe there's some kind of binary coding, in twos. You know, like computers. Could this be part of some computer programme?"

"Possibly," Kate said, concealing her excitement. "Look I didn't expect you to crack it straight away, or at all, but would you take a look at it? Here's my mobile number."

She scribbled it on the paper.

"If there's somethin' to crack, I'll crack it," Douglas said, finished his drink and stood up.

"Can I give you a lift back to college?" Katie said.

"No, I better go and humour Dirty Doris over there. I don't want to seem standoffish. Ta-ra."

Chapter 10

Miles and Paul were walking in the Fellows' Garden at St James, just over the other side of Skimble's Bridge. They were both being ultra-cautious, but they had decided that the implications of what only a handful of people knew must not get out in an uncontrolled way. Miles had a flask of Turkish coffee Leila had made. Although it was a sunny autumn day which showed Cambridge at its best, it was bitterly cold under the blue sky.

The two men sat on a bench, looking across at the 17th-century block which had formed the nucleus of the college. An undergraduate was leaning out of a first floor window and talking to another on the ground below. A boy and a girl on bikes cycled over Skimble's Bridge, past the gate to the Fellows' Garden, on their way to the University Library.

"I told Leila last night," Miles said, handing Paul a small paper cup of coffee.

"So what did she say?"

Miles told Paul about Leila suggesting that they tell the PM, or someone higher up, that they know that the Message as published by the Russians is a fake, but not reveal the whole message.

"I doubt they'll fall for that," Paul said, "Even if they believe that we don't have the original – " Paul patted his jacket outside the pocket that contained the memory stick – "they'll want us to lead them to it, and that will end up with them pressuring Terry, even though he's destroyed his copy. They're not stupid, these government people. And they've got GCHQ to do the heavy lifting."

"Maybe we can make a good argument for why the Message, the real one, should be kept back from the public for a while?"

"Actually, I'd be surprised if they didn't think that was a good idea anyway. They'd probably make us sign the Official Secrets Act to stop us releasing it."

"The problem is, deciding who to tell and how to keep it confidential."

"Well, you have a hotline to the PM."

"No I don't, I have a hotline to Mr Martin Paul or is he Paul Martin?"

Paul laughed.

"Miles, you can remember intimate details of the rituals of the Trobriand Islanders. Why can't you remember a simple thing like that man's name?"

"If I ring him," Miles went on, ignoring Paul's jibe, "he'll want me to explain why, and I don't even want to give a hint."

A young woman cycled over Skimbles Bridge and dismounted by the college gate, before putting her bike in a rack.

Miles looked at her vaguely and then sat up sharply.

"I have an idea," he said.

Back in his study at the Master's Lodge, Miles called the college administrator's office.

"Peter," he said, when he was put through "Do you have Dido DeWaal's next of kin details? She is a second year."

"I'll look," the man said. "Is she okay, Master? Has something happened?"

"No, no," Miles said, "Just an administrative thing."

Miles took down the details of Dido's parents' addresses – one in Little College Street, within reach of the Commons division bell, and another near Chipping Camden, along with three phone numbers, including a mobile.

"Surely that's a state secret?" Miles said to himself as he copied the mobile number onto his computer contacts, and decided to ring the London number later in the day, when the Foreign Secretary might be at home. He had checked that DeWaal wasn't out of the country on government business, but it was Friday evening, so he supposed the man might be on his way to the country.

Miles' heart raced as he dialled the minister's London home number and waited. A woman's voice answered.

"Is the Foreign Secretary there?" Miles said, hesitantly.

"Who wants him?" the woman said.

"Miles Cadogan, Dr Miles Cadogan, Master of St James' College Cambridge"

There was a pause

"Is Daphne all right?" the woman said.

"Daphne?" Miles said.

"Yes, our daughter. I believe she's a student at St James. At least that's what she tells us."

"Oh, is that Mrs DeWaal?"

"Yes. Is she all right?"

"Oh, I'm sorry, she calls herself Dido in the college. She's fine, as far as I know. I'm not ringing about her. In fact, she's been a delight this term. Her Lady Macbeth was chilling. But could I speak to your husband? Is he there?"

"All right. That's a relief. I'll get him."

The Foreign Minister came to the phone after about half minute.

"Yes? Dr Cadogan, is it?"

"Yes. The Master of St James," he added unnecessarily. "It's about the Message, from the extraterrestrials. I have something very important to say to someone senior, in absolute confidence."

"Is it really important? And if so, should you approach the PM directly?"

Miles felt slightly embarrassed.

"Look, Foreign Minister, I'm slightly reluctant to go to the PM's Office since I might have to explain myself to his advisor, Mr..." Miles hesitated and then took a chance"... Mr Paul."

The Foreign Minister laughed.

"Oh, Martin. Yes, he can be a bit fierce. He's only being protective. Well, can you give me a hint?"

Miles squirmed. He really didn't want to give anything away on the phone.

"Could I meet you personally. I'm sure within thirty seconds of me telling you, you'd understand the importance of what we have to say."

"We?"

"Oh, Dr Paul Spearman and I are working on it. He is head of the department of astronomy."

"If you're serious about the thirty seconds" he said, "You could come to see me tomorrow but I'll be in the country."

"Chipping Camden?" Miles said, his heart sinking. It was a half day trek from Cambridge to the Cotswolds.

"No, Chevening. The Foreign Secretary's official country residence. We have the US Secretary of State visiting, so you'd have to come early. For a bit of breakfast?"

"Where is Chevening?"

The Foreign Secretary told him, and Miles realised that he'd still have to get up early to drive to Kent by eight o'clock. But it was an opportunity he couldn't afford to miss.

"Bring your passport," the Foreign Secretary said.

"Are we going on somewhere?" Miles said, as a joke.

"No, you need it for ID at the gate. And one other thing. That production of *Macbeth* in the Fellow's Garden was terrific. I don't just mean Daphne's performance – the whole thing. Birnam Wood really did come to Dunsinane."

"Oh thanks. Yes, the head gardener wasn't too happy about that." Miles said, "We had to make the students put all the trees back and they were half dead."

"Well done, anyway. See you tomorrow."

Miles got up at six, leaving Leila sleeping, and made a quick cup of espresso which he carried in an insulated mug to his car. He put the postcode he had been given into the satnav, and set off in the early morning darkness. He had a transcript of the new part of the real message in the inside pocket of his jacket. It was the only copy. There was not even a word processor version of the message, after Ravi deleted the decryption from the laptop. Apart from this piece of paper, the real message now existed only in the raw file on Martin's memory stick and, of course, in Russia.

Along a country lane, Miles drove past an ancient brick wall and up to a five-bar gate flanked by an old brick-built lodge. As he approached the gate it swung open. He presumed his number plate was already in the system. He hadn't given the details to the Foreign Secretary but the government has a way of knowing these things.

He stopped by a red-and-white bar across the road about fifty yards further on and showed his passport. A uniformed man checked the photo against his face and then said "Park your car in the visitor's car park on the left and then walk to the main house. Don't go to the main door but round the corner on the left to the side door. The Secretary of State will meet you there."

'The servants' entrance, presumably,' Miles thought as he parked the car. He got out, patting his pocket nervously, and walked across gravel to the main house and round the side. At a door, Fergus DeWaal was waiting for him.

"Dr Mason," he said, holding out his hand. "Good to see you again. We'll have to have breakfast in the family kitchen. The dining room is being prepared for brunch with the US Secretary of State. Do you know Rob Delmonico?"

"Of course I know him by sight," Miles said.

"He'll be arriving here about 8.30. His plane landed at 7.30. We should be able to fit your thirty-second presentation in there somehow."

He smiled, and then showed Miles down a corridor to a large warm kitchen, with a scrubbed pine table in the middle and an Aga against one wall.

"No briefcase?" DeWaal said.

"No, nothing," Miles said, patting his pocket. "Just one piece of paper."

"Filter or espresso," DeWaal said putting his hand on a cafetière.

"Espresso, please."

"Cereal? Toast?"

Miles quite liked that idea – he'd eaten nothing since last night – but thought that what he had to say was too important to be interrupted by having to eat spoonfuls of granola or put marmalade on toast.

"Nothing at all, thanks," he said. "I don't want to use up your time."

The Foreign Secretary sat at the head of the table and Miles sat near him across the corner. He reached into his pocket and took out a folded sheet of A4 paper. Clearing his throat, he began to speak.

"The Message the Russians released to the world is not the original message sent by the Outpost. As you know, the Russian version threatened the annihilation of the human race. The real version promises something very different – help in dealing with the global problems of climate change, pandemics, extinction of species, and famine. I think that was about thirty seconds."

DeWaal's face showed a succession of emotions. Mild interest, followed by concern and ending up with incredulity.

"That's the Message there?"

"It's just the paragraph about helping humanity rather than destroying it. The rest of the message is unchanged," Miles said, handing over the piece of paper. DeWaal read it twice.

"Okay," he said, "Now you know what I'm going to ask. How do you know this? Where is the original? And how can you be sure you are not being hoaxed?"

"I know you don't have a lot of time so I'd rather you believe me, both that what I'm saying about the Message is true, and that the method by which we have seen the original pretty well rules out the possibility that we are being hoaxed."

"Pretty well?" De Waal said.

"Well, until someone finds some irrefutable evidence that shows it couldn't be the fabrication of a human mind I think we have to take it that on balance of probabilities it is not a hoax. Apart from anything else, since we got the previous version from the Russians, it's presumably they who changed it before releasing it to the world. If it was a hoax, why wouldn't they just have started with this version."

Miles pointed at the paper in De Waal's hand.

"Well, Dr Mason," DeWaal said, looking at his watch "We still have a bit of time. But if you won't give me the background – I have to take it on trust, I suppose – what do you want from me?"

"Actually, your advice. The advice of someone senior in government, about what should be done with this knowledge. Do we tell the world? We – the college or the department of astronomy – could just issue it as a press release –"

"No," DeWaal said, "You mustn't do that."

"But if we just handed over to you – to the British government – it's out of our hands, and there are a lot of issues raised by it, to do with science, public reactions, and international politics, and so on."

"Of course, but do you think you could make decisions about those matters better than the government?"

"Well, the government might have different motives."

"More coffee?" DeWaal said, and stood up.

"No, thanks," Miles said. "Actually, can I use the bathroom?"

"Of course. Can I read this again?"

"Sure," Miles said, and DeWaal indicated a door along a corridor leading from the kitchen.

When Miles returned to the kitchen, DeWaal was looking out of a window on to some trees. Beyond them were glimpses of the driveway and the main gate.

"I do believe the US Secretary of State is arriving," DeWaal said. "I'm very sorry I haven't more time. Can you leave this with me?" He had the paper in his hand.

Miles shook his head.

"Look, I'm very sorry. I don't want to let it get out of my sight. It's the only version. You know the gist of it anyway. Can we talk later today? About the next steps?" Miles put a business card on the table.

DeWaal said "I'm sorry. That won't be possible. I'm busy all today and tomorrow. Call me on Monday. Here is my office number. It will get to my assistant, Melanie. I'll tell her you'll call."

"You won't do anything –" Miles wanted to say 'silly' but thought that would be a little too impertinent "– anything precipitate?"

The Foreign Secretary smiled.

"Of course not," he said.

As Miles settled into the seat of his car and started the engine, he wondered if he had done the right thing. He drove out of the visitors' car park, past three large black limousines which, a few minutes before, had disgorged the US Secretary of State, three advisers, and six security men.

Inside the house, DeWaal was shaking hands with Rob Delmonico, as the rest of the party bustled around, taking cases up the wide oak staircase, and familiarising themselves with the layout of the house, floorplans in hand.

"Rob," DeWaal said, "Can you come with me for a moment?"

He led Delmonico down the corridor to the kitchen, taking his phone out of his pocket. A security man tried to follow the US Secretary of State, who shook him away

"There's something I'd like to show you," DeWaal said, and called up a photo of Miles' piece of paper on the screen of his phone.

Delmonico started to read it.

"This is just a summary of global problems from someone who is rather exercised about them."

"Read on. It's partmof the original Message, sent from the Outpost. We think the Russians changed it, to include the threat of annihilation, which wasn't in the original paragraph 4."

Delmonico read more.

"Fergus, are you sure about this?" he asked. "And what comes after 'we propose to intervene in the following ways…'" he said.

"It's the stuff about supplying various solutions to these problems, using their technology…"

"What stuff?"

"Further down the page."

"There is no 'further down'. Look."

Delmonico showed DeWaal the screen. In his hurry to take a photo before Miles came back, DeWaal had positioned the camera and paper badly, and captured only the top half of the sheet.

"Shit! shit! shit!," DeWaal said, "and I thought I was being so clever."

"Nevertheless," Delmonico said, "if this is correct, it proves the Russians have changed the Message and sold fake news to the world. Can you email this to me? And how about getting the rest of this para? Surely, the guy who showed it you will be happy to give it to you? Or you can make him."

"I'm afraid not. Leave it with me," DeWaal said, still annoyed with himself. "We'd better get on with our discussions. There's brunch in the dining room."

On the drive back from Chevening, Miles wondered whether he had done the right thing. Maybe DeWaal would take him seriously, and escalate the matter, but maybe he'd tuck it at the back of his mind and get on with whatever business he had to do with the US Secretary of State. Maybe Miles should have left him the piece of paper, he thought, but he and Paul had decided to keep tight control of the original message until they knew how it was going to be used.

'I'd rather deal with the behaviour of Melanesian tribal groups than British politicians,' he thought, 'Much more predictable'.

He unloaded some of this on Leila when he got back to Cambridge about 10.30.

"You see, we still have control at the moment. DeWaal has seen the Message so he knows its significance, but he can't show it to anyone else until we let him."

"Really?" Leila said.

"Yes, really," Miles said, irritated at being doubted.

"You kept the printout with you at all times?"

"Of course. Well, he held it to read it through. But I was with him."

"You didn't go anywhere? Use the loo?"

Miles thought.

"Well I did use the loo. It had been a long drive."

"And took the printout with you?"

"Yes." He thought. "No. He wanted to read it once more."

Leila smiled.

"Do you think the Foreign Secretary has a smartphone?"

"Of course he does!" Miles said, "He's bound to."

Then he thought.

"He wouldn't have!"

"Wouldn't you have taken a photo of it in that situation? Suppose you had crashed the car on the way home and it burst into flames and destroyed you and the piece of paper."

"You do have the wickedest imagination, Leila Cadogan. And if he did photograph it, it wouldn't be for that reason."

"No it wouldn't. And I'd be surprised if he didn't."

Miles slumped into an armchair.

"I'd be a hopeless politician," he said.

"But you are a brilliant anthropologist. Have a coffee and a piece of carrot cake I just made."

"I thought I smelled baking when I came in," Miles said. "That will be lovely."

As Leila surmised, Miles and Martin's attempts to control the original message had not been as successful as they had hoped.

President Jennifer Billings, wearing furry cat ears and a leopard skin top, was dishing out candy to the children of military families in the Rose Garden when one of her mobile phones buzzed, the one with the highest level of security and encryption. As she handed out goody bags with Presidential M&Ms and cookies, she looked at the phone and then turned away from the young visitors and staff.

There was a text from Rob Delmonico, saying "Can we talk?" He did tend to overuse this particular phone number – it was his first White House post after all – but she knew she had to call back as soon as possible. He had returned from the UK yesterday and she wondered what he had to report.

Followed by her Chief of Staff, President Billings went back to the Oval Office. A security man muttered into his sleeve "POTUS on the move to the Oval" as she walked by.

"Michael, can you give me the room?" she said. "I'm going to have to make a call."

"Sure, madam president," the chief of staff said.

"Rob," Billings said when she had reached the Secretary of State. "How was the UK. Something up?"

"Well it is and it isn't," Delmonico said.

"Gee, that's really helpful," Billings said, "but you could've told me that on the Oval office phone. Then all posterity will be able to consider its significance when the transcripts are released."

"It's quite important that what I want to tell you doesn't get transcribed anywhere by anyone at the moment, until you've decided what you want to do. Can I come over now?"

"I was about to go upstairs. It is Halloween, you know. Haven't you got a family too?"

"I think you you'll want to see this. I can be with you in half an hour."

Billings sighed. She pressed a button on her desk phone.

"Alice, can you tell Harrison I've been delayed?" she said, "The usual apologies."

"He's here," Alice Bendixen, her assistant said.

"Tell him to put his head round the door."

The door opened and her husband gave her a wave.

"Jenny, will you be up soon?" he said, "Your mother misses you."

"And my husband doesn't?" she said.

"I do, and you know that goes without saying."

"Look, Rob Delmonico has something he wants to talk about. From his tone of voice I get the idea that it can't wait. I'll be as quick as I can. Manuel is not starting the meal till five, right?"

"Right. We'll just have to drown our sorrows in Napa Valley's best."

He disappeared, and President Billings sat back in her chair. To tell the truth, when things are moving fast, like all these preparations for the promised annihilation even though it was five years away, she was afraid of losing concentration by taking time off, even for important family occasions.

She fingered two reports on her desk. Each of them had coloured stickers poking out of the edges of pages that her two main advisors, on space and defence, considered to be important. Kent Branton had used yellow markers and the deputy defence secretary, Grant Mowbray, red.

She flicked through the nearest report, of the UNACC commission set up to consider the options. A red marker drew attention to a comment by the Russian representative, offering to convert a secret Russian program of unspecified purpose to be able to defeat and destroy incoming missiles or craft from elsewhere in the solar system. Grant had scribbled by this "This is their secret military satellite destruction program – see DOD7/C/AN365/V."

"Not so secret, then," Billings thought.

The other report was from Billings' own committee, set up to report to her on a weekly basis, and involving Kent Branton from NASA, Grant from DOD and a number of representatives of other US government departments. Kent's sticker was on the last page where he had scribbled in handwriting: "Sherry Walker's team have a Russian contact who's suggested that the version of the Message promising annihilation may not be genuine. It's only one source with no idea of reliability but we are following a lead with a Brit astronomer who has been recording data from Saturn. Since the Outpost is believed to be in that vicinity we're hopeful he may have something to confirm – or deny – the genuineness of the annihilation message."

(Kent was being very optimistic. All he had to go on was Sherry telling him about Gary's phone call, and Bernard's conversation with a Brit who had suddenly clammed up in mid-conversation, perhaps because he knew more than he let on. But he had no idea whether there was anything they could do to get at the man's data.)

Billings looked through some of the other marked pages and wondered whether any of it was worthwhile. Any advanced civilisation – at least one more advanced than ours by a million years or so – would be bound to outwit anything we could devise to thwart the annihilation plans. It would be like an Amazonian tribe trying to bring down a US drone by waving big sticks and throwing stones at it.

Her phone buzzed.

"The Secretary of State is here," Ellis said.

"Show him in."

Jenny Billings got up and walked towards the sofas as Rob came in.

"Happy Halloween," she said.

"And Happy Halloween to you."

He shook her hand and sat opposite her.

"It's about the Message," he said.

"Oh, I've just been reading the UN report. And our committee's report too. No brilliant insights yet."

"What would you say if I told you the Message – the one we are familiar with – is a fake."

"I'd say it supports a rumour coming from the SETI team at NASA. But have you got anything more than rumour to go on?"

"Our British friends may be ahead of us in this matter."

"Really? And they didn't tell us? Did DeWaal tell you something?"

"No, that's the odd thing. Or rather, yes he did but not officially. Before I arrived – just before I arrived – he had been visited by someone who claimed to have had sight of the original message, one that he says the Russians received and then edited."

"To say what? I mean what did the Russians change – according to this mysterious visitor?"

"Read this," he said, and handed her his phone with the photo of part of the original paragraph 4.

President Billings read it, and looked up at him. "Where's the rest?"

Delmonico look sheepish.

"Unfortunately DeWaal is not great at taking pictures on his phone. He only copied some of the document. But he seemed worried enough by what he read."

"But it's garbage, isn't it? Someone's idea of a joke?"

She was rather irritated.

"I waited for you instead of joining my family. Do you have any proof of this?" she said

"Don't you see the significance of this, Madam President?"

"Of course I do, Rob, or rather the significance if it was real. That's why it's important not to get excited about it until we are 110% certain. This 'friend of a friend' stuff could be anything, from Russian interference to a QAnon prank."

Delmonico stuck to his guns. He explained the background – the status of Miles Cadogan as a leading academic, working with astronomer Paul Spearman; Cadogan's role in a group consulted by the Prime Minister Carla Baker, and the efforts Cadogan had made to keep the new paragraph to as few people as possible.

"What did DeWaal say about this?"

"He was inclined to believe it was genuine. And he felt that you should know about it so that we could coordinate some kind of action. Press release, maybe, or even a contingency plan before we publicise it."

"But we would need the whole thing." Billings said. "Do you think Carla Baxter knows?"

"I doubt if he would show it to me without telling his own prime minister."

Then he thought.

"Though it all happened very quickly. The guy left just as I was arriving, and DeWaal showed it to me within a few minutes."

"But he must've told her by now. And they will be looking for the original file as much as we will," Billings said.

"But we looked, according to Branton, and we didn't find it."

"Well, his latest position..." – she fingered the report with Kent's handwritten note – "is that they may be on to a British astronomer who could have an original version. The fact that your photo comes from the British Foreign Secretary may confirm that. But we can't put the world into a handbrake turn on the basis of a smartphone photograph, a photograph of half the original. Should we get in touch with this Cadogan guy?"

"If anyone does," Delmonico said, "it should be his own government. If the file is in a British computer, GCHQ should be able to find it. They've still got a few more keys to try on British computers than we have."

"Well," Billing said, "My family needs me, and so does yours. Let me think about this."

During the Halloween supper, Jennifer Billings was preoccupied. The Message, real or fake, wouldn't go away. Even a hint of a possibility that it no longer threatened annihilation mustn't get out. The stock markets would go crazy; people would be angry at having been misled by their governments; some families had lost members to suicide, others had cashed up all they owned to buy space in deep earth shelters; and without cast-iron proof, the conspiracy theorists would have a field day and the Russians would do everything to attack and dismiss the accusations against them of fakery.

But she knew that she'd have to talk first to Kent Branton and his SETI team. How come they hadn't found the file, if the Brits had? As long as Delmonico told no one, and she felt sure the British PM – assuming she'd seen the same Para 4, or part of it – would talk to their 'closest ally' without doing anything about it, it could probably wait until tomorrow and she would enjoy time with her family and Kent enjoy time with his.

But she was so jittery over dinner, losing concentration, and serving a slice of beef filet to her vegan child, that Harrison said, after the plates had been cleared, "Now, instead of looking at home videos of previous Thanksgivings, as we traditionally do at this time, mommy is going back to her office to sort out some urgent business, and then she'll join us later."

Jenny Billings was worried. Did Harrison know about the Message? She took him to one side.

"What do you mean?" she murmured. "How do you know I have urgent business?"

"Something's on your mind," he said "You've been away with the fairies during the whole meal. Why don't you get it out of your system?"

She was relieved, and kissed him on the cheek.

"Thank you, darling," she said. "I owe you," and she left the room.

At his home in Arlington, Kent Branton was dozing in his lounger, half watching two television sets. His wife was talking to their Filipino maid in the kitchen. Suddenly he started. His secure cell phone buzzed on the table next to him and he reached across to grab it, knocking over a glass of brandy.

"Shit!" he said as he answered the call.

"Nice," said President Billings, dryly.

"Sorry, Madam President," he said, sitting upright in the chair. "You surprised me."

"You surprised me, Kent," she said. "You told me there was no original message that was different from the one the Russians released."

"To be absolutely correct, I said we had been unable to find one but we had a lead."

"I know. I'm just giving you a hard time. Your lead may be correct. We have it from another source."

"What!" Kent said.

"I'm torn about this," Billings said. "On the one hand, if we can prove that there was no different message, it excuses your inability to find it. On the other hand, the possible original version, part of which I've seen, says nothing about the annihilation of the human race. Quite the opposite in fact. They're apparently offering to help solve all the world's problems, which I think you'll agree is good news."

As Kent listened, his wife came into the room, and rotated her hand to say 'What's going on?' He pointed to the red cell phone, and she went back to the kitchen, closing the door.

"What have you actually seen? Is it believable?"

"No, it isn't. It's just a photo of a piece of paper with some typing on it. You need to help me decide if it's genuine or not, preferably by finding the file that generated it. My office, 7.30 tomorrow morning, and tell no one."

"But I may make a couple of calls. We've already been looking for the possible file, after all."

"OK. And I'll call the British PM before you come, see if we can get anything from her."

Kent picked up his regular cell phone and dialled Sherry Walker's number. He knew he mustn't give too much away but needed to get some background before he met President Billings the following morning.

In Georgetown, at Sherry's house, the Halloween activities were in full swing. Sherry's sister and brother-in-law, Mary Beth and Tarrant, and their two sons were playing a raucous game which involved virtual reality goggles and a lot of arm waving accompanied by shrieks of laughter.

Sherry couldn't hear who was on the phone and had to walk into the hallway where it was quieter.

"Oh, Kent," she said, "It's you."

"Can you find somewhere quiet? Somewhere you won't be overheard?"

"Wait a moment," Sherry said, and went into a small study off the hallway, shutting the door behind her.

"Have you and your crew got any nearer to an original version of the Message?"

"Well, no," Sherry said, "We haven't got anything out of the scientist who just possibly might have picked up something. Why the sudden interest? Can't it wait?"

"We heard another rumour," Kent said. He knew he was in danger of breaching confidentiality, but thought he would phrase it vaguely enough.

"This one has slightly corroborated what your guy got from his Russian friend."

"What I don't understand," she said, "is what an original message might have said that would make the Russians want to conceal it, and invent the annihilation threat instead."

Of course, Kent knew what the real message was supposed to say, the gist of it, anyway, but with even that knowledge he agreed with Sherry: why didn't the Russians just pass that on? But the Russians offer to adapt their so-called 'Papirosi' program with financial support from the rest of the world could provide a motive, as well as Russia claiming a global leadership role in any response to the Message and its implications.

"Do you think it would be helpful to let the Russians know that we think they altered the original message," Kent said. "Maybe your guy – what's he called...?"

"Gary," Sherry said.

"Maybe he could get a message back to his contact."

"She's told him not to call back. Her phone may be tapped. And what good would it do? The Russians would just clam up, and we'd still never see the original. Now, please can I go back to my family?"

"Yes, of course, Sherry. But we need to some more answers if we are not going to be left behind by the Brits. Don't be afraid to call me if you think of something."

"Sure. Anyway, Happy Halloween."

Chapter 11

The following morning, at 7 a.m. Washington DC time, midday in London, Paul Martin picked up the desk phone in Number 10. There had been an overnight email from the White House, setting up a call to the PM. Martin buzzed through.

"It's President Billings, Prime Minister," he said.

Jennifer Billings had decided that her approach should be to imply that the US already had a copy of the file. She hoped that might lead Carla Baxter to let drop some clues about what it contained, or where it was.

"Madam President, good morning," Carla said, "I'm always so glad the time difference means you have to be up early when I can take your calls at a civilised time."

The US president laughed. "But we have been known to disturb your evenings, or even your nights, when we are still at the office."

"What can I do for you? The Message and the annihilation I suppose. There's little time for anything else these days. We are just preparing a draft of a possible joint US/UK position paper on the Russians."

To Billings this sounded like bluffing - business as usual, making plans for how to deal with the annihilation. But it could just mean that Baxter had decided that the Para 4 she must have been shown was not worth worrying about.

"I'm wondering if we should take seriously this file with an alternative version of the Message, one that's supposed to be the original."

There was a pause. Then Baxter spoke.

"Of course, Fergus showed me what he'd been shown. But it's a long way from a full file of an alternative - an original - version of the Message. Anyone could have written it. It was just a piece of paper. It's only because this man is such a distinguished academic that Fergus agreed to see him at all."

"But if what it says is correct, it totally changes the whole situation, for the world," Billings said. "And of course, obtaining the actual file strengthens the likelihood that it is true."

Billings hoped she had planted the idea that the US already had a copy.

Carla Baxter decided that she couldn't be bothered playing games.

"Look," she said, "we've done a bit of work to find the copy of the file Dr Cadogan showed Fergus, and haven't done so yet. It's tricky - I'm told - because it's not a state secret or anything. It's just some scientific data, and so the people who have it quite rightly are saying they want to decide for themselves what to do about it."

The US president was astonished.

"Carla, you can't take that lying down!"

She immediately regretted being so forthright.

"Sorry, that came out wrong," Billings said. "But surely this is too important to risk leaving it in the hands of 'the people who have it'?"

"So you don't have the file?" Baxter said. "If you did have it, you wouldn't be so worried about what the scientists might do."

"We'd be more worried," Jenny said, "because we wouldn't have control. At least if just you and I had it, we could plan how to release the news, backed up with some kind of joint plan."

"Well, we are obviously both still looking. And whatever we do - if we are 100% certain that the new message is genuine - we need the cooperation of the scientists who've discovered it. There are so many questions no one has answered yet - about the other civilisation, the so-called Outpost, their technical capabilities, their motivation, the claims that they somehow seeded homo sapiens with language. All of those will become much higher profile questions if we don't have to worry about annihilation and, instead, work out the best way to save the globe with the help of these people. But I say again, until we have established with certainty that the earlier threat is false, we shouldn't do anything rash."

"I know our State Department and NSA are working with your people on the Russian front. Are your people any nearer establishing what they are up to? What they will get out of this if they are not unmasked?"

"Not really. One group of Moscow watchers thinks it might be something to do with a power struggle between Pavlov and Gromov, head of the FSB. But another group disagrees and thinks it centres on a power struggle between the space people and the defence people."

"Well, we've made a pretty exhaustive search for the file," Billings said, massaging the truth, "and by the sound of it you haven't found a copy either. Why don't you just ask the scientists to give you their copy?"

"We can't make them, Jennifer, and it seems that for the time being they don't want to hand it over. It's all so murky but there's nothing we can do at the moment. We're just going to keep an eye on their activities. We have to bear in mind that they may have been fooled too, even though they think it's genuine."

The call ended without anything having been decided. But at least President Billings knew that the British government didn't have a copy of the file either. It was all very frustrating.

Much of the media coverage was still about the annihilation - reports of the UN Committee meeting, leaked, of course, although it was so early in their deliberations that there was nothing startling, other than the suggestion by the Chinese representative that the whole thing had been dreamed up by Russia and the West to isolate China, perhaps as a punishment for them creating the Covid virus, which they hadn't, of course.

There were newspaper stories about the sort of things rich people were doing to try to avoid the consequences of the annihilation. They all seemed pretty futile - buying islands, building bunkers, setting up new and improved cryogenic preservation complexes.

There was the increase in new religions, promising ever more ingenious forms of prayer for action, requiring, of course, large financial donations to obtain special treatment for their adherents, although it was the aliens, not God, who was threatening destruction.

Then there were the communicators – groups of hackers who claimed to be in regular contact with the Outpost and offered to carry out a negotiated deferral or even cancellation of the annihilation if they were given donations, in bitcoins of course. They offered platinum-plated ID cards to donors to be shown to the aliens when they appeared – assuming they could only carry out the annihilation in person – guaranteeing immunity from annihilation, along with a form of rapture which consisted of being taken up to the Outpost on Saturn to continue their lives there. If they had known that the Outpost was barely larger than the Super Bowl, these donors might have thought twice about changing life on Earth for the increasingly cramped conditions of a floating computer-cum-nanotechnology factory.

All the while, the Outpost orbited Saturn, its antennae sucking in terabytes of information every second from Earth's wireless emissions, which were amplified and processed by unimaginably fast quantum computers, powered by fusion generators which extracted tritium from the surrounding rocks which made up Saturn's rings. And the extraterrestrial civilisation which had devised all this, back on a planet around Tau Ceti, was unaware of the fact that its Outpost had finally made contact with homo sapiens, because the automatic message confirming this had a journey of twelve Earth years before it would reach them.

Katie Flynn was itching to hear from Douglas about the sequence Mary had found. When she sent him an email after she hadn't heard from him for a day, he sent back a curt reply. "Sorry, busy."

She thought of approaching Ravi again, but decided not to push. It was probably nothing at all, anyway, so she swallowed her impatience and went off to her lab to look at a new parcel of bones that had come in from a field palaeontologist in East Africa.

Douglas was deep in the work he had been doing on the Goldbach Conjecture, which had thrown up some new leads he was keen to pursue. As he settled down on the floor of his room he noticed the Post-It he had stuck on his computer with the sequence of bases Katie had given him.

'I'll take a quick look,' he thought, 'and if nothing emerges I'll go back to Goldbach.'

As he had noticed, there was a very uneven distribution of the four letters, and that didn't really give him a clue. He then thought 'Supposing each letter stands for one of the first four integers.'

He started with G=1, T=2, C=3 and A=4 and wrote out the sequence of numbers beginning 1233321223343… and ending …3212. Nothing leaped out at him from that sequence.

Then he thought 'Why four?' He would have understood if there had been only two symbols, representing 0 and 1, because then the sequence could represent binary digits. He took out a pad and a battered pencil with a chewed end and started playing around with different values for the four letters and then writing the first few numbers in the sequence they represented.

There were quite a lot of possible combinations but he persisted, looking at the first few digits for some significance. He didn't notice the time but his stomach told him he had missed lunch.

'Just one more,' he thought.

The next substitution, G=2, T=3, C=1 and A=0, gave the first few digits as 2311132331101…

He stared at this sequence for a minute or two, letting it sink into his brain. Then rapidly he typed it into his laptop and put spaces between combinations of numbers:

2 3 11 13 23 31 101 113 131 133…

"Yesss!" he said out loud, and scrambled up from the floor.

There was no answer from Katie's mobile. She usually kept it off during tutorials. It was only fair to the students. Douglas didn't want to leave a message, and decided to microwave some leftover Chicken McNuggets. He was taking a while to grasp the idea that, as a Fellow, he could eat free food, but when he did take advantage of the college cook's menus he didn't always like the dishes and often returned to his old habits, though yesterday's Chicken McNuggets were purchased, rather than retrieved from a rubbish bin.

On Sunday evening, three unmarked cars drove up to St James and parked on the cobbles outside St James' front gate. Two men in bulging suits walked into the Porter's Lodge while several others waited outside.

One of the men asked for Dr Miles Cadogan, and the senior porter, Harry Golding, said that the Master was in the chapel at the annual service for town and gown. When the man asked Golding to fetch him out, he stretched to his full height of 5' 2" and said "I will do nothing of the sort."

The man produced an impressive but unclear badge of identity, and said "Special Branch."

Mr Golding was a quick thinker and said "Surely you know that Cambridge colleges are independent entities with the status of… foreign embassies. I could have you thrown out!"

The man looked astonished, and because he wasn't sure whether what Golding had said was correct, he took out his phone.

"But you may go into the chapel yourself," Golding said, "and after the Master has done his bit in the service, you may identify yourselves to him at the end, and I'm sure he will be happy to talk to you. It might do you some good too," he added. "The chapel is across the First Court, through the passageway in the corner on the right and the door is on the left. You might hear some singing."

The two men started walking diagonally across the lawn in the middle of First Court."

"Oy!"

A shout came from across the Court. Bob Patch, the assistant porter, was assiduous in making sure college rules relating to lawn privileges were observed. He knew that the two men were not senior members of the college, and that meant they were in breach of regulations.

"Off the grass!" Patch called.

The two men looked at each other and then at the young man who was coming towards them, waving his arms. One of them, Dave, put his hand inside his jacket, and the other, Ben, said quickly "Don't be stupid, Dave. It's just another Jobsworth."

Ben and Dave walked to the nearest path and followed it round to the passage in the corner. They found the door to the chapel and pushed it open with a loud creak. A voice from the congregation said "Shhhh!" and the two men saw that someone was speaking from a pulpit. It was Miles Cadogan finishing the annual address the Master of the college gave to the people of Cambridge. He was reading from notes.

"... We will, God willing, be here at the same time next year. It will be an unusually uncertain year as we try to grasp the significance of the first communication from an alien civilisation."

He had meant to go on and say, "We all face death. As the writer in Ecclesiastes says 'There is a time to live and a time to die'. But most of us have never had to deal with the knowledge of when that might be. Nevertheless, the signs are that the world is coming together in an unprecedented way and much can happen in the face of what is an existential challenge..."

Instead, on impulse, knowing what he now knew, he tried to be more positive, without giving anything away. Looking up from his notes he said, "I am not a priest but I am more inclined to use priestly words at a time like this and say, let us have hope for the future, and faith that the ingenuity of the human race, working together, will lead to a future which will surprise and hearten those of us who are confused and disheartened about what lies ahead."

As Miles came down from the pulpit, the college chaplain led the congregation in prayers. The Special Branch men rather uncomfortably followed the responses of the people around them.

The chaplain then said "Let us offer one another a sign of peace," and everyone stood up. The young man next to Dave turned to him and thrust his hand towards him. In a flash Dave had spun the man around and forced one arm behind his back in a half nelson. The man gasped in pain and people around them looked astonished. After Ben had shaken hands with the person on his left he turned to see what David had done.

"Dave!" he hissed, "What are you doing?"

"He was after my gun!" Dave said.

"No he wasn't," said Ben, who had been brought up C of E, "He wanted to exchange the Peace!"

"That's what I said – he wanted my piece."

"Let him go! I'll explain later."

Dave reluctantly released the young man, who nursed his arm. Dave patted him on the shoulder.

"Sorry, mate," he muttered.

At the end of the service, people in the rows around Ben and Dave gave them a wide berth. Ben led Dave to the back of the chapel and the two men waited by the door for Miles, who had noticed some sort of disturbance around the two strangers near the back of the chapel.

He stopped by the two men and said "What was the fuss about?"

"It was nothing" Ben said, "My colleague was unfamiliar with that key moment in the Anglican service where the congregation share the Peace. I think he's a pagan."

Dave looked daggers at Ben.

"Could we speak to you, sir?" Ben went on, and showed his badge.

Miles was surprised, though he suddenly had an idea of what this might be about.

"What for?" he said. "Is it about one of the students?"

"I'd rather not say till we are somewhere private."

"You can come to the Lodge," he said. "Do I need to have someone with me? A lawyer perhaps?"

"I hope not," Ben said. "I hope we can achieve what we want without bothering any lawyers."

As the three men left the chapel, Harry Golding, the head porter was waiting.

"Excuse me, Master, could I have a word?"

"Of course, Harry, what is it?"

"Your visitors seem to have parked three cars on the cobbles. Professor Clark can't find a space for his mobility bike."

"Oh," Miles said and turned to the two men.

"I'm afraid the cobbles are sacred. Parking space is so restricted in Cambridge, we have to have rules. And how come you have three cars when they're only two of you?"

"There are six more of them, sir, sitting in their vehicles."

"Do they need to talk to me as well?" Miles said to Ben and Dave.

"No, not talk," Dave said, sinisterly.

"Oh, you mean beat me up?"

Miles was enjoying this. Although he knew it might not end well, he couldn't take these men seriously, with their bulky, ill-fitting suits and - he suspected - a gun or two underneath.

"I just need to make a call, while your men re-park the cars," he said. "The car park near the Round Church will probably have spaces."

Ben muttered something to Dave, who walked off towards the college gate.

Miles called Paul's phone. He had seen him among the fellows at the service and hoped he hadn't gone back to the department yet.

Paul answered and Miles said, out of the hearing of Ben, "I think we've been rumbled."

“What?”

“I’ve got two visitors from Special Branch, with another six on the way. It can only be about… well, you know what. I’m going with them to the Lodge. Can you join me there?”

“Sounds as if I’d better,” Paul said.

Neither Miles nor the remaining Special Branch man spoke as they walked across Skimble’s Court to the Master’s Lodge. On the front step, Miles held up his hand to stop Ben in his tracks, and opened the front door.

“Loo!” he called and Leila came out of a cloakroom where she’d been taking off her coat after the chapel service. She had slipped away from the service before Miles and not seen the two men.

“We have … guests,” he said, and when she opened her mouth to speak, he went on “Don’t ask.”

He turned and beckoned Ben in, who was joined by Dave, panting after running back from the main gate. The men came through the door sheepishly and wiped their feet thoroughly on the doormat.

“This is Mr… Ben and Mr Dave,” he said, introducing them to Leila, and then, to the men, he said, “Tea?”

The two men mumbled yesses and Miles said brightly to Leila “Could you make us some tea? And you might like to join us.”

“Oh, no,” Ben said “that won’t be necessary.”

“Oh, yes,” Miles replied, “It certainly will. And I have a colleague on his way, so whatever this is about, you may have to wait.”

“Look, Mr… Dr Cadogan, we really just want a little chat. There’s no need for anyone else. Is he a lawyer, this colleague?”

“No he’s a scientist. Head of the department of astronomy. I’m sure he’ll be interested in your ‘little chat’ whatever it’s about. Or do you think I need a lawyer? We have a couple of those in the college too.”

“No, no,” said Ben, the one who seem to do all the talking. “I’m sure that won’t be necessary.”

“Do you mind taking your coats off?” Leila said with a smile, echoing Miles’ matter-of-fact approach. “You can hang them there, in the cloakroom.”

“And could you take your shoes off, too,” Miles said. “We’ve recently had new carpeting in the living room.”

Mikes knew how uncomfortable people felt trying to carry out normal business in their stockinged feet, particularly when, as with Dave, a big toe pokes through a hole in the sock.

Dave looked daggers at Miles and then obliged, and the two men followed him into the sitting room, perching themselves rather uncomfortably on the edge of a sofa, with a view through French windows onto the Master’s garden.

“Would you excuse me for a moment?” Miles said as he turned and started to leave the room.

“I’m afraid not,” Dave said suddenly.

"So, Garbo speaks," Miles said to Ben, making a cultural reference he was sure the men wouldn't understand, "And he seems to want to tell me what to do in my own house."

Dave then had a muttered conversation with Ben, in which the word "computer" occurred a couple of times.

"We'd prefer that you didn't," Ben said.

"Well, Mr Ben, whoever you are, you can prefer what you like but I'm just going to talk to my wife in the kitchen."

Before either of them could stop him, Miles left the room.

Ben took out his mobile phone and called one of his colleagues waiting outside the college gate.

"This could take a while," he said quietly.

There was a ring at the doorbell and Leila opened the front door to Paul.

"You could have walked in," she said, "You know the door is usually unlocked when we are here."

"I wasn't sure what was going on," Paul said. "Thought I'd be cautious."

"Don't ask me, " Leila said. "There's two men in the sitting room who look like characters from *The Godfather*. Go in."

Miles came out of the kitchen and had a quiet conversation with Paul.

"They're from Special Branch. Obviously, my little jaunt to see the Foreign Secretary backfired. Maybe spectacularly."

"Don't worry," Paul said, "If they haven't got a warrant there's not much they can do. And since we haven't done anything illegal I don't see how they could be granted a warrant."

In the sitting room, as Miles and Paul came in, Ben and Dave stood up.

"This is Professor Spearman," Miles said, "and look, although I know your first names, would you mind introducing yourselves formally."

"Formally?" Ben said.

"You know, by name. Mr Ben Franklin or whatever your second name is. Maybe you have a card?"

"Oh, I'm Carney and this is Buckle. Ben Carney and David Buckle."

"Good, and do sit down and tell me what I can do for you."

Ben Carney cleared his throat.

"We have reason to believe that you are in possession of a computer file that is of great interest to the British government."

"Oh, really?" Miles said, "Can you describe this file?"

"It relates to a message from an alien civilisation," he said looking at some notes in a notebook. "You know, the one there's been all the publicity about."

"Oh, you mean the one about the annihilation of the human race?"

Leila came in with a tray of tea things and put it on a low table in front of the sofa.

"Milk? Sugar?" she said to the men.

"Yes, please," said Ben, "One spoon."

"Yes, please," said Dave, "Three spoons," as if it was a competition.

"Do you have a copy of that file?" Miles said to Paul.

"I'm sure we do," Paul replied, "most university astronomy department, and a few others, are bound to. I'm surprised Special Branch don't have their own copy."

He turned to Ben. "You're talking about the file obtained by the Russians and publicised by them on September 1?"

"No," said Ben, "I'm talking about another one, which I believe you, Dr Cadogan, showed the Foreign Secretary last week."

He handed him a printout of the photo from DeWaal's phone.

"I showed him no computer file," Miles said.

"Yes, you did," Ben said, "or is the Foreign Secretary lying?"

"I've no idea what the Foreign Secretary said to you or your boss. But all I showed him was a page of printed text."

"Well, of course," Ben said, "When I said a computer file I meant the file used to generate that text."

"Ah, I see. Do we have that file, Paul?"

"No, Miles, or at least I don't. Do you?"

"No, Paul. I don't either."

It was clear to Ben and even to Dave that the two academics were playing games. The next bit was going to be tricky.

"Do you mind if I ask some of my colleagues to inspect your computers?"

"Of course," Miles said pleasantly.

Ben was relieved. He opened his phone, pressed a button, and said "You can come in now. Ask the porter to show you to the Master's Lodge."

"Hang on," Miles said. "Why are you summoning your colleagues?"

"To inspect your computers."

"You can't do that," Miles said, "unless you have a warrant, and I can't imagine how you would have achieved that."

"But you said we could!" Ben said indignantly.

"No, I didn't. You asked if I minded if you inspected my computers, and I said 'Of course'. In my universe that means 'Of course I mind if you inspect my computers'."

Ben was deflated. This wasn't going the way he wanted. He picked up his phone, pressed a button, and said "Temporary abort."

Miles, Leila and Paul sat and looked at the two men, and wondered what they would do next.

"What do you think, Paul? Supposing we had such a file, should we give it to these men?"

"We certainly don't have to," Paul said. "They have no legal powers to take it from us. But I would be inclined to let them have it anyway. We are reasonable people."

Ben looked relieved.

"Yes, we are," Miles said. "What a shame there is no computer within 100 miles of this place that has a copy of the file that generated the text that was on the piece of paper I showed the Foreign Secretary, and which, against all rules of decency and ethics, he must have photographed on his phone. I can see his kitchen table in the background."

Miles threw the photo on to the coffee table and stood up.

"Mr Carney, Mr Buckle, I think it is best if you leave now. I think you would give Inspector Clouseau a run for his money, don't you, Paul?"

"'A beumb'," Paul said, imitating Peter Sellers in the *Pink Panther* films.

"Oh, I think that's a bit harsh, Miles," Leila said, and turned to the two men. "You don't want your tea? Maybe I could put it in paper cups?"

Ben brushed Leila's offer aside.

"Come on," he said to Dave, and the two men left the room. As they let themselves out, the men heard Miles, Paul and Leila laughing.

"I'll top up the teapot," Leila said. "You need to talk about what happens next."

"She's right," Miles said, "They're not going to give up. The next couple they send will be brighter and maybe more determined than Bill and Ben."

"It's clear that DeWaal told the prime minister and she told Special Branch to get hold of the file. But why wouldn't they have just called and asked you for it?"

"I can only think there's been crossed wires somewhere. Maybe the PM meant Special Branch to hack into our computers, or break in and steal them, and they decided to try the direct approach and just ask for it."

Leila came in with the tea, overhearing Miles' last remark.

"But does it matter now, Miles?" she said. "The cat's out of the bag. Why not just give them the file?"

"We lose control," Paul said. "We decided to try to approach DeWaal in confidence, without handing over the computer file, because we knew that even if they have a copy of the original wording they won't publicise it unless they can be absolutely sure that we – or someone – didn't just type it out on a piece of paper. Without the data file of the full, original, message with its headers and metadata, they can't publicise it, because they wouldn't be able to prove the new paragraph is genuine."

"Do you think DeWaal and Baxter have told anyone else? The Americans for example?"

"Does that matter?" Leila said.

"Well, if the UK and the Americans know, they're likely to want to gang up against the Russians, rather than go their own way."

Miles slapped his thigh. "Blast!" he said, "DeWaal had the US Secretary of State visiting the day I saw him. What are the chances he didn't show him the paragraph?"

"So can we expect a visit from an American SWAT team now?" Leila said, "That front door is 18th-century. I don't want it smashed in."

"Look," Paul said, "whether or not the US know now, they're bound to soon. Let's look at what cards we still have in our hand. We are the only people who know where the only copy of the file outside Russia is – at the Goonhilly Satellite Earth Station."

Miles was puzzled and was about to speak, when Paul put his hand over Miles' mouth before continuing.

"There's nothing we can do to publicise the message and anyway it's too explosive to launch on the world without a lot of thought. Let's just leave the matter for a few days and get on with our other work. Maybe we'll have a better idea when we've slept on it. Now I need to get back to Dee and Ellie. I enjoyed the service, by the way."

Paul held his finger to his lips and then wrote on a paper napkin which he took from the tea tray.

"THEY MAY HAVE LEFT A BUG. THAT'S WHY I SAID GOONHILLY."

He stood up and said, "We should talk about the new list of research fellowships. Maybe tomorrow morning? You could come to my house. I have to wait in for a washing machine repair man."

Miles read the note, and understood.

"Yes, that will be fine," he said

Two days later, the Penzance local newspaper reported on a break-in at the Goonhilly Satellite Earth Station outside the town.

"ROBBERY AT GOONHILLY" was the headline, and underneath "Valuable computers stolen from space research company. Years of data lost."

Chapter 12

After the visit from Special Branch, Paul Spearman was worried. There seemed to be two options: to hand over everything to the government and let them decide what to do, or to organise in secret a way of publicising the Message at a time of their choosing and with all the context it needed to understand it properly.

"With the first option," Paul said to Miles as they walked in the Cambridge Botanical Gardens, "We lose control from the moment we hand over the full file. They can do what they like with it, and I'm worried that it will seem like some piece of do-gooding by climate change activists, scaremongering to wake people up. When this is released, everyone has to believe it, so that as quickly as possible there is some kind of global response, supported by all governments and all citizens. What we need is Option 2 – a detailed, considered, scientifically authentic publication that persuades anyone but the most prejudiced that we must welcome the help of the Outpost and its civilisation."

"That sounds like an entire book. Look at all the angles that one needs to provide context – astronomy, biology, space science, computing, how you found the original – etc, etc. We have to get all those bases covered and watertight."

"Not a book," Paul said "an entire issue of a newspaper, or a supplement to one. Look how many words are published every day in a paper like the *Times* or the *Guardian*, say. Some organisation like that is used to doing detailed investigations of a story in secret and then publishing it, without anyone knowing ahead of time."

"But so many people would have to be involved, it would be bound to get out," Miles said.

"Not if they are people we know, and if we can keep it to a tight circle for as long as possible."

Miles suddenly thought.

"Did you say the *Guardian* because of Dee?"

"Exactly," Paul said. "I think the editor would trust his Managing Editor if she said in very general terms that she had a world-shattering story that could be published as a supplement, say, with a front-page news story on a certain date. Then we could organise the copy for the supplement and supply it for printing a day or so before the date.

"Baldrick would be proud of your cunning plan," Miles said.

"Baldrick who?" Paul said.

"Not a Blackadder fan, then?"

It seemed unfortunate that, when Leila took the train to London the day after Miles let her into the plan, she left a folder of papers on the table where she was sitting while she went to the lavatory. When she came back, the folder and the papers were still there, so she carried on working with them, making notes in a moleskin notebook.

When she left the train at King's Cross, she either didn't notice – or didn't care – that she was being followed. She walked a quarter of a mile to the offices of *Nature*, the science journal, just off York Way, and was seen to go inside.

In Leila's folder of papers was a schedule for a series of events. It read as follows:

HIGHLY CONFIDENTIAL:

Circulation: Dr Miles Cadogan, Leila Cadogan, Professor Paul Spearman, Clark Clements, editor of Nature

Timeline for major paper on the Message, publication date, February 5, 2025

Weeks 1 to 3 – Mason and Spearman prepare papers on astronomy, exobiology, the Outpost, candidates for the planet, its civilisation.

Also identify others to write on AI, nanotechnology, possible history of civilisation's observations of Earth.

Week 4 – meeting (away from Nature offices – St Pancras hotel?) to discuss section, illustrations, graphics, maps, et cetera.

Week 5 – rewrites, graphic work, circulation of final drafts.

Week 6 – publication. Embargoed press releases circulated globally on February 4th.

NB: We suggest that as far as office staff are concerned, a dummy issue is prepared and the Message issue substituted at the last minute.

The man who had followed Leila from Cambridge waited in a café near the *Nature* offices, at a table where he could see the front door. Over his coffee, he emailed several images from his phone to his contact at MI5. After two hours and four coffees there was no sign of Leila, who had changed into a man's suit in the toilet, and put up her hair under a trilby, before heading back to the station, pleased with the success of her first experience as a decoy.

The following morning, Carla Baxter found a memo on her desk from her National Security Advisor, Joseph Parry. It said:

We have established that Dr Mason and Professor Spearman are planning to release the original Message, via a special addition of Nature being prepared in secret. The current publication date is February 5, 2025, which gives us eight weeks to find a copy of the full data file and decide how to release it ourselves, before the Nature issue. The reason Nature is being used seems to be that the scientists want to prepare contextual material that will make the strongest case for the Message being genuine. This is something we would require too – to release the original Message, whatever it says, on its own, would lead inevitably to conspiracy theories, claims of a hoax and, indeed, a possible rearguard action by Russia, seeking to discredit the original version and hold to its fake text.

I suggest that you convene a committee – obviously not including Mason and Spearman – to prepare a Green Paper for a release date that will pre-empt the Nature issue by at least two weeks. Although any accompanying material we prepare will, of necessity, be less detailed, it should still cover the sort of topics mentioned in the Nature schedule (attached). This way, we regain the initiative. In consultation with our allies, we could also make sure that the content of the Green Paper covers some of the global political issues which are important to UK/US but which the scientists may well ignore.

Carla Baxter heaved a sigh of relief. At least there was a breathing space for the government to plan the release of the Message on its own terms. But of course, that still required a full version of the Message. She asked Paul Martin to get Parry on the phone.

"Joe," she said, "This is good work, and quick. But we still have one major problem. If we are going to plan a release of the real Message, I should have thought we need a copy of it, which you haven't found yet."

"Of course, PM, we are working on that," Parry said. "I'm sure that if worse comes to worst, as the special issue is being prepared, we can find a copy, either in the *Nature* office or at the printers. But we hope to find a copy sooner than that."

"Indeed we do," Baxter said. "We want to release it days or weeks before the *Nature* piece, not a day or two ahead.

"It seems that Dr Cadogan's wife is playing some sort of courier role in the affair, so we are keeping an eye on her as the thing evolves."

"How about the text DeWaal photographed? Is there any way of finding the content of the rest of the piece of paper Cadogan showed him?"

"Not really. It obviously doesn't exist anywhere on his phone. We asked the Foreign Secretary to put down what he could remember of the rest of it, and by using that we can cobble together a full Paragraph 4 from the photo and what he remembers. But it's a real last resort."

"Here's an idea," Carla Baxter said, "How about this as a fall-back plan? We could do what the Russians did and make an announcement that we have a full version of the original, maybe quote what we do have from DeWaal's phone, and then say we will be releasing the fuller version when we have considered it in more detail. That will then spike the *Nature* issue – they might decide that the wind has gone from their sails, and it might even lead to them letting us have the file."

"Good idea, Prime Minister. But we'll still do our best to find the original file."

The following morning, US President Billings sent messages to a small group of senior officials who had been kept informed about the possibility that the Message as publicised was a partial forgery. Most of this group assembled in the Situation Room at lunchtime.

It included Kent Branton by videolink from NASA's Goddard offices, Tonk Wilbraham from CIA, Rob Newbury from NSA, Grant Mowbray, deputy defence secretary, and Secretary of State Rob Delmonico.

The President summarised the situation so far.

"As I see it, unless something new has happened in the last 24 hours we are pretty sure the original Message was obtained from a terrestrial source by the Russians, who then altered it, inserting the threat of annihilation in five years' time, and then published it."

There were gasps of astonishment from those in the room who had not yet heard the full story.

"That is the good news," she went on, "'Good' in the sense that we shall not all die in five years' time. The bad news is that we do not have, and cannot find, the original Message

"So how do you know this?" Grant Mowbray said.

"It's complicated," she said, looking across at Rob Delmonico. "And while I said we are pretty sure about this, we don't have enough to act on. The odd thing is, that scientists in the UK appear to have a copy, but they have been very successful in concealing it from our hackers."

She looked pointedly across at Wilbraham and Newbury who were sitting next to each other, both looking uncomfortable.

"Although we do not have a copy of the original Message, we do have the wording of part of it, a section that we believe was changed by the Russians. This is what it says."

She signed to a young man sitting in the back of the room and an image appeared on a large screen, showing the wording of the first part of the new Paragraph 4, ending "…So we propose to intervene in the following ways, using levels of artificial intelligence and nanotechnology which we have developed over a much longer period than your own technology…"

"That's it?" said Branton.

"I'm afraid so," Billings said.

As even the partial paragraph sank in, there was a chorus of comments.

"This is great news!"

"What a relief!"

"Is this for real?"

"No notes please?!" Billings said as she saw people starting to copy the words. "And no leaks! Now, we have to decide what to do about this messy situation. Do we release this incomplete paragraph to the world as soon as possible? As you will appreciate, we see the negative effects of the fake version every day. Suicide, people going into survivalist mode, stock exchange volatility. And we know that there will be similarly dramatic effects - if less predictable - when the truth comes out. And of course, releasing this paragraph when we don't have the full message will damage our credibility, if that fact comes out."

"If we don't, who will?" Branton said on the video link, "The Brits? We had a bead on a Saturn researcher at the University of Manchester, but he never returned our call."

"People who have secrets they want to keep are like that," Wilbraham said dryly. "Why didn't you give us his name?"

"What would you do? Thumbscrews?" Branton said. "I think Sherry's team got as far as they could. And we don't know it was this guy, anyway.":

"In fact, the Brits will release the correct Message, and we know when and how, thanks to CIA and GCHQ actually talking to each other. The scientists who have the original message are planning a special issue of the journal *Nature*, in seven weeks' time."

"They've told you this?" Sherry said.

"Of course not, Dr Walker. They want it to be a surprise, but also they have good motives. They believe it should be published with background material, to put it all in context, to quash theories that the Message is a fake. Astronomy, biology, the background to SETI, the statistics of likely inhabited planets and civilisations, that sort of stuff. They also, we believe, want to ensure that there is no hint of a political motive in the way the Message is released. 'The purity of science' sort of thing. Commendable really."

"So we could leave it to them?" Branton said.

"We could. I'm hopeful that we could have advanced sight of their text, right, Mr Director? Or perhaps you, Rob, could even persuade the British government to get off their asses and find it before the scientists release it." She looked at Delmonico challengingly. "And maybe, Kent, you could try a little harder with your SETI people."

"I'm not sure how we do that," Kent said. "Do we say we know the real Message, in which case what are we asking them to do? Or do we say we are still looking, in which case, since they've been trying already I'm not sure how they can try harder."

"We believe it shouldn't be too difficult," Wilbraham said. "We know where *Nature* is printed – they even do a simultaneous print run in the US – and the copy will obviously be laid out and typeset a few days beforehand. And of course, we may be able to hack it online."

"Is there a chance that we can still find the original Message somewhere else, before it even gets into print?" Grant Mowbray said, "So that we could start making plans for how to respond? It's going to require a huge change in global politics to take up the offers of help to fight the perils they list in the new Message."

"Well I'm sure we are still looking," Billings said, "but don't hold your breath."

"One thing that worries me, Madam President, is how the Russians will react?" Mowbray said, "After all, as we've seen, they stand to benefit financially and politically from the version we now believe to be fake. We are already discussing in the UN Funding Group how to calculate contributions to the effort to counteract the annihilation, using the Russian

Space shield technology. And just the way they have been trying to take control of the global response to their fake Message is paying off in prestige, and in enhancing the reputation of Pavlov, particularly in the light of elections early next year."

"Rob, do you have any thoughts?" Billings asked the Secretary of State.

"They're not going to be very pleased. And of course, they will say that we are publishing a forgery and insist that they have the real Message. It could be stalemate."

"Particularly because, if we publish only part of paragraph 4 – the part we know – we'll effectively be admitting we don't have the full version," Kent said, in a dig at Delmonico, whose fault it actually wasn't.

"So we just sit on our hands?" Billings said, in a frustrated tone.

"Surely at the very least, Madam President, we should start organising a US response to the real Message – as far as we know it – as soon as possible, whoever ends up publishing it," Kent said. "We should also consider the harm done to our population by letting people continue to believe in the annihilation message."

"Is it worth you talking to President Pavlov on the hotline?" Delmonico said "Warning him that we have the message?"

"But we don't, and anyway it will just alert him to our belief that their message is a fake and give them time to fabricate all sorts of 'evidence' to bolster their forgery," Billings said. "I have to say that until someone, which can't be us at the moment, reveals the full text of the original Message, the Russians will stick to their guns. And that means if all else fails we wait for the Brits to do their thing."

"At least that gives us nearly two months to prepare," Delmonico said.

Katie was, of course, unaware of the discovery of the genuine Message, although she sensed that something odd was going on, from the bright and yet guarded reactions of Miles and Paul when she spoke to them in the Buttery queue to order sandwiches in the SCR. She hadn't heard any more from Douglas about the ACGT sequence, and the Message was very much on her mind, but when she asked Paul if there was any more news about the Message or the Outpost, the two men quickly glanced at each other and then turned to her and Paul said, rather noncommittally, "No. The threat of annihilation still hangs over the world."

Thinking about it afterwards, they seemed to have answered a different question from the one she asked, as if she'd said "Is the Message genuine?"

When Douglas finally reached her later that day, he launched into a rushed and profanity-laden phone call saying that he had discovered a pattern in the sequence of bases but wanted to tell her the details in person.

"Can't you give me a hint?" she said.

"Too fucking dangerous," he said. "Can't take a chance. Where can we meet? As soon as possible."

Katie suggested her home, a two-up two-down terraced house in the Kite area of Cambridge. She knew they wouldn't be disturbed – unfortunately. She wouldn't have minded her life being a bit more disturbed these days. She had so buried her life in her work that there appeared to be no time for socialisation. Even the unexpected drinking session in the pub with Douglas had lifted her spirits – so to speak. Meeting Douglas at her home would also give her the incentive to do a bit of housework, though she knew that someone used to sleeping on the ground under a stall in the Market Place might not be particularly fussy about such things.

At 6 p.m. her doorbell rang and she let Douglas in. He had smartened himself up. His jeans looked as if they might be a bit damp from a hurried wash in the college washing machines in the basement of N staircase, and he was wearing a jumper inside out, perhaps to conceal stains.

With no preliminaries, Douglas, having spotted a dining table, put down his laptop, and opened it up. He put a file on the screen and said "Look at that."

Kate leaned down and looked. There was a sequence of numbers:

2311132331101103113131133211221223233311323

"This is one representation of that string of letters you gave me. I chose symbols from 0 to 3 to represent ACTG. There are four of them so I thought that someone might be representing numbers in quaternary form, to the base 4."

"You don't say," Katie said.

Douglas sighed.

"Sorry, going too fast."

Taking out his chewed pencil he rapidly took Katie through the basis of the decimal system, the one based on tens, which we use all the time, and then showed how you could base a system for writing whole numbers on any number. In the system everyone was familiar with, the decimal system, the symbol '100' represents a hundred ($\mathbf{1} \times 10^2 + \mathbf{0} \times 10 + \mathbf{0} \times 1$). But in binary, based on 2 instead of 10, '100' represents 4 ($\mathbf{1} \times 2^2 + \mathbf{0} \times 2 + \mathbf{0} \times 1$) and in a system based on 4. '100' represents sixteen ($\mathbf{1} \times 4^2 + \mathbf{0} \times 4 + \mathbf{0} \times 1$).

"If you treat the string of 0s, 1s, 2s, and 3s, the equivalents of A,C,T and G, as numbers based on 4 , and change them to decimal numbers, you get this," Douglas said, and turned the laptop towards Kate, to reveal:

2, 3, 5, 7, 11, 13, 17, 19, 23, 27, 31, 37, 41, 47, 53, 59

"These are the first sixteen prime numbers, however you write them. And anyone, anywhere in the universe would recognise them. And they were carried by those letters you gave me which you said were in a gene."

"Could that happen by accident?" Katie said, hoping the answer was 'no'.

"Shit, no!" Douglas said. "Someone must have put them there."

Katie poured two glasses of whisky and sat opposite Douglas in the living room. This finding was amazingly significant but she didn't know what to do with it, whom to tell. Douglas was more affected by having spotted the quaternary primes than by learning that extraterrestrials had seeded life on earth to produce humans.

"You know this confirms that the Message is genuine, right?" Katie said. "So there won't be any doubt that we're going to be annihilated in five years?"

Douglas had a strange expression on his face. He wasn't sure what to say. He had been sworn to secrecy by the Master about his other code-breaking feat, but he thought Kate's discovery might affect what was done with the real Message.

"I think you should tell Dr Cadogan about this," Douglas said, "As soon as possible."

"I was going to try to catch his ear on Monday," she said, "In Hall."

"I'd say sooner than later, Dr Flynn – "

"Katie, please."

"How about now?"

Katie and Douglas sat in the Cadogans' sitting room.

"He's got to go to a Senate House dinner, for heads of colleges," Leila said. "You're sure it can't wait till tomorrow?"

"I'd – we'd – rather not," Katie said. "I think he'll be interested in what we want to say."

She looked at Douglas, who was perched rather uncomfortably on the settee, as if he was afraid of falling back and being submerged in the upholstery. He nodded.

They heard the front door open and then shut, and Miles came sweeping into the room.

"If I have to listen to –" he said, and stopped. "Hi, Katie. And Douglas. Did we…?"

"No, we didn't make an appointment. We need to show you something urgently. It's about the Message."

Miles looked at Leila, who shook her head.

"O.K. Well I only have a few minutes. Can it be quick?"

Katie couldn't contain herself any longer.

"We have proof that the Messengers did seed intelligence and language in homo sapiens, as they said in the Message. This is independent proof. Unfortunately, it confirms that they are telling the truth."

"Unfortunately?" Miles said.

"The annihilation?"

Miles pulled a dining chair round from a long table and sat on it.

"Douglas didn't tell you, I imagine?" He looked at Douglas. "Good for you."

Katie looked at Douglas. "Tell me what?"

Miles decided he had to admit Katie to the inner circle. "We've discovered, with Douglas' help, that the annihilation message is fake. There is a real message and the Russians altered it."

"So what does the real Message say?" Katie asked in astonishment.

Miles quickly filled her in with the details of how Ravi and Douglas had deciphered a copy of the real Message and how the Messengers were offering to help the Earth to deal with the global environment crisis. Katie sat there stunned, and delighted.

"But this mustn't leak out until we are ready to reveal it," Mikes said.

"Who knows? Have you told anyone? The government?"

"No one outside St James, apart from..." Miles hesitated. "There was a bit of a mix-up and the Foreign Secretary knows that we have something, but no one knows the details. We have the only text. But what have you discovered?" Miles said. "If you have independent proof of extraterrestrial interference with the evolution of humankind, that removes any doubts about the genuineness of the Message."

Katie explained about the FOXP2 gene and that if anything was responsible for the rapid acquisition of language in homo sapiens, it was the mysteriously sudden appearance of this in the human genome. She then described how she had asked Mary Sheridan if she could find anything odd about the FOXP2 gene and she had come up with a repeated sequence of bases which Douglas had then shown represented the first 16 prime numbers, something which could not have evolved naturally.

"Have you told anyone else?" Miles said.

"No, we came straight to you."

"Not even Dr Chandra?" Miles said, looking at Douglas.

Douglas shook his head.

"Don't you think maybe we should give him a look over your discovery before we get too excited?"

Douglas leapt off the settee with a volley of tics and curses.

"I'm sorry," Miles said. "I shouldn't doubt you." He looked at his watch. "Can you just take me, a humble non-mathematician, though the key steps."

He turned to Leila.

"Can you tell Sir John I'll be fifteen minutes late?"

A quarter of an hour later – Miles was a quick learner – he had to agree that the steps from the values Douglas mentioned for A,C,T, and G, to the first sixteen prime numbers were pretty extraordinary, and entirely unnatural.

"And it's the first sixteen prime numbers because of the base 4?" Miles said.

"Probably," Douglas said. "I don't know many aliens to ask."

Miles went on, "Paul and I, and Paul's wife, Dee, had been working on a plan to release the new message to the world though a special newspaper supplement so we can give the proper scientific context without governments interfering. But your new information is so important we'll want to include that with proper background material. Can you help with that?"

"Of course," Katie said.

"Paul and I had arranged a meeting tomorrow morning to do a preliminary layout and farm out writing tasks. Can you come to that? I'll rephrase that – you must come to that. It's at Paul and Dee's house. And another thing – you must absolutely obey the rules of computer silence. We know that the British government and probably the Americans, will be doing everything they can to hack into our activities. Thanks to Leila here, we hope they believe that we are preparing an issue of *Nature* for eight weeks' time..."

Leila did a little wave.

"...and so we think they will use that time to plan their own response, which they can't really do without a copy of the real Message. So far, we're pretty sure they haven't got it, and anyway our supplement will take them by surprise when it comes out in four weeks' time, as long as we all stick to the secrecy rules."

About a week after Leila's trip to London, Miles' phone rang while he was in Heffers bookshop, leading to 'tut-tuts' from some browsing customers. He looked at the phone and saw the call was from a withheld number and so he turned it off. As he walked down St James's Lane through a sudden shower to the college, he remembered to turn it on again and saw that there were three missed calls and a message, all saying "number withheld".

'Somebody is in a hurry' he thought, and, sheltering under the arch of the main gate, he listened to the message

"This is Quentin Stewart from GCHQ. The PM received a report from Special Branch that I'd like to talk to you about. Please ring 01242 221007 as soon as possible."

Miles walked back to the Master's Lodge and into his study where he dialled the number.

It was answered by a man's voice.

"Dr Cadogan, good of you to return my call."

'Did he have caller ID because he just called me?' Miles thought, 'Or do these people have automatic Caller ID for everyone in the UK? It's possible, I suppose.'

"What can I do for you? I presume this is about the Message."

"Right first time, Dr Cadogan. I think it's time to stop playing games."

"I wasn't aware that you were?" Miles said

"Not us, you. It was unfortunate that you showed only part of the real Message to the Foreign Secretary,"

"Actually, I showed him all of it. But in a breach of confidence he photographed only half of the important paragraph."

"If I can't persuade you to hand us over the full Message you have – which may, of course, just be another fake, and we have the tools for deciding that – can I at least ask you to give me your word that you will hold off publishing your supplement in *Nature* until we give you permission to do so."

Miles was quietly glad that Leila's decoy work had borne fruit. He let a silence hang in the air before he said "A supplement in *Nature*?"

Stewart was pleased that this news had apparently come as a surprise to Miles Cadogan.

"Yes," Stewart said, "We know all about that. The Prime Minister is very keen that while there are ongoing discussions with the Americans and others, we do nothing to make the situation worse. Releasing the correct Message could cause incalculable harm."

"More harm than letting people believe they are going to be annihilated in five years – no, four years and ten months – time?" Miles said.

There was silence on the line.

"Do you know who you're talking to?" Quentin Stewart said, irritated.

"Well, you told me where you work, but very little else so far."

"The PM has asked me to use the resources of GCHQ to coordinate things, with a view to the interests of national security. Global security really. And that means no uncontrolled releases of information. Can I ask you at least to give me – us – an undertaking not to release the supplement you are preparing for *Nature* in seven weeks time if we, the government, have not obtained a copy of the Message by that date. We expect to find it through other sources and then, in return for the favour, we can consult you about some kind of participation in the release of the correct Message."

"If we don't publish the *Nature* supplement, how do we know that you will involve us in any official release of the Message?"

"I'm afraid you don't."

"Can you get the Prime Minister to send us a brief email to that effect?"

Miles knew that it wouldn't be necessary but kept up the pressure.

Quentin Stewart was irritated.

"The Prime Minister is too busy for that sort of thing herself. I'll ask the cabinet secretary to send you something. Do I have a 'yes'?"

"Yes," Miles said, "We will not publish anything in *Nature* if you have not found the text of the Message by then," and put the phone down.

The College Admissions Committee was meeting, and Paul Spearman was addressing the group about the growing numbers of students applying to study the sciences.

"The figures are in front of you," Paul said, "and you may be surprised that I find this a bad thing."

There were murmurs from the other fellows around the table.

"Of course, I want good scientists to come to St James. Twenty years ago, the figures were the other way round, and we put in a big effort, with the science fellows doing a rota around secondary schools to promote the college's science offerings. But with my senior tutor hat on, it's best for the college to have a good balance across all subjects."

As various fellows contributed to the discussion, Miles thought about Stewart's phone call. Who did they think they were? Of course the Message had national - global –importance. But too often, major scientific advances had got out of the hands of the scientists and were misused by politicians. Here was a chance for scientists to have their say before the politicians got their hands on it.

"Perhaps the Master agrees?" Ravi Chandra said, shaking him out of his reverie.

"Importance of maths," Paul muttered from his seat next to Miles.

"Yes, indeed, Dr Chandra, maths," Miles said.

"The science and the maths undergraduates should go hand in hand…" Chandra said

"I know quite a few who do," Miles Cadogan said, to a few titters,

"…but we have fewer maths applicants this year," Ravi went on.

As the discussion continued, Miles slid a scribbled note across to Paul. It said "GCHQ want to stop *Nature* paper," underlining 'Nature' to show that their ruse had worked. Paul glanced down but didn't read it until the meeting moved on to discuss whether or not to continue a Latin translation prize set up 150 years ago with an endowment which paid £10 to the annual winner.

Martin's eyes widened as he read the note.

"Hook, line and sinker," he said quietly to Miles. "Talk about it after this?"

Miles nodded.

Chapter 13

When Miles, Leila, Paul, Dee and Katie met at the Spearman's house the following morning for a meeting about the *Guardian* supplement, Katie was trying to suppress the excitement she felt. She knew that what she had discovered was big, but she hadn't anticipated what an important part her discovery would play in validating the new version of the Message.

The group sat around Paul and Dee's dining table and Paul put a large coffee pot and four mugs in the middle.

"Okay," Paul said, "Let's go through the content. Dee had prepared a layout for four pages, rather like the Long Read the *Guardian* publishes sometimes. But I was thinking, with Katie's amazing discovery, maybe we should try eight pages. We'd then have room for more graphics, which would make it more readable."

Dee passed round an A3 sheet with blocks of nonsense text laid out.

"I'm suggesting that the front page is entirely taken up with the original message. It's about 600 words so we can use quite a large font, and the graphics surrounding could have an astronomical feel, maybe based on Saturn. I don't want to involve a separate graphic designer but I can play around with some NASA pics and Photoshop them myself."

"I could help with that," Leila said.

"Right," Miles said "but wait, should we say something about the forgery?"

"Possibly, though I imagine we will also have a news story about it on the front page."

"Yes, but we need something a bit more technical in the Supplement – maybe hint at how we discovered it?"

"Okay." Dee made a note. Then she had an idea. "How about including an interview with Douglas Burnside? His story is quite a powerful one but from what I gather, he's not much of a writer. Do you think you could do that, Leila? At least, record it and transcribe it, and we could edit it into shape."

"Sure," Leila said. "It could be fun. I could take a portrait photo of him as well, and maybe a pic of Market Square, where he used to 'live.'"

"Do you think he'd be all right with that, Miles? You knew him before anyone. Does he mind being reminded of those days?"

"I can ask," Miles said. "He knows what we're doing and why, after all."

"So," Dee went on, "If 2 and 3 are the discovery and the interview, 4 could give some background to the search for extra-terrestrial intelligence over the last decade, mentioning some of the false alarms, starting with pulsars… Paul will do that, right?"

Paul nodded. "And on 5 and 6 I will write what we know of Tau Ceti and its planet, and what we can infer about the Outpost. Now, here's where we decide how to present Katie's discovery –"

"Mine and Douglas Burnside's," Katie interrupted, "and Mary's. And even my research assistant, Rosie, played a small part."

"Sure. That's a pretty important finding, so we should maybe make a big thing of it. What was a hypothesis when we started this process is now a certainty, if I understand it right."

He looked at Katie, who nodded.

"The finding confirms the likely truth of the key part of the message that no one had corroborated up to now," Katie said, " – the statement that, in a way, homo sapiens is the progeny of the civilisation that sent the Message, which makes it even more likely that they'd want to save us – and have the skill to do so – rather than destroy us."

Paul turned to Dee.

"I think this deserves a whole page, don't you? Page 7. Even with a bit of mathematics, if it doesn't frighten people off."

"Of course. It's getting better and better. I've not said too much to Sean, the editor, but I promised him it will be sensational, so we've got no trouble now fulfilling that promise"

"Right, so that leaves page 8," Miles said.

"That's where you and Paul might write something about the implications for the world, and the way forward."

"Why don't you do 'The Way Forward'" Paul said to Miles. "You're our representative of humanity, if you like. We just study atoms and molecules and stars and galaxies.

Miles laughed. "I humbly accept the role," he said.

"That must be a first, Miles," Leila teased, "to accept anything humbly."

"I could finish up with a sort of general survey of the problems facing the world," Miles said, ignoring Leila's remark, "with suggestions for how some of the problems could be fixed, if we have access to even a fraction of what a million-year-old technical civilisation can achieve,."

"God!" Paul said, sitting back in his chair, "The world is not going to know what's hit it. Shall I make some more coffee?"

The following day, as Katie set to work drafting her contribution to the supplement, she realised how much she enjoyed thinking about what to say to a non-scientific readership. She was freed from the constraints of writing for a scientific journal and was quite pleased with some of the explanations she came up with for how a new genetic sequence might have become inserted into the human genome. Although all of this was highly speculative – the methodology – the end point, the sequence of primes which could not have been achieved artificially by any human agent, was unarguable. It wasn't just that the sequence was extremely unlikely to have arisen by chance. It was also that it would be in every human genome on Earth. Then she paused for a moment. Of course, the gene sequence had only come from an internet database. Maybe she should do a DNA analysis of the FOXP2 gene in some random human genome, just to be absolutely sure. She parked that idea and took a sip of a mug of coffee that had gone cold.

Now, she just felt the need for some kind of rousing peroration, something that crystallised what she really thought about the whole situation, something more personal, to round it off.

With the speed the supplement had to be put together, Miles and Paul had told her just to get on with it and say what she wanted to say. They'd comment on it, sure, if she asked, but they gave her the freedom to say what she wanted.

Her fingers hovered over the keyboard and then she typed the following:

In analysing the technology which, I believe, was sent to us initially to create humankind, I can't help thinking of the phrase 'in their own image'. Whatever physical form the inhabitants of the planet round Tau Ceti take, and we can be sure that it exceeds our imaginative capacity, there must be embedded in what we would call their 'consciousness' a degree of humanity which is enviable. The commitment shown by the Tau Ceti Messengers to benefit our much inferior civilisation must have persevered for thousands if not millions of years as a defining characteristic of a civilisation which may today have become extinct. But even so, it has left us an incomparable gift, and whatever happens next in this extraordinary tale, we should remember this and, rather as good parenting lays the foundation of a good life for a child, we should recognise and honour the civilisation that will make our future more secure, so that, with their help, we will learn how to respect and cherish the planet that is our home.

As a piece of writing, this was unlike anything she had written before, but she felt rather pleased as she re-read it. What she didn't realise was something which only became apparent a month later, and the degree to which this paragraph would change her life.

In the months since the content of the Message had swept the world, a strange sense of calm held sway, and Christmas celebrations were planned in the same way as every year. Most people just got on with their lives, leaving it to politicians and scientists to digest the news of the forthcoming annihilation and, it was assumed, come up with a way of preventing it. The attitude was similar to people's reaction to the increasingly doom-laden facts about the global climate crisis. A minority of people were really distressed, and their lives were changed by the dreadful news in all sorts of ways. Some people contributed their votes and their money to parties and organisations that promised to do something about it, and left it to them; others knew that someone somewhere would do something to prevent it without having much idea who or how, and a small proportion just 'knew' that the threat would go away, somehow or other.

On both sides of the Atlantic, key figures involved in the cover-up, as it had to be termed, tried to deal with the knowledge that they were likely to be withholding from the rest of the world the most precious piece of information they could ever have known. The weight was heaviest on those who had responsibility for entire nations, and knew that every day that passed with people believing in the annihilation was a day that brought misery and depression to many.

President Billings made daily calls to Wilbraham and Bob Newbery, as if the presidential pressure would somehow magically open a door somewhere for US spies to break in and find the full Message, an essential requirement before the world could be told. She also spoke more often than usual to Prime Minister Baxter, whom she didn't entirely trust to share with the US if the British government found the full Message before the US.

One issue she pondered was how to relate to Russia. Should they drop hints that they knew of Russia's fakery, when they didn't? Should they go along with the whole annihilation story to show that they didn't suspect? In the end, she called the small team who represented the US at UNACC to discuss a decision she had made.

Knowledge of the likelihood that the world was not going to be annihilated in five years was still restricted to a small number of senior officials, not including the US delegation to UNACC, so when Billings recommended to the UN team that they go easy on the Russians at the next meeting, on December 22nd, there was a chorus of reactions. At all previous meetings, the US had put up strong objections to the way the Russians seemed to be running the show, under the chairman Sergei Gromov.

"Madam President, some of their suggestions are outrageous!" said Patty Moore, the rapporteur on the team. "They are asking the world to fund a project – at a greatly inflated price – that we know behind the scenes has little chance of working on its own terms, let alone being able to defend against an attack by a civilisation a million years older than ours!"

"We're just going to look silly," said Ed Campbell, the head of the US UNACC team. "We've been gung ho up to now. Now you want us to lie down and have our tummies tickled?"

"I'm not sure that's a very good metaphor, Ed. But in any case, I have made the policy. Now you have to carry it out."

When UNACC met two days later, Gromov was ready for a battle. Dmitry Ilyich Pavlov had told him not to come back without an agreement for full funding of Papirosi, and with a start date for cashflow of January 7th. It was a tough call. The Brits were the first to speak, with Wendy Carthew, the British representative, saying that they needed more details about the system, how it works and how it was costed, as well as a timetable for prototype demonstrations and a cutoff point beyond which UN members would not be committed to pay if the thing didn't work. Other nations' representatives spoke, some ready to contribute, others more reluctant. Then the American delegate, Ted Anderson, gave a brief speech in which he accepted everything the Russians had asked for. The British looked astonished, and asked for a recess.

When they returned, they changed their vote and agreed to everything Gromov asked.

A call from Billings to PM Baxter, followed by a call from Baxter to Carthew had done the trick, and Gromov flew home, knowing that he could give his President the present he wanted for Russian Christmas on January 7th.

Swept up in the excitement of the discoveries they had made, the St James' group's Christmas was dominated by planning and writing the *Guardian* supplement. But there were occasional anguished exchanges between the various members of the group. On Christmas Eve, at drinks in the Master's Lodge after the college's annual Christmas service, Dee Spearman cornered Miles and said "Are you losing any sleep over this?"

"Over what?" Miles said.

"Over the fact that the world is dying to know what we know but we can't tell them? Should we at least discuss releasing the full Message as it stands – just ring the BBC, send them the text and make a lot of people happy…?"

"Without any background, any context, any of the scientific justification, any proof that our version is genuine? I just think there would be too much wiggle room for vested interests to ignore it… That's why the idea of the supplement is such a good one."

There was a certain amount of special pleading in Miles' reply to Dee. He had got so wrapped up in the Plan that it would have been difficult to pull back at this stage. The events that would follow the publication would focus world attention on St James' College – and on him. He persuaded himself that another couple of weeks with people believing in the annihilation several years away would be a price worth paying to achieve widespread belief in the iron-clad evidence for the truth of the revised message.

Katie Flynn was in a quandary over Christmas. Last year she had spent it with her mother, whose dementia was not so bad that her family – her sister and husband and two boys – couldn't experience some of the spirit of Christmas, Ginger Wine in her mother's case and a very nice malt whisky in Katie's. This year she couldn't face a similar experience, with her mother's worsening condition, and she knew she'd be spending Christmas in Cambridge. Sure, there would be parties to go to and drinks at the Lodge, but she felt she might have to cook a solitary turkey breast to eat alone.

Then she thought of Douglas Burnside. He had done her a big favour by cracking the FOXP2 code, and although she found his personality a little off-putting – well, more than a little – she wondered if he might want to share Christmas Day with her. In fact, she wasn't sure if she'd like to spend Christmas Day with him, but decided to take the plunge and invite him.

As it turned out, once she got past his tics, Katie found that Douglas was a rather interesting man. The first half hour or so after he arrived at Katie's house was a little awkward. They sat opposite each other drinking coffee – hers espresso, his Nescafe Instant – making stilted conversation about the college. Occasionally, Katie would get up and go to the kitchen area to check on the turkey breast she was cooking. At one point she began to lay the table with some nice china she rarely used. As she did this, it occurred to her that another sort of guest might have called out "Is there anything I can do to help?" but Douglas was silent. As she looked through to the sitting area she saw Douglas scanning her bookshelves.

'Doubt if he'll find much there,' she thought, but as she watched he took down a book and went and sat down to open it.

Katie went and sat down and said "Should be another fifteen minutes."

Douglas looked up from the book. "Thank you," he said.

"What have you found?" she asked.

He looked at the cover. "It's called the Merck Manual. A medical book."

"Oh, yes. A doctor friend told me it was the best guide to medical problems. Doctors use it, so on the whole you get the truth. And getting a GP appointment these days is like tickets to Glastonbury."

She decided to take the plunge. "Are you looking up about your Tourette's?"

Douglas experienced a bout of ticking and swearing.

"Fuck! that's all you see, innit?! The mathematician with Tourette's! How about the Tourette's guy who's a brilliant mathematician?"

Katie was taken aback. She had avoided ever mentioning the condition, like everyone at St James because they wanted to make Douglas feel like a normal academic.

"Is that how you'd rather be seen?" she said, cautiously.

"I'd rather people accepted me as I am. I live with my Tourette's. Why can't they?"

There was a buzz from a kitchen timer, and Katie was relieved. She said "Let's hold that idea – we'd better eat."

"Sorry," Douglas muttered, as he stood up to go to the table. "I need to pee."

"It's up the stairs to the first landing. Straight ahead."

As she put the turkey and vegetables on the table she thought about what Douglas had said. It was true that, as a form of shorthand, when Douglas had just arrived, it had been a lazy way to describe him. But once his extraordinary talents became clear, she felt he had become a valued member of the college. And – as far as she could understand it – his contribution to the whole Message business had been key to the plan the small group had formed.

During the meal, Douglas had calmed down after his explosive reaction. Conversation roamed over other college fellows, the history of St James, Katie's career path, Douglas's friends, including Dirty Doris, that he'd made during his homeless phase. Katie had bought some nice Vouvray and by the time they were into the second bottle, she felt it was time to pull the crackers she had put by their plates.

After the Christmas pudding they put on paper hats and read the bad jokes inside.

"What does yours say?" Katie said.

Douglas unfurled the small piece of paper

"Why can't a bike stand up by itself?"

Katie thought. "Because it's tired?"

"Very fucking good," Douglas said, "Because it's two-tired."

"Wow. A mathematical joke."

"Nah," Douglas said. "But there are real mathematical jokes..."

"Tell me one," Katie said, sensing that the wine and the atmosphere of jollity was relaxing Douglas.

"Here's one I like: Two plus two equals five for sufficiently large values of two..."

Katie was puzzled.

"But two is two. It can't be any larger."

Douglas sighed. "That one separates the men from the boys, the mathematicians from the non-mathematicians. Sod it, what's yours?"

Katie looked at her cracker motto.

"Oh, another mathematical one: What has four wheels and flies?"

Douglas quickly replied, "Two bikes in the hold of a 747, a car driving off Beachy Head, a pair of trousers with a toy car in a pocket, a..."

"Stop, stop," Katie said, taking a mouthful of wine. "Those are much better than the answer they give, 'a bin lorry'. You know, you are a lateral thinker. Maybe that's why you're so good at maths."

Douglas reddened slightly. "I don't know what that is but it sounds nice." He stood up, a little unsteadily. "I'd better go. Leave you to the rest of your Christmas."

"How about a brandy?"

"I had some. That brandy butter was full of it."

"Have some more."

Douglas slumped into an armchair.

Katie decided that in his current mood it was worth exploring his Tourette's a bit more.

"So Douglas," she said, "You think people just see your condition? You don't think you're appreciated for your talents? For God's sake, look what you've done over the last couple of weeks. You've saved the Earth!" This was meant as a joke, but Douglas had never shown much of a sense of humour.

"It started when I was about twelve," he said, answering a question Katie hadn't asked. "My mum chucked me out of the house when I was fifteen."

"So how did you learn your mathematics?"

"Before I bunked off school one of the teachers gave me a book called *Mathematicians Delight*. It was an old paperback, a bit battered. I've still got it. I found it made me calmer to think about some of the things the man went on about."

"But that must have been very different from university level maths? How did you reach that?"

"In one of the squats I stayed in there was a telly and I watched Open University programmes. When they recommended books I went into the public library and pinched them."

"So you were entirely self-taught?' Katie said, astonished.

"Well, no one would take me seriously in my state."

"You know some people would admire what you've been able to do, in spite of your Tourette's. It actually makes you even more admirable."

Douglas thought for a moment.

"So you think if I didn't have it, I wouldn't have become a fellow?"

"Well, literally that's true. As I understand it, the college only knew about you because you accosted Miles in Market Square."

"Shit! I didn't accost 'im. I just needed money for a burger. For fuck's sake!"

"No, I'm sorry. I just mean, it was the unlikely combination of you, homeless, and the papers you had which Ravi thought were brilliant."

Douglas was silent.

"So how would you feel if the Tourette's could be cured?" Katie wasn't sure where that question came from but in unleashed a torrential reaction from Douglas.

"Are you stupid?! When anyone says that, it means they despise me! I can see that it will never go away! And maybe I like the having it! Maybe I need it, because it sets me apart!..."

"But you said…"

"I know what I said. But sometimes, I lie awake at night and I can hear my voice saying things calmly in my head, without swearing and ticcing, and it seems like a dream. But I can't afford to hope."

"Have you followed research in the area?"

"I was looking in your medical book. Nothing new there."

"How about online?"

"Nothing."

Katie remembered something she had heard on the radio recently. At the time she had thought of mentioning it to Douglas but it had slipped her mind.

"Do you know about the Nottingham University work? On a device to attach to the wrist that reduces the effects of the Tourette's?"

She described what she had read, which made the research sound like a real step forward.

Douglas looked dubious but interested.

"Do you want me to find out more?" she said. She knew that one of the St James' fellows who was a neurologist had run a department in Nottingham Medical School before coming to Cambridge.

"Knock yerself out," he said, and then said in a quiet voice, "No, I really would be chuffed. But I'm not getting my hopes up…"

He stood up and, impulsively, Katie gave him a hug. Douglas resisted for a moment and then sank into her arms. She felt him give a sob, but said nothing. He then turned away, with a grunt and a burst of tics, saying "Thank you for a lovely Christmas," before letting himself out of Katie's house.

At the Master's Lodge, the Cadogans and the Spearmans were sitting around with coffee and mince pies. The television was on in the background.

"Nearly time," Miles said.

"I didn't realise you were a monarchist, Miles," Paul said.

"I'm interested in all forms of government," Miles replied. "And the King has made only three Christmas speeches so you can sometimes pick up some interesting nuances about how he sees his role."

After a picture of Buckingham Palace with a caption, 'His Majesty King Charles III', the broadcast began.

"I would like to give a short message of hope to the British people," the King began. "We are all preoccupied coming to terms with the substance of the extraterrestrial Message about the possible Annihilation, and I want to reassure everyone that however it seems on the surface, your government, in collaboration with others round the world, is working hard to establish whether the event will happen in the way the Messengers tell us. Or, indeed, if it will happen at all. I cannot say any more at the moment, but there are reasons to think that in my message next Christmas, perhaps considerably sooner, we will learn of a significant change in our understanding of the situation, brought about by the efforts of scientists and astronomers, some of them in the United Kingdom."

"Jesus," Paul said, "He's going out on a limb. He's all but said the Message is a fake. He must have got that from Baxter."

"You're reading too much into it," Dee said. "He could just be saying that we've been in touch with the Outpost and have more information that will be useful in some way."

"But anyone who knows it is a fake, like the Russians, will know they've been found out!"

"It might send journalists digging around a bit more than they have been," Leila said.

"Could we bring forward the release of the supplement?" Miles said to Dee. "I think the King's speech does change things a bit."

"Well we're currently scheduled for January 14th," Dee said. "I could talk to Sean about bringing it forward a week."

"You know what would make that a very good idea," Paul said, with a wicked grin. "January 7th is Russian Christmas. It would be a great Christmas present for Pavlov."

There was a sense of achievement, and of letdown, in Paul and Dee Spearman's house on the evening of January 5th. Paul lay sprawled on the sofa; Dee on the floor, finally checking for the fifth time the layout of the supplement, on several A2 sheets of paper; Katie was checking on her laptop to confirm that the website addresses for the background information given in the supplement were correct; Leila was finalising the exposure and cropping of some photos she had taken or downloaded to make the supplement more reader friendly – the rings of Saturn, Jodrell Bank, the Rift Valley in Africa, a variant of the familiar graphic of the evolutionary succession from monkey to man, with a man looking out of the page and apparently speaking.

"You can send it, love," said Paul. "You've checked it to buggery – there can't be any mistakes now."

Dee sat up on her haunches.

"Sometimes, you miss the same mistake, however often you look."

"My case exactly," Paul replied. "Anyway, isn't Sean standing by? When did you say you'd send it?"

Dee glanced at the clock.

"Twenty minutes ago, but he always gives artificial deadlines."

She turned to Leila and Katie.

"Can we go?"

"The addresses seem fine," Katie said.

"The high res versions of the pictures are going on a separate file," Leila said. "You can send off the layout."

Dee stood up and went over to the large desktop computer with one of the spreads laid out on the screen.

She sat down, looked it over once more, and then picked up her phone and rang Sean at the *Guardian*.

"It's coming now," she said. "The future will never be the same again, as you will see when you read it."

"'Trebles all around,'" Miles said, "as they say in *Private Eye*."

"You read *Private Eye*?" Paul said. "I thought it was a scurrilous rag."

"It is, and very funny."

Dee had sent the files and swivelled in her chair

"The deed is done. And 'yes' to the trebles all round idea, scurrilous or not."

"Would champagne be an acceptable substitute?" Leila said, going over to her camera bag.

"Of course," Paul said, easing himself up from the sofa. "I'll get some glasses."

There was a thoughtful silence in the room as everyone pondered what they had set in motion.

"To global prosperity," Miles said.

"That sounds too 'wealth creationist'," Leila said, "How about to a clean and habitable earth?"

The others raised their glasses and repeated the toast.

"Now, we can get back to our day jobs. I have grant proposals gathering dust in my in tray," Paul said."

"Hang on, hang on!" Leila said. "Where do you guys think that you're going to find the time for this?"

"What do you mean, Loo?" Miles said

"Do you know what's going to happen ten times an hour from about one a.m. the day after tomorrow?"

"What?" Miles said.

"Your phones are going to be ringing off the hook, if they have hooks. The world's media will be beating a path to your doors. You, Miles, and Paul and Katie, for starters. And you've got colleges and departments to run and research to do."

"We can just say to reporters that we said all we want to say in the supplement…" Paul said.

"Oh, that's bound to work," Miles said, "No, Leila is right. Even if we say nothing, we'll be door-stepped and chased and followed wherever we go, at least for a while."

"I think Leila is right, actually," Paul said. "And we should respond to the media. It's a good chance to do a bit of science education, and to get our point of view over before too many others pile in."

"But what is our point of view," Miles said. "What do we want to say that others might not?"

"First of all, we don't know how Russia will react. After all, they've got egg on their face, or will have in two days' time. They might want to cling to the story that their version is genuine. If they don't, suddenly all those financial commitments to support their Papirosi program will fly out of the window. We can hammer home the story of how we discovered that their message was a forgery. And how will the Chinese respond? They might not want to toe the line and restrict their own emission levels on the orders of a spacecraft in the Rings of Saturn. We will need - they, the Outpost will need - total global commitment, and that's going to be difficult," Paul replied.

Dee stood up.

"Look it's late and we've all been working hard. I'd like to make a suggestion. Leila, supposing the group nominates you as a spokesperson and any calls to the college or Paul's lab are routed to you first. It doesn't mean the others won't have to say anything at all, but I'm sure you'd be great at dealing with persistent journalists."

Leila looked surprised.

"Do you think so? I've never done this sort of thing before."

"Loo, you used to work at Number Ten," Miles said, "You must have mingled with the mighty, not all of whom are sweet and charming, I'm sure."

"Okay, let me think about it," Leila said to the others. "Miles and I will talk about it tomorrow when we have clear heads."

"Good girl," Miles said, and put his arm through hers. "Home to Saint James's and don't spare the horsepower.

Chapter 14

Sergei Gromov's phone rang at two a.m. on Christmas Day, January 7th, 2026. Sleepily, he answered the call. It was Irina Lyubimova, head of TASS.

"Sergei Alexandrovich! There is bad news!"

Gromov shook his head and thought. What could it be? Irina wouldn't have said that if Pavlov had died suddenly.

"What?" Sergei said.

"The British have discovered that the Message is a fake. They've published the real message with a lot of scientific data, leaving people in no doubt."

Gromov jumped out of bed and tried to put an arm through a sleeve of his dressing gown while listening to Irina. His wife, Elena, stirred and turned away from him, putting her head under her pillow. It wasn't the first night-time call her husband had received.

Gromov walked into his study and looked out of the window at the Moscow river and the Kremlin floodlit beyond.

"Does Pavlov know?"

"No, I called you first."

"But lots of people must know if it's in the British newspapers."

"They're only just being distributed. Georgi in the London embassy sends a man to pick them up at midnight."

"Call Pavlov and tell him we are coming to talk to him."

"We?"

"Sure. And I'll get Ivanov too. Pavlov can face the security forces, the media, and the army all at the same time."

"What are we going to do, to say?"

"I'll think of something. I'm sure this is an opportunity, but we must act quickly."

"Okay. I'll call him."

Gromov begin to dress. He put on a tracksuit.

'I'm blowed if I'm going to put on a suit and tie in the middle of the night. He'll be in pyjamas anyway,' he thought.

He kissed his sleeping wife.

"Lenka, I have to go to see Pavlov. Back later."

He took the lift downstairs to the underground garage, got into his Land Rover – no need to call for the official car – and pressed the button to open the garage door. It was a cold night and the heater hummed into life.

He was starting the journey not knowing quite what he was going to say to Pavlov, but he knew he had to have a plan by the time he drove through the Kremlin gates.

At the door of Pavlov's private apartment, Oleg Kozlov greeted him. He looked half dressed with a formal jacket and crumpled tracksuit trousers.

"Come in, Sergei Alexandrovich. Happy Christmas. The samovar is hot and I have some bulochki in the oven. The president is still getting dressed."

"Is Irina Lyubimova here?"

"Yes, she arrived five minutes ago."

"And General Ivanov?"

"Not yet."

Pavlov came into his office at the same time as Oleg showed Sergei in.

Irina was looking out of the window, down into one of the Kremlin courtyards.

"How did this happen?" Pavlov said angrily to Sergei, "You told me there were no more copies."

"Crazy Bear are good but even they can't hack into every computer in the world. They hacked all the main astronomical databases. Anyway, let's not waste time on post-mortems. We must decide what to do, and quickly. It will be around the world in an hour. Probably already is."

"What do you propose?"

"Well, it depends whether you want to admit what we did, or find a way to deny it and hope people believe you."

"Of course I want to deny it. We had a whole plan to benefit from the annihilation threat. We were beginning to take hold of the global effort to deal with it, using Russian technology – Papirosi – for sake of speed. Why give all that up?"

"Because it isn't true. There's not going to be any annihilation."

At that moment, General Ivanov was shown in.

"Yuri Pavlovich, did I invite you?" Pavlov said.

The general was taken aback.

"No. Sergei Alexandrovich called me. I thought, at this time ..."

"You do not need to think. I can think enough for all of us. But stay since you're here. Now, this is what we are going to do..."

"No," Sergei Gromov said, "*This* is what we are going to do. The three of us sat with you at the dacha when you told us you wanted to change the Message, with faked new material. We are the only senior figures to know this. Of course, there are a few others, translators and cryptographers, but I trust them, and they know what would happen if they spoke out. So we, in this room, could all agree that the forgery didn't happen, and dismiss the British newspaper story as a fake in its own right. But we are not going to do that."

Pavlov looked at Gromov, astonished and a little afraid. They were old friends. That's why, when Pavlov rose in the hierarchy, Gromov rose too. But Gromov had rarely questioned Pavlov directly, knowing that he would benefit more as a faithful supporter than as a potential rival.

But Gromov's manner now, taking control, seemed to suggest a new approach. Perhaps a worrying one.

Oleg came in with warm pies on a tray, but Pavlov brushed them away.

"Wait," said Gromov to Oleg, "I'll have one. I'm a bit peckish."

Pavlov turned and walked to his desk. He sat in the large leather chair to assert his authority.

"It seems to me that you must abandon the original idea of the annihilation," Gromov continued. "You couldn't possibly keep that up for five years. Who knows? There may be other copies with material, or from sources, which would make it impossible to deny each one as fake."

"You can deal with anything like that, Sergei Alexandrovich," said Pavlov, trying to head off what might be coming.

"I could. We could, but actually I'm not sure I want to."

"I'm not sure that what you want has any relevance at the moment. After all, I am the president."

"Well, Dimitri Ilyich, I suggest that if you want to stay president – for the time being – you listen to my plan – our plan," Gromov said, looking at Irina who had joined Ivanov, standing next to Pavlov's drinks cabinet. The two of them shifted uneasily. Gromov hadn't told them what he was about to suggest but he hoped they wouldn't break ranks.

Pavlov tried once more to assert himself.

"I'm not sure I want to listen to any more of this shit," he said. "I make the decisions in this country, and I'll call you when I've decided. Don't go far away."

"I'm not moving from this room," Gromov said. "And I think when you listen to me, you'll think it best to opt for one or other of my suggestions."

"Do you realise I could have you arrested?"

"Could he?" Gromov looked at General Ivanov.

Ivanov said "Probably not, Mr President, at least until you've heard what… what we have to say. I still control the army, Sergei Alexandrovich is the FSB, and I'm not sure if the Moscow police chief is even awake at the moment."

"And if he is, he'll be drunk," Gromov added. "But look, Dmitri Ilyich, just hear me out. We go back a long way and I know you are not an unreasonable man."

Pavlov sat back, looked out of the window at the lightening sky, and said wearily, "Oh well, go ahead."

Gromov sat down in a chair and indicated to the other two that they might like to do the same.

"The cat is out of the bag and I think it can't be put back," Gromov said. "But let's look at two possibilities. I can produce a dossier – we are skilled at producing *'dodgy dossiers'*" – he used the English phrase – "as the British call them, that proves that the Americans actually sent us a fake file, via a double agent. So we were perfectly within our rights to decipher and translate it, and react the way we did. Of course – we say – we regret what happened but are relieved, along with the rest of the world, that we now don't face annihilation, and we strongly criticise the US for its 'dirty tricks', trying to blame Russia for faking the message, having caused great unhappiness with the forgery. If we go along this route, you will put me in charge of the Russian team who will work on the global effort to save the Earth from the effects of man's exploitation of the environment."

Gromov didn't mention it, but he knew that if he did play such a crucial role on the world stage he would be in a good place to stand for the presidency in the election after next.

"And if I don't agree with that plan?" Pavlov said.

"I think you can guess what would happen," Gromov said.

"Nevertheless, spell it out."

"Well, first, there are three witnesses to the plan - entirely concocted by you - to fake some of the message." Gromov looked at General Ivanov and Irina Lyubimova, who nodded warily.

"Second, we can produce a dossier - not dodgy at all - which sets out in exhaustive detail, starting with witness statements from us and going on with emails and memos, to prove that the idea and the fakery were yours, designed to destabilise the West, and suck in funds, even more than we needed for your extravagant Papirosi weapon program, disguised as a 'Save the World' program, which you knew would never be necessary anyway."

Pavlov was quiet, thinking.

"Would the first one work?"

Gromov knew he had hooked Pavlov.

"The fake dossier, the anti-US one, could be on the front page of Pravda tomorrow." He looked at Irina, who looked dubious.

"Well, in 48 hours. Actually, more time will help us make it more authentic."

"What will the Americans do? Won't they just deny it?" Pavlov said.

"Yes, but we each always deny any outrageous claims against ourselves. The main thing to worry about is if they go deeper and prepare some more detailed dossier and prove that they didn't send us a fake message. But people may get tired of the battle of dossiers, particularly with all the good news that we are not going to die and the Earth will be saved."

Pavlov was silent. He fiddled with a ballpoint pen, flicking it in and out, as he pondered. The others watched. Then he sat up, pulled his chair nearer the desk, and spoke.

"Right," said Pavlov, "I have made my decision as president of Russia."

"Yes, Mr. President?" Gromov said politely.

"Yes. We will announce to the world that we have been persuaded by the British discovery, and that we will be publishing evidence that we have been tricked by the Americans. We condemn such trickery as a prime example of creating 'fake news' and hope they can put aside their anti-Russian stance to join in a global effort to benefit from the offer in the real Message to fix the problems of the environment and the biosphere."

"And who will be in charge of this global effort from the Russian side?"

"You will, Sergei Alexandrovich. I can't think of anyone better."

"Such a good decision, Mr President," Gromov said.

He turned to Irina.

"Come to my office at three this afternoon, Irina Semionova. I should have the basis of the dossier by then, but I need to get some graphics people to prepare US letterheads and typefaces and so on. We can do that by lunchtime the day after. And General, we should talk about liaison between my security people and the army. We are going to face some sad, bereaved relatives of suicides, including those members of the community in Semipalatinsk who all killed themselves. We can probably make sure people blame the Americans first, but they also blame us for being taken in."

Gromov turned back to Pavlov to say goodbye.

"You made a good choice, Mr. President," he said.

"Mrs Lyubimova," Pavlov said, "Make sure I get a copy of the *Pravda* piece as soon as possible."

"I will arrange it," Irina said.

The three men left the room, and after he heard their footsteps die away Pavlov picked up the desk phone and asked Oleg to connect him to the home of the Moscow police chief.

While he waited, he watched the sun peek over the Moscow rooftops.

A woman answered the phone.

"This is Dimitri Ilyich Pavlov," he said. "I wish to speak to Sviatoslav Nikolayevich."

The woman hesitated.

"He's not… He is not here," she said.

"Where is he?"

"He's in bed."

"So he is there? I need to speak to him."

"I'm sorry, Mr President. He cannot come to the phone."

"Is he ill?"

"Sort of," she said. "Is there a message?"

"The message is that if he doesn't cut his consumption to less than two bottles a day, he's fired. In fact, he may be fired anyway."

Pavlov slammed the phone down, and turned to his computer. He called up a copy of the original message and started to read it.

In the flat of the Moscow police chief, his wife put the phone down, and one of Gromov's most trustworthy operatives, standing over her shoulder, nodded and patted her on the back.

"How the hell can this land, fully formed, on British newsstands, without us knowing?!" Jennifer Billings shouted at Tonk Wilbraham down the phone. "I thought you were the Central Intelligence Agency, not the Central Idiots Agency! You told me we had another month before the Brits released the real Message, and that by then you would know the whole thing rather than the scrap on Delmonico's cell phone."

It had been seven in the evening in Washington, midnight in London, when a duty clerk at the US Embassy in London dumped the following day's newspapers on the desk of the Third Secretary whose turn it was to do the night shift. He got on the phone straight away to the State Department duty officer, who caught Delmonico in his office as he was about to leave for the day.

With a muttered 'shit!' under his breath as he speedread the emailed front page of the *Guardian*, he knew his evening plans were blown. He phoned the President's office and she called back immediately from the bowling alley in the basement where she had hoped to spend an hour or so with her daughter on her birthday. She got the summary of the situation from Delmonico and then disrupted Wilbraham's poker game just as he had been dealt four tens and an ace, and he discovered from the phone call that his luck had run out for the evening.

The only consolation about the whole SNAFU was that the British security service had been singing from the same, erroneous, song sheet and had also expected the Brits to release their bombshell in *Nature* in early February.

"I'm going to talk to the British Prime Minister soon – we'll let them make the running and I'm sure they'll make some kind of statement, but we should hold a press conference tomorrow. Can you coordinate with MI5 over any security issues? I'll make sure we get a good team for a press conference – you'd better delegate someone who can think on their feet. I imagine the media here will carry the Brits' conference, and I need to get some common line with the Brits beforehand, over the next step."

Billings then rang Kent Branton.

"What do you think we should do with your SETI office, who signally failed to do the only job they were set up to do?"

Kent had only just heard the news and was reading the *Guardian* supplement on his computer.

"They're not spies, Madam President," Brandon said. "That's Tonk's job. The CIA has $60 billion a year. SETI has $10 *million*."

"Well, you're going to have to work the ass off them now. Get them poring over the Message and the stuff the Brits have written about it, all night if necessary, and I want that Sherry woman in DC tomorrow at my Press Conference."

Although the flea in his ear wasn't their fault, Sherry Walker got the sharp end of Kent's tongue when he rang her on a conference call.

"As you are about to find out," he said, "the original Message sent from the Outpost has been released by a team of Brits who discovered it. I wonder why they did and you didn't?" Kent said.

"What did it say?" Sherry said.

"'No annihilation' is the main thing. It will be all over the internet soon if it isn't already. Instead of killing us all, the aliens are saving our asses."

While she was listening Sherry was calling up the Message on her phone.

"I can't process this quickly," she said.

"You're going to have to," Branton said. "The President wants to hold a Press conference at the White House tomorrow, in which you will take part."

"I wasn't planning to be in Washington tomorrow," Sherry said, peeved at the way Branton seemed to want to shift the blame to her unit.

"I think you know my answer to that," Kent said. "The next few days and weeks – I suspect – you're going to be rather busy.

"What do you want me to cover tomorrow?"

"You can put the discovery in context – the result of a long search – success for US science –"

"Wait," Sherry said, "We failed to find it!"

"But you were the first to identify Saturn as the location of the Outpost."

"And how do we deal with the Russian side?" Sherry said, "'Those lying, cheating frauds'?"

"Not by calling them that. In fact, you don't say anything about that. Refer it to President Billings. I have a hunch she will have a call to President Pavlov in the next twelve hours, and we'll hear their version."

After Kent rang off, Sherry sat down and read the entire *Guardian* supplement. Suddenly she felt out of her depth. The moment she had waited for her entire adult life had arrived. Of course, it had seemed to arrive when the Message was first publicised, but there was always a lingering doubt, a doubt that had now been removed by this other extraordinary piece of news she had read in the supplement, evidence of the planting of a 'signature', by the Messengers in the gene that coded for speech and intelligence. That really clinched it.

She also felt anxious. 'We only have one shot at getting this dialogue right, between humanity and the Messengers', she thought. 'Will our politicians rise to the occasion?'

She admired Jennifer Billings as the first woman president, but knew that she was surrounded by advisers in her administration who were not so admirable. Or intelligent. Suddenly she had the idea of putting on paper – well, pixels really – some thoughts about how to approach the Messengers, now that there was no doubt about their existence, and how to respond to their offer – or their order, really. It would help her with whatever she was called on to do at the Press Conference and, in fact, she might even send it to Billings, not as an official NASA communication but as one human to another. One woman to another, really. If it pissed Branton off, so what? This whole thing was bigger than office – or Administration – politics.

Although it was getting late, Sherry knew she shouldn't delay the task, and she sat down at her computer and started to write. By 2 a.m. she had a piece of text she was happy with:

SUBJECT: HOW SHOULD WE RELATE TO THE 'WRITERS' OF THE MESSAGE?

In considering how we talk to a civilisation that contacts us, a topic I have thought a lot about at NASA, there is a danger that we will think only scientifically about the content and tone of any reply. This is understandable, because any such message will have required the participation of science to detect, decrypt, translate, and understand. And indeed understanding the source of the Message itself involves astronomers, exobiologists, physicists, and computer modellers.

There is an extra factor in the current situation – the fact that the Message itself comes from an artificial construct, the Outpost, in which there are unlikely to be any intelligent lifeforms, but merely (merely!) a cleverly constructed simulacrum of intelligence, capable of surpassing the Turing test many times over, in its ability to communicate with us, detect and interpret our own languages, thought patterns, reasoning processes and – I would say – psychology. All of these are, of course, human terms, but if the Messengers were clever enough to instil intelligence and humanity into the lower primate that was our ancestor, they are clever enough to understand and deal with the consequences of that achievement.

There is a possibility that the original civilisation is not extinct. The reasoning that would lead to this conclusion is as follows. Tau Ceti is 12 light years away. The initial genetic manipulation that led to homo sapiens took place 250,000, plus or minus 100,000, years ago. It is likely that this was preceded by millennia of observational research by the civilisation, in order to understand the evolution of life on Earth. In addition, it is difficult to see how this was achieved without earlier space probes, evidence of which may still exist somewhere on Earth. This could be necessary to take samples and either return them to their planet, or, using advanced technology – such as our Mars Perseverance mission but far more sophisticated – to analyse the genetics of Earth's life forms and transmit the data back.

This minimum of two major visitations of spacecraft – many thousands of them, possibly – would require a civilisation already much further advanced than our own. They will have been observing us for say, 250,000 years at a minimum and at that point they would have developed technology sophisticated enough in its computing capacity, power generation and, as it seems, nano-technology skills, to far exceed what we are capable of. Who knows what the subsequent history of this civilisation might have been, after they sent the Outpost to await the results of their intervention in our evolution? We have no way of knowing, but it is likely that the Outpost is both the source of the original intervention technology and the site of its monitoring capacity over the last 250,000 years, which would mean they were programmed to expect many millennia of radio silence before the first useful signs of our intellectual life in the early part of the 20th century, although they would probably have been capable of detecting signs of industrial pollution in the 19th century along with street lighting in the major cities.

But there is a second possibility, one which I am coming to believe in, that the Outpost is the only active remnant that now exists of the civilisation. We have detected no direct attempts to communicate from Tau Ceti, such as we would expect if there was still life on the planet. Surely over the last fifty years of SETI programs we would have detected any direct communication from them. And we have to assume that the recent message from the Outpost was a response to some preprogrammed "trigger" event on Earth, related to man-made deterioration in the global environment.

Where is this leading? It is late at night so I may not be thinking clearly but I want to explore the nature of any reply the world sends to the message.

It seems to me that however sophisticated the language of the Message - however cleverly they have learnt our languages and discovered how to express themselves comprehensively - this is analogous to the way our anthropologists approached so-called primitive societies in the early days of anthropological discovery. We should not be deceived into thinking that "Oh, they think like us." We do not know that, any more than Malinowski thought like a Trobriand Islander when he addressed them in their own language.

There is a danger, it seems to me, that any globally composed response to the Message may give the impression that we think we are at least equal to the Messengers and therefore try to haggle, or bargain, or argue, or in some other way imply that we are happy to share the task of cleaning up the Earth rather than do whatever they suggest. These people(!) know what they are saying. They have put more 'thought' into how to solve our problems than we could ever have devoted to them, because of the likely nature of their intelligence, their ability to reason and, of course, their far advanced knowledge of physics, chemistry, and computing.

I realise that I'm straying into areas that are outside my competence. The psychology of humans sometimes baffles me, let alone trying to understand the likely psychology of extra-terrestrials. But however falteringly, I think we have to do our utmost to understand the likely reaction to any reply we send to the Message, before we fire off some pompous, politically naïve, response in which the Outpost's AI computers will undoubtedly detect any insincerity, cover-up, posturing, or attempt to deceive. Remember, they have the capacity to monitor all our communications, and if in some international committee of world leaders, each nation attempts to get something for itself – the sort of thing which must be behind the Russian fakery – the recipients of the Earth's reply will already be aware of this.

On rereading this, it seems rather muddled, but fundamentally, Madam President, it is a plea for caution and humility. We have one opportunity to get this right. It is a once-in-a-lifetime offer and we cannot rely on it being repeated if it is mishandled.

Sherry sat back; reread it and then realised that she didn't know how to get it to Jennifer Billings. Then she remembered the woman she had to ring to pass on her details for the White House visit back in October. She scrolled through her messages and found Kent's original text. Then she wondered if the woman would even be there at this time of night. Of course she wouldn't. But someone would.

It took Sherry a while to convince the young man on duty in the President's office but he finally gave her an email address, and said that he'd leave a note for Mary-Ellen when she came in at 7 a.m. and she could decide whether the President needed to see it.

'Well, I did my best,' Sherry thought as she pressed the 'Send' button. She wondered if the whole tenor of her message would seem silly or presumptuous to the President, if she even had time to read it, but then she thought 'What does it matter? If she does think it's silly she can just delete it. And it's helped me organise my thoughts.'

Chapter 15

The phone rang by Miles's side of the bed at 3 a.m. It was the college phone, not his mobile, which he had turned off before he went to bed.

"We'll try to get one night's sleep before the storm," he said to Leila the night following the meeting to finalise the document. "I told Harry Golding on pain of death not put any calls through till 8 a.m."

"I'll kill that man!" he muttered as he picked up the phone.

"Master, I'm really sorry to call you," said Robert Patch. "Mr Golding put a big Post-It on the switchboard saying "Do not put calls through to the Master till after 8 a.m. on pain of death!"

"What is it, Bob?" Miles said.

"It's Number 10 Downing Street. They were most insistent. Rude, even. I told him about the Post-It but the man said 'I'll tell you where to post it unless you put me through.'"

Miles sighed.

"All right," he said, "I'll speak to him."

There was a click on the line, and Miles heard the familiar voice of Carla Baxter, the PM.

"I'm sure you don't like being woken up at this ungodly hour any more than I do, Dr Cadogan," she said, "But we have to move quickly over your supplement about the Message. I haven't time to discuss how and why you have managed to pull the wool over the eyes of Special Branch – obviously the ivory tower has a more down-to-earth basement. But all hell is breaking out and we need to plan the press conference."

"What press conference?" Miles said, as Leila stirred in the bed next to him.

"*A* press conference," she said, "We have to answer all the questions the real Message raises, including how do we know it's a real Message?"

"We try to answer them all in the supplement," Miles said.

"This suggests that you believe the entire nation reads the *Guardian*."

"No, but the other papers will report it too."

"Report it, not reprint it. And do you think the *Sun* will report it with the same detail and nuances that you have?"

"I suppose not."

"I want a major press conference at five this evening, with you attending."

"Don't you think Professor Spearman would be better? He is professor of astronomy at Cambridge, after all."

"You are a social anthropologist," Baxter said, "And a lot of the issues are to do with how society responds."

"Do you think people even know what social anthropology is?"

Baxter ignored his remark.

"So if we have you, who else?" she asked.

"Well, what strikes you is the most unusual part of the message, the real Message?"

"You know, I don't know if the media will concentrate on this, but I think the most interesting thing about the whole business is this suggestion that the human race is only here because of what these people – this civilisation – did hundreds and thousands of years ago to create us. The piece by –" she paused.

"Katie Flynn?" Miles said.

"Yes, Dr Flynn. We should have her. Good to have a woman instead of two middle-aged men."

Miles knew that the exposure would be good for Katie's career, if she could rise to the challenge.

"It'll be like those Covid press conferences five years ago," the PM said.

"Oh, you mean the ones with two middle-age men, three, really if you include your predecessor."

"They had women as well. Jenny whatever she was called, Harries was it?"

"True"

"If, say, you and Dr Flynn can come, we will field the Foreign Secretary and Quentin Stewart from MI5. He's taken an interest in the Message because of its security implications. And then I'll be there too. We'll do it in the Number 10 TV studio. Can you come here at three so that we can go through any possible tricky questions?"

"I suppose I have to do this?" Miles said.

"Yes. I'll leave it to you to make sure Dr Flynn comes too."

After the call, with Leila now wide awake, Miles explained what was going on.

"Your weekly visit to Number 10?" she said. "They should have a coffee mug with your name on it."

"Monthly, more like it," he said. "Now let's try to get some more sleep."

Katie was delighted, although nervous, to be invited to take part in the prime minister's press conference.

'Me,' she thought, 'an insignificant palaeogeneticist.' But of course, she knew her own growing worth to the group of scientists working on the implications of the message. Without her analysis there would be no actual evidence for the claim that the extra-terrestrials had seeded intelligence and language in homo sapiens.

When Miles had called her at 6.30 a.m. – he couldn't wait any longer, he said – she was half awake anyway. For the last two nights she had not slept well.

The first night, her head was abuzz with the work the group had done at Paul's house; the second night, she tossed and turned, eager to see what the world reactions would be to the *Guardian* supplement. So when the phone rang she was halfway through getting dressed, eager to see what the day would bring.

That the day was going to bring participation in a televised press conference chaired by the Prime Minister, and no doubt seen round the world, raised a very important question: what was she going to wear? Should she try to look like the brainy, sometimes nerdy, academic she was, or confound people's expectations and dress up, or at least dress differently. Whatever she wore, there was nothing in her wardrobe that fitted the bill, so she knew she'd have to go into town as soon as the shops opened and splash out a bit.

Miles had booked a taxi to take the two of them to the station at one o'clock, and offered an early lunch in the Lodge at twelve, so she didn't have much time.

She had one other thing to do before she went shopping – to ring her mother and try to tell her about the press conference. She knew that if it was a good day, the carers would call her aunt and uncles, and invite into her room some of the other carers, and two or three of the residents of the home, and that they would all talk over the things she said and say things like "That's a nice dress she's wearing" and "What's she done with her hair?" and "Fancy, she walked in with the prime minister." But it was nice to be able to show that what she did for a living was not just working in a dusty old lab. Or rather, it was, but it had some profound implications.

When Miles and Katie arrived at No 10 they were shown into the Prime Minister's meeting room, next to her office. By the door was Paul Martin who offered a damp hand to each of them to shake. There were four other people: Quentin Stewart, the MI5 man, the Foreign Secretary, Fergus DeWaal, the PM's spokeswoman, Bryony Pemberton, whom Miles recognised from previous television appearances, and a man introduced as a Special Advisor, who looked about twenty.

"He's a SPAD," Miles muttered to Katie after they had been introduced, and sat together at a green baize table.

"What's a SPAD?" she said.

"Special Advisor," Miles replied.

"Doesn't look very special to me," she said quietly. "Look, his shirt tails are hanging out."

"That proves he works so hard giving advice that he doesn't have time to dress properly."

"How can someone as fetal as that advise the government on anything? What does he know that senior civil servants don't."

"Beats me," Miles said. "Oh, here she is," he went on as Carla Baxter came into the room, and sat down, opening up a copy of the *Guardian* supplement.

Stewart stopped his call and came and stood next to Miles and Katie.

"We haven't met," he said "I am Quentin Stewart, MI5."

"I feel we have," Miles said, "After our phone calls and email exchanges."

"I'm surprised you pulled that Goonhilly stunt," Stewart said. "We had to find money from my budget to repair the damage."

The man was every bit as unpleasant as he had been on the phone. Tall, with receding hairline, half-moon specs, and an Armani suit, Stewart towered over Miles, a stance he seemed to think was justified by his elevated status and intelligence.

"This is my colleague, Katie Flynn," Miles said, ignoring Stewart's jibe.

Katie offered her hand.

"His job is very secret," Miles said to her.

"Oh, I wouldn't say that," Stewart said, giving Katie a toothy smile, which made her shudder inwardly. "Most people have heard of MI5 and what goes on there."

"What they think goes on there," Miles said.

"Ladies and gentlemen," the PM said, "Thanks for coming at such short notice. Like me, and like Bryony here, you've probably been fending off press queries all day, so people's tongues will be hanging out for this press conference. We've told the broadcasters to set aside an hour and I'm sure the press will be wanting more, but we need to keep it tight. The Americans will be doing the same thing at five their time, so I've got a conference call with President Billings after six to compare notes."

For the next hour and a half, the SPAD and the PM's media advisor threw questions at the PM, Miles, Katie, the Foreign Secretary and the MI5 man, quite often stopping to reshape an answer, making it briefer, clearer, or more accurate.

At 4:30, the PM got up.

"I have a small international crisis in the Gambia to deal with," she said. "More electoral fiddling, and the EU needs our help. There is tea and biscuits in the anteroom to the studio and then we go in at five on the dot."

She gave Katie and the others a reassuring smile.

Katie felt pleased that the answers she had given in the mock interviews had gone down well with the PM.

There was an air of suppressed excitement in the No. 10 TV studio. As Katie walked in just behind the PM – she knew her mum would be pleased to see that – she smelled the odour of damp clothing, from a torrential downpour as journalists had assembled. There were about forty of them, thirty seated and others standing around against the walls. At the back was a battery of TV cameras.

There was a raised dais with five chairs in front of a large video screen, with smaller screens facing the dais from either side. The screens carried the words "Prime Minister's Press Conference – The Message from Space," with the date and the names of the speakers.

Paul Martin stepped forward from the side of the room and positioned each of the speakers so that they were sitting in the same arrangement as the names on the screen. There was a standing microphone in front of each speaker with a small video screen on each, facing the audience of journalists, which showed the speaker's name and affiliation.

Katie noticed that many of the journalists had the *Guardian* supplement on their laps and were taking notes. She looked down at her copy, open at the page with her article, though she knew exactly what she was going to say.

At 5 p.m. exactly, the words disappeared from the large video screen and were replaced by a closeup of Carla Baxter. The buzz in the room subsided, and Baxter tapped the microphone in front of her, and started to speak.

"I don't think any of us can remember quite as momentous a series of events as those that have dominated the headlines since October 15th last year," she said. "And among those momentous events, none can be more important than what happened last night when the details were published of what we now believe to be the correct version of a Message directed to our planet by a civilisation which exists, or did exist, on a planet orbiting a star about twelve light years away from our sun. There is much we still don't know about the real Message, but virtually everything we do know is in the supplement prepared by Dr Miles Cadogan here, and his colleagues, including Dr Katie Flynn, another member of the group, all of whom are at St James' College, Cambridge. They are here to answer your questions, as is the Foreign Secretary, Fergus DeWaal, to whose international responsibilities I have temporarily added the territory of Outer Space."

A titter ran through the audience.

"And Quentin Stewart of MI5 is here to talk about any security issues."

As she named the panel, the video screen showed their faces, names, and titles.

"Each of the speakers has been asked to summarise in one or two sentences how they see the significance of the message. Dr Cadogan..."

Miles cleared his throat, looked down at his notes, and started speaking.

"For weeks, the world has lived in fear of annihilation as a result of the fake extraterrestrial Message released by Russia. Now that a team of Cambridge researchers have found the real message, we have different, but more pleasant, concerns - how best to take up the offer in the Message to benefit all humanity. And dealing with those concerns is a task I hope we researchers in Britain will be able to help the government with."

Miles had though carefully about how to take advantage of the limelight and stake a claim for Cambridge participation in whatever happened next

"Admirably brief," the PM said. "Fergus, can you emulate Dr Cadogan?"

The Foreign Secretary was not known for his brevity of speaking or concision of thought, but tried his best.

"Good international relations have been increasingly necessary as the truths about threats to the biosphere have become apparent. Before the

Message was discovered, while there was a fruitful momentum towards global cooperation, the predictions for how soon these problems could be fixed were not promising. But suddenly, with the arrival of the Message, and particularly the correct version of it, we have been handed a beacon of hope, but to take advantage of this, we will have to strain every sinew to put aside international differences and work together. Whether this is possible –"

"That's enough, Fergus," the PM said, followed by laughter from the floor. "I'm sure you can elaborate during the questioning. Mr Stewart?"

Quentin Stewart leaned back in his chair and said, "In spite of the apparent disappearance of the annihilation threat, we really have no way of knowing whether this extra-terrestrial civilisation poses a threat to the UK or the world, although its expressed intentions are benign. But the next steps, whatever they are, will have to be taken with great care so as not to leave ourselves open to being attacked rather than helped. The story of the Trojan Horse comes to mind."

"Now, Dr Flynn, whose ingenious research you will have read about, described admirably clearly in her *Guardian* piece," the PM said.

Katie's heart was racing and her mouth was dry. But she had taken seriously Baxter's plea for brevity.

"The idea that humanity was seeded in some way from outside the Earth is a very old one, and it is sheer good luck that my research into the origins of intelligence and homo sapiens has helped to confirm a key element in the message – that we are all in some sense the progeny of this extra-terrestrial civilisation. It is because of that that I believe the attitude of the civilisation is as benign to us as a parent's solicitousness for her child."

Quentin Stewart rolled his eyes at Katie's last remark.

"Thank you, Dr Flynn," the PM said. "And now, we're open to questions."

A forest of hands was raised in the air, and the PM pointed to Palab Ghosh for the BBC.

Ghosh looked at his notes.

"Can I ask Dr Flynn what we know, if anything, about the inhabitants of the Tau Ceti planet and what makes you think that they can deliver the help they are offering in their Message?"

"I can tell you absolutely nothing about their biology," Katie said. "The best I can do is tell you what we think they have achieved. They have monitored the biosphere of the Earth for maybe half a million years; they have built a space station capable of travelling a distance of twelve light years – that's 100,000,000,000 km – on a journey that could have taken it centuries, while still having the capacity to navigate to the Rings of Saturn, install itself, with the computers still working, so that it could send what we believe were small exploratory spacecraft to analyse our life forms a quarter of a million years ago and decide to enhance the abilities of one of those species and change it into homo sapiens. Now, I don't know whether they are green men, multi-fingered plants, gaseous balloons or black clouds; but one thing I would say, since they have been able to do what I have just described, I think saving homo sapiens from the results of his own activities by creating a new biosphere would be a doddle."

Journalists tapped away on laptops, and there was an underscore of amusement.

"Michael Binyon, the Times," the PM said.

"Can I ask the Foreign Secretary whether anything in current British foreign policy is useful in deciding how to respond to this Message?"

DeWaal smiled. "Good question," he said. "Actually I think there is. I think Prime Minister Baxter has brought two new elements into foreign policy since she was appointed. Where there was a choice between confrontation and collaboration, she has favoured the latter, with great success. Who would have thought that the Iran nuclear stand-off would have been solved by arguing for lifting sanctions rather than imposing more. But we all know the result. And she has also argued for a global response to global problems, even when the economic price for our country seemed more than we can bear. Both of these principles will be essential going forward as we try to come to terms with the Message."

For the next fifty minutes, Miles, Katie and the politicians fielded a wide range of questions, some intelligent, some stupid ("If we don't answer, will they leave us alone?" was one). Carla Baxter looked up at a clock on the wall and was about to wrap up the press conference, when she noticed a number of journalists suddenly looking down at their phones, as if they had all received the same message. One of them interrupted an answer from Quentin Stewart and shouted "Prime Minister, do you have a comment on what the Russians have just said?"

Baxter looked puzzled, and gave a quizzical look to DeWaal, who shook his head.

Then Paul Martin, who had left the room unnoticed, returned with three sheets of paper which he put in front of the PM, the Foreign Secretary, and the head of MI5.

There were anguished sotto voce questions to their colleagues from those journalists unlucky enough not to have received a Russian press release just issued in Moscow. Baxter read the short communiqué once, and then read it again. "We know nothing about this," she said. "I have just seen it for the first time."

"What is it?" Several voices called from the floor.

"Fergus, since this will now be all over the place," Baxter said, "would you like to read it out for those of our colleagues who haven't been sent it? And by the way I'm not going to make any comment at the moment, however many people wave their hands and shout at me."

DeWaal gave the PM a look at seemed to say 'Do I have to?' and then read the brief statement:

Having read the British newspapers' allegations that the Russian government somehow faked the alleged Message from an extra-terrestrial civilisation, we repudiate absolutely the suggestion. We did, in good faith, issue a decrypted text which contained the threat of annihilation. But we will shortly issue a dossier with an analysis of the raw data, along with other incriminating material, which will show that the original Message, now released, was first received by the Americans, who tampered with it and then planted it in such a way that when detected by Russian astronomers it was assumed to be genuine. We are of, course, happy to take a leading role in any global response to the new message, and, like many around the world, we rejoice in the fact that the threat of annihilation was merely an irresponsible example of American fake news.

The room was in uproar at this news. With difficulty, Carla Baxter managed to quieten things down by putting up her hands and showing that she wanted to say something.

"I want to say only two things," she said. "First I think no one need doubt that the new Message – the offer of help – is genuine, and second, I am going to say nothing more today until I have talked to US President Billings. Thank you."

With that, she ushered the others out of the studio, pursued by shouted questions and handwaving.

Much of the Presidential press conference an hour later was spent fending off queries about the Russian press release. Jenny Billings was determined to say nothing, but it didn't stop journalists persisting. In the end, Billings brought that line of questioning to a halt.

"Look," she said, "I read this Russian allegation an hour ago for the first time. Bearing in mind the propensity of Russia to fabricate alternative facts whenever it is called out, it seems to me this is possibly more of the same. Certainly, as I've said ten times already in the last half hour, at the moment I have no knowledge of any US plan to trick the Russians into publishing the annihilation message. Now, do you want to talk about anything else, or shall I close the conference down? We have some very bright people here who are dying to talk about important things, like the first civilisation we have ever detected outside the solar system, or the mysterious Outpost that we think sent the message. Anybody?"

She looked across the room and picked one of several hands that were going up.

"Tom Shepherd, *LA Times*, and I warn you..." She said mock menacingly.

"Can I ask Dr Walker to tell us what we know so far about this Outpost? Shape? Size? How it works?"

"I'm glad you asked that, Tom, because we do have some interesting new information. Could you show my image please," Sherry said into the air.

The image of Saturn's rings came on the screen, the picture used in the supplement, with the suspected Outpost as a small white rectangle. There was a torrent of clicking as people took pictures of the image on the screen.

"We believe that this shows an object about the size of a large building circling Saturn in the midst of other elements in the inner ring of Saturn," Sherry said, "which are rocks of a range of sizes but with different reflectivity. The much brighter surface indicates a possible metallic structure."

The image changed.

"Now, here's an image you probably haven't seen."

Jenny Billings had told Kent to get Sherry to bring this second image as a way of giving the media something new.

"This is a closer view and you can see that it is a much more regular shape than its surroundings, suggesting a manufactured structure, rather than a naturally occurring piece of rock."

"What telescope was that taken by?" Tom Shepard asked

"Actually it wasn't taken through a telescope. It was an image from the Cassini flyby mission which went round Saturn in 2011, and sent back thousands of images of Saturn and its rings. No one spotted this image until we went back over the files after the Message was first received, with the fake content. From Earth, no telescope would show the rings at that resolution, so unless we get another mission organised to approach Saturn, we're not going to see it that close for a while."

President Billings chose another raised hand.

"Laura Steiner, *Science*."

"Can I ask Dr Walker whether there is any chance that the Outpost contains representatives of the civilisation that sent the Message?"

Sherry shook her head.

"We believe the Outpost has been in situ for thousands of years, and that it took more thousands of years to reach the solar system from its home planet. Of course, I suppose we can imagine life forms which remain alive and capable of acting for that length of time, but it seems much more likely that the civilisation, detecting a star like our sun as a possible site for planets on which life could form, would send some kind of automated space outpost to lodge somewhere in the solar system and observe any likely planets, like ours, as a biosphere develops."

Another journalist was chosen by President Billings, Parry Geraldo from the *Washington Post*.

"What is the next step, Madam President. Who is going to reply to the Message and what will we say?"

"Parry, twenty four hours ago, I believed, like most of the rest of the world, that we were all going to be annihilated in five years. I – we, I suspect, – all the governments of the world would like a bit of time to consider what to do next."

"But there will be a reply?" Geraldo persisted.

"Stay tuned," Billings said.

Chapter 16

The reply which was sent from Earth to the Outpost was a carefully composed 700 words assembled after seven meetings of the UN Alien Communication Committee – UNACC.

It was measured, authoritative, and boring:

> "Whereas," it began, "our global nations have received, read and appreciated the Message transmitted on September 14th, 2025, to our planet, we set out below in Clauses 1 to 10 a response to the concerns expressed in the Message, concerns which, as you will be aware, we have already expressed ourselves, at conferences like Cop 26, Davos 23, and numerous other meetings of national leaders..."

The reply continued in a similar bureaucratic vein, itemising what the nations of the Earth had decided to do in the light of the Outpost's "kind" offer to help solve global environmental problems and remedy the harm being done to the biosphere.

While each nation had been asked to submit a report based on drafts from international leaders and scientists, there was little agreement by the countries' governments on the specifics to be incorporated in the reply. In any case, many of these reports merely recommended their own preferred solutions.

As Miles Cadogan, who had drafted the UK report to the UN, wrote "There is no point in suggesting the sort of 'primitive' solutions the world has discussed so far to a civilisation that is so unimaginably more advanced than ours," and the UK report concentrated on the need for some global scientific consensus to accept whatever the Output suggested, rather than squabble about the effect of any particular solution on an individual nation.

One big question was how to transmit the reply so that it would be detected by the Outpost amidst the cacophony of radio signals emanating from the Earth every second of the day and night.

UNACC decided to use the well-tried hydrogen line frequency to transmit the reply, coded into binary and with prime number precursors, simultaneously on a loop from six major radio telescopes around the world. This would start transmitting on February 1st, a date chosen arbitrarily once the final draft had been agreed. The same radio telescopes would then set up an alert to receive whatever reply might be forthcoming to take the rescue of the Earth to its next stage.

On February 1st, at noon GMT, a time reluctantly accepted by those nations to whom the time would be inconvenient, Katie, Miles and Leila, and Paul and Dee were in the Master's Lodge at St James', watching the BBC news channel on television. Miles had supplied a bottle of champagne and Katie had brought some nibbles, but none of this would be consumed until it was certain that the reply had been transmitted.

At twelve noon in the UK, as Big Ben struck the hour, Carla Baxter appeared on television and said "In a momentous day for the world, a message on behalf of all citizens has been sent to the Outpost in the rings of Saturn. If the original Message is to be believed, this will mark the beginning of the restoration of the Earth to health, after decades of human-caused deterioration."

In St James' College, a champagne cork popped and Miles poured out five glasses of bubbly. Katie passed round the nibbles and then the group sat around in silence.

"This is big, isn't it?" Leila said, after taking a sip of her drink.

"It is," Miles said. "It's a day the world will remember."

"When do you think we'll get an answer?" Leila said.

"Today? Tomorrow? Presumably there has to be some process to digest a reply and prepare an account of what the next steps are going to be."

"Meanwhile, we get back to work," Paul said.

"I suppose the UN has a group to translate the binary back into English," Leila said.

"Why do you think they'll reply in English?" Katie said.

"Well, you're right. I suppose they'll do what they did before - send an answer in several languages," Miles said.

"'They'," said Leila, thoughtfully. "What a limiting word that is. We only use it of humans and animals but what on earth does 'they' mean applied to the writers of the original message, or to the Outpost, which may not have any 'they' there at all?"

Miles's mobile phone rang and he answered the call.

"Oh yes, Prime Minister," he said, "It is an important day. I just hope that the UN Committee knows how to deal with the next step."

"Look," Carla Baxter said, "they're all politicians. They wanted to have their moment in the sun. Once some actual recommendations are received we'll have to rely on the scientists to guide us."

Miles had made known his feelings to the PM after it became clear that international politics would drive the wording of the reply.

"Well, it's not as if we're short of things to do. Regardless of any answer to our reply, there's a lot scientists still need to research about Tau Ceti and its civilisation," Miles said.

"You and Professor Spearman were thinking about all this very early on. I'm sure you'll have an important role. Please stay in touch. I've valued your advice. And Dr Flynn's too."

Miles closed his phone.

"The Prime Minister sends her love, Katie," he said.

"Sweet," Katie replied.

Leila stood up.

"I'll lay out the lunch. It'll be a light meal, because I know you've got things to do."

After a leisurely lunch the five of them chatted. The television was on in the corner of the room, with various commentators guessing when a reply might come and what it might say. The Earth's reply would take about an hour and a half to reach the Outpost, and then, after 'they' had considered it and prepared a reply, it would take another hour and a half to travel back.

"Well, I've got some work to do," Katie said. "Do you mind if I come back later, when there's a chance there might have been a reply?"

"Of course, Katie," Miles said. "We're all in this together."

Back in her lab, Katie was discussing some new PCR tests with Rosie. She wanted to see if there were any significant variations between samples taken from different areas in Africa. Her phone on the lab bench buzzed. As Katie looked at the sender's name, she froze. She then peered more closely to make sure she had read it correctly. The one word sender name said "Outpost".

"I've just got to look at this, Rosie," she said, and went into her small office in the corner of the lab. There, she opened the email, addressed to Katie, and to Sherry Walker at NASA, and started to read.

This is how it began:

> WE RECOMMEND THAT YOU KEEP THE CONTENTS OF THIS EMAIL TO YOURSELVES, AT LEAST UNTIL YOU HAVE HAD TIME TO DIGEST ITS CONTENTS.

Katie continued reading the email, trying to conceal her growing astonishment:

> Our AI system has read and understood the UNACC reply, sent to us today at 12 noon GMT (received at 13:21:17 GMT) and we find the tone unhelpful to us in planning the next steps. We are, of course, glad that some kind of consensus has been found, although, reading between the lines, this reeks of a rather dodgy and unenthusiastic compromise. So we are reserving judgement at the moment on the issue of how to respond.
>
> But we were already aware of a more informed and sensitive attitude to the issues, expressed in Katie Flynn's contribution to the *Guardian* supplement. This had a similar level of understanding to that expressed in a report sent to the US President and written by Dr Sherry Walker, Director of SETI at NASA, headed "How should we relate to the 'writers' of the Message?". What we have decided, therefore, is to communicate our future messages to you both initially, in private, for you to analyse and react directly to us, rather than us using the suboptimal channel offered by UNACC. While, of course, we can anticipate, and even predict, the likely course of negotiations with UNACC, while Earth organisations tried to agree to abide by the solutions we offer valuable time could be lost.
>
> We could instigate the solutions we propose unilaterally, and will probably do that, whatever responses we get from UNACC. But having someone on Earth as our point of contact – our ambassadors, if you like – will mean that some discussion of the issues can take place using conventional communication methods, without the hassle of back-and-forth messages via radio telescopes.

You may wonder why, in view of our immeasurably greater technical skills and information-gathering capability, we should need the kind of insights you might provide. But we have reached the stage in our civilization where logic and rationality are the determinants of our decision-making. What you call 'politics' has played no part in our society for half a million years and this is the one area where our analytical skills fall short. We literally cannot imagine how the kind of decision-making occurs that leads to outcomes for your people and society which are harmful to large numbers of humans, merely in order to achieve the survival or prosperity of small group or even one individual. Such decision-making must play no part in how humans collaborate with us in their own salvation, but it will help us if you can at least direct our attention to the key human obstacles that global politics may try to put in the way of the swift and effective solutions we will offer.

To assure you that this message is genuinely from the Outpost, in our formal reply to the UNACC message, transmitted by radio on the hydrogen line, you will find that the English version will contain two sequences of words which begin with the letters of your first names, 'Katie' and 'Sherry'.

Please indicate your willingness to play the role assigned to you, by replying merely 'Yes' or 'No' to this email, once you have satisfied yourself of its genuineness.

"Let's finish for the day, Rosie," Katie said, trying to conceal the astonishment at the email. "Can you clear up before you go?"

Rosie thought there was something distracted about Katie's manner. Perhaps the email had some bad news.

"Of course, Dr Flynn. See you tomorrow."

As Katie cycled back to St James' her mind was in a whirl. She obviously couldn't tell the others about this, but wondered how she would conceal her excitement and her confusion. But when she arrived at the Lodge, the others were clustered around the television, preoccupied by what was going on.

A newsreader was saying "We have just heard from the UN that a reply has been received to the message sent by UNACC at 12 noon today to the Outpost, accepting the offers of assistance in dealing with major environmental problems. It was announced by the chair of the committee, Sergei Gromov."

There was a shot of the Russian Deputy President at a UN podium. He said: "In an almost unbelievably quick turnaround, the Outpost sent a reply to a message which they will have received at about 13.21 GMT. We received that reply ten minutes ago, at about 14.45, suggesting an instantaneous deciphering and analysis of our message. Once the Outpost's reply is fully translated, we will release it to the world's leaders and the media."

"How can they have achieved such an instantaneous reply?" said Leila, "Surely 'they' must have prepared their answer beforehand?"

Paul laughed.

"Leila, you underestimate the speed with which technology can progress. If the Outpost's computing power is thousands of years ahead of ours, they could achieve in a second what would take us hours or days. I don't just mean the physical computing speed. Remember we don't believe it likely that there are actual wetware brains on their post, but even if there were, they would be able to receive, translate, digest and make decisions in infinitesimally small amounts of time. Remember too," he continued, "that they are likely to have been able to tap into the UNACC discussions, however secret those meetings were, so that they were as likely as not prepared for what its message would say."

Well," Leila said, "I'm flummoxed. More champagne anyone?"

"Are you sure you mean 'flummoxed', Loo?" Miles said, "Rather than 'flabbergasted'?"

"Of course you are right. They are both stupid words and I got them mixed up."

Katie stood up, trying to look casual.

"I'm sure it will be a while before we get the full text of the Outpost's new message. I just have one or two housekeeping tasks. I'll be in my rooms."

She walked out of the room quickly before anyone noticed her shaking hands.

Sherry Walker was up at five a.m. on 'the day'. She sat outside on the deck watching early morning scullers on the Potomac. It was still cool, and she had wrapped a furry throw around her shoulders and warmed her hands in an irregularly shaped mug her niece had made her with love.

She had her phone on the glass topped table, tuned to National Public Radio. She knew the event would be covered by all TV news channels but couldn't bear the jokey, punning, 'little green men' banter that accompanied all coverage of the Message story these days. It was bad enough having to deal with it when she was interviewed - as she had to be, it was part of her job - and had to explain, once more, that a light year was a measure of distance, not time.

Sherry heard a buzz from her phone on the table top and picked it up, to find an email which started:

> WE RECOMMEND THAT YOU KEEP THE CONTENTS OF THIS EMAIL TO YOURSELF, AT LEAST UNTIL YOU HAVE HAD A FEW DAYS TO DIGEST ITS CONTENTS…

The Outpost's swift reply, three hours after UNACC's response was sent - it couldn't arrive any sooner because of the limitations of the speed of light - found the world's leaders unprepared. This could have been foreseen if anyone had thought seriously about what would be necessary for the Outpost to compose a reply. The only explanation for this failure was that no one at a senior level was able to break out of the anthropomorphic straitjacket that went "We will send them a reply, they will sit down and read it, consider their answer to us, and in the fullness of time, compose and sent us their reaction."

It was clear to anyone who thought about it that the computing power in the Outpost would be many orders of magnitude greater than anything that could be envisaged by computer scientists on Earth and therefore the process involved in reading, analysing, deciding, composing and sending could take place in a nanosecond or so. As a result, the Outpost's long and detailed reply to UNACC's message was on its way to Earth within less than a second of receiving it.

"Do you know Sherry Walker, Paul?" Katie said as the group sat around in the Cadogans' sitting room.

"We were on a panel once," Paul said, "at the AAAS. She seems bright, and no nonsense."

"A bit like our Katie," Miles said.

"Our Katie!" Katie said. "Do you mind? I'm nobody's Katie thank you very much."

As instructed, Katie had not shared the email with the group, but she was intensely curious about her 'co-conspirator', Sherry Walker, and knew that - secretly or with a fabricated excuse - she'd have to meet her if this apparent instruction from the Outpost was not a hoax.

"I've been thinking of starting to write a book about all this, a popular science book, maybe a mix of journalism and science. I read a good piece by Sherry Walker in the *New York Times*," she went on. "She has the right mix of scientific rigour and a popular approach."

'That's not a bad idea," Miles said. "There's bound to be a lot written about this whole affair, but you have an inside track. And with your unique palaeogenetics angle too."

"Look!" Leila said, drawing the group's attention to the TV screen. "There's an answer from the Outpost!"

There was a preliminary statement from the newsreader, saying that the text had been released in English on major websites - NASA, the BBC, gov.uk, and so on - and that it would be scrolled up the screen in a moment.

Immediately, each member of the group in the room looked for the text on their phones.

On television, a voice started to read the text:

> We will propose a series of technological solutions for each of the problems which affects the global descent towards an uninhabitable planet. These solutions will, necessarily, be nanotechnological in nature, building on expertise developed in our home planet. Clearly, as an unmanned - if you will pardon the word, we prefer 'unentitied' - space station, we would need an impracticable amount of time to build major space vehicles

capable of travelling to Earth and acting as laboratories and factories to solve the wide range of problems. Instead, we have designed a variety of nanotechnologies, similar to viruses, using ideas embodied in our language insertion devices which transformed *Homo erectus* into *Homo sapiens* and these will be sent to Earth once a timetable is decided...

By now, each of the group in the sitting room was ignoring the television and speed reading the printout of the full message.

Katie was scanning the text for what was promised in the email – her first name spelt out "in a sequence of words".

When she read "...keeping a technology in existence for the necessary duration will require supranational harmony, ensuring real responsibilities yet adaptable to future developments..." she knew her email from the Outpost was genuine, and that Sherry Walker was her collaborator.

The newsreader was approaching the end of the message:

We have another condition for our assistance. We find your reply alarmingly short of detail when it comes to a total acceptance, across all nations, of our offer of aid. We are beginning to understand the ways in which Earth politics can affect the survival of a civilisation composed of a variety of competing interests. Our own civilisation went through a period when a series of wars almost destroyed our planet, and it was only with great effort that a planetary government emerged which set aside national differences and devised what you would call 'eugenic' methods to ensure that all future members of our species would emerge with an absolute inability to do anything which would deliberately destroy another member of our species. While we would not propose such a solution to your global problems, which are in any case unconnected directly with your propensity to wage war on each other, we see signs of decision-making on Earth being driven by excessive self-interest.

Your own 'United Nations' seems anything but united, judging by your reply to our message, and by what we know through a hundred years of observation of your society. Before we start an intensive aid program we will need some assurance that there will be leaders who put global interest above national interests and some body which genuinely acts on behalf of all nations without the kind of veto powers that your own so-called Security Council has. To help give us this reassurance, we have identified individuals who will advise us as we consider the communications of whichever body you create to handle the important events of the next decade or so. Those individuals will be charged, by us, with advising us whether to accept or reject the Earth's response to our proposals, and whether there are stipulations we could make to increase the likelihood of any solutions we propose being accepted unconditionally.

"That's extraordinary," Paul said. "If they have the superhuman abilities they suggest, why would they need any advice from anyone on

Earth? Surely they can see through any political manoeuvrings that might get in the way of dealing with global problems?"

Katie thought about how to answer Paul's point without seeming too well-informed.

"Well, who knows?" she said, "Maybe they are prisoners of logic, of rationality. Sometimes *I* can't believe how stupid world leaders are or even the people who elect them. Things happen that we can't anticipate – Trump, Johnson, Putin – that have huge effects on the world, but are hardly the result of rational processes. Perhaps the Outpost hasn't built the irrational into its AI systems, because by any sane assessment of how to behave, the irrational should have been evolved out of humanity, and maybe will be one day."

"That's very pessimistic," Miles said. "Do you really think that national leaders will put their own nations' interests ahead of global needs? Hold on," he went on. 'I hear what I just said. Of course, you're probably right, Katie. But I don't envy whoever the Outpost choose as their advisers. They'll hold a lot of power. I hope they're up to it."

"So do I," said Katie, with feeling, and she was glad when her phone rang.

She looked at the screen and saw "Number withheld."

When Katie listened, the voice said "'Supranational harmony ensuring real responsibility yet' here. Is that 'Keeping a technology in existence'?"

"Just a moment," Katie said, her mind racing, "I just need to check my diary."

She left the room, went out of the front door of the Master's Lodge and walked across the court to a passageway that led towards the river. It was deserted.

"Hi," she said. "This is Katie. Is that Sherry?"

"Look," Sherry said, without preamble, "I haven't decided to help yet. I wanted to talk to you first. I thought your piece in the supplement was very good. Who'd have thought the Outpost read the *Guardian*?"

"Should we be talking like this" Katie said. "You know, because of phone-tapping…?"

"You're right. So the next question is, your place or mine?"

"Where is your place?"

"Washington DC. And for logistical reasons, if you can come here it would suit me better. I have a department to run which is red hot at the moment."

"Do you mean come to the US?"

"Difficult to get here without it."

"Let me think about it. Can you text me your number?"

"Sure, Katie. It's good to know you."

The call ended.

Katie walked back to the Lodge. Miles was addressing the group as she went back into the sitting room.

"It's a bit of an anti-climax really," he was saying. "We made all the running in revealing the original message. Now, we just sit on our hands and let the world leaders get on with it."

"I'm sure our dear prime minister will continue to want your advice, Miles. And Paul's," Leila said. "And meanwhile, you can get on with your own work."

"You know it's odd," Miles said. "Somehow, working through the evolution of matriarchy in three generations of Trobriand Islanders seems rather pointless when a quick word with the Outpost will tell me all I need to know about the history of any human society…"

"Hi, Katie. Everything OK?" Leila said.

"Yes. Just an MOT reminder," she said, knowing that she was going to have to tell a lot of white lies in the next few weeks and months.

Not surprisingly, a big topic of discussion, once the answer from the Outpost had been digested, was the extraordinary statement that individuals had been selected as a conduit of communication between Earth and the Outpost, and that these individuals, whoever they were, would have the final say in discussions about how the nations of the globe related and responded to the Outpost.

"We can find these people, right?" President Billing said to Tonk Wilbraham.

"We can find these people, right?" Prime Minister Baxter said to Quentin Stewart.

"Мы можем найти этих людей, верно?" President Pavolv said to Sergei Gromov.

But it soon became apparent that they couldn't. No one even had an idea of what sort of person it would be. How many of them? What nationalities? What criteria would the Outpost have used to choose these all important go-betweens?

The media of course abhorred the vacuum.

The *Daily Mail* said it had it from a very good source that one of the Go-betweens was the Duchess of Sussex, and even mocked up a possible memo sent by her to the Outpost.

The New York Daily Post said one of them was almost certainly Donald Trump, whose whole campaign and presidency had been controlled by the Outpost, which suggested to some that the Outpost had failed to study how US presidents were supposed to behave.

Pravda let it be known that one of the Go-betweens was an orthodox priest with a long beard who lived in Krasnoyarsk, and the large Orthodox cross on his roof was really a communications antenna.

But the Outpost had made sure that the identities of Katie and Sherry were protected.

One important thing about codebreaking is that you need to know something about the people whose message you are trying to decrypt. Where are they? What communication system are they using? Even if they communicate 'in clear' you need to know what kind of content their messages might contain so that it's easy to carry out an automated search. The problem with trying to find messages which might be sent between the Go-betweens and the Outpost was that everybody in the world – every media outlet, every journalist, every email writer, really – was discussing the momentous events of the recent days. Some were even writing the sort of messages they thought should be sent to the Outpost. Attempts made by intelligence services in the US, Russia, China, and the UK, to use AI to trawl electronic communications threw up thousands of suspects based on keywords and concepts which, it was hypothesised, would be in messages exchanged between the secret Go-betweens and between them and the Outpost.

A further problem was that the world's intelligence services started searching as soon as the latest message was received from the Outpost, which explained the use of the Go-betweens and the reasons for this decision. But in fact, Katie and Sherry made no attempt to communicate with the Outpost and received no message from it for three weeks. For a week after the Outpost's reply, SETI at NASA was inundated with media queries and Sherry's face became very familiar on the world's TV screens. Of course, she was frequently asked if she knew or suspected who the Go-betweens might be and she had to claim ignorance.

At one meeting at the NSA, to which Sherry had been invited to help draw up a list of potential candidates, she could barely conceal her amusement at some of the suggestions. But as the meeting ground on and on, in the face of increasing exasperation by the participants, senior figures from the intelligence community who were frustrated by a problem they couldn't begin to handle, Sherry burst out "Look the Outpost is cleverer than us! Why on earth do you think they wouldn't make it as difficult as possible to find out who they were communicating with? They don't want us to know?!"

There was a moment's silence after this, and Sherry wondered if she'd gone too far, and drawn suspicion on herself. But there were several nods around the table, by people agreeing with her.

The meeting was chaired by Bob Newberry who, in order to come to some conclusion, said "Let's spend the last half hour drawing up a profile of the sort of person who might have been chosen. Nationality, qualifications, social class, connections…"

As the meeting wound up, Sherry looked at her notes of the last half hour, where she had written people's suggestions: "Chinese, linguist/ anthropologist, expatriate (free from Chinese Government control)", "Brit, GCHQ, science graduate, supportive of environmental movement," and, weirdly, "Pacific Islander, perhaps political leader, follows indigenous religion, uses native language."

These suggestions seemed born of desperation, seeking perhaps someone as far as possible from the conventional perception of a global politician. The reason for seeking to cast the net so widely was put well by Ted Anderson, the US representative at the UN.

"If they've seen what a shit show every Security Council meeting turns into when it tries to do something useful, why would the aliens go anywhere near a conventional global structure set up to deal with their offer of aid? They know the urgency of the situation better than we do. They clearly want to do it with some level of genuine collaboration from us, and this is the way they suggested of bypassing the fossilised procedures we use. I actually don't see much point in trying to find out who they've picked. What would we do if we find them? We'll find out when they want us to know. If they want us to know

"But surely," Newberry said, "you'd want to have some say in how these Go-betweens communicate with the Outpost? And in what they say to it?"

"We might want to," Anderson said, "but then we'd be back in a situation where we were trying to do something they don't want."

When Sherry got home after the inconclusive meeting at the NSA, she sat on her own on her deck with a glass of wine.

So much had happened since she got the email from the Outpost that she hadn't had time to catch her breath. She wondered how she would keep the secret of the role she and Katie had been chosen to play and for how long. And what was Katie like? Sherry wondered how they would get on? Would they agree on whatever tasks faced them in the next months or even years? How would they communicate with each without being monitored by the world's security agencies? And how would they communicate with the Outpost?

Sherry had read Katie's contribution to the supplement, of course, and was impressed by her discoveries about how language might have been genetically engineered by the Outpost. She also tried to read some of Katie's more technical papers, and understood enough to know that she seemed a very good scientist. 'Maybe after all this is over,' Sherry thought, 'I can pick her brains about our exobiology program, to look at what lifeforms might be possible with non-carbon-based molecules.'

They had decided in a deliberately innocuous email exchange, to wait at least a week before deciding on the next step. Katie was all for meeting straight away but Sherry knew she was going to be busy and anyway they both needed to think through some of the questions that must be answered or at least considered before they met.

That week was up in two days' time, and Sherry made a decision. She drained a glass of Shiraz to the last drop, got up from her comfortable chair, and went indoors to bed.

The following morning, before going to work, Sherry sent an email to Katie:

SUBJECT: DISCOVERY OF BONES

Message: A friend of mine at the University of Maryland has been digging in Pig Park, near Lothian, and has made some interesting discoveries of prehistoric human bones. It seems like the sort of thing you might be interested in. I'd be happy to show you around.

Sherry Walker

As she walked into her office an hour later, Sherry said to Mary Onofrio, "It's been a pretty hectic week or so. I'm going to take a break from the day after tomorrow for a couple of days. I have an archaeologist friend coming to visit so we'll tour around. Can you talk to people and draw up a list of urgent decisions before I leave?"

Chapter 17

It was unfortunate that Telesforo Dessança was trying out his new telescope in the garden of his house in Acton, in West London, at a time when a man in the next door house, a keen follower of the Tau Ceti saga, overheard Telesforo showing his son, Joanes, a view of the Orion nebula and explaining what it was.

The neighbour, Robbie Matching, had been fascinated by the story of the secret Go-betweens, and said to his wife, Desirée, "I wonder who they are. It could be literally anybody. Even our next door neighbour."

Robbie already had his suspicions of Telesforo, who had moved in only a month ago and had been heard to speak to his wife in a foreign language, although when the two men exchanged words over the garden fence, Telesforo's English was almost faultless.

"Almost too perfect," Robbie said to Desirée, after this conversation.

Robbie had several books on alien abductions, and when the Message was first publicised he formed the idea that there might be reverse abductions, when aliens infiltrated themselves into the population instead of taking people out. If the Outpost was actually in the region of Saturn it would be easy for them - he thought - to send people down to Earth, and of course they would speak perfect English, as well as their own language.

The day after their first conversation, a Saturday, Robbie hovered near the window that looked onto the street so as to 'accidentally on purpose' bump into Telesforo who he hoped would leave the house some time in the morning. He was lucky. Telesforo needed to take Joanes to get some new trainers, and as the two of them opened the garden gate, Robbie came bounding out with some garden shears in his hand.

"Good morning, neighbour!" he said cheerily.

"Good morning to you," Telesforo said. "Esan 'Good morning' gizonari," he told Joanes.

"Goo' moan," the boy said, doing his best.

"Just moved to England?" Robbie said.

"Yes. We came a month ago, and then rented this house."

"From where?" Robbie said, and then added, "You came?" He then realised that he sounded like a foreigner.

"From Spain," Telesforo said. This was literally correct, although he was Basque and supported the independence movement. But it was often too complicated to explain the situation, particularly to the sort of insular British people he met all the time.

"Oh, nice," Robbie said, and clicked his fingers over his head to mimic castanets, a gesture that just puzzled Telesforo.

Desirée taught Modern Languages at a local comprehensive, and the following night, when Robbie heard Telesforo and Joanes talking in the garden, after he came back from putting out the wheelie bin about 9 p.m., he went back into the house and asked Desirée to come out and tell him what language they were speaking.

"He said he was from Spain," Robbie said. "Tell me if he is speaking Spanish.

Telesforo had moved to London to be the first manager of the Basque Tourist Office in the UK, in Camden Town, as part of an attempt by the Basque region to counteract the image of the Basque people as terrorists. At home in the town of Getxo, Telesforo and his wife Pilar spoke Basque together and brought up their son to take pride in his culture and language. As an amateur astronomer, Telesforo was spoiled by the clear skies of the Pyrenees but because he was particularly interested in the moon, he decided to bring his telescope to the UK. Even though the stars, galaxies and planets were likely to be visible less often, if the sky was clear at all you could always see the moon.

The night when he was overheard by Robbie and Desirée, the sky was particularly clear, for London anyway, and because Joanes was at an age where he had started to take an interest in space and stars, Telesforo decided to set up the telescope in the garden.

"Ikus dezakezu," Telesforo said to his son, "Bola borobil handi bat bezalakoa da…"

"Baina laua dirudi, aita," the boy said.

Robbie and Desirée were crouching behind the wall, trying to hear the conversation.

"Do you recognise the language?" Robbie whispered. Desirée shook her head.

Telesforo looked through the finder of the telescope to point it to the right area of sky, and then made small adjustments to bring the moon into the field of view.

Joanes gasped as he saw the craters along the line dividing the lit area of the moon from the part in shadow. There was more conversation in Basque, which Desirée failed to recognise.

The two of them went back into the house and sat at the kitchen table.

"It's definitely not Spanish," Desirée said.

"This is serious," Robbie said. "They are not who they say they are. Weird language, perfect English, and now a device they are pointing at the sky…"

"Isn't it a telescope?" Desirée said.

"Telescope! Who ever saw a telescope where you looked into the side of it. It must be some kind of communication device." (Robbie had never seen a reflector telescope in use.)

"And that torch with a red light, and the way he was shining it on some kind of chart."

Nor had Robbie understood that when you are looking at a star atlas in the dark, red light would be easier on the eyes and allow you to look back into the eyepiece without being dazzled.

"We could tip off the *Daily Mail*. They pay for this sort of thing."

Desirée had given up trying to persuade Robbie that some of the conspiracies he believed in were unlikely to be true. She had even got secretly vaccinated against Covid a few years ago rather than risk his wrath.

Two days later, the pavement outside the neighbouring houses of the Dessanças and the Matchings was lined with photographers, reporters and TV cameramen, eager to get a glimpse of the first Go-between to be identified.

The next putative Go-betweens were two deaf brothers in Uttar Pradesh, whose signing to each other - based on a sign language they had devised for themselves - was taken as hand signals to the Outpost, observed, some believed, through extremely powerful telescopes from Saturn. Day after day, crowds assembled outside the small house the brothers shared with their parents in the village of Titarwara Khurd, watching every exchange between the brothers themselves, and between them and their parents. Reporters made notes of the gestures and got 'experts' to interpret them. One day, when the village experienced a huge, torrential rainstorm after several weeks of drought, one of these 'experts' looked though the notes of the previous day's signs and pointed out how the storm had been caused by the Outpost after instructions from the brothers. In the following days, gifts were piled up outside the family's hut, with notes requesting various other favours for the brothers to request.

Slightly more plausibly, an Australian, Barry Flice, in Derby on the north coast of Australia, attracted a lot of attention. He lived on his own after his wife ran away with a member of the MalakMalak tribe, and he was a passionate amateur astronomer as well as having an impressive radio aerial outside his single story home. He was often outside at night, looking though his telescope at deep-sky objects from Messier's catalogue of 110 galaxies and nebulae, trying to tick off every one of them; at other times adjusting the tall aerial to get the best reception on his ham radio. These activities attracted the attention of his neighbours, Marge and Cecily Banting, once the news broke of the existence of the Go-betweens. What made it even more likely - at least to the Bantings - that he was one of the Go-betweens was that he drove an old Saturn car, called a Saturn Outlook. The last Saturn car rolled off the General Motors assembly line in 2009, so clearly, since 2009, Flice had been in cahoots with the Outpost and its 'inhabitants', and was now regularly communicating with them. So enamoured was Flice with the attention - journalists would drive seventeen hours from Darwin to interview him - that he never denied a role as a Go-between, but dropped heavy hints about the sorts of things the Outpost might be asking him, and the sorts of answers he might be giving.

Katie had set off for Heathrow at 5 a.m. from a still-dark Cambridge and the overcast sky was barely light when the taxi driver took her bag out of the cab's boot and pulled up the handle for her.

"Have a nice time," the driver said "Don't break a leg skiing"

After the hectic few weeks Katie had had, no one had been really surprised that she needed a holiday. She hadn't skied for years but she used to enjoy it, so it wasn't an unusual choice to make.

Katie had never been able to get over the feeling that, when you go on a plane trip, the weather at the other end would be the same as it was when you left. And the fact that her body was telling her it was 6 p.m. on a late February evening made the bright sunshine seem even weirder when she arrived in the US and was met in the baggage claim by Sherry.

The two women chatted brightly and inconsequentially in the car trip from Dulles airport to a nice hotel Sherry had booked in the Chesapeake Bay. It wasn't that far from the archaeological site they had no intention of visiting, and Sherry suspected that the combination of food, drink, pretty views, spa, and – most important – a lot of meaty scientific, societal and political issues would keep them entirely occupied.

"I've booked a table for dinner. Do you think you can stay awake?"

"I've only been to the US three or four times," Katie said, "but I usually find I can stay up on the first night but the following couple of days are the worst."

"Okay" Sherry said. "I can tell you what I have planned for us, over dinner."

"Do I get to see NASA?"

"Do you know, I'd rather not? I've told people I've got an archaeologist friend visiting but someone might make the connection between my friend and the woman who wrote that brilliant piece in the supplement."

"Okay. I agree we have to do our best to keep the whole business secret for now."

Sherry dropped Katie and her bag under the hotel canopy and then went and parked in the car park.

After the women had checked in, Sherry said "Knock on my door – 211 – when you feel like a tea or a drink."

Sherry had handwritten a list of questions to start their discussions. She had decided not to type anything on any of her computers about the tasks they faced. Now, with a glass of iced tea, she put her feet up with the paper on her lap and the TV on CNN with the sound low in the background. As she read through her notes she thought she heard the word 'Go-betweens' on the TV, and she turned the sound up:

NEWSREADER: So far, the subcommittee set up by UNACC after the Reply was received has narrowed down the hundreds of claims from people saying that they are 'Go-betweens' to 17 who have at least a degree of plausibility. Our science correspondent Tom Wade has this:

WADE: Since the reply was received from the Outpost a week ago carrying the shock announcement that the civilisation represented by the Outpost did not want to deal initially with the Global Committee but would instead deal with people it had nominated, there has been a race to identify who these individuals might be. Of course, whoever they are, it is in their interest and that of the Outpost to keep the names secret – that's the whole point. But that hasn't stopped scores of individuals from around the world coming forward to announce that they are the Go-betweens. Of course, the question arises, why on earth would these people, chosen as intermediaries between the global community and the Outpost, reveal their identity? Surely they are all just hoaxers and attention seekers. I put this question to Sergei Gromov, Chair of UNACC:

GROMOV: Whatever the Outpost offers to help us deal with world's problems must be carefully considered by the global community, through UN committee that was set up for the purpose. The idea that there might be – do you say 'freebooters'? – with power to say what they like to Outpost and be treated as presenting the collective wisdom of the nations of the world is one we just can't have. I'm not saying that it's bad idea to have one channel of communication between Earth and Outpost, but surely no individuals can have wisdom and knowledge to make all the decisions the world needs in this vitally important situation.

WADE: But I understand that you have set up a subcommittee to go through the names of all the people who have come forward claiming to be Go-betweens. Surely, the real Go-betweens will be preserving total secrecy, rather than revealing themselves?

GROMOV: The situation is so important that, as we say in Russia, we must leave no eggs uncracked. Who knows? Maybe one of these people has been chosen as Go-between and has decided he or she doesn't want to be. If that's the case, they may have been communicating with the Outpost over the last week and can give us some idea of the Outpost's thinking.

WADE: (to camera) It seems to me that is clutching at straws. The wind has been taken out of the nations' leaders' sails by this Go-between stipulation and until there are further communications from the Outpost UNACC has nothing to do.

NEWS READER: Thank you Tom. Now to other news...

Sherry turned the TV sound down, and made a note in the margin of her list of questions. "Deflect attention with decoy?"

At about 5.30, Katie came in to Sherry's sitting room, rubbing her eyes.

"I just closed my eyes for a few minutes," she said. "I shouldn't have slept so long but I couldn't help it. Now you can take me anywhere."

"How does the Dockside Canteen sound?" Sherry said.

"It sounds a bit like a restaurant," Katie replied.

"It does scallops," Sherry said, "I've been wanting someone to try it with."

Things had happened so fast that Katie hadn't even thought to ask if Sherry was married or in a relationship or divorced. She decided to leave that issue for now. It would probably emerge.

"Well, now you have someone," she said, with a bright smile.

There was a crescent moon low down on the western horizon as Sherry drove to the restaurant. The sky was darkening and the brighter stars were visible pinpricks against the prussian blue background.

Katie felt in an unreal state. Twenty-four hours before, she had been finishing some lab work and briefing her assistant, Rosie, about the various tasks to be done while she was away on a week's 'skiing holiday'.

"I'm going to try a total blackout on communication," Katie said. "I'm not going to answer emails or phone calls unless they seem really urgent. And I certainly don't want to have any more conversations with journalists about how the aliens managed to alter our genes to give us language."

Sherry parked the car, and the two women walked through a small shopping mall, with a McDonald's, a Whole Foods, a Kinko's and an unprepossessing shopfront labelled 'Dockside Cantina'.

"In my experience," Sherry said, "there is often an inverse relationship between the appearance of the restaurant and the quality of the food. Let's hope that's the case here. After you."

As she opened the door, Katie was assailed by a fragrant mixture of unfamiliar smells.

In the course of a meal of entirely unfamiliar – to Katie – courses, she discovered that Sherry wasn't married, had had a number of relationships (nature unspecified), adored her sister's children, and was a little overcome by the events of the last three months. She confided to Katie, "To be honest – and I already think I can be open with you – I sometimes think I've been whisked from a backwater to the biggest wave a surfer has ever ridden. When NASA set up its SETI section, funded by the government, for the cost of a couple of new tanks for the army, the high point of SETI was over. Carl Sagan was long dead, and there were very exciting things happening in other fields of astronomy. Dark matter, inflation, deep sky galaxy clusters – that's where the astronomy money went. New instruments like Hubble and ALMA and VLA and James Webb – they got the big bucks. Of course, we got some crumbs. We knew that if there ever was a signal from an intelligent civilisation it would be detected by one of those devices. But I'm not sure anyone within the Beltway believed there would be a signal."

"Beltway? Is that an astronomical concept? Like the Milky Way?"

Sherry laughed.

"It's a road that goes round DC, within which all the government movers and shakers can be found."

"Oh," Katie said, "a bit like the M25, I suppose, and yet I imagine a bit more glamorous."

"Your drinks," the waiter said, a young man called Clark according to his badge, and he put two wide glasses of something in front of the two of them.

"I have had a margarita before," Katie said, "at the Hilton in Cambridge. I'm hoping this is better."

"I'm pretty sure it will be," Sherry said. "The newspaper reviewer commented specifically on the Dockside's margaritas."

Somehow, the two women got through their meal without addressing the issue that was uppermost in their minds. But for Sherry, this was deliberate. She wanted Katie to have a good night's sleep and a clear head, though the second margarita she asked for – "this is delicious," she said – might make the latter a little unlikely.

As they got out of the car back at the hotel, they both looked up at the sky.

"Do you know where they are?" Sherry said.

Katie knew what she meant.

"You know, I have a friend in my college who is an astronomer and yet I don't think he has ever shown me in the sky where Tau Ceti is. Mind you, that's maybe because only about one night in ten do we get clear skies in Cambridge."

"Well," Sherry said, "It's about there."

Sherry stretched her arm at about 50° above the horizon. "See those three stars making quite a bright triangle? Well, it's just below the bottom star of the triangle."

"Oh," said Katie. "How sweet! Hello little people..."

Sherry looked at Katie quizzically.

"How many margaritas did you have?"

"Only two," Katie said, yawning, "but I think they may have been quite strong."

"To bed with you, straight away," Sherry said as they walked into the Lobby. She guided Katie towards her room, and went next door to her own. "We need all your brainpower tomorrow. We have a lot to think about."

Katie was up at 6 a.m., unable to sleep any more. She read some instructions by a coffee machine and set it brewing. Then she went on to the balcony, with a mug in her hands, and looked out over the Chesapeake Bay, watching a large heron poke around in the reeds. It was still cool and Katie wrapped herself in the robe she found in the bathroom. Still in a daze of jetlag, she let her mind coast over yesterday's events and over the things Sherry had told her. Katie had no black friends in Britain, but had had a good friend at school, Sandra, who was Nigerian and they'd become very close.

But even on brief acquaintance, she found Sherry's 'black' was very different. Not the skin colour itself, of course, but the way in which – it appeared – life as a black woman in America shaped some of her ideas and attitudes. It was clear that, having arrived at a senior level job in a significant scientific field, she felt she had, in some sense, "put it to them", 'them' being people who, as she was growing up, had ignored her or her ambitions or just passed the voting laws which made it more difficult for black people to vote.

And now, even though they hadn't spoken much last night about the Go-between roles, it seemed as if Sherry thought she might have been chosen because she was black, or at least partly for that reason, a factor in her favour maybe.

Katie had wondered about something slightly different: why had two English speakers been chosen? Of course, it made sense to choose two people who speak the same language but why not two Russians or two Chinese?

"Morning!" Sherry said as she came on to the balcony next door, separated by a wicker screen. "They have croissants downstairs. Why don't you get yourself one and come and have pre-breakfast in my room. We can have more later in the restaurant."

After she had dressed, Katie went downstairs for more coffee and *two* croissants. She was feeling peckish. Then she went to Sherry's room, and the two women sat either side of a coffee table with laptops and notepads.

"I've made some notes," Sherry said, "My item 1 is how do we communicate, you and me?"

"Well, let's go through the issues. Who is going to be looking for the Go-betweens and what methods will they use?"

"It could be the security services of the entire world..."

"Okay, no pressure then."

"Emails will be searchable and text and phone calls if they have - and use - audio transcription software."

"But that means all emails, etc, between everyone in the world. The Outpost can do that sort of thing, we know that, but the CIA? MI6? FSB?" Katie said.

"Right. So they would have to narrow down the search. No Slovakian peasants in their villages, no Chinese barefoot doctors, no food stamp families in the suburbs of Detroit..." Sherry said.

"On the other hand, 'yes' to all of those precisely because they are unlikely and so could've been chosen."

"Well, I think we have to take a chance that email exchanges between two women scientists across the Atlantic will be lost in the huge amount of email traffic over this issue, so long as they don't have any specific reason for suspecting either of us."

"OK," Katie said. "I haven't any better ideas at the moment so I'll go with that. Now, I was wondering how we'll work with the Outpost? Do you have any ideas?"

"The first thing I thought," Sherry said, looking at her notes, "was that there is no need for the Outpost to communicate with us directly. There is only our first two emails, to you and me, and I think you should destroy yours if you haven't. Those are the only unambiguous emails that show we are Go-betweens. From now on, we are just two people discussing interesting scientific ideas triggered by the Message. If the Outpost detected my memo to Billings as well as your piece in the *Guardian*, they must be monitoring our communications. Surely we just need to send things to each other, and the Outpost will read them."

"And anything they want to say to us, they can say to the world?"

"That's right. Even if they want to comment on something we've said to them – "we disagree with item 3 on your list" – it won't make much sense to anyone else.

"So," Katie said, "The sequence goes: a message from the Outpost, sent by the usual method and decoded by those nice people at CIA or some other government organisation; we then email each other about how the world should reply, and then we agree a draft that just gets read by the Outpost as part of their monitoring."

"Right. How about some other issues? How much do you know about the kind of problem they're offering to solve and some of the solutions?"

"Only what I read in the main message."

"Well I've been doing some research, and I've compiled a file of global problems, the likely impact, and a kind of order of priority based on global need rather than how they affect each country. Presumably, the Outpost has chosen the Go-between method because they know that we will be honest brokers and not be swayed by arguments or vetoes by the big national players, even our own countries."

For the next couple of hours, Sherry talked Katie through the dossier of problems and made notes as Katie made observations or raised objections.

"You're pretty good at this stuff, even though…" Sherry said.

"Even though I'm not an astronomer or earth scientist?"

They both laughed.

"I meant even though you haven't got access to the sort of data I have," Sherry said. "Some of this has come from background papers for high-level meetings in Washington."

"When we get to the stage of suggesting things, or accepting or commenting on their suggestions, do we involve anyone else at all?" Katie said. "I mean it's a big responsibility, even if our recommendations are based on the best possible information we have about the environmental problems."

"Of course. Even if we don't reveal our identity, our ideas – after we've 'discussed' them with the Outpost – could be put to the world, maybe through UNACC, for their comments. It's just that we don't need their approval, only their comments in case we got something wrong."

"And how do we tell UNACC our ideas without revealing our identity?"

Sherry thought. "I've got it?!" she said. "We ask the Outpost to transmit our recommendations. 'We have been advised… etc, etc' Then everyone can read them and comment on them and we can take that into account before we make a final decision."

"Of course," Katie said, "that will work."

Chapter 18

Two days after Katie arrived in Maryland, the Outpost released its Master Plan to the world. It was not an easy read. It was headed "Summary of Proposals for a Cleansed Earth", and, when printed out, ran to a thousand closely-printed pages.

"Some summary," Jenny Billings said to herself as she flicked through the pages on her computer. Headings flashed past her eyes as she skimmed the document – "Atmosphere: molecular dispersion, ozone reduction, albedo, particulates, etc, etc. Water: desalination, temperature control, plastic elimination, marine biosphere readjustment, etc, etc. Surface renovation: forests, soil, reduction in urbanisation, volcano control, earthquake warnings,..." The list went on and on and whenever she dipped into one section, she found many closely printed pages of technical descriptions, usually way beyond her comprehension.

Katie and Sherry, too, rather balked at sitting down and reading it page by page. They knew that the UNACC members and their scientific secretariat would divide up the sections for different experts to consider and in the coming days there would be executive summaries which Sherry would receive from Kent Branton to keep her in the loop.

On the day before Katie left the US, the two women drove back to Washington, to Sherry's apartment. That evening, they sat round the dining table in Sherry's house, each with her own laptop, with the Master Plan on the screen, and discussed what to do next.

"It seems to me," Sherry said, "that they won't expect us to comment on the measures set out in the Master Plan. It's hardly likely that we would spot something they hadn't taken account of. The measures I can understand are astounding. Take this, for example. Go to page 371."

The section was headed "Nano-distillation of salt water," and Sherry read out:

> We propose to assemble and send to Earth millions of nano-devices which use electrodialysis and electrodialysis reversal to liberate the hydrogen and oxygen atoms from seawater to provide fresh water for humans. There are about 620,000 kilometres of coastline on Earth and we can send, in the space of a year, enough nano-devices to operate on water within a few metres of half of the coastlines, those areas which are not already occupied. It will require barriers to be built, like artificial reefs, to separate out the seawater to be processed from the main body of seawater, using the nano-devices. If this is done by local communities, the fresh water produced by the nano-dialysis devices will float on the concentrated residue underneath and can be pumped out for drinking purposes. When most of the seawater confined by the barriers has been divided into potable and non-potable volumes, the barriers can be opened to let in a new supply for more fresh water to be created...

"Now," Sherry said, "we can both understand that and, apart from one huge implausibility, we can see how that might be achieved. And it's the same with some of the other solutions I've read. The implausibility is always the manufacture and transportation of the devices, although maybe it's the other way round – the 'factory' is sent first and then the manufacturing takes place on Earth or in Earth orbit. But it's still a massive task – I nearly said superhuman but of course that's exactly what it is."

"That's right," Katie said, "I looked through their albedo-increasing technology, to reflect more sunlight from the Earth's atmosphere and reduce global warming, and the physics and chemistry seem fine – you'd expect that since we all live in the same universe – but the sheer amount of technology at a nano-level – devices and complex molecules floating in the stratosphere – is far beyond us to manufacture but that is what the Outpost is offering."

"So I suggest that our role as Go-betweens is to observe how the nations of the world respond to the Master Plan and help the Outpost overcome any political or psychological problems that might prevent the solutions being used."

"How do we do that?" Katie said.

"Well, I spoke to Kent Branton – as a member of his staff not as a Go-between, of course – and he's asked President Billings if we can have access to the confidential UNACC discussions. That will give us an insight into how ready different national leaders are to take up the offers in the Master Plan…"

"You don't sit about do you, Sherry? When did you make that call?"

"Well, you were having a nap – to deal with your jet lag, maybe…"

"Yes, well I think I've got over it now. But of course, I'll have it all over again when I get home tomorrow. God knows how I explain getting jet lag after a trip to Switzerland!"

The discussion of the Master Plan at UNACC was a stormy one. It seemed that few of the national delegates had read the whole document. They were all relying on Executive Summaries produced by their own scientific advisers, who were often imbued with a parochialism that meant they criticised and recommended non-acceptance of anything that might benefit the global environment at the expense of their own national well-being.

These were closed sessions, but Sherry had privileged access, and of course the Outpost knew every word of what was said and written. The transcript was larded with self-serving comments from different delegates: 'Perhaps clean up the oceans away from our coasts to avoid affecting our fishing industry.' (Or alternatively, 'clean our coastal waters first, to overcome our regular droughts'.) 'Of course, give us a new source of energy, maybe fusion, but not so soon that it bankrupts our oil companies.' 'We don't mind you tackling deforestation as long as you can give us a way to replace the profits for our logging companies.' And so on.

In a slightly guarded phone conversation once Katie was back in Cambridge. the two Go-betweens identified the main problem as the usual chauvinism that got in the way of so many important global decisions.

"Honestly, at the PTA meeting, everyone was arguing for their own child," Katie said, hoping that if anyone was listening they would not realise that she had no children. "We're not going to get anywhere in ... cleaning the asbestos out of the school roof if parents want someone else to pay for it."

"You'd think some of them, maybe the ones who had younger children, would realise that helping to pay for it now would benefit their other children at least, and their grandchildren."

"The trouble is," Katie said, "that there's no organisation above the PTA to make them toe the line."

Sherry was silent, thinking.

"What about finding a way to expel the dissenting nations - parents, I mean. Maybe if there are enough parents who support the - asbestos removal, did you say? - they could vote the others off the Committee."

"But then they'd complain that their own children were disadvantaged in some way."

They both felt a little uneasy - well, intimidated, really - to be discussing how to improve the take-up of the Outpost's offer among the world's leaders. Perhaps that wasn't the key issue at all. The early voting at UNACC might not mean anything.

The first day back in Cambridge after her 'skiing holiday' brought with it a series of small problems Katie should have anticipated. Although she had spent some time in the early spring sun in America, she didn't have the bronzed appearance her friends and colleagues expected.

"Not much of a tan, Katie," Miles Cadogan said as he passed her in First Court. "Après-ski all day?"

Paul Spearman just said "Had a good break, Katie?" without turning it into a joke about fractures.

She dragged herself out of bed the following day about 9 a.m., her body still on East Coast time. She and Sherry had decided to wait a week or two for another UNACC meeting to try to break the impasse, although both of them were pessimistic about the necessary unanimity ever being achieved.

They tried to take their roles seriously as Go-betweens. But there was no handbook for the task. The main change in Katie's behaviour was to read the newspapers assiduously, and try to monitor the broadcast media. With the removal of the threat of annihilation, the coverage of the Outpost and its offer to save the world from its own negligence was relegated to the pages that dealt with environmental matters, along with coverage of climate change deniers - who felt the news stories about the Outpost, whether the thing existed or not, were just another way for environmentalists to keep their alarmist rhetoric in front of the public.

Every new message from the Outpost was, of course, widely publicised. One message picked up by radio telescopes pointed in the direction of Saturn was headed "Question to Go-betweens". Of course, no one knew how to draw the attention of these mysterious Go-betweens to the message but since it was widely publicised, Katie and Sherry soon knew its contents.

The message said:

> Hey, Go-betweens, what's with these guys? Do they know what deep shit they are in? We can hand them solutions on a plate, and yet they are acting as if they can pick and choose what we are offering depending on how much their own countries will suffer. Are they even ready to receive our carefully prepared Master Plan or should we keep them dangling a few months, or even years, while everything goes to hell in a handbasket? I hope you like our attempts at colloquial speech.

The Outpost's attempt at a more relaxed language style than its previous messages wasn't entirely successful, Katie and Sherry thought, worried that its message wouldn't be taken seriously, or even that it might seem like a hoax from some Earthling. But for those who believed it, it had a double purpose. First, of course, it sought advice from the Go-betweens but, second, it told the members of UNACC - and the world - that their current approaches to the Outpost's offer of help fell far short of what the Outpost expected or was willing to respond to.

Katie and Sherry felt a huge weight of responsibility. This wasn't even a scientific question. It was more political or psychological. Of course they had both read UNACC's first reply, and, like the Outpost, they were appalled at the politicking that had already started among the various nations. In their next phone call, they discussed some options.

"How's the PTA?" Katie said when Sherry called her.

"I think we need to compile a list of questions to … the Governors," Sherry said. "For example, would they accept a majority vote rather than unanimity?"

"Seems unlikely," Katie said. "How do you … mend part of a roof? Some parents are just not convinced that the authorities can achieve what they are promising to do? Maybe they need some kind of demonstration?"

"You mean the way the US 'demonstrated' that they had the atom bomb by dropping it on Hiroshima and Nagasaki?"

"That sort of thing, yes, but with more benign results. It did end the war."

"There are some who would disagree about that," Sherry said, "Do you have something in mind?"

"Not yet, but I have a half-formed idea. Supposing the school had a pond and there were animals in the grounds that liked to drink from it, and the water got so polluted, salty perhaps, that the animals were in danger of dying of thirst, and someone came along who claimed that, in an instant, they could make it fresh, and then they did, that would be pretty impressive, wouldn't it?"

"Yee-ee-s," Sherry said, puzzled.

"So the lake, having been dead," she emphasised, "could be brought to life with fresh water."

There was a pause while Sherry tried to understand what Katie meant.

"Of course!" Sherry exclaimed. "That would be impressive."

They decided that Katie's idea might jog some of the more recalcitrant world leaders into line and lead to a more unanimous acceptance by the UNACC members of the help that was being offered.

Two days later, after a long and guarded phone conversation with Katie, Sherry left the office about five, and sat down at home to write a very important message to Katie that would be conveyed to – or intercepted by – the Outpost, and no one else, she hoped. It said the following:

> We believe that the difficulties with getting global approval for your Plan are partly political and partly to do with credibility. And the two can be linked – if a national leader sees political problems in putting his nation's future in your hands, he will cast doubt on the genuineness of the Outpost and its capacity to do what it promises. We think that a practical demonstration of what you can do for the Earth will make it much more difficult for those doubts to remain. Picking up on the 'Nano-desalination' section of your Master Plan, we would like to suggest the following, if you agree that it is practicable:...

She then set out a plan to desalinate the Dead Sea ('In for a penny...' she thought) so that people on either shore, Israelis and Arabs, could access limitless supplies of fresh water for their own uses, and show the rest of the world what the Outpost could do.

Known for its speedy replies, the Outpost responded within eight minutes, with a reply which was picked up by several radio telescopes.

> To the Go-Betweens:
>
> We have considered your suggestion carefully. It is certainly feasible. We could assemble a nano-factory specifically designed for the demonstration you suggest, and, using the 'slingshot effect' of our position in one of Saturn's rings, combined with nuclear fusion propulsion, the demonstration could take place in about a month's time, say March 20th?

Within an hour, President Billings was on the phone to Kent Branton.

"What the hell is going on, Kent?" she said. "What is this 'demonstration' they're talking about?"

Branton had to admit that he hadn't the foggiest.

"No doubt, they'll tell us when they're ready," he said, rather forlornly.

"How come these Go-betweens are communicating merrily with the aliens and we still don't know who they are?"

"We're on the case," Branton said weakly. "At least we're pretty sure they're English or American."

"I don't see how you can even say that. You don't have to be English to speak English. Maybe it's just that the Messengers would like their messages to be read by as large a number of people as possible."

"If that was the case, they'd have replied in Chinese," he said.

Billings then rang Bob Newberry.

"These Go-betweens must have made some proposal that the Outpost is replying to. Can't you track down their original message?"

"Madame President, we've had this discussion before." Newberry said. "Clever as we are, we can't spy on every single email that anyone sends to anyone else. And it's illegal, anyway. We can just collect metadata."

"Oh, my goodness, Bob, I'd forgotten that the NSA never does anything illegal."

"We did get a tip-off that one of the Go-betweens might be a pizza-maker in Dubuque. He's offering a 'Saturn pizza' with a half beefsteak tomato in the middle. Someone thought that a piece of pineapple on the edge might represent the Outpost."

There was a click as Jenny Billings put the phone down in a fit of anger. She turned to Rob Delmonico and Ted Anderson, the UN ambassador, who were sitting opposite her desk.

"They know *bubkis*," she said. "Now back to what we were talking about. How did this whole thing became political? I've told you, Ted, that we are willing to do anything – even at the US's expense – to move this thing along. If the Outpost is serious, this is the one chance for the world to solve a whole clutch of problems all at the same time, and yet, few of the other nations seem to see that. The UK, OK; the rest of Europe, lukewarm but OKish; then most of the others just keep holding back, putting objections, some of them contradictory, and each time there's an UNACC vote there's little change in the numbers."

"Some of the leaders might be susceptible to bribery," Anderson said.

"I'm not against that," Billings said. "It's been done before – not in my presidency," she added, "but I can see the value sometimes. But it would go against the grain to bribe someone to do something that's for their own country's benefit in the long run."

"Don't you ever bribe Samantha to do things for her own good?" Delmonico said.

"Funnily enough, no," Billings said. "Harrison tries to do it all the time, and I can't always stop him. But anyway, the numbers are too great. This thing is so important that we can't save the world with a simple majority. It's got to be unanimous or nearly."

Back in Cambridge, Katie was pleased and a little overawed at the speed with which an idea she had had, and Sherry approved of, had become accepted by the Outpost. Things were moving to a whole new level. Their job as Go-betweens seemed to be producing results. But now they would have to wait a month for any new developments, a month during which endless discussions would take place at UNACC, with no likelihood of any major change in voting figures.

But if course, Katie had her research, and Sherry had the running of SETI to think about, so, after another guarded phone call they decided to set aside Go-between business and go back to their 'day jobs.'

The next message from the Outpost arrived, unexpected, on February 28th. It was headed "TO THE WORLD" and it said:

> This is to forewarn you that we will be conducting a demonstration somewhere on Earth on March 20th. The evidence of its effectiveness should be clear by noon on the following day. The purpose of this demonstration will be to show that we can deliver what we promise, by revealing how our advanced technology can fix some of the Earth's problems with an efficiency and speed which is far beyond your capabilities. We do not propose to tell you where this demonstration will take place. It will not involve any harm to the biosphere and so there will be no need for people to be afraid. Its results will be apparent soon enough and we hope that they will help to resolve some of the doubts that seem to be getting in the way of humanity making a unanimous decision among your nations to accept our help.

Of course, this message triggered huge amounts of speculation, rumour and fake news. Since no one – apart from Kate and Sherry – had the faintest idea what the 'demonstration' might involve and where it would occur, ideas ranged from the realistic to the wildly improbable. Some people thought that the Earth would be encased in some kind of giant screen or filter which sucked carbon dioxide out of the air and shot it into space. Others, more reasonably, guessed that the atmosphere would be seeded with trillions of tiny reflective particles to bounce sunlight away from the atmosphere. Then there were those who suggested that in some way the Outpost would install some localised temperature-lowering system over the Poles to reverse the warming of the ice caps, which would then have a knock on effect on the rest of the climate.

The massed armies of clairvoyants and psychics which arise on these occasions gave a number of definite predictions, all of them mutually contradictory. Something would definitely happen in Death Valley, California, the hottest place on earth, or the Mindanao Trench, the deepest part of the ocean. One psychic was sure that whatever it was would happen near the village of Parsley Hay in Staffordshire in the UK, where a large number of ley lines were said to cross; another said she was sure it would be somewhere in the Tokyo-Yokahama conurbation in Japan, the site of the largest agglomeration of people on Earth. Her prediction was that all 40 million inhabitants would be taken up into a fleet of spaceships and cured of every ailment they might have now or be susceptible to in the future, before being returned unscathed.

UNACC, which had been moribund after a series of inconclusive votes, now had something new to talk about, and discussion raged over several days about whether to sit back and await the demonstration or make every effort to anticipate and prevent it in case the Outpost was lying in whatever passed for its teeth and was really planning to annihilate humanity, as originally set out in the (fake) first Message.

Sergei Gromov, as chair of UNACC, suddenly saw the advantage to his country of reviving the idea of mobilising the Papirosi space defence system, to monitor whatever the Outpost did to make sure it really was benign, and he argued strongly for this. But China also had a satellite surveillance and attack system, Distant Water, which could be adapted, for 270 billion dollars or so collected from other UNACC members, to look out for, and – if necessary – deal decisively with, any conceivable Outpost technology aimed at the Earth. That argument raged for several days, dividing the members of UNACC into three groups – pro-Russian, pro-Chinese, and pro-sitting on their hands. Once again, the result of the voting was nowhere near the unanimity required by the Outpost.

In early March, Katie was queuing at the cashier's in Sainsbury's when Leila Cadogan came up behind her.

Katie always enjoyed talking to Leila, though it usually seemed to be in some gathering with her husband and others. On an impulse, she said "Coffee?"

Leila looked at the time. "Sure," she said.

"Shall we go to St Michael's café?"

They hadn't really had a relaxed conversation since the frantic few days finalising the *Guardian* supplement. After they'd collected their coffees and sat down, Leila talked about her relief and, in particular, about how it lifted the emotional obstacle it had created to the idea of her and Miles starting a family.

"I hope you don't mind me sharing this. That's not too much information?" she said.

"Of course not," Katie said, "Though don't ask me for child-rearing tips. I haven't taken the plunge yet."

"No, it's OK," Leila said. "It's just that I don't have many close women friends. Dee is nice but she's a bit forbidding. And other fellows are older than Miles, with older wives."

As they chatted, Leila mentioned that she was planning a trip on her own to see her mother in Jerusalem. She had been much affected by the annihilation threat and Leila hadn't seen her since the fakery of the Message was revealed.

Katie asked when Leila was going, and realised that it was exactly at the time the Outpost had suggested for the demonstration. The idea of actually witnessing it – if it happened – hadn't occurred to her before but now she saw an opportunity.

"You know, I've always wanted to go to ..." She hesitated, trying to choose the right word. "...Palestine," she said. "Maybe I could go with you – well, not with you, but at the same time. Would you mind if I did that? We could travel together but of course I wouldn't need to be with you all the time."

Leila's face lit up.

"Of course!" she said. "That would be lovely. You could meet my mum, and my aunties, and I could show you round."

"Don't worry about that," Katie said. "I'll just need a few hints for how to get around. To places like the Dead Sea..."

"That might take up half a day," Leila said. "There are many more interesting places I could tell you about."

Two weeks later, after an overnight flight to Ben Gurion airport, Katie checked into the Al-Quds Hotel, recommended by Leila as a good place to stay if you are on a budget. Katie would have preferred somewhere more luxurious for such a momentous occasion, but she didn't want to draw attention to her real motive for coming to the area.

In fact, the place was OK. It was in an old Arab mansion overlooking the bus station. "Easy for you to start your travels," Leila said.

Although they were at Katie's hotel by 7 a.m. after the ridiculously early arrival of her overnight flight, and no sleep, the nice Arab woman at reception said to Leila that if her guest wanted to have some breakfast in the hotel restaurant, they would get her room ready as early as possible.

"Have some breakfast with me?" Katie said to Leila.

"Thank you, but my mum is dying to see me, and I her, of course. I've kept the taxi waiting to take me to her in Sheikh Jarrah. I asked the woman at reception – she's called Hanan – to give you some brochures. You might like to walk on the walls of Jerusalem to get a feel for the city. I hope you'll come to supper with us this evening. I'll come and pick you up."

Although she'd never been before to this part of the Middle East, Katie had difficulty summing up any enthusiasm for sightseeing. Until 'the Demonstration' happened – or didn't – she would feel on edge. For the first time she would be faced with the possibility of some hard proof, not only of the existence of an alien civilization hanging around in the solar system but also of their abilities. This would entirely rule out the slim possibility that, all along, the communications from 'the Outpost' had some terrestrial origin.

In the hotel's restaurant, which was in a large permanent marquee in front of the hotel, Katie had helped herself to some breakfast from a simple buffet: hummus, Arab bread, boiled eggs, cheese, ham.

Katie looked around the marquee at the dozen or so people having breakfast. Two backpackers, a young man and woman, both wearing very short shorts. 'That won't go down very well in the Old City,' Katie thought. An elderly English couple, the man with grey hair and rimless spectacles and wearing a clerical collar, the woman with a smiley, wrinkled face and her hair in a bun. They were both wearing sandals, and there was a rucksack hanging on the chair. She heard the man say 'Shukrun' to the waiter, the Arabic for thank you, with a distinctly unArabic accent. Three youngish Arabs drinking Turkish coffee were comparing notes on an open laptop. A professorial older Arab was inspecting his mobile phone.

'Who are these people?' she thought, 'and how will they react tomorrow when they learn that they were within a few miles of a pretty momentous event?' Perhaps, like her, they were even planning a trip to the Dead Sea tomorrow. She felt a jolt, a small twinge of fear, as she thought about what the Outpost would actually do. Who knows? She knew nothing about how the demonstration would work, other than it would be some unique and technologically far advanced form of desalination. Would it - could it - be restricted to the water itself? Or might the process spill over on to the land and the people around it in some way?

A polite man with a curly moustache brought her a pot of coffee, and while she was eating, Hanan from reception brought her a small pile of tourist leaflets.

"*Sahtein,*" the woman said, and Katie looked puzzled.

"Enjoy your food, it mean," she said. "Your room will be ready in an hour."

The room had stone walls and a high ceiling, with a window that overlooked the open area where buses arrived and departed, with a distant view of a minaret. Once she had unpacked a small bag of her belongings, and had a shower, Katie set off, map in hand, to find the Damascus Gate and the steps up to the city walls. She was accosted from time to time by little boys selling chewing gum or an elderly man offering - very politely - to be her guide.

Her walk round the walls was interesting - she was able to pick out from the map the Church of the Holy Sepulchre and the Dome of the Rock - but her heart wasn't in it. She was not the sightseeing type, at least not for touristy places, and anyway, her mind was too full of other things. For this reason, she was also rather dreading the meal with Leila's family, though, of course, she couldn't say 'no' to the invitation.

On the way back to the hotel she passed an English bookshop and saw that it had a cafe too. She bought a book about the Dead Sea, with a good map, and a ordered a cup of cappuccino before climbing the stairs to a small area on the mezzanine, where there were chairs and tables. She sat down and flicked through the book, noting that there were various places down the west side of the Dead Sea where it might be possible to sit at 2 p.m. the following day, which would be 12 noon GMT. There was a hotel in the southern part, quite a distance from Jerusalem, but she thought a glamping resort on the northern edge might have a café, or even somewhere to sit and eat an ice cream.

The book contained some facts about the geology and hydrology of the Sea, really a lake, and she wondered how on earth such a high concentration of salts and minerals could possibly be transformed in a way, and on a timescale, that would convince the world of the power of the Outpost.

Leila called for Katie at about six.

"Got some comfortable shoes?" she said. "We can walk to my mum's in about twenty minutes. You'll get more of an impression of the place."

As they walked, Leila explained how her family had lived in East Jerusalem for two centuries, but were now worried about the Israeli policy of evicting Palestinians to give their homes to Jewish residents.

"But that's outrageous!" Katie said, and Leila gently explained some of the realities of life for Palestinians living in Israel.

After they had crossed several dusty, rubble-strewn roads, and penetrated an area of narrow streets with a jumble of two- and three-story stone houses, Leila pushed open a faded green-painted iron gate into a small courtyard. Three children were playing with a mangy cat, and an elderly man was sitting smoking on an old wooden dining chair.

"He is my *jiddi* – my grandfather," Leila said to Katie in a low voice. "He's blind."

She went up to him, took his hand and kissed him on the cheek. His face lit up and he lifted his head.

"*Ahlan, ahlan, habibti*," he said.

An hour later, after meeting a bewildering number of Leila's relatives, some of whom just popped in to greet Leila after her long absence, Katie sat down to supper, presided over by Leila's mother, known as 'Umm Hasib' – mother of Hasib, Leila's brother. He was there too with his wife, a shy young woman with dark eyes and eyebrows and a pale skin. It was their children who were playing in the yard. Leila's grandfather came in too, and Katie watched with fascination as he moved around the house effortlessly, avoiding obstacles, finding his chair, and using a knife and fork to eat as effectively as a sighted person.

Katie was plied with food by Umm Hasib, who made her taste a little from a dozen or so dishes covering the surface of the table. She spoke no English and would occasionally look at Katie and turn to Leila to ask a question in Arabic.

"She says you are very pretty but too thin," Leila said. "That's why she keeps pressing you to eat more."

Then Umm Hasib said something to Leila which made the others look at Katie and laugh.

"What did she say?" Katie asked Leila.

"It was nothing," Leila said.

Katie was now worried and a bit irritated.

"It can't have been nothing. Why did everyone laugh?"

Leila sighed.

"She asked if you were married and when I told her 'no' she said she had just the man for you, my uncle Farid."

"So why did they laugh?"

"I show you," said Hasib, who understood some English.

He stood up, went over to a dresser and picked up a framed photo which he brought to Katie. It showed a portly man in his fifties, wearing a fez, in a three piece suit. He was holding a musical instrument, an 'oud, a bit like a mandolin.

"My mother is the oldest of twelve children," Leila said, "and Uncle Farid is the youngest. He composes music for films and television, and plays the 'oud in cafes and at weddings and so on."

Her mother said something else in Arabic.

"She says that you would not need to work if you married him, because he makes good money. You would just need to produce children."

Katie's mind raced. What could she say to this sweet woman that wouldn't upset her? She turned to Leila, and said quietly "I don't want to be rude but..."

"It's OK," Leila said. "Leave it to me.

She explained something to her mother in Arabic, and the woman looked at Katie with a sad expression.

"*Maskeena*," she said. 'Poor one.'

"I told her that the doctors had discovered that you can't have children," Leila said. "That was enough to put the idea out of her mind."

At breakfast at the hotel the following morning, Katie was joined by Leila, who had offered to spend the day with her, showing her some of the sights. Katie knew that if the events of the day went as promised by the Outpost, she would have to tell Leila that she was a Go-between. The coincidence would be too weird, particularly once Leila learned that Katie wanted to spend the day in one of the driest, lowest, hottest parts of the earth, with little to see apart from sand, rocks and water, rather than visiting some of the historic sights of the Holy Land.

"The Dead Sea?" Leila said. "Well, we could, I suppose. It's about an hour out of Jerusalem – Hasib can drive us. But are you sure you wouldn't rather visit the Dome of the Rock? The tiles are magnificent, and anyway the whole area, with the Al-Aqsa mosque as well, is the heart of the city."

Katie put her hand on Leila's.

"Trust me. This is what I want to do. I can't explain more now, but might be able to later. But I'm very happy to get a taxi – do you have taxis here? – and go there myself. We could maybe meet up later in the day."

"No, that's fine. It's intriguing, what you want, so I'm happy to wait to find out why."

"I don't need to be there until about one. Why don't we do something else until then?"

"I'll take you into the Old City. The souqs are fascinating and maybe you want to buy presents?"

'Who would I buy presents for?' Katie thought, but went along with the idea.

It was one p.m. before Hasib picked the two women up at the Damascus Gate. Katie was a little worried that they might have missed whatever the Outpost had organised, but she was partly to blame. She could not resist a cave-like shop in the Old City containing a series of connected rooms which seemed never-ending. One was full of Russian ikons, brought to Israel as currency by Russian Jews who weren't allowed to take money out of Russia; another had Palestinian dresses with – as Leila explained – embroidery which was different depending on the village it came from; Palestinian jewellery, some of it almost too heavy to wear, but put on show at weddings; and even a collection of possibly Neolithic artefacts, which Leila warned her against.

"They make them in a workshop in Abu Dis," she said. "They're unlikely to be genuine."

They set off on the road to Jericho, with Katie asking Hasib if he could speed up a bit. But in fact, halfway down the twisty road that led to the Dead Sea, they stopped behind a long line of traffic. Katie could see the water in the distance, and hovering above it were several military helicopters. Then, with a loud blare of sirens, several police vehicles coming from Jerusalem rushed by on the wrong side of the road.

Hasib got out of the car and walked along the line of traffic, trying to find out what was going on. The two women got out and leaned on the car, catching the sun, but it became too hot and they got back in to benefit from the air conditioning. Hasib came back fifteen minutes later, and got back into the car.

"Security alert," he said. "'Terrorism', they say. They always say terrorism, whatever it is. We should go back."

Katie was frantic.

"Is there no other way to get to the Dead Sea? No side roads?"

"There are, but I'm too sure they would be blocked also."

Katie realised that the alert was probably associated with the Outpost's demonstration. In fact, she rather hoped it was. But she was bitterly disappointed to miss having a front row seat.

Traffic was slow on the road back to Jerusalem, and it was about five by the time Hasib dropped Katie at the hotel. Leila invited Katie back for another family supper, but Katie shook her head.

"No, thanks. I rather fancy a quiet evening. I might walk around a bit and have a drink somewhere."

"The American Colony has a good bar if you're not on a budget. Very pleasant, in a garden. It's only ten minutes' walk that way."

Sitting in the garden with a glass of chilled wine and some delicious salted almonds, Katie puzzled over what had – or had not – happened. She had switched on the television in her room and watched the BBC News channel, but there was no news of an extraordinary extra-terrestrial demonstration on the Dead Sea, and when she turned to an Israeli news channel, although there seemed to be a story about some security event on the Dead Sea, with pictures of road blocks and distant shots of the water, it wasn't presented in a dramatic enough way to persuade Katie that something earthshattering had taken place.

As she was drinking, she overheard a conversation at the next table. A man in sand-coloured jacket and buff chinos was talking to another man, red-faced with half-moon spectacles, rather over-dressed for the climate.

"I'd hoped to go to Amman today," the red-faced man said. "I'd arranged an interview with the prime minister. But my car never got to the Allenby Bridge. It was stopped by a terrorist alert. At least it gave me a chance to say 'yes' after all to that drink you suggested, Charles."

"It didn't seem to be terrorist-related," the other man said. "Our attaché told me that his contacts in the police said they had been called by the army after some drone footage last night, using night vision, showed something suspicious in the Dead Sea. It didn't seem like a boat, and it appeared suddenly, not from one of the coastal areas but instantaneous, as if it had suddenly come up from the bottom."

"Do you think it's a new weapon? From Jordan or the West Bank?"

"Difficult to say. The police weren't allowed to go out on the water and our source only saw something that might have been floating seaweed, which you wouldn't think would harm anyone. Anyway, I'm glad you stayed over. Meryl was saying she wished she could give you supper, but she's got a charity thing at the King David Hotel."

'It's happened!' Katie thought to herself, and wondered how she could find out more.

After she got back to the hotel, she switched the television on again to see the BBC World News. Although there was nothing specific about the Dead Sea event, there was news of another message from the Outpost.

The newsreader began by saying, "Another message from the Outpost was received today at several observatories around the world. It said..." and a brief text appeared on the screen:

> Today, as promised, we caused a major improvement in the environment in one small area of the globe, as an indication of what we could do for the whole Earth. Although we note that the nations involved are trying to keep it secret, we are confident that within twenty-four hours the effects of the demonstration will be impossible to conceal.

Chapter 19

It was the Jordanians who were able to reveal what was going on. There was enough access from the east side of the Dead Sea for them to put patrol boats out towards the 'seaweed', which was actually a large and growing blob of some kind of gel. By night time, it covered almost the entire water surface from north to south and east to west. Biologists and hydrologists from the University of Jordan were able to take samples before the extent of the gel made it impossible for boats to travel on the surface.

By the following day, the gel had disappeared, apparently beneath the surface, and the water seemed clear again. But something odd occurred when the first boats set out to see what they could find. It was clear that there was something different about the water. The boatmen, who were used to the increased buoyancy given by the very salty water of the Dead Sea, found that their boats were floating much lower in the water, and when one of the scientists guessed why this might be, a sample gathered from over the side of the boat proved that she was right. The water was no longer salty, but pure and fresh. None of her colleagues believed her, until they tried for themselves, drinking from improvised receptacles. Another scientist stripped off to his boxers and jumped into the water, where he floated much lower than he was used to on his occasional trips to the beach at the Holiday Inn Dead Sea resort.

Back at the Al-Quds hotel, Katie telephoned Sherry to tell her of the situation. Sherry told her that she had heard from Kent at NASA that, through contacts at the US Embassy in Amman, the US was pretty convinced that some kind of Outpost demonstration had taken place in the Dead Sea.

"We did our best to guess where in the world it would be, after the Outpost gave us the date, but we were all fooled. I suppose the Go-betweens must have known," Katie said, knowing that the call could be tapped.

"I suppose so," Sherry had said, non-committedly.

By the time Katie was back in Cambridge two days later, she had told Leila of her role as a Go-between but swore her to secrecy, even from Miles, at least for the time being. By now, the world knew that the Outpost had separated the waters of the Dead Sea into two layers – a top layer of about 100 metres, entirely made up of water from which all dissolved minerals had been removed, and a bottom layer with an even greater mineral concentration than before. The 'gel' which had been dropped into the Dead Sea after a three week journey from Saturn (at a tenth of the speed of light) was made up of nano-factories which separated the pure water molecules out of the seawater, allowing them to rise to the surface while the saltier water sank. It then formed a barrier between the two layers of water, preventing them from mixing again. Now, there were abundant supplies of fresh water which could be siphoned from the sea by the countries which bordered it.

Government observers and journalists from all over the world headed for the Dead Sea to try to discover how this amazing feat had been accomplished. After it became clear that the Israelis were placing severe restrictions on access, the majority of observers flew to Amman and hired cars to get them to any part of the Dead Sea coast in Jordanian hands. Jordanian scientists had gathered samples of the gel before it sank beneath the surface, and made small amounts in sealed capsules available to scientists from other countries to analyse. There was also a flourishing black market in samples among residents of Jordanian towns and villages near the Dead Sea, which journalists from all over the world tried to get their hands on. Some of them were disappointed to find when they returned home that their samples had exactly the same chemical composition as a proprietary brand of cellulose wallpaper paste.

In a phone conversation with Sherry, Katie had difficulty containing her excitement at the success of the Outpost's first attempt to show the world what it could do.

"Surely people will take things more seriously now," Katie said. "UNACC has to pull its finger out and accept the Outpost's help wholeheartedly."

There was in fact a different tone to the UNACC discussion, in the light of the Dead Sea demonstration. The motion being discussed was:

> Granted that: the demonstration by the so-called Outpost had introduced a new urgency into the topic of accepting the assistance of the Outpost in dealing with a number of major and urgent problems threatening the biosphere, this committee delegates to the drafting subcommittee the task of replying to the Outpost and deciding whether to accept the proffered solutions.

Sherry and her team at NASA watched the debates at UNACC and saw the strong resisters changing tack, from 'we still really don't know whether this is genuine at all' to 'desalination is only one small part of the problem, and anyway we have more fresh water in my country than we know what to do with.' The delegate from Slovakia pleaded with other delegates to take the demonstration seriously and unite behind a concerted effort to consider in detail the list of measures proposed by the Outpost. His prime minister was a woman. The female delegate from Malawi, dressed in national costume, said that to go outside our planet in search of some will-o-the-wisp when Jesus had promised to look after every soul on earth was rank blasphemy. Her prime minister was a man, an ordained bishop of the Glory Zone Ministry.

The vote on a motion to accept the Outpost's measures after seventeen speeches, including supportive speeches from the British and American delegates and a more non-committal one from Russia, was 20 for, 147 against and 29 abstentions.

Two months of arguing in UNACC, backed by national leaders who "weren't going to be pushed around by aliens," had led to an impasse. Even the demonstration of the power of the Outpost's technology in the (formerly) Dead Sea, did not shift the views of a significant number of leaders, some of them heads of major powers. The Outpost's messages to the Go-betweens, seen – as intended – by all the world, expressed increasing frustration at the inability of the human race wholeheartedly to accept the means of their own survival. The figures had barely changed since the last vote, pre-Demonstration. Perhaps half a dozen countries had moved in a direction more accepting of the Outpost's offer, and several of those were countries where a more significant and effective desalination programme would relieve major water shortages.

Back in Cambridge, on the day of the UNACC vote, Miles watched the proceedings on C-Span on his computer. Over the last few months he had got caught up in the whole Message saga. Partly, of course, because he'd become an unofficial spokesman for the St James' team but also because he knew how momentous the Message was for society, and how varied the reactions were across different cultures, providing unique research material for an anthropologist. As he had watched the UNACC voting results come in, an idea had struck him. After the vote was finished, he found the full list on the *New York Times* website. He set up a spreadsheet on his computer and started entering data, occasionally checking facts about the country concerned on Wikipedia. When he had finished he sat back, looked at the summaries of the data and pressed "Print 2 copies".

The following day, Katie was having supper with Miles and Leila. The two women had grown closer after the Dead Sea event, but Leila had kept her vow of secrecy about Katie's Go-between status. She knew she'd have to face Miles' annoyance one day, when he found out that Leila had known all along, but she knew why it was important for now not to reveal the secret.

Miles was glad to have the two women to talk to over supper. He wanted to try out an idea that had emerged from his analysis of the UNACC voting patterns.

"If you don't mind talking shop," Miles said, "if we can call the saving of life on earth 'shop', I've something I'd like to show you."

"Really, Miles?" Leila said, "Can't we eat in peace?"

"I think you'll find this interesting," he said, retrieving the printouts from his bag.

"Tuck into the meat loaf," Katie said. "Help yourself to potato salad."

Katie sat down opposite Miles, intrigued. He had printed out a list of the UN member countries in alphabetical order, and by each country name he had put an 'A' or a 'B'. Katie scanned the list, and Leila looked over her shoulder.

"There are more 'B's than 'A's," Katie said, and took a mouthful of meatloaf. "This is delicious. Did you make it, Leila?"

"Yes. An old recipe of my mother's."

"That's right," Miles said, "D'you see anything else?"

Katie looked again.

"No," she said.

"Now look at this." Miles slid another list across the table.

Katie and Leila looked carefully.

"This is the countries divided up by votes," Miles said. "'Yes' for accepting the Outpost's help, 'No' for rejecting it, and then the abstentions."

"O.K." Leila said. "Now, I see something. There's a bigger proportion of Bs in the Noes votes list, and smaller in the Yeses."

"More Bs abstained as well," Katie said.

"Have some more wine," Miles said, topping up two glasses. "You're both doing well."

"So what's going on?" Katie said, intrigued.

"As are female, Bs are males."

Leila looked at the list.

"But that's not true," she said. "I know for a fact that the delegate from Italy is a woman, Carlotta Muccino, but you've put 'B' by Italy."

"Aha, well spotted. But does she decide how to vote?"

"Doesn't she?"

"I shouldn't think so. With an issue as important as that, it's the country's government, led by the Prime Minister or President who decides, don't you think?"

"And the leader of Italy is a man?"

"Exactly. A right-wing nationalist."

Katie cut some more meat, and heaped it on a fork with some potato salad. Then she looked at the voting list again.

"So the majority of countries that support cooperation with the Outpost to save the world are led by women?"

"Exactly."

"And if the world's nations were all led by women, we would be home and dry?"

"Yes."

"Problem solved, then."

They both laughed, then Miles lifted his glass

"To the monstrous regiment of women," he said.

"Seconded," Leila said. "But where does that phrase come from?"

"It's by a Scottish clergyman who believed that female rulers are contrary to the Bible. Thank God he was wrong. In fact, 'regiment' in that phrase means 'rule' rather than a group of thousands of soldiers."

Katie concealed her excitement. Perhaps Miles' insight would be useful for the Outpost. She knew she needed to discuss the implications with Sherry.

"Could you email me a copy of those two lists?" Katie said to Miles. "They're rather interesting…"

After she left the Master's Lodge, Katie went to her college office and sent a text message to Sherry. "New idea worth discussing. Call soonest."

She then sat impatiently, waiting for Sherry's call. She knew Sherry would give it priority, but she also knew that Sherry's role as 'SETI Queen' in the US meant that she was often in very important meetings.

A ping on her computer showed that an email had arrived. She looked and saw that it was from Miles.

MATRIARCHY

Katie, Here's the voting figures. I'm glad you find them interesting. If you haven't read my recent paper on Matriarchy you might find it relevant…

Katie opened the pdf attachment.

It was called HOW MATRIARCHY PRECEDED PATRIARCHY: THE SURVIVAL CHARACTERISTICS OF FEMALE RULE IN THE EVOLUTION OF SOCIETIES.

The abstract began:

It has been reported (Taylor, Bateman, Kryztowski, 2012) that location of a species along the 'selfishness-altruism' spectrum is connected to gender imbalance and the genetics of sex determination. This has been shown for sea snails, jerboas and snow geese, but there has been no reliable data for homo sapiens. This paper reports a study of the Khasi people of India...

She was halfway through the paper, absorbed in its provocative arguments, when her phone rang, startling her.

"A new idea?" Sherry said, without preamble.

Katie summarised Miles' insights into the UNACC voting patterns, and the implication that it was the male national leaders who were holding back the drive for acceptance of help from the Outpost. Sherry was intrigued by the observation, although she wasn't sure how it could be useful to the Outpost.

"What could they do about it?" she asked.

"I've learnt it's not worth even asking that question," Katie said. "Their capabilities, their knowledge, is so far beyond ours. We just make suggestions. I think their one blind spot may be human psychology. They have evolved to be such rational, logical beings themselves, they can't believe that humans, or any evolved intelligent life-forms, would do anything that is irrational, against their best interests. Maybe we can shape some kind of advice based on the figures. We might need to back it up with some more data. Not figures, but some kind of theoretical underpinning. Miles himself has written a very interesting paper which I can send you."

The following morning, Katie cornered Miles when she saw him in the SCR.

"I read your paper on the Khasi in Meghalaya," she said, "and had a few questions I wanted to ask."

Miles was very surprised.

"A bit outside your field, I would have thought," he said, "but fire away, anyway."

"Like you, I read *Scientific American* – and other journals outside my subject," she said. "You never know where new insights will come from."

"I doubt if the Khasi's matrilineal society can tell you anything about the origin of language."

Katie brushed the remark aside.

"Is there anything in that society that tells us about the role of women in other societies, and what the benefits might be if other societies became more – matriarchal?"

Miles thought.

"Well, there is a measure of empathy that you can apply to whole societies rather than individuals, and there seems to be a rough correlation between matrilinearity and empathy, as judged by how a society treats its poor or deprived or disabled individuals. The Khasi are at one end of that spectrum – the good end – and that's usually put down to the role of women."

"How about long-term planning? Are they better or worse at taking the long view of their society rather than going for short-term gains?"

"That's a very specific question, Katie. Where is all this coming from?"

Katie knew she'd have to come clean about her intentions, at least partly.

"Look, I have a friend in the US who is involved with the UNACC Committee and is looking at whether the Outpost's recommendations, which are regularly rejected by a majority of the members, would be more readily accepted if more national leaders were women. I mentioned your data," she said, "and she was very interested."

It took Katie a whole evening to write her and Sherry's new recommendation to the Outpost. Miles Cadogan had written a paper at Katie's suggestion, intrigued by the possibility of playing some indeterminate role in advising the UN Committee, and Katie had sent it to Sherry. The paper began:

> Female decision-makers in matriarchal societies consistently make decisions towards a more altruistic end of the spectrum than male leaders, and altruism, expressed as a greater concern for others even at the expense of one's own well-being, leads to fundamentally different policies, which may have more beneficial effects for the society in the long run. This fact, supported by data from a number of societies round the world may help to explain

the difficulties currently faced by UNACC in accepting the Outpost's recommendations...

After some more back and forth between Katie and Sherry, a document emerged which the Outpost had no trouble detecting, reading, and seeing as a brand new approach to the question of how to push Earthlings towards doing something which was for their own good anyway.

The first fruit of Katie and Sherry's recommendations was the death of South Korea's president, Yoon Suk-yeol. It seemed inexplicable at first, the result of a fatal accident when he was being driven back to the presidential offices in the Blue House in Seoul. The president's driver, Yang Jeong-Hoon, had been appointed when Yoon was made president, after a hotly contested election dominated by the issue of his anti-feminism. Yang had had a spotless driving record for the previous ten years, and yet on the surface the accident seemed a simple matter of driver incompetence.

The president's car failed to stop at a red light at the end of Jahamun-ro 28-gil where it joined Changuimun-ro. After colliding with a coach-full of Japanese tourists, the car careered across the road, through a wire mesh fence and embedded itself into the wall of no. 89-11 Cheongunhyoja-dong. Yoon was found dead, with a bamboo curtain pole through his head, from the window the car crashed through. Yang was fortunately unscathed, but for a day or two he was held in police custody while closed circuit video from the surrounding streets and buildings, as well as the car's internal and external dash cams, was analysed.

When the Kia K900's inbuilt computer was retrieved from the wreck and analysed two days later, a different story emerged. All safety measures to prevent such an accident - collision detection, airbags, automatic seat belt release - had been immobilised in the master control panel. In addition, the car had accelerated wildly as it approached the traffic light, even though pressure data from the pedals showed that the driver's foot was not on the accelerator but the brake pedal, which the computer had made inoperative.

Strangest of all was that there was no way these shortcomings in the computer could have been triggered manually. Some sort of hacking must have been involved, but no one had ever seen such a complex hacking operation, changing settings on all the major safety features which were, in any case, triply redundant.

The situation only became clearer - and more worrying for world leaders - when Hungary's prime minister, Viktor Orban, was killed in a helicopter crash on the way back from an official visit to the Dunaújváros paper factory on the tenth anniversary of the installation of a new biomass power plant. Again, it was blamed initially on operator error - though Orban's personal pilot had a clean record - until examination of the black box showed an unaccountable clash between the main rotor blades and the stabilising propeller at the rear of the craft, as if one of the elements had suddenly changed rotation speed, a situation which has been 'designed out' of all helicopter flight systems. Nevertheless, it had happened here, and analysis of the computer's control systems showed a sequence of computer commands which overrode the normal operating software to produce the crash. Like the Korean car crash, the Hungarian accident could only be explained by a never-before-encountered type of hacking of the helicopter's control system.

A week later, Senior General Maha Thray Sithu Min Aung Hlaing, a member of the Burmese junta, was electrocuted after opening the door of his new Fisher and Paykel fridge, recently imported from California and installed by a very competent electrician. It was one of the new 'intelligent' fridges, but not quite intelligent enough to prevent the entire metal case of the refrigerator becoming live with 230 volts, sending the general's body juddering across the room where it collided with a rack of knives on the wall, one of which severed his carotid artery. In fact, he was already dead from the electric shock, and the whole scene was messier than it needed to be. Again, inspection by experts showed that the fridge's control centre had experienced a chain of extremely unlikely – in fact, impossible to explain – events, interferences really, which seemed to be caused by changes in the inbuilt operating system, a system which was hard-wired into the microcircuits.

It was significant, but not really commented on at the time, that these three leaders, all men, had been among the most reluctant to accept the Outpost's offer, discussed by their representatives in UNACC, to cleanse the biosphere to prevent the environmental disaster that would otherwise occur. They each felt that harm would befall to their country's economy if they took part in a global acceptance of the Outpost's offer.

There had been no warning by the Outpost and therefore no reason to connect the three deaths, although they seemed too similar to be coincidences. But about a week after the death of Senior General Maha Thray Sithu Min Aung Hlaing, the following message arrived at the world's Outpost monitoring posts:

> Clearly, the desalination of Dead Sea water was not dramatic enough to convince all the world's leaders that our offer of assistance in cleaning the global biosphere is genuine and that we are capable of carrying out the task. We propose, therefore, to change our approach. Since, almost without exception, the only leaders who seem to understand our approach and are willing to put long term benefits above short term gains are women (see the attached list of voting choices at the last seven meetings of UNACC) we propose to wait for a year, in the hope that many more nations elect or install women leaders. Although we are loath to postpone our programme of measures to clean the Earth, we feel that a delay of a year in order to obtain the whole-hearted support of the world's nations is a price worth paying. To encourage such a change in national governance, it is worth pointing out that although we do not have a binary structure in the reproduction of our own species, your own scientists have shown that leaders carrying XX chromosomes consistently make decisions

towards the more altruistic end of the spectrum than male leaders, and altruism, expressed as a greater concern for others, even at the expense of one's own well-being, is what is necessary to solve the global crisis. (See the paper by Dr Miles Cadogan of the University of Cambridge at the end of this message.)

Of course, this will not be achieved merely by hoping, and it will not have escaped notice that three of the most recalcitrant leaders, who have stood out against our programme, have died in recent weeks. Such deaths may continue, and other methods may be devised to ensure the rapid replacement of all male leaders with females.

Carla Baxter received the Outpost's latest message as she was entertaining the Prime Minister of Tunisia, Najla Bouden. Paul Martin came into the office with a printout in his hand.

"Very sorry, Prime Minister, I thought you'd want to see this straight away," he said.

"Excuse me, Dr Bouden," Baxter said, and took the piece of paper. After skimming it, she looked up and said, "I think this affects both of us," and handed her the message.

"Thank you, Paul," she said. "Can you get hold of Dr Miles Cadogan after my press conference with Dr Bouden? In fact, make that before. I don't see how we can avoid this message trumping questions about Anglo-Tunisian relations."

She turned to the Tunisian P.M.

"Are you good at thinking on your feet?" she said.

Half an hour later, Miles Cadogan received a call on his mobile phone from Paul Martin. He was on his knees in the Lodge kitchen trying to unblock a waste pipe from the sink that had become blocked with fat. He had rashly offered to do the washing up after Leila had cooked a duck at lunch for a visiting alumnus who might be tempted to donate to the College's Supplementary Grant Support Fund, and it seemed a good idea to empty the roasting dish down the sink.

"Oh, hi, Paul," he said, having finally got the man's Christian name into his head. "Can I ring you back a bit later? No? Well, let me get my head out from under this sink. Yes, that's what I said."

Miles sat, a little out of breath, on a kitchen chair. As Patrick spoke, Miles reached for a TV remote control and turned on a small TV set on a surface near the cooker. The screen was showing the text of the new message from the Outpost.

"Yes, I see," he said. "Of course, I'll talk to her."

"I have a press conference in fifteen minutes," the Prime Minister said. "and you seem to be the Outpost's favourite scientist. Can you give me anything coherent to say about this message? I'm bound to be asked, even if we're meant to be talking about security for tourists visiting Tunisia after the latest terrorist attack."

"What sort of thing would you like to say at the press conference?"

"Should we take this seriously? Can the Outpost actually create more women national leaders in twelve months?"

"Well, they've made a pretty good start by killing three of the biggest critics of their proposals. If they carried on like this, that would achieve the effect pretty quickly. What man will stand for office if he thinks he'll die a mysterious death within days of becoming a leader?"

"Of course, as you can imagine, I'm not against the idea," Baxter said. "Women standing for office, not killing men. But I'd like to be able to give some kind of useful answer to journalists. Can you jot me down something in an email? In the next ten minutes," she added.

Half an hour later, Miles, Leila, and Katie were all watching Carla Baxter's press conference on television.

For the first five minutes the questions were about mundane topics to do with relations between the UK and Tunisia but then there was a bustle of activity among the journalists as the news spread on their phones about the latest message from the Outpost. One journalist put up her hand and said "Prime Minister, do you have any comment on the Outpost's call, just spelled out in their latest message, that all national leaders should be women?"

Baxter took a breath, looked across at Dr Bouden, and said "What do you think, Najla?"

There was laughter among the journalists, and then the questioner said, "But seriously, Mrs Baxter, isn't this a major development in the whole saga?"

"It's too soon to make any sort of policy statement – we've all only just seen the message – but without wishing to sound smug, the two national leaders standing before you today have already demonstrated that, perhaps, women leaders can bring a different approach to some of the world's problems. And it is certainly the case that we both ordered our UNACC delegates to vote wholeheartedly for cooperation with any of the solutions offered by the Outpost to the world's climate emergency, because we believe that, unlike some of the other nations voting on the topic, we have to take a short-term hit to our nations' well-being in order to achieve long-term benefits."

In the Kremlin, President Pavlov was talking on a secure phone to Sergei Gromov in New York.

"So what are we to make of this message from the Outpost?" Pavlov said.

"Well," Gromov replied. "It's as clear as it can be. They are trying to encourage – no more than encourage, force – nations to adopt female leaders."

"How are they going to do that?" Pavlov said

"Well, one way is to carry on doing what they're doing, which is to kill male leaders. Until we are so terrified that no man stands for election."

"And if we ignore this message?" Pavlov said.

"Well, if you're happy to wait and see, I'm sure we'll find out soon enough."

"Do you think there's anything we should do?" Pavlov said.

"Well, we could look towards a situation in which the President of Russia is a woman…"

Pavlov was astounded.

"You can't be serious," he said.

"Of course I am. You have put me in charge of efforts to try to make the best use of the Output's offers, and I have done a certain amount of that here at the UNACC committee. As you know, on your instructions, I have actually voted for at least a measure of cooperation, even though I had to include certain caveats, which you insisted on, so as not to jeopardise the Russian economy or threaten the future governance of the country. So, if my job is to try to find the best way towards cleansing the biosphere, which is what the Outpost wants, then I think we have to do what we can to fit in with their wishes."

So," Pavlov said, "You think that in the upcoming election for president, I should not stand again?"

"Well," Gromov said, "you said it, not me. But it would certainly be a possible way ahead. Put it this way, if you do stand again and get elected, do you want to risk dying in a car crash or your refrigerator electrocuting you?"

"That's silly," Pavlov said. "First, we can't be sure that those three deaths weren't random accidents."

"Oh," said Gromov, "Reading this message, I think we can."

"All right. But second, if I'm prepared to take the risk, we – you, as executive director of FSB, can take all the precautions necessary. If they are killing people, they may be doing it with some kind of hacking techniques. We have the best computer hackers in the world. Surely they can invent ways of preventing the sort of tricks that the Outpost is using."

"Mr President," Gromov said, with a sigh. "That's like saying that the Native Americans should have found a way of avoiding the smallpox carried into their communities on blankets sold to them by the white man. Our technology and theirs, the Outpost's, are much further apart even than Stone Age man and us. The only way to pacify the Outpost is to do what they want."

"Or pretend to…"

"Dimitri Ilyich," Gromov said, "You still don't get it. The Outpost has access to all our communications in real time, all the time. They'll be listening to our conversation now. We could never hide anything from them."

"You are sounding like an alien yourself, Sergei Alexandrovich."

"I just understand their power and abilities better than you. They are limitless."

"Perhaps you could use our presence on UNACC to go a bit more in the direction of the way a woman would vote. That might appease them."

"I don't think 'a bit more in the direction' is good enough," Gromov said. "In fact, if you want my view, it's the following: you should stand down and Katarina Bondarchuk should stand as the next president of Russia and be unopposed, unless perhaps by another woman. She is my campaign manager, so I know her quite well."

There was silence for a moment.

"You know, that is treason," Pavlov said quietly.

"I don't think it's treason at all," Gromov said. "It's what happens in democracies."

"But we are not a democracy," Pavlov said, "and we are all the better for it."

"Nevertheless, if Russia wants to be in the forefront of accepting the Outpost's help and still trying to do what's best for Russia, then it is one way forward."

"And why Katarina Bondarchuk?" Pavlov said. "I hardly know her. You introduced me to her as your campaign manager, after I told you I had found out that you were plotting to stand against me. But how does anybody know if she is President material?"

"I don't think that's the point," Gromov said. "The real point is, how is Russia going to get ahead of the field in dealing with the problem of the Outpost so that we can still retain some measure of control over what happens next? Your instinct was right when you faked the first message, which - by the way - the world still doesn't know, and I think..." He paused.

"Were you about to make a threat?"

"Look," said Gromov, "You know, and I know that if you stand again as president, if it became apparent that it wasn't the Americans who faked the message but you, and that you had been responsible for the world panic that occurred when the fake message was released, that would not do your presidential campaign any good. I'm suggesting we find a way of you bowing out gracefully, and Russia having a woman president"

"But you would be behind her?" said Pavlov. "You would be pulling her strings?"

"No," Gromov said, "Katerina is her own woman. And I think the more we know how much power the Outpost has, and what it's capable of, there is no alternative."

"I don't like this idea," Pavlov said, "I don't like it at all."

"You may have no choice as to whether to like it or not, Dimitri Ilyich," Gromov said. "This maybe the only way of keeping ahead of the field and doing what is best - or at least, least worst - for Russia."

Jennifer Billings felt a warm glow of confidence as she took her daily run on the treadmill in the White House, the morning after the latest Outpost message. She had been encouraged over the last few years to see how many women leaders had been elected in nations around the world. There were now more than twenty - a small proportion of the 193 UN members, but still it was a start. If the Outpost really could change the situation radically – and they'd shown what they could do pretty impressively so far – perhaps there was hope for the world after all. She thought of her daughter, Samantha, and the whirlwind of concerns she had had for her future over the last year, first with the growing crisis in global warming and climate change, then with the (fake) threat of annihilation.

But now, there was a new factor. Perhaps inadvertently, Samantha could look forward to a world in which women would play the role they were meant to, a role which would benefit civilisation as a whole, rather than principally those members who had XY chromosomes.

In Cambridge, Katie asked Miles and Leila if she could meet them at the Lodge, and invite Paul and Dee to join them for coffee. Miles was a little puzzled but agreed a time, if Katie could get the others together. When he mentioned this to Leila, she gave him a knowing look and said "I think I know why, but I'll leave it to her," she said.

It was, of course, to tell all her colleagues that she was one of the Go-betweens. Katie felt that the business had reached a whole new level. She and Sherry had also admitted to each other a sense of discomfort at the deaths of three world leaders and felt that the Outpost's actions – derived from their recommendations admittedly – had crossed some sort of line. It wasn't that they wanted to stop playing the role they had done up till now, but they felt they'd rather do it in consultation with others.

The others were of course astonished.

"How long have you been doing this?" Miles said.

"We were asked in January," Katie said.

"Did they follow your recommendations?" Paul asked.

"Pretty much."

Leila interrupted. "The Dead Sea demonstration was hers, right, Katie?"

"Well, between Sherry and me," she said.

Miles chipped in. "So you really were in direct contact with them? That's how they got my matriarchy paper? So what happens now?"

"Well, I think we wait and see," Katie replied. "I just don't hold out much hope for male candidates in the next few national elections."

"But surely it's broader than that," Miles said. "And I now understand how my thoughts about matriarchal societies were relayed in an Outpost message – thanks for that, Katie. But their last message seems to be looking for the whole of homo sapiens to become matriarchal. Do you want to stand down as master in favour of a woman, Miles?"

"It would be a relief," Miles said. "I could get back to my research."

Epilogue

EXTRACT FROM UNIPEDIA ENTRY ON 'THE OUTPOST FROM TAU CETI'

The War on Males Message (WAMM)

… In 2026, after six months of wrangling at the UN committee set up to negotiate with the Outpost (UNACC) over its offer to cleanse the biosphere, the Outpost announced that it would no longer allow a series of indecisive votes to continue. It had expected that its Dead Sea demonstration would 'bring homo sapiens to its senses' but after the two Go-betweens (later revealed as Dr Katie Flynn and Dr Sherry Walker) suggested that the impasse might be due to the preponderance of male national leaders, the Outpost adopted a new and more interventionist policy.

The first manifestation of this was the seemingly accidental deaths of three national leaders, of South Korea, Burma, Hungary, (the April 'accidents') which were shown by investigating inquiries in each country to be caused by interference on a hitherto unseen scale with computer software. In a message from the Outpost, no. 27 in the Outpost Message Archive, the Earth's nations were told that if the gender imbalance among world leaders had not changed within a year, the Outpost would close down and no further assistance would be forthcoming. A subsequent message revealed the identity of the Go-betweens, and said that thenceforth any official replies should be channelled through them. When UNACC asked, through the Go-betweens, whether the Outpost insisted on all world leaders being women from now on, or whether they would accept male leaders if they voted to accept the Outpost's help, the following message (no 29) was the reply:

> The advice we have received, and our own researches into the history of homo sapiens, suggests that the inability of existing male leaders to take a long-term view of the benefits to humanity, in spite of the Dead Sea demonstration, is a manifestation of a broader difference between male and female leaders which has harmed humanity in other ways and which could continue if some male leaders were still in post. The most egregious of these is, of course, the propensity to wage war, seen at its starkest in the 2022 war on Ukraine by Russia. There is also the use of guns in society, almost exclusively a male phenomenon, to kill their fellow human beings. There is no evidence that, if some male leaders accepted the benefits of our assistance with the problems of the biosphere, they would simultaneously stop the use of violence in these other ways.

This Message, which became known as the War on Males Message (WAMM), is considered the first and most succinct statement of the Outpost's policy towards Earth which broadened the arena for the events which followed.

The 'Regiment of Women' Begins

There were five national elections in the six months that followed the WAMM. In the first, the Philippines, there were only male candidates for the presidency. The winner, Manuel Garcia, in his inauguration speech, offered a lukewarm welcome to the Outpost's offer of help, and made certain conditions to protect the tourism industry. A week later, when he and his wife went to stay in the newly-built presidential beach house in Cebu, he was killed by a roof collapse in his office. The disaster was put down to faulty construction workmanship, but a later investigation showed that, although the correct ingredients for the concrete had been ordered, the computer-generated list of proportions of cement, sand and water for the mixture had been altered between the calculation by the project management team and the instruction received by the construction workers. No Earthly explanation was found for this mistake. In a hurried vote of the Philippine parliament, a woman, Rosa Magsaysay, was created president by acclamation.

The second election was in Uruguay, after right-wing President Luis Alberto Lacalle Pou died suddenly of Covid 19. (No suspicious circumstance could be identified.) On election day, when all seven candidates were male, all electronic voting machines malfunctioned, printing the name of an eighth, the Uruguayan singer, Natalia Oreiro, (who was not a candidate) and assigning 100% of the votes to her. When this happened a second time, at a restaged election two months later, electing a character from a Uruguyan children's book, Micaela, all candidates stood down. At the third election, Natalia Oreiro, who had not considered a political career up to that point, stood unopposed and became the new President.

In the third election, in Gabon, Lucie Milebou Aubusson was elected president, in competition with three other women candidates and one man. Two days before the election, the male candidate, who was expected to win, an adherent of the Bwitl religion, had a fright, when his computer started talking to him in the Fang language and told him his ancestors were looking down on him and didn't want him to stand. The following day he withdrew his candidacy.

In the fourth election, in Italy, the only male candidate was Federico Silva, associated with several corruption scandals in which he had allegedly bribed judges so as to avoid conviction. A month before the election, his accountants discovered that every single one of his bank accounts had been emptied and evidence of all his shareholdings had disappeared. Since Silva was now unable to pay the accountants' bills, €700,000 in arrears, they severed relationships with him. Now with no resources at all, Silva withdrew his candidacy. The day after Eleanora Montisi was elected president, Silva's money and shares reappeared as mysteriously as they had vanished.

Within six months of the WAMM, it was clear that the transition to all female national leadership was going to happen much faster than had seemed possible. Clearly, the capacity of the Outpost to influence activities on Earth was far greater than anyone had anticipated. The ingenuity of the methods the Outpost used to discourage or prevent any males anywhere standing for national or international positions of power meant that within a year very few men nursed political ambitions and many women, who would had never thought before of becoming candidates for major posts, stood in elections. Most lists became all-female, and as a result the calibre of elected officials rose considerably.

It had been thought that a sticking point would be in those countries where no election was scheduled or where there was a tradition of rigging elections. Turkmenistan, for example, had had elections two years before the Outpost's first message, in which Serdar Gurbangulyýewiç, the son of Gurbanguly Mälikgulyýewiç Berdimuhamedow, the man who had ruled for fifteen years, was elected with 83% of the vote in an election which was deemed by international observers to be "neither free nor fair." But in an astonishing volte face, Berdimuhamedow resigned within days of the WAMM, citing ill-health, even though he was only in his early 40s. The story took a bizarre turn when a female candidate appeared from nowhere, to stand, unopposed, in the subsequent election. She claimed to be named Gulshat Berdimuhamedowa, a cousin of the former president. She bore a strong resemblance to her cousin, and the reason for this became clear when a CCTV camera in the presidential palace was hacked and showed 'Gulshat' kissing the former president's wife and hugging his children before swimming in the presidential swimming pool, flat-chested and wearing only swimming trunks, revealing that the new president had been just the old president in drag.

Within 24 hours, the palace was besieged by thousands of women, from the capital Ashgabat and bussed in from outlying areas, calling for the nullification of the elections and a ban on all male candidates. The new president, Galina Abdulova, was elected by 56% of the electorate, and accepted all the conditions sought by the Outpost in the WAMM.

These events led to an agreement by the Outpost to start the Great Cleanup in 2027, as it was clear that the momentum towards universal female leadership was unstoppable. Over the years from 2027 to 2030, the number of women national leaders increased five-fold, and was accompanied by similar increases in women members of parliament, leaders of major companies and even army officers and lower ranks.

The Great Cleanup

This mass movement, instigated - some say forced - by the Outpost, led to an immediate start to a number of different technological programmes to rectify some of the Earth's most serious problems, with the willing consent of a majority of the members of UNACC, which had transformed itself into a clearing house for the Outpost's proposals, and which involved major universities and scientific institutions in the programme of activities.

Environmental problems

A series of nano-factories were dispatched from the Outpost in 2027, to arrive in 2028, and instructions were sent to the designated scientific establishments to prepare backup resources for when they arrived. (See Communication 112, Outpost Archive). On each continent a landing area was prepared, about fifty kilometres square, next to which mineral resources were stockpiled, to be broken down and reassembled by the nano-factories when they arrived. Each continent had at least one of these complexes of nano-factories and resource stockpiles, controlled by a central quantum computer, also dispatched at the same time as the nano-factories, and programmed to control several different processes, from water distillation and cleansing to clearance of air pollution, replenishment of ozone, rapid regrowth of depleted forests, etc. These nano-factories were assembled and programmed at the landing sites to produce millions of nanobots which were then distributed worldwide and operated using feedback loops to gauge the state of the atmosphere, water, etc, and carry out the necessary chemical reactions according to need.

Human issues

In addition to the landing/resource areas, a series of smaller robotic 'campuses' were created near cities, to receive computer-controlled genetic manipulation labs, designed to provide solutions to problems of health and disease, nutrition and food supply, energy and power, and aggression and criminality. UNACC subcommittees had drawn up a list of priorities in these areas. In health, these ranged from diseases which would benefit from new vaccines, to cancers for which gene repair could provide a solution; in food and nutrition, new molecular foods, improved yields of pulses, and vitamin enhanced grain crops; and in the area of aggression and criminality, genetic solutions by viral implantation of female mitochondrial DNA in male babies, as well as brainwave manipulation to 'detune' aggressive centres in the (mainly male) brain.

Rapid progress

One of the unforeseen consequences of the rapid replacement of male rule by female rule was the speed with which even in the early years, humanity's own solutions, cumbersome and inefficient as they were, took off rapidly. Governments all over the world gave a far higher priority to such solutions than they had been able to when competing interests – business and political – had prevented the immediate adoption of such quick fixes as wind and tidal power generation. And when the nano-factories started to arrive and were brought online, any obstacles that might have been foreseen to the adoption of their solutions world-wide were removed by the rulings of the World Female Forum, a body with representatives from all national governments whose rulings were binding. When the dwindling number of fossil fuel companies, at least the ones that had hung on to male leadership, tried to slow down or prevent the wide manufacture and adoption of nano-fusion power generators, one for every home in the world, the Outpost returned to the harsh policy which had set in motion the female leaders movement, and several male CEOs found, mysteriously, that they had lost the power of speech and writing as a result of a brain virus which seemed targeted specifically at them. When they resigned from their positions, their communication powers returned.

No more war

The Russian war on Ukraine was the last big act of national aggression before the Outpost set in motion its programme to save homo sapiens from its own misdeeds. In fact, human violence and aggression as a whole diminished markedly between 2030 and 2040. Some of this, as expected, was due merely to the different approaches to conflict which female leaders adopted naturally. "Peace games" replaced wars, and international conflicts, which still arose occasionally, were settled by combatants taking part in a complex and challenging series of rounds of a game devised by the Outpost and based on their own, long-dead, society's method of resolving conflict. The nearest equivalent on Earth was chess, but this new game was played on a three-dimensional board, a cube with a hundred units per side, and each participant having 100 'pieces'. Their complement of pieces could be augmented by dividing (fission) or reduced by merging (fusion) with a piece from the other side. (See Outpost Peace Game rules) Each game was time limited, usually by agreement, and the side with the most pieces remaining was deemed to have won the Peace.

Learning about the Outpost

By 2035, when it was clear that the proposed solutions were working even better than had been hoped, UNACC set up a new committee – UNFUEL, the UN Committee for Understanding Extra-terrestrial Lifeforms. Contact with the Outpost had been on a 'need to know' basis over the previous ten years, since so much information needed to be exchanged about the massive transformation of the global environment. But since the whole motivation for the world's SETI programmes had been to discover and understand extra-terrestrial civilizations, astronomers and astrobiologists had been intensely curious about the Outpost and the civilization which had created it. But attempts to get answers to their questions had met with a blank wall, apart from the initial information contained in the Outpost's first message. (Outpost Archive No. 1). Even when a delegation of leading scientists from the US, Russia, Europe and China approached the Go-betweens in 2032, who were still consulted from time to time by the Outpost, the list of questions they sent were not addressed in the Outpost's reply, which included the comment (Outpost Archive No. 7325) "All in good time."

In fact, by 2038, when it was clear that the Earth was well on target for the major transformation of the environment and biosphere, the Outpost issued a series of 'handbooks', as they called them, covering questions which had been the focus of intense scientific curiosity over the last fifteen years.

The first was called "Who are we?" (Outpost Handbook, No 1) and was a 500,000 word account of the civilization which had existed on the planet round Tau Ceti, with brief accounts of the biology, biochemistry, anatomy and 'neurology' of the members, although it made clear that the way they 'thought' and communicated used entirely different modalities from anything in use on Earth. The second Handbook was called "How and Why the Outpost" (Outpost Handbook, No 2) and told the story of how the idea arose of trying to save from themselves the life form (homo sapiens) whose intelligence and language had been 'seeded' by the Tau Ceti civilization.

The third Handbook was called "Mathematics: A universal language" (Outpost Handbook, No 3) and in the first 300,000 words laid out basic mathematical concepts which were recognizable by human mathematicians, but then devoted the next million words to developments in mathematics which addressed, and solved, all current mathematical problems, and laid the groundwork to keep mathematicians busy for the next millennium with a whole range of new concepts and issues.

There have so far been seventeen Outpost Handbooks (See list with links to full text: Outpost Handbook catalogue)

The Pioneers

There was a group of people - scientists, statesmen (and women), administrators - who were involved in the initial detection and interpretation of the original (fake) version of the Message, and in discovering the real Message and its implications, as well as taking part in the early months of communication with the Outpost. They were instrumental in facilitating the eventual acceptance of the offers of help in rectifying the problems that world governments had been wrestling with unsuccessfully. Several of them have written accounts of the parts they played (see Further reading) and have told of how their lives were changed by the experience.

Dr Katie Flynn was a scientist whose work on the evolution of language developed into a proof that what the Outpost said about 'seeding' language in homo sapiens was true. In collaboration with **Dr Ravi Chandra** and **Dr Douglas Burnside**, she went on to show that the gene FOXP2 had been implanted in homo sapiens by the Outpost, and the three of them were awarded the Nobel Peace Prize in 2033. **President Jennifer Billings** was re-elected in 2028 for a second term with a massively increased majority, and played a leading part in mentoring the new crop of female leaders who were elected in the years after the WAMM. After her second term, she was replaced by another Democrat, **Alexandria Ocasio-Cortez,** whose two terms were marked by a movement to encourage more women to go into government, management and administration, as well as encouraging girls to take up science, computing and maths to serve the growing need for scientists to work through the huge amount of new scientific data supplied by the Outpost in its handbooks. President Billings became UN Secretary General in 2033 and led a root and branch reform of the organisation which expanded the Security Council and took away veto powers from its members, using a new body, the UN Arbitration Service, to resolve issues when a Security Council member had difficulty accepting the view of a majority of the other members.

Dr Paul Spearman continued as Director of Astronomy at Cambridge, and raised funds for a new Institute for Public Education in Mathematics and Science (IPEMS) in collaboration with the Outpost, whose quantum computing facilities produced a series of learning packages which increased public literacy tenfold in science and maths. As a result of the Outpost's database of human genetics with reference to intelligence and speech, by 2035 children were forming sentences at the age of ten months, an average of eight months earlier than usual. The knock-on effect of this, combined with similar instructional material given to all children on free iPads, led to children attending university at the age of 12, many of whom gained first class degrees at the age of 15. **Mrs Dee Spearman**, who had assisted her husband in compiling the *Guardian* supplement which revealed the correct text of the Message, was appointed editor of the *Guardian* in 2029.

Former Russian President **Dimitri Illych Pavlov**, responsible for ordering the faking of the original version of the Message, tried to stand for re-election in 2028, but during his television address to the nation a few days before the polls, a mysterious computer glitch led to a sound track in which an entirely different speech emerged from his mouth on television sets around the nation from the speech he was actually giving in the Kremlin. The effect was enhanced by visual distortions of his lip movements which made them fit the alternative speech accurately. In the fake speech, believed to be a result of the Outpost hacking into the Kremlin's TV system, Pavlov confessed to ordering the Annihilation version of the Message to be issued. Instead of hearing Pavlov set out his ten-year plan to create peace and prosperity in Russia, listeners heard him appear to say that he didn't really care about the people who had been alarmed by the fake Message and even some who killed themselves, and that, frankly, he was only standing in this election for reasons of personal aggrandisement and to gather and stash away a fortune in revenues from Russia's mineral resources which were expected to become even more valuable as the need for nano-techonology and quantum computers increased. As for this nonsense about women taking over senior roles in government and administration, he thought Russian women should keep their mouths shut and confine themselves to the kitchen and the bedroom. The negative impact of the faked speech plus a good campaign by a female candidate **Katerina Bondarchuk** led to a resounding victory for Bondarchuk, and Pavlov's arrest by the FGB at his dacha outside Moscow. He has not been seen or heard of since.

Sergei Alexandrovich Gromov moved to the USA after the election of President Bondarchuk, and was appointed by her to be Russia's delegate to the UN. At the request of President Billings, he established the US-Russia Coordination Centre, set up to explore a whole range of issues which might lead to friction or competition between the two nations before they presented serious problems. Its co-directors were **Natasha Firestone**, from the US State Department, and **Olga Cheliuskina**, an academic and translator from the University of St Petersburg.

Dr Sherry Walker, the second Go-between with Dr Katie Flynn, became Director Emeritus of NASA and headed a research facility to exploit the many innovations in propulsion, energy supply and navigation which had enabled Tau Ceti to colonise the rings of Saturn and send spacecraft, large and small, to Earth. The ultimate aim of the programme was in keeping with NASA's new mission, which Dr Walker helped to devise, by which the new aim of space travel was to exploit planetary and solar science to help Earth. It was felt that the old aims of exploring and colonising the Moon and planets and investigating the outer atmosphere of the sun was superseded by the vast array of information now available in the Outpost Handbooks. (See, in particular, Handbooks 58, 59,and 60).

Dr Miles Cadogan, Master of St James' College, Cambridge, and one of the original group which revealed the text of the genuine Message from the Outpost, resigned both posts in 2027, in keeping with the world-wide move towards female governance in major institutions. He was succeeded by **Dr Katie Flynn** as Master (the title of heads of house at Oxford and Cambridge was finally changed to the non-binary 'Leader' in 2032.) Cadogan then became deputy director of a new government establishment, the Outpost Knowledge Research Council, refusing to be director and helping in the search for a female scientist. Dr Cadogan's wife **Leila** gave birth to twin boys in 2027. They were named Tau and Ceti.

The science behind this book

Most of the science and mathematics in this book is reasonably correct. There *is* a gene called FOXP2 which *did* arrive rather suddenly – on an evolutionary time scale anyway – in the primate genome and is intimately connected with human language and intelligence. No one knows how this gene came about, so an extraterrestrial origin is as likely as any.

When the first Message arrives, it is almost certain that we will recognise its origins only through some mathematical content, probably involving prime numbers. The likely computing abilities of a civilisation in advance of ours will be unimaginably more powerful than anything we can conceive today, involving quantum computing, a technology in its infancy on Earth today.

Nanotechnology, also in its infancy, will eventually be capable of assembling any complex molecular structure, from viruses and proteins to space probes and power stations, controlled by quantum computers.

If extraterrestrial civilisations exist, they are likely to be either behind us in their technologies, or a huge way ahead of us. The universe is 13 billion years old, and the likelihood that another civilisation is within, say, a thousand years of our state of technology is vanishingly small, even smaller than the chance that a person sitting next to you on the bus was born at exactly the same second as you were. What is far more likely is that such civilisations are millions of years *ahead* of us, giving them a comfortable advantage in developing science, mathematics and technology. (There are about two billion seconds in a human life, so even if life in the universe did not arise until two billion years ago, the 'person on a bus' analogy would hold.)

The Arthur C. Clarke quote at the beginning of the book is meant to suggest that, however extraordinary – even magical – the sort of technologies used by the Outpost seem, they may be feasible one day. The specific actions carried out in the book against recalcitrant male leaders – however impossible they may seem – could become only too possible as our everyday lives, transport, and communications become more and more dependent on AI and computers.